A Game of Chance

ALEXA ASTON

OLIVER HEBER BOOKS

All rights reserved.

No part of this publication may be sold, copied, distributed, reproduced or transmitted in any form or by any means, mechanical or digital, including photocopying and recording or by any information storage and retrieval system without the prior written permission of both the publisher, Oliver Heber Books and the author, Alexa Aston, except in the case of brief quotations embodied in critical articles and reviews.

PUBLISHER'S NOTE: This is a work of fiction. Names, characters, places, and incidents either are the product of the author's imagination or are used fictitiously. Any resemblance to actual persons, living or dead, business establishments, events, or locales is entirely coincidental.

COPYRIGHT © Alexa Aston

Published by Oliver-Heber Books

0 9 8 7 6 5 4 3 2 1

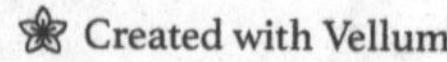 Created with Vellum

PROLOGUE
NEW YORK—1845

The whispers sounded like screams echoing in her head. All Cara Lee's senses had magnified over the last twenty hours while she labored to bring forth the baby. She weakly gripped the cheap coverlet in her fists, willing the pain to go far away.

"The blood loss is great, sir. If you had only called me earlier, I might have—"

"Just leave. Give me a few minutes... with my wife."

Gordon's voice. Full of anguish. *Oh, he was good.*

The midwife walked reluctantly to the door. "Five minutes only, sir. The babe will soon be here. Please—"

"Yes, yes." He eased the woman out the door and leaned against it, his long frame graceful as he removed a handkerchief from his pocket and dabbed his brow.

What had she seen in him?

Cara Lee wished she could reverse time, return to being the naïve schoolgirl she'd been before she listened to his flattery and lies. He was so handsome on the stage. She'd almost taken leave of her senses when he actually spoke to her after the performance.

Suddenly, another pain gripped her belly. She gave out a low, guttural howl.

"My God, Cara Lee. You sound like a wolf in the wild."

Gordon pulled up the lone rickety chair, fixing the crease in his trousers before turning his attention to her.

"The midwife says you're dying. Something about losing too much blood. Don't worry about the baby. I'll take him to Max."

She eyed him suspiciously. "What if it's a girl?" She wouldn't have been bold enough to cross him before. *Funny, how dying changed everything.*

Her husband shrugged. "I suppose a girl will do. Either way, I'll get my money."

So, it was true. He'd married her for reasons other than love. She'd been tempted to go to Maximilian Fisher but was too ashamed of what he might say to her. And by marrying a penniless actor, her Boston Brahmin parents disowned their foolish only child. Her father's word had always stood stronger than the law. If she'd appeared at her childhood home seeking assistance, the door would have been shut in her face. Not slammed in the heat of the moment, but quietly closed in cold admonition, locking her out from a much-needed refuge.

She had nowhere to turn in these last minutes. Not a friend left in the world. No one would mourn for her. Especially her cruel spouse.

Gordon removed his money clip. He placed a few bills on the bed, soaked in her sweat and water and blood.

"That's enough to satisfy the midwife. Sorry I don't have enough for your funeral, love."

Cara Lee bit back the scream and held it in her

throat. The contraction ended. She refused to give him another reason to belittle her.

To her surprise, Gordon pecked her on the cheek. He reeked of cheap perfume and another woman. He'd left her alone soon after her labor pains began, locked in this dismal bedroom, only returning an hour before with the midwife. Not that she could have gone anywhere with the crippling pains, or that she knew anyone in this city of strangers.

"Try to hurry up, dear. I've got an appointment, and I'll still need to take the baby to a wet nurse that I've found. She'll care for it a few weeks before I present it to Max. I'll share with him how you passed in childbirth while I was on stage in Boston, and that I buried you there." He chuckled. "You know, Reverend Monty could do your funeral."

Cara Lee remembered the jovial man who had married them. He had smiled broadly at her throughout the brief ceremony.

"That would be nice," she murmured, as she floated away. The odd feeling of euphoria was short-lived as she gasped, torn apart once again. She was past tears now. She only wished she were past the never-ending pain.

"No, come to think of it, he's in Chicago. Doing *King Lear,* if I'm not mistaken."

She tried to focus on what her husband said, but he didn't make any sense.

Gordon beamed at her. "You didn't really think we were married, pet? I thought you realized long ago Monty was a fellow thespian."

The banging on the door interrupted him. "Please, sir. Let me back in."

"Oh, all right." Her lover—her great deceiver—

opened the door and ushered the stout woman in. "Shall I wait in the hall?" he asked pleasantly.

The midwife came to the bed and lifted the covers. "The head! My God, the baby's coming out. Push, missus, push. Push for your life!"

Cara Lee gritted her teeth and bore down hard. A great relief washed over her. She closed her eyes, unwilling to see the man who had meant everything to her and who now betrayed her in her greatest hour of need.

"There, little one, there you go."

Cara Lee heard a slap and a hearty cry. She opened her eyes and saw her baby. Love burst from her.

"It's a boy, missus. Hale and hearty. Even got a nice head of hair on him."

Rustlings and soft noises were all Cara Lee heard as she faded in and out. Then in her exhaustion, she sat up.

"He's mine," she spit out, glaring at Gordon Fisher. "You can't take him."

"Oh, I can and I will, dear girl. This child is the meal ticket to my trust fund. You didn't think Max would loosen his grip and leave all his money to a worthless actor now, did you?"

He took the baby, now clean and wrapped in his mother's ivory shawl. He spoke in low tones to the midwife before turning back to her. "This child will prove I'm respectable. I thank you for all you did, my dear."

Gordon retreated from the room. She let out an anguished cry.

"Well, I never..." The midwife shook her head. "Let's see if I can make you comfortable, dearie."

Cara Lee began to moan as the woman fussed over

her. She was having trouble breathing again, just like before. A great weight pressed upon her.

"The worst is over now, missus. Let me just deal with the afterbirth. Maybe I can staunch the bleeding."

As the midwife lifted the sheet again, she gasped. "Oh, no. Oh, my lord."

Cara Lee broke out in a cold sweat. The pain was back again, this time even worse. Her body, her spirit, her faith in her husband. All had been broken. How much more could she bear?

The midwife clucked loudly. "Another one's coming, child. You'll have to be strong a little bit longer."

She sat up again. The burning urge to push herself to her limit had returned. It was stronger than the first time. She bit her lip hard and willed the baby to exit the birth canal. The burden eased from her, and the midwife cut the cord as before.

"It's another boy. Spittin' image of the other tyke."

Cara Lee smiled weakly at the newborn. The room began to grow dark. She reached out to touch her child. "I love you, sweet boy," she croaked.

The baby gurgled happily.

"You mustn't call him back. Don't ever let..." Her voice trailed off.

A wet cloth glided across her forehead. *What I wouldn't give for a sip of cool water.*

A few minutes later the midwife pulled the stained bedsheet over the woman's head. She stared blankly at the wide-eyed baby in her arms.

"Lord Almighty. I never even knew your mama's name."

1

CALIFORNIA—1870

The sheriff dragged in another drunk and threw him into the overcrowded jail cell. "Just one more to add to the smell, fellas."

He cackled as he hooked the key onto the ring hanging on the wall. He lumbered over to his chair and sat, throwing booted feet up on the desk. In under a minute, snores began.

Jed shook his head in disgust, wondering how this beer-bellied swine ever got elected to office.

He raised his hands above his head in a bored stretch. He had no room to move them anywhere else. The small cell was a temporary home to nine other men, ranging from their early twenties to a balding dentist that had to be over seventy. Most had committed petty crimes. Two were horse thieves and would hang with him.

Jed had landed in this jail for robbery and murder. The Landrey gang had held up two trains in Nebraska and another three in Texas. They'd shot a conductor trying to disarm one of the robbers. Killed an elderly passenger refusing to part with his gold pocket watch. Gutted a third they caught sneaking off one of the trains.

Hanging Hal, Stockton's local judge, was getting married for the fourth time today. He'd promised his betrothed there'd be no killing on her wedding day.

Jed had until noon tomorrow to live.

Trouble was, he didn't belong to the Landrey gang. The sheriff arrested him eight days ago in a saloon as he tried to find a pick-up card game. He protested his innocence while being escorted to the nearby jail. Once there, the sheriff thrust a flyer into his hands. One look at it silenced him.

Jed had stared at his picture on the wanted poster. Below the image were the name Cal Hart and a description of his crimes. He'd spent most of the past eight days trying to understand the fact that he had a double wandering around.

And he would hang for Cal Hart's crime spree.

His trial consisted of little more than the charges being read. Hanging Hal decided that Jed would 'hang *from the neck until declared dead by an attending physician.*' With the way the judge thundered the phrase, he knew with certainty that Hal had delivered it often over the years.

He closed weary eyes, tired of staring at the peeling paint. He wondered idly if Louis had been partner to such despair in his last hours, as he awaited the hangman's noose for a murder he didn't commit.

The thought of his closest friend brought a bittersweet smile to his lips. Louis, the amiable drunk, told him over and over again, "I see big things for you, Jed Stone."

Big things, indeed.

Jed regretted growing the heavy beard that itched unmercifully. It made him start every time he caught his image in a mirror, thinking a stranger glared back at him. His plan had been to alter his appearance

"Even the harmless drunks?" Ezekiel asked. He pointed to the far right. "I know that one is Lenny the barkeep's cousin. I don't think anyone wants Lenny mad at us."

"Then let the drunks go." A large, muscular man stepped forth, a knotted rope in his hands. "We'll just string up the others, one at a time." He coiled the rope around his hands and pulled it taut.

Jed took a calming breath. He'd been in worse situations before. The war saw to that. He'd learned to stay focused and always keep thinking. Too many men acted from their gut without playing out a scene first.

Jed knew what he would have to do.

The rabble pressed closer. The man with the torch shoved his way to the front as others began to press and nudge up to the bars.

Ezekiel took the ring of keys from the wall and slipped one into the lock. As he turned it, the crowd anxiously surged forward. Someone knocked the torch from the hand of its holder. It hit the man along his pants leg as it fell to the ground. The trousers caught fire.

Screaming, the man clutched the bars in front of him. The instant smell of charring flesh permeated the room. Shouts for a blanket were lost as the mob rushed to help.

Jed forced the cell bars back, springing from his prison. The other prisoners followed behind him. As fists flew, the kerosene lantern went out. He crouched low and moved along the floor toward the desk. He felt its leg and rose up, skimming his palms alongside the surface.

He grabbed the items on the desktop the sheriff left behind. In the general confusion and darkness, he rushed in the direction of the door. He found the knob and turned it, squeezing through a narrow slit.

Darkness closed around him. Night had fallen a couple of hours before. Jed hustled down the main street, keeping close to the buildings for cover. He pocketed the cuffs and slipped the pistol in at the small of his back. The badge he pinned on his chest.

He saw a lantern in the distance. If memory served correctly, it was near the livery. He was in need of a horse. He couldn't outrun the mob on foot. Sooner or later, someone would realize he'd escaped.

He prayed Rascal was there, but would take any mount.

Jed vaulted the fence silently. The corral was empty. He made his way to the barn door and opened it noiselessly. The sweet smell of hay and horseflesh greeted him.

"Rascal?"

A nickering response told him to steer to the right. He located the top of the first stall door, and by touch moved along the inside of the barn.

"Rascal?"

A loud snort echoed near his ear.

"Well, excuse me, boy, but I was detained." He slipped into his horse's stall and rubbed the animal's alert ears with affection.

"We need to shake the dust of this sorry place from our feet."

He found Rascal's blanket and saddle. Jed had experience slipping out of darkened towns so tacking Rascal up took only a minute.

He stroked the horse's blaze. "Let's go, fella."

His eyes adjusted to the unlit barn. He quietly led the gelding from the stall. They crossed the pen and he eased open the gate. Once through, he swung into Rascal's saddle.

"We need to fly like the devil," he told the bay.

Rascal responded to the slight touch of his boots. Jed raced west down the dirt street of Stockton, determined to find Cal Hart before the law found him again.

2

J ed surveyed the lighted house from across the street. Two men wove drunkenly up the stairs leading to the front porch, both laughing loudly. They paused and knocked. A moment later, the door opened. Music wafted out into the night air as they entered.

It was near ten. Jed desperately needed a few hours sleep. He'd constantly looked over his shoulder to make sure no one followed him from Stockton. After three days of hard riding in all kinds of circles, he hoped he'd shaken off anyone on his trail. He figured the only person who would receive less sympathy than an accused murderer would be an escaped murderer, regardless of whether he proclaimed his innocence or not.

The night air caressed his face. He'd taken time yesterday to rid himself of the cumbersome beard. The image reflected in the still pool he'd used as a mirror showed a very different man from both the clean-shaven and bearded Jed Stone. He was still amazed how a mustache and a change in his hair's part and length made such a difference. He doubted even Elmira, who'd been at his birth, would know him at this point.

San Francisco had been his eventual destination. He'd just hastened his arrival here. He knew next to nothing about the place, other than it flourished during the Gold Rush of Forty-Nine. Now the tenth largest city in the country, it was famous for gambling fever. Miners and entrepreneurs who overran the place twenty years ago brought that element of thrill with them. Fortunes were won and lost here on the turn of a single card.

It was his kind of place.

Louis had been the one to mention Lucky Lil's. He said it was a smaller house on Kearney Street, one with pretty girls of all races and any game of chance imaginable. Jed had nowhere else to go. He might as well start at Lil's.

He hitched Rascal to a post across the street and gave him a pat. "You should be full. That hay wasn't two hours ago. Let me grab some shut-eye and then we'll figure out our next move."

Jed crossed the street and strolled up the walkway. Louis said Lil's serviced all kinds. After his long, dusty ride, he prayed they'd still welcome him. Of course, a whorehouse was a whorehouse, and he did have money to spend. At least, he had what he hid in his boots before that ornery sheriff arrested him and pocketed his money clip.

If he ever found Simon Morgan, he'd have a whole lot more. Jed intended to get back every dime Morgan took from him and then some.

A tall Indian answered his knock. His smooth skin was a deep brown, the color of fine leather. He could have been anywhere from thirty to fifty years of age.

"Welcome to Lucky Lil's."

The Indian ushered him inside, where the piano player tinkled the ivories with *Camptown Races*. The thick carpet was a bit worn, as was the wallpaper, but Jed recognized it as Aubusson. A quick glance told him the furniture was Italian and of good quality. It had seen better days, but he supposed Lil's did business year-round.

He glanced up at the crystal chandelier in the hallway, polished to perfection.

"Might I recommend a certain girl to you, or are you here for a game of chance?"

The low voice came from his left. Jed turned to see a raven-haired woman with hard eyes staring up at him. She was pretty in a garish way. Heavy make-up made it impossible to discern her age. Her eyes, rimmed with thick, black eyeliner, glittered like amber. Bright red lipstick and rouge made her pale skin even paler.

"I'm Lil. What can I do for you?"

"A friend recommended the place. I'd like a woman and a room for the night."

The madam frowned at him. "I can provide the first easily but you'll have to be out by three. House policy."

He snorted in amazement. "You're joking."

Lil glared daggers in return. "I never joke about business, *ma cherie*."

She gestured to the Indian who'd received him. He stepped immediately to her side.

"Find Gertie."

The man nodded and headed up the staircase.

"You'll like Gertie. Actually, she'll like you. She has a thing for men with intense blue eyes." Lil sized him up. "She also likes them tall. A little cleaner than you but I'll send up hot water. I'm sure you'd like to freshen up after a long ride. You have just arrived in town?"

Jed fought the chill that raced through him. Lil was one wise cookie. "Hot water would be much appreciated."

A petite blonde flew down the stairs, holding her red skirts high to show off trim ankles and more than a little of her calves. She stopped directly in front of him. "Ooh, Lil, he's a looker, even with the grime." She slipped her arm possessively through his. "Come on, sugar. We can think of all kinds of things to do between now and three."

Gertie guided him up the steps. As they moved higher, Jed surveyed the open room off to the right, seeing gaming tables. Suddenly, he froze.

"What's wrong, sugar? Someone walk over your grave?" Gertie giggled girlishly, a sound that seemed out of place for her line of work.

"Nothing. Let's go."

They turned left and went down a long hallway peppered with many doors. Gertie paused at a door third from the end.

"Go on in and get comfortable. I'll see to that hot water." She gave his cheek a pat and winked seductively.

He entered the room and let out a sigh.

Simon Morgan was here, in San Francisco, right at Lucky Lil's. Jed wished he could deal with his nemesis tonight but he was bone tired. Besides, he would need all his wits about him when they did meet. He also didn't want Simon to know how little cash he had at the moment. Before he could embark upon any scheme, he needed to up his stakes considerably. Still, he'd been on a lucky streak before he'd hit Stockton. He knew it hadn't tapped out yet.

When he was ready, he would meet up with Simon Morgan—on his terms.

Gertie returned with hot water in two tin buckets, easily maneuvering them for a woman, though she sloshed water everywhere in the process. "Let me help you clean up. What's your name, sugar?"

"Bret." He rarely used his real name, like many of the gamblers he knew, since they often danced along the edge of the law. Jed doubted he would respond to it if a passerby called out to him.

"Well, Bret, you and me are going to have a fine time. I just feel it in my bones." She unbuttoned his shirt as she spoke and slipped a hand inside. As she stroked his chest, she looked into his eyes.

"My, you have the bluest eyes I've ever seen, just like a clear pond. I ain't never seen eyes so pretty on a man."

She pulled his shirt away from his shoulders and leaned closer. "Let's get this off, sugar. I think you'll cool off a spell if we do."

He let Gertie fuss over him. It was a luxury he'd done without, growing up. Elmira wasn't much of a toucher, despite being a midwife. Jed never saw her deliver a baby, but he was hard-pressed to think of her as nurturing.

Soon he was fairly clean, although he worked up a nice sweat sporting with Gertie. She was easy to please and now lay cuddled against his side. He'd never been able to sleep with a woman in his bed, though, and he needed rest desperately.

"Gertie?"

"Hmm?"

He kneaded her shoulder gently. "Do you think you could leave and let me get some sleep?"

The girl's mouth turned into an instant pout.

"Didn't I please you, Bret?" She took his hand and entwined her fingers with his. "I was just getting started, sugar. Surely, you don't want to stop now?"

He gave her a smile, the one that he knew melted most women to their core. He reserved it for when he wanted something badly enough. He seldom had to use it.

"You were grand, honey. I just need to get rested up, is all." He gave her a sensual look. Lowering his voice a notch, he said, "I won't be able to if you stay right beside me."

Her eyelashes fluttered prettily. "I won't cause you a bit of trouble."

He grinned at her. "I'd say '*Trouble*' is your middle name." He kissed her, a slow, deep kiss, one that would please any woman. "I just have to get some shut-eye."

"As long as you're out by three."

Jed sat up. "What is this obsession with three? That Lil woman gave me heck for questioning her about it."

Gertie's eyes grew wide. "Oh, you don't want to get on Lil's bad side, Bret. Her rule's hard and fast. She's had it nigh on twenty years, ever since she came here from France and set up business back during the Rush."

He brushed a soft kiss along her jaw. "I bet we can break it just this once."

Her mouth set quicker than concrete. "No. Lil's good to her girls. It took me three years to work my way in here. I ain't going to give her a reason to kick me out. Not even for the bluest eyes west of the Rockies."

Jed knew only one thing would change Gertie's mind. He reached for his trousers and removed a ten dollar gold piece. He placed it in her palm and wrapped her fingers around it.

"Just bunk in with a friend for a few hours. If I can sleep until five, I'll be outta here. Maybe there's a back staircase I could slip down?"

Gertie opened her hand to stare at the money. He saw her toss the argument back and forth in her mind. When she made a fist with the piece inside, he knew he'd won.

After all, he was a gambler.

"Promise you'll be quieter than a dead mouse?"

Jed crossed his heart. "On my honor as a former Union soldier."

She left the bed and slipped on a wrapper. She opened the door a crack before motioning to him. He pulled on his trousers and moved to her.

"Poke your head out and look left," she instructed. "And do it quickly."

He did so, spying a heavy door at the end of the dimly lit hall. He leaned back into the room. "Outside door?"

Gertie nodded. "It's a separate staircase that goes down into the back yard. There's a hen house and a small barn. Lil is sweet about us always having fresh milk and butter. Says it's good for our complexions."

She stared at him anxiously. "You can't tell anyone about this. Don't go bragging or nothing after you leave."

He gave her a solemn look. "I wouldn't do anything to hurt you, Gertie. I may want to see you again."

She beamed at him, pleased at his words. "Then I'll be two doors down, toward the staircase. Same side of the hall. That's if you need me. You will be out by five?"

He nodded. She left the room and he returned to

the bed. Too tired to remove his pants again, he sank back onto the feather pillow and a dreamless sleep.

JED AWOKE TO THE PRICKLING. It had always been a warning sign. He went to the window. In the faint light he consulted his pocket watch. Quarter to five. Time to go.

In less than a minute, he slipped into his boots and shirt. His hat sat back in the Stockton jail. Fortunately, he had the grace of a jungle cat. He doubted anyone would hear him leave. If the three o'clock rule was as sacred as he'd been led to believe, he assumed all the whores and help would have bedded down a good hour ago. They'd all be in a deep sleep.

He cracked open the door. No sounds stirred from the hall or below. He eased open the door and looked out.

Holy Moses! A woman. Coming down the darkened hallway.

Jed ducked back inside the doorframe. Before he closed the door, a loud banging sounded downstairs.

3
___

The knock startled her—but not half as much as the man who grabbed her. He snaked his left arm around her waist. His right hand covered her mouth.

Lily struggled as he snapped her back close against him. Through her thin silk wrapper she felt hard chest. Her hands, locked onto his forearm, touched tension coiled tightly around muscle.

She heard Ben hollering, "Hold your horses."

Instinctively, her gut told her the visitors below would be looking for this man.

He whispered the same into her ear, his mustache tickling as he asked, "Can you buy me some time?"

She nodded, not sure if she would or not. The stranger dropped his hand from her mouth but still kept her next to him.

It surprised her when she said, "Follow me."

Reluctantly, Jed let her go. She had a freshness about her. The scent of strawberries. He wondered why she was in a place like this, with her silk wrapper and sweet curves.

She moved quickly to the room on the end, the one by the back stairs. He heard the front door being opened below. Muffled voices caused his prickling to ignite like wildfire.

Hot on her heels, he followed her into the darkened chamber. In the faint light he made out a bed and a shape within it. Maybe others had broken the sacred curfew.

The room had an odd smell, almost medicinal in nature which his mind didn't have time to process. He felt along the furniture. Must be a bureau from its shape and length.

The girl opened a wardrobe door. He heard the swish of clothes being pushed aside, then a spring popping.

"Get in," she whispered. "It has a false front. It may be a while. Be patient."

Jed climbed in on blind faith. He willed his muscles to keep from moving when he heard noise at the door.

"Miz Lil. Men lookin' for someone."

The house madam's deep voice answered. Jed bit the inside of his mouth. This must be her room. The girl who brought him here had grit. Lil herself must've been the shape he saw in the bed. He wondered if old Lil knew who graced her wardrobe.

"I'm not my usual beautiful self, gentlemen. Sorry I can't receive you now."

He imagined she barely opened her door, not wanting her visitors to see her rumpled from sleep. Even whores liked to look good for men.

Jed heard the sneer in their voices as they spoke. He strained to remember if any of the muffled voices sounded familiar and thought he recognized the Stockton sheriff's.

"We're looking for a man, ma'am."

Lil chuckled low. "Aren't we all?"

"We tracked him here. Found his horse hitched across from your place. He's about two inches over six feet. One-eighty or one-ninety. Dark blond hair and a beard. There's a reward for his sorry hide."

"Sounds like a lot of men who come here," the madam purred. "Maybe you can help jog my memory, boys."

He listened at the long pause. He assumed someone was pulling out money and counting it into Miz Lil's greedy little hand. He hoped he'd go higher than thirty pieces of silver but he wasn't counting on it.

"Yes, he was with me, gentlemen. Left here shortly before three. You know my famous rule."

Jed heard the nonchalance in her voice. "I don't know or care where he went. Wish I would've known about the reward. I would've turned in his sorry hide. Especially since he wasn't much in bed."

Laughter echoed. The tightening in his chest loosened a bit. So, she wasn't going to tip her hand. But did she have to save his hide at the expense of his reputation?

He shook his head. He'd choose being alive with a reputation in shreds any day. It was better than accompanying the voices he heard to God knew where.

Their conversation grew dim. Jed relaxed further until he heard Lil bark out, "Go back to bed! Catch up on your beauty sleep, *mes amis*. I'll expect smiling faces and no dark circles come the morrow. *Vite! Vite!*"

Silence reigned for a good half-hour. Jed grew tired on his feet, being used to conducting most of his business seated at a gaming table. Little air circulated in the small space. At least he hadn't buttoned his shirt before. That gave him some small relief.

Before he realized it, his hiding place was revealed.

The shape of a woman stood before him in the growing light. She wore the same low-cut gown from the previous evening, her make-up caked on. He wondered if she slept in it.

In an angry whisper she hissed, "May I have the name of the only fool who ever broke my rule?"

"Maybe I'm the only fool who's ever been caught." He stepped from the wardrobe, causing her to back up.

"If I'd been gone five minutes earlier like I planned, you would've never known I hung around."

The madam shrugged, a Gallic gesture he recognized from his time with Louis. It could mean many things.

"You can't go now. They might be watching despite what I said." She walked to the window and pulled the curtain aside. "Although they said a man with a beard," she mused.

Jed stretched his arms over his head. The bedchamber seemed large as a barn after his cramped sojourn.

"Miz Lil?"

She turned and studied him thoroughly. He swallowed. It couldn't hurt to ask.

"I'm running a bit low on cash now. I was wondering if you might want to split that money they gave you."

The look she gave him would ice hell over and the Seven Seas, to boot. Miz Lil was one tough customer. He doubted she serviced anyone nowadays. He wondered if she'd been any good at it in younger times. Despite her lush figure, he didn't picture her tenderly cooing over any man.

"Go back to Gertie's room. I'll deal with her later."

Jed remembered the fear the girl had at being

kicked out of Madam Lil's establishment. She'd risked her neck for him. He wouldn't abandon her.

"You can't blame Gertie for what happened."

Lil's smoky voice dropped. "I can, and I will. She knows the consequences of breaking my rules."

Jed stepped close to the madam. "I threatened her, ma'am. Slapped her around. Told her I'd do worse if she didn't leave me to get a couple hours of shut-eye."

Lil laughed harshly. "You don't strike me as the type who'd swat a fly."

He grabbed her, his fingers digging into the soft flesh. His face was inches from hers as he revealed, "I did a lot worse in the war. Those things stay with you. Don't push me, Lil. I'm not as affable as I look."

He broke his hold and backed off. He didn't catch any fear in her eyes. He only saw admiration.

"Go back to bed," she ordered. "And get cleaned up before you see me. The staff eats around four. I'll expect you after that in the upstairs parlor."

Jed understood the dismissal and retreated back down the hall. The bed called invitingly to him. He slipped out of his boots and crawled onto it face down. He snuggled up with the pillow, the tension dropping from his body in waves.

As he drifted away, he wondered what happened to the girl who hid him. What troubled him more, though, was why a woman twenty years his senior had him feeling so randy.

4

———————

Lily sipped from the Waterford tumbler on her dressing table. The brandy slid down her throat and settled in her stomach, spreading its magic glow. She twirled the crystal glass in her hand, watching the amber liquid slosh lazily.

She set down the drink and reached for her cigarette, taking a long drag and exhaling. She would never acquire a taste for tobacco but her mother was known for smoking. That and years of hard drinking helped create the low, musical voice which purred like a cat for men.

She wondered what her schoolmates would say if they could see her now. They wouldn't be half as shocked by the smoking and drinking as they would if they heard about her attendance at this morning's suffragette meeting at Dashaway Hall. The convention drew women from all backgrounds, but not the Boston blue-bloods and other East coast socially prominent girls from her boarding school. They would be appalled by her presence at such a gathering.

Lily loved every minute of it.

She'd read from an early age, thanks to her nanny.

She'd been lucky to have the time with Sarah Hall. A proper Englishwoman whose husband had been caught up in Gold Fever, Sarah eventually joined him in California, only to learn he'd been shot dead over a disputed claim. With little money and no connections, Sarah wound up at Lucky Lil's, desperate to do anything.

Even the unthinkable.

Fortunately, Lilian Frontiere recognized Sarah's intellectual talents, and put her to work as nanny to her only child. Sarah exposed Lily to literature and art and gave her an appreciation for the city of San Francisco.

When Sarah passed on from an unexpected heart attack, Lily was desolate. Her mother decided at thirteen it was time her daughter spread her wings and so she'd been sent to school back East just before the war broke out. The next several years, she'd been safely ensconced in a female academy. Despite her background being so different from the other students, she thrived.

"Lily?"

She sprang from her chair and went to the bed.

"*Maman*? How do you feel?"

She fussed over Lilian, straightening her pillows, brushing her raven hair, giving her lukewarm tea. She didn't have much success with the latter. Lilian ate or drank very little nowadays, saying most things upset her stomach.

"I have things to tell you, Lily." Her mother sighed. "I have made a mess."

Lily clucked her tongue. "No worrying. We'll deal with it, *Maman*. I have gone through the books. I will fix things, even if I am rather put out with you."

Lilian's eyebrows raised. "*Oui*?"

"Oh, *Maman*, you spent far too much on our trip to Europe and all those fancy clothes. I'm sure my education cost a fortune, too. Why did you do it? I would have been content to stay in San Francisco and be with you."

"You worry too much, *ma cherie*." Her mother stroked Lily's cheek gently. "I wanted you to see Paris. To show you the places of my youth. I needed you to see your roots, Lily. Feel the spirit of the people. Taste remarkable wines and melt at desserts that only those in Paris can create."

She sniffed. "Well, I saw a lot more than my roots. Look where that trip got me."

Lilian sighed. "Not all men are Pierre, *ma petite*."

Her mouth tightened more than the Mona Lisa's at the mention of Pierre's name. "At least I found I don't need any man—except as a client."

She removed the tray holding the tea from the bed and placed it on the floor. "The gaming is going well. Simon Morgan had a good run last night, but he draws in a crowd willing to risk more, so we came out fine."

"Did he bother you?"

Lily kept her face a mask. "Simon always irritates me. You know that."

"You are being evasive, *ma douce*." Lilian winced, her face screwing up tightly.

"I'll get the belladonna."

She went to the dressing table. Placing several drops into a tall glass, she poured water over it.

"Drink this," she told her mother.

Lilian fought to get down the contents. Lily was grateful that belladonna was so readily available. Many of the girls at Lucky Lil's took it for the pain they suffered from being laced so tightly into their corsets. It had been the one thing that offered her mother any sort of relief in recent weeks.

"Before I fall asleep, we must talk, Lily."

She took her mother's hand in hers. It was cold to the touch. She rubbed it and held it close to her face.

"Nothing is that important. Wait until tomorrow."

"We are running out of tomorrows. There can be no more putting it off." Her mother stared into her eyes. "I've been gambling."

She dropped her mother's hand. "Gambling?"

Lilian Frontiere had two cardinal rules. One was that all guests were escorted off the premises by three each night. It had set up exclusivity to Lucky Lil's. Men came in droves to their house. Lily remembered in the early days how they had to turn men away, only accepting those who brought a letter of introduction from a previous, steady customer.

The second rule had been no gambling. Ever. From the house madam at the top down to the lowest kitchen maid, Lilian Frontiere demanded that gambling not touch their lives.

"It's a disease," she'd drilled into her daughter and her staff many times. "It only brings heartache in the end."

That's why this new information startled her. Of course, it would explain where such vast amounts of money had gone with nothing to show for it.

"Why?"

Lilian shrugged. "Why? Why not? How does anything like that ever start? I ran a little short one month. It's expensive to run a proper house. The payoffs to the police. The fees for licensing. All the salaries."

Lily mentally ticked off just how many salaries. The domestics that kept Lucky Lil's sparkling clean. A large cook staff that fed the girls before business began and set up the lavish buffets for which the house was known. The bouncers, rarely needed, but always evident in case trouble broke out. Raymond, their long-time piano player, and the nightly string quartet that played during his breaks.

Thank goodness they didn't pay the girls themselves a salary. Lilian simply split fifty-fifty with them, taking the girls' wages from what they collected from their clients.

"I thought I knew enough after all these years. I can spot a cheater at any given table." A fat tear slid down her mother's cheek. Suddenly she seemed old to Lily. "I was wrong."

Lilian shifted, grimacing again. "I had a short run of very good luck but I had caught the fever by then. I couldn't stop. When the bad streak hit, I thought just one more toss of the dice would begin another good run.

"It didn't."

She worded her question carefully. "How much are we in for, *Maman*?"

Lilian shook her head sorrowfully. "I confess I put the house up at the bank. It is mortgaged to the hilt."

"When does the first payment come due?"

"At the end of February."

"Next month," echoed Lily.

"I don't know what to do." Lilian's words began to slur. The belladonna was taking affect. She watched her mother drift into sleep as her own anger bubbled up and threatened to spill over.

She went and sat down at the dressing table again, her thoughts returning to Simon Morgan. If she were dressed as herself, he would've pawed at her again last night. She knew Morgan wanted her—and Lucky Lil's.

Did he know the bank now held the deed?

She rearranged the jars in front of her. She was furious at her mother, frustrated by what she'd learned. She finally calmed herself, and skillfully smoothed on the layers of cosmetics as she thought how Simon would pounce on them like a wolf among tender sheep. What could she do to prevent that? Ideas flitted through her mind.

None of them held the answers she longed for.

When she completed her work, she stared at the image in the mirror.

She was Lilian Frontiere.

At first when Lil's health began to fail, she took off the occasional night. Lily noticed a subtle shift in attitude at those times. From the clients. From the girls themselves. People had a tendency to slack off without her mother's constant presence to keep them in line.

Respect came to Lil through her hard work and determination. Lily realized she couldn't step in and command a room the way her mother did.

Instead, she became Madam Lil.

They had always been the same size. That was a blessing. Though Lily never had dressed provocatively as Lilian did, she filled out the clothes as well as her mother. She covered her cinnamon-colored hair with an expensively-made wig. With the right touches of make-up and the raven-black hair, she was a dead ringer for Madam Lil.

Lily enjoyed the challenge of her charade. She had excelled in dramatic arts, winning the lead in many school productions. Many of her mannerisms were already similar to Lil's. Her impersonation was the challenge of a lifetime.

She had pulled it off. Of course, Ben and her mother knew but she had the others fooled. Her gestures, her pitch, her stance—they all had become Lil's.

The staff thought Lily was staying with a friend on and off. Her infrequent appearances received little notice. Her mother had never allowed her to partake of life in the whorehouse.

She knew the other girls, many younger than she, thought her aloof and intellectual. Lily did enjoy chatting with the kitchen staff. She had spent many good times there, gossiping while the bread rose and fruit was sliced and diced. Other things she picked up after many years of observing, blending into the background, making herself as oblivious as possible.

The act gave meaning to her life. She had longed to go on stage when she finished school, but Lilian strictly forbade it. Her dream had been to go to the university, but females weren't allowed to do so by the State of California. At times, she even wished to settle down and raise a family.

But where would a girl like her meet a decent gentleman? In the next bedroom? Or shooting craps at the tables downstairs?

Suddenly, she remembered the feel of the man against her. His muscled chest. The strong arms that had encircled her.

"He was totally fooled," she said aloud.

The notion pleased her. She had also liked how he took up for Gertie. Most men wouldn't have given the whore a thought. This one actually lied about beating Gertie, simply to convince her to keep the tart on. She royally chewed Gertie's ears afterwards. But she gave the girl one more chance. Simply because the man had seemed so... *nice*. And he had a smile like an angel.

A soft tap sounded at the door. Ben entered with her dinner tray.

"How's Miss Lil?"

"About the same," she told the Cherokee. He'd always been in her life. She didn't know his connection with Lilian, but he was one of her mother's closest friends.

"Go ahead and eat. I'll sit with you and then with her a spell."

Lily daintily bit into the baked chicken. She glanced across the room at her sleeping mother. Feelings of love washed over her.

She had to forgive her mother for her indiscretions. They all occurred for Lily's own benefit. However misguided, Lilian loved her only child very much. Now Lily had to find a way to make money–and fast. If she didn't, the only home she'd known would soon belong to another.

She wondered if the stranger down the hall could help.

5

Jed sat in the upstairs parlor, awaiting his appointment with Madam Lil. He'd slept the morning away. Upon arising at noon, he went to care for Rascal and was bitterly disappointed when he found the horse gone. He assumed the men looking for him had taken the bay when he hadn't come back to claim it. Although he hadn't owned the animal for long, he would miss him.

He stopped in at the local bathhouse. For two bits, he had a bath and a closer shave than he'd been able to give himself while on the run. He looked good. And felt even better.

He was leery, though. He kept a watchful eye wherever he went, not wanting to repeat his arrest in Stockton. He didn't spot his face on any of the wanted posters he passed. He wondered where Stockton's sheriff got his copy, the one with Cal Hart's picture on it. Thank goodness he'd taken the time to shave his beard. With the mustache alone and another change in his hair, he held no resemblance to the outlaw Cal Hart.

Jed stood and circled the room, antsy for the meeting to begin. His thoughts turned to Simon

Morgan and the memory of Sherry, a young dance hall girl who was sweet on Louis. Pictures of her broken body filled his mind and thickened his throat. He owed revenge not only for what Simon had done to him, but to what Morgan and his men did to that poor girl, placing the blame for her death on Louis.

Most important of all, he would finally pay his debt to Louis. The Frenchman saved Jed's life during the war, bayoneting a Billy Yank in the back as the soldier raised his own bayonet to finish Jed off while he hunched over a downed man from his unit, unaware of the danger at his back. He was unable to return the favor when Louis was thrown into prison. Now, he would. It would just take a little more patience on his part.

The click of the door caused him to jump.

Lily looked at the man's air of vulnerability. She watched him visibly shake it off and like magic, the cocky stranger from the early morning hours returned. He was appealing but she needed to get rid of him. She didn't know why those men came looking for him and didn't know if they'd be back.

They may have asked for a bearded man but she knew they were after this handsome stranger. She only wanted someone now to help her hold onto Lucky Lil's. She'd given it much thought and determined the stranger before her couldn't aid in any way. In fact, she considered him nothing but trouble.

The quicker she got rid of him, the better.

"You look different than before, *monsieur*."

"A bath will do wonders for a man's disposition, ma'am." He ran a hand through his thick, dark blond hair. "I would like to thank you for your hospitality last night."

"Lucky Lil's is nothing if not hospitable."

"As long as a paying customer's out by three."

He beamed then like warm sunshine. Lily's heart leaped. A man with a smile like that would steal many hearts.

She ignored it. "I have provided sanctuary for you long enough. You will leave and not return. Agreed?"

"Of course. I need to push on. Previous plans and all. I do have a question, though, about a man I saw last night at your gaming tables."

"Do you know this man's name?"

"I can't quite remember it."

But Lily saw in his eyes that he did.

"He was about five-ten with a stocky build. Mustache. Black hair and black eyes. Probably mid- to late-forties."

For the second time her heart skipped a beat. He described Simon Morgan.

"Several customers fit that description, *monsieur*."

"He sat at a poker table last night. Dark suit. Wait a minute. Simon something."

Lily decided to play it out. "Oh, Simon Morgan?"

He nodded. "Yes, that's it."

"Why do you ask?"

The man shrugged. "Met him on a steamer once going from St. Louis to New Orleans. Thought he was a card player then. Seems to me he won a heap of money."

She nodded. It seemed plausible they would meet on the Mississippi. Simon often played on the steamers before the war. He still traveled back East on occasion, New Orleans being a special favorite of his.

"That would be Simon. I've heard it said he's a card sharp."

The stranger's blue eyes bore into hers. "You mean he cheats."

Lily laughed harshly and dropped her voice a bit lower. She was glad she'd just finished a cigarette before she came in. The booze and tobacco already affected her voice. Between that and her dramatic training, she was able to pitch her tone close to Lilian's.

"Not here he doesn't. But he tries anywhere he can to get away with it."

The stranger grew thoughtful. "Does he play at Lucky Lil's often?"

"More than I would like." Lily wondered why she divulged so much information, and thought it must be that smile. "But he frequents the gambling halls around Portsmouth Square. Will you try your hand at gaming there?"

"Which would you recommend?"

She paused a moment. "The Alhambra and El Dorado are well known, but many prefer Parker House or La Souciedad."

"Does Simon Morgan play any of those?"

"I know he's often seen at Bella Union and Mazourka. Why do you ask?"

The man looked at her sheepishly. "I need to avoid him for the moment. We had a problem that I'd rather he not be reminded about for a while."

Lilian was nothing if not direct. In character, Lily shot back, "He cleaned you out? He does it all the time. As I said, I won't tolerate cheating, but other houses and their players do. Especially if they bring in the kind of cash Simon Morgan does."

"Has he ever used other... means of winning?"

Lily frowned. *"Je ne comprehend pas.* What do you mean?"

The stranger himself scowled. "Has he ever applied pressure in any manner?"

She thought of the weekly pressure she experienced when Simon came around, as he touched her and played word games with her.

Jed watched her shudder. Suddenly the older, experienced madam looked very young and vulnerable. It made her very appealing.

He grinned. She was old enough to be his mother and then some.

"Well, thanks again for your hospitality." He headed for the door. As he reached it, he stopped and turned.

"I know Gertie's still around. She told me so at dinner. What happened to the other girl?"

Lil looked at him blankly. "Other girl?"

"Yes. The one that smelled like strawberries. She's the one that put me into that trick panel in your room."

Lucky Lil shook her head back and forth like he was crazy. "I don't know whom you speak of."

He started to protest, then thought better of it. "Never mind."

Jed left the room and walked down the hall.

Had she been a ghost? Or possibly his guardian angel?

Maybe there was a heaven after all. He rubbed his pocket watch for good luck just the same.

TWO DAYS LATER, Lily readied herself with care. For once it was nice to look into the mirror and see her undisguised image reflected in the glass. She smoothed a stray hair and screwed on delicate earbobs that matched her sapphire dress.

She loved going to tea at Max's house. The Nob

Hill estate was the largest in the area, bigger than those she'd visited back East with her classmates.

Lily reached for her shawl and wrapped it around her. January in San Francisco was never as cold as Boston had been, but she would take the wrap all the same. She had a tendency to be cold-natured.

Her mother slept now, as she did most days. Lily would return in time to feed her before the evening's activities began. She slipped downstairs, only passing one of the girls. Most of the others would just be stirring. The domestics were hard at work, sweeping the carpet and dusting furniture as she moved through the lower floor.

"Ready?" Ben asked, holding the door of the carriage.

"Yes."

Ben drove her each time to Nob Hill. Tea was always from three to four, and Lily knew well enough to be punctual. She and her mother had gone to tea with Maximilian Fisher for as long as she could remember. She regretted that both her mother and Max's health were such now that they hadn't seen each other in several months.

On the way over, she read the notes she'd taken at the suffragette meeting. She wanted to share a few points the speaker had made. Max approved of her interest in politics. He'd given her books on government and history, philosophy, and architecture, from the time she was young.

Until last year when he'd broken his hip, he'd always taken her to the opera and theater as well. Even now, with his access limited by where he could go in his wheelchair, they still would tour his sumptuous mansion, looking at *objects d'art* and discussing their significance. As far as Lily was concerned, Max knew everything.

Ben stopped the carriage and handed her down. "I'll be back by four. Gotta check on a few things."

She nodded. She trusted Ben implicitly. Only he knew of her ruse and the sad shape of their financial affairs. She had shared the latter with him once her mother revealed it.

Lily ascended the steps leading up to Fisher House, eighty in all. As always, she turned back to take in the magnificent view. She loved this look of San Francisco as much as one from out in the bay.

Harold answered her knock.

"Good day, Miss Lily. Master Max is in excellent spirits this afternoon."

"I'm so glad to hear that, Harold."

The butler paused before adding, "He did have an unexpected visitor arrive several minutes ago. The young man was most insistent. Master Max is with him now. Would you care to wait in the parlor?"

Lily shook her head. "No, I think I'll just wander around in the hall."

"You do love the armor, miss."

She smiled. "Yes. When I was little, I was certain that real knights hid inside it. I couldn't wait to be the first to report when they came to life."

"I'll wager your imagination is as good now as then."

"Perhaps even better, Harold."

"Then I will excuse myself." He consulted his pocket watch. "I shall have Margaret ready the tea tray. It will arrive in fifteen minutes. Master Max should be free by then."

Harold retreated down the long hallway while she walked along in the opposite direction toward the library. Outside it in the circular hall were seven sets of armor, with lances and shields, all polished to the point of blinding any visitor. She looked at them fondly. Max had instilled a love of learning in her. He read to her about Sir Gawain and Sir Lancelot from the time she sat upon his knee. Arthurian legends still fascinated her.

Raised voices caught her ear as she passed close to the library doors. What on earth could be going on? Max, angry? It seemed out of character. In twenty years, she had never heard him speak so loudly.

She didn't think twice before she pressed her ear against the massive oak door. She'd learned from an early age that eavesdropping was a very effective tool.

Muffled voices did her no good, though. She could catch the rage but not the actual words. She quietly turned the brass handle and cracked the door open an inch.

"You were spoiled from day one. Day one!"

"No thanks to you. You're richer than King Midas, but you expect me to work like a day laborer."

"There's much to be said for hard work, young man. How do you think I got where I did?"

"I don't care. All I know is you're sitting on a fortune. Why don't you just die and get it over with? I'll know how to spend the money. With relish."

"You insolent pup. Twenty-five and still no manners? I blame Gordon. No, I blame Crenshaw. If he hadn't been such a worthless drunk with an empty-headed doll for a wife, he would've handled your father with discipline. As it is, Gordon would still rather chase pretty women half his age. I'm sure you two compete for the same strumpets."

"You go too far, Max. You'll regret every word."

"You are a good-for-nothing scalawag. Get out!"

"With pleasure."

Lily eased the door back into place and stepped away. Moments later, it crashed open. She glanced up, ready to act startled. She didn't have to act.

The stranger who'd hid in her wardrobe stormed into the hall.

6

———

Lily realized she didn't even know his name. She hadn't wanted to and he certainly hadn't volunteered it.

He brushed by her, his arm catching on her bent elbow and twirling her around so hard she faced the opposite direction. Her mouth flew open, outraged that he would be so rude. Then he turned. Those crystal blue eyes flashed with anger, quickly masked. And he smiled.

It was that brilliant, touch-you-from-your-head-to-your-toes smile, she thought. One meant to be open, honest, and make her feel like anything was possible. And very flirtatious.

Lily saw it turn sensual in the blink of an eye, as he closed the half-dozen steps between them.

"Sorry, ma'am." He removed his hat and held it over his heart. "I hadn't noticed that a beautiful lady lurked outside."

Even though Lily knew the compliment to be insincere, she smiled politely. Boarding school had drilled exquisite manners into her.

"I am here to visit Mr. Fisher." She lifted her shoulders in apology. "I didn't mean to get in your way."

Fury flitted across his face. Instead of masking it, he swore softly under his breath. "That bag of bones is as useless as a busted French letter in a whorehouse."

Lily stiffened at the vulgarity. "How dare you speak in such a crude manner! You will apologize. Immediately." She glared at him, daring him to do otherwise.

He frowned for a bare instant, then mumbled, "Sorry."

Something was wrong, Lily thought. It wasn't the fact that he didn't recognize her. She knew he wouldn't. It had been dark that night and he never really saw her in a good light. She'd also whispered, due to the danger that knocked loudly at the front door. It wasn't as if he could distinguish her voice.

He acted so differently. His stance was the same, as was the dark blond hair that fell across his brow, even the smile. And yet... it was an attitude, the way he put his words together. He'd been rude to Max, but what about the vulgar remark he just made to her? He even sounded different from the man she'd spoken to while disguised as Lilian.

"How do you know Max?"

He snorted. "Know him? I'm *related* to him. I'm his great-grandson. Cal Fisher." He held out a hand to her.

Lily took it, the shock slipping around her like the fog that gathered mornings around the bay. *This man was Max's flesh and blood?*

He was tall, as Max had been in his younger days. Few reached the age of ninety and retained all their height, though. And in the two decades she'd known him, Max had always been bald. Had he once had blond hair that looked as if it were kissed by the summer sun?

She studied the man's face. Tanned, high cheekbones. A strong jaw. It was possible she saw a little bit of her friend in this man.

Fisher gave her gloved fingers a quick squeeze. "How do you know the old son of a bitch?"

Lily glared at him and pulled her hand away. "He's a family friend." She resented Cal Fisher's attitude. She disliked everything about him, now that she was seeing his true colors.

He laughed deeply, a belly laugh that rang throughout the hall. "You prefer him over me. Now, ain't that a shame?"

Something in his burning blue eyes frightened Lily. She nodded briskly. "It was nice to meet you, Mr. Fisher. If you'll excuse me?" She turned and walked toward the library door.

"Sure. Maybe we'll meet up again."

Lily refused to turn but she sensed his eyes on her. She entered the library and closed the door behind her, exhaling the pent-up nervousness he'd caused.

Max sat in his wheelchair at the picture window. He looked frail and lonely, every bit his age.

"Max?"

When he faced her, she gasped. His face was a deep purple. Lily ran to him and grabbed his wrist. His pulse raced like he'd just fought a fire on Geary Street.

"What on earth happened?"

Max shook off her hand and wheeled his chair to the fire. "Worthless brat. They're all scum. Every single one of them."

Lily followed him and sat in the wing chair next to him. "The man that was here?"

"You saw him?" His bushy eyebrows seemed to have a life of their own.

"Yes. I ran into him in the hallway. Who is he, Max?"

"That piece of rubbish is my great-grandson."

He took a handkerchief from his pocket and mopped his brow. His face had gone from purple to red. Lily hoped that was a sign he was calming down.

"Never told you about my family. No need to." He took her hand. "You and Lilian have been all the family I could ever want."

Max had been sweet on her mother since he'd arrived in San Francisco. He'd set up a branch of his business in the aftermath of the Gold Rush and never returned to New York. She wasn't exactly sure what had passed between her mother and Max, but he'd always been very generous with his time and gifts to them both.

"I'm an old man who's been unlucky in love, Lily."

He reached for a glass on the table next to him and sipped at the water in it. His hand shook as he tried to replace the glass.

"I married at nineteen. Ah, sweet Geraldine." He smiled. "Prettiest girl on the Lower East Side. Childbirth killed her a year later. I wish I could have known Crenshaw would be such a sorry man. I would've killed him on the spot, too, for taking away my precious wife."

Lily hid her shock. Max had never mentioned his family before. Curiosity helped hold her tongue.

"Crenshaw never took an interest in my businesses. Sent him to the best schools. Married him to a colleague's daughter. Now Rebecca, she was an empty-headed lass."

Harold tapped at the door and rolled in the tea cart. He looked at Max and asked, "Shall I have him shot if he tries to set foot inside Fisher House again?"

"No, no. You wouldn't deny me the pleasure, Harold. If he shows his face, I want the honor. What could they do to me? I've already got one foot in the grave as it is."

Harold poured out tea for them, adding two sugars to each and milk to his employer's. He handed them their cups.

"Eat your scones, Master Max. If you feel well enough afterwards, perhaps you can remove your foot from your grave and we'll choose the coffin that will fit in there."

Lily suppressed a giggle. Only Harold could get away with such outrageous talk. She only hoped that Max wasn't sidetracked. She wanted to hear more about his family.

Harold left and they dug into the blueberry scones, piping hot and plentiful.

"You were telling me about Crenshaw," she prompted.

Max snorted. "Wretched fellow. Took after Geraldine's side. She had one no-good brother. If Crenshaw would've lived, he might've turned out like his uncle."

"He was killed?"

Max tossed his head back and roared with laughter. He laughed for a full minute and then took his napkin, wiping his eyes.

"You could say that, I suppose. Crenshaw drank himself to death. Like Poe. Rebecca blubbered the whole way through the funeral. Caused a huge scene. Said she couldn't live without him, while half those in attendance had slept with him behind her back.

"A year later, she killed herself."

Lily almost dropped her teacup. "Did they have any children?"

"One. Gordon. Good-looking devil. Became an actor. Traveled all up and down the east coast in one play or another. Too hammy for my taste. Threatened to disinherit him if he didn't straighten up and get a real job. I wanted him to come to work with me. Settle down, marry, provide an heir for all the money I'd stockpiled."

Lily was fascinated by this unknown family saga. "Did he?"

"Yes and no. He married in Boston. Some young girl with no family. Cara Lee. Met her twice when they were first married and Gordon was doing a play in New York that his friend Monty wrote. Sweet little thing. Totally fooled by Gordon. Probably thought he was a man of good character and a loving husband. She died back in Boston during childbirth while Gordon was performing on the stage. The idiot you met in the hallway is their son."

So, that's how the stranger was connected to the Fisher family tree. Lily tossed it all about in her mind.

"The buffoon got kicked out of several good schools. A few mediocre ones after that. Got a girl with child at sixteen here in San Francisco. I demanded he marry her but she killed herself before a wedding could be arranged. Her family said it was an accident but I know better."

Max stared hard at her. "Between the two of them, Gordon and Cal have chiseled away at what money I've given them. Never done a decent day's work. Wouldn't know the meaning of the word. By God, I'm tired of them trying to bleed me dry. There'll be no more for them. No more!"

Max slammed the porcelain teacup into the fireplace. The delicate china shattered, scattering broken pieces. Lily swallowed hard.

She had come today ready to ask Max for a loan.

After hearing how his own family took advantage of him, she couldn't do it. Max had been so good to her—to them—in the past. She didn't want to seem ungrateful and treat him as shabbily as his own family had.

Knowing she would be mad at herself later, she pulled the sheets of paper from her reticule.

"Changing the subject, would you like to hear about Dashaway Hall and my suffragette meeting?"

Max shook his head. "No, not now, child. But did you hear about Mrs. Meehan? Sixty if she's a day, and fined two hundred dollars for horsewhipping Colonel Murphy. He insulted her, you know, and she wasn't standing for it."

Even though her heart wasn't in it, Lily settled back for her regular gossip session with Max.

CAL FISHER LEFT Nob Hill full of bitterness. He hadn't seen the old man in years, and look how things turned out. His father had warned him not to visit.

"Max'll chew you up and spit you out in tiny pieces, Cal. Some things never change."

He couldn't bring himself to tell Gordon how much trouble he was in. How he'd fallen in with not just the wrong crowd again but a gang of cutthroat killers. He was now wanted in several states. He didn't know how long it would take the flyers to reach California, but he was certain they would. He would hang if caught—there wasn't a doubt in his mind.

At least he'd rid himself of the beard he wore while a member of the Landrey gang. He had a barber shave all but a mustache from his face. He'd asked for a different haircut, too, telling the barber he wanted to surprise his new gal. The man had worked wonders. Cal didn't resemble the wanted poster any longer.

He'd hoped to squeeze enough money from Max to get the hell out of the country altogether. Canada? South America? He only knew he needed to leave fast before anyone connected Cal Fisher to Cal Hart's crimes.

He decided to turn to Simon Morgan. His father's friend let him hang around as a boy, taking him up and down the Mississippi on steamers. They'd work everything from monte and faro scams to poker games, with Cal signaling Simon what cards his opponents held.

It all fell apart when the war came, and those dammed Southerners lost all their money. They'd been easy marks. Great drinking companions, too. Why they went and ruined everything was beyond him.

He'd find Simon at Bella Union or Aquila d'Or if those gambling dens were still around. Both gaming houses had the best liquor and cigars, and walls that displayed life-size paintings of naked women. If not there, Simon would be somewhere around Portsmouth Square.

Or maybe Lucky Lil's. She always had the prettiest whores in town—fresh, sassy, and lots of fun. A gaming room, too. Nothing on a grand scale to compete with the big gambling halls. Just something for her customers to while away their time if they waited on a certain girl.

Yes, he thought he'd check Lil's first. If Simon weren't there, he'd turn up eventually. It had been a long time since Cal had a poke. A Lucky Lil tart was as good as any.

7

J ed entered the bank on Second, just north of Mission. He'd never set up a bank account before and wasn't sure what to expect.

"May I help you, sir?" A tall, gangly clerk about his age smiled at him. Open face. Honest. Would never be able to hide what he held in his hand. If he drew a pair of aces, he'd probably light up like a Christmas tree.

"I need to set up an account."

"Of course, sir. Cleveland Armstrong, at your service."

The clerk attempted to make small talk with him. Jed could be charming when he wished. Right now wasn't the time. After a few nods and grunts on his part, the bank employee gave him lots of paperwork to fill out. No wonder he'd never bothered before. He did want a safe place for his earnings, though. This bank had branches in several major cities, which was why he chose it. Circumstances being what they were, he didn't know if or when he'd light out again and wanted his funds available to him.

Name.

He paused a moment. He'd gone by so many

monikers over the years. He hated to tie himself to one. But maybe it was time he stayed in one place. Once he solved the mystery of the wanted poster and made sure Simon Morgan got what he deserved, he figured California was as nice a place as any to settle down. It would be interesting to roam the state and see what it had to offer.

Jed wondered what it would be like to live in one place all the time, go to work and come home at regular hours, have three squares a day right when the chimes sang out, sitting at a kitchen table he'd purchased. He never experienced that growing up. Elmira Stone was gone odd hours and sometimes for days at a time.

"A midwife's work never finishes, boy. Babies choose the most peculiar times to make their appearance."

He thought of her homely face, the small, strong hands, the dowager's hump that she developed before the consumption claimed her. He had to feel more than a little grateful that she took him in.

Jed Stone.

He printed the letters on the application form in his firm handwriting. He made up most of the rest, but it still got him the passbook he desired.

"And if you'll just inscribe your name on this signature card," the clerk told him. "That way we'll keep this on file." He grinned. "Wouldn't want anyone taking out your money but you."

Jed scrawled his John Hancock where the clerk indicated.

"I see you're a southpaw, Mr. Stone. So am I. Not too many of us. My daddy always said that not all great men are left-handed—but all left-handed men are great."

Armstrong smiled at him shyly and adjusted his

spectacles. Jed regretted his earlier, brusque behavior. The poor fellow was just doing his job. He returned the man's smile and handed him the card.

"Do you have safety deposit boxes for rent?" he asked in a pleasant tone. He wanted something he could access fast but that would still be secure.

"Of course. Follow me, Mr. Stone."

Fifteen minutes later, Jed held the key to his own protected box. He placed most of his recent winning stake inside the box. Two thousand remained in his pocket for gaming. He'd deposited another fifteen hundred in the checking account, which was why he received such nice treatment from the eager clerk.

He slipped the gold locket from his pocket and studied it a moment. Elmira said his mama was wearing it when she died. He touched it gently. Deep sorrow welled within him. Elmira hadn't known the girl's name but on the back were engraved the initials *CLF*. Jed knew one day he would learn her name.

And the name of the bastard that walked out on them.

He'd studied the picture inside the locket time and again. Many times he wished to rip it out and throw it away. Yet it, too, might someday provide a clue as to who *CLF* was.

He also unfolded a copy of the wanted poster. The sheriff in Stockton gave it to him when he swore the lawman had the wrong fellow. Jed brushed his fingers over the picture. Even in sketch form, the resemblance startled him. His eyes fell to the description below.

WANTED: DEAD OR ALIVE. Cal Hart of the infamous Landrey gang. Murder, train robbery, and rape. Armed and considered highly dangerous.

Jed wondered about the man who'd committed such heinous crimes. Sure, he wasn't in the most honorable profession himself, but he made a point of playing fair and square—unlike most gamblers. What kind of man could take money, a woman's honor, and even people's lives?

Would he ever meet this bearded outlaw face-to-face?

He placed the necklace and the wanted poster alongside the cash and closed the box. Locking it, he called for the clerk, who slipped it into its numbered slot. 722. Two of his luckiest numbers were seven and twenty-two. It was a good sign.

"Will there be anything else, Mr. Stone?"

"No. Thank you for your time, Mr. Armstrong."

He pocketed the key and account booklet and left the bank. He had enough cash to take on Simon, thanks to his lucrative two-week swing through neighboring towns, but how? He had to do more than simply take his money. He wanted to take Simon Morgan's soul, strip him of everything that meant something to him, yet Jed was fresh out of ideas.

He'd never been in the revenge business. Hell, he'd even had trouble shooting at Southerners during the war. Never saw one before the conflict began. He only enlisted to extricate himself from a messy situation. Not of his own making, strictly speaking, but one he took the blame for, nonetheless.

Jed left the bank and strolled along the Financial District. It was late in the business day and many workers streamed from their workplaces. He liked San Francisco—the buildings, the variety of people, the breeze from the Bay. Once he made Simon Morgan pay, he'd find a place to hang his hat. It'd be nice if it were here.

Maybe a card game would raise his spirits. He turned and headed toward Portsmouth Square. He'd make sure not to frequent any of the places Madam Lil had mentioned in conjunction with Simon Morgan. But he would face Simon. When he was ready.

"WHAT'S *HE* DOING HERE?" Travis nudged his companion. "It's not on until *tomorrow* night."

Monty looked Cal over. "Dressed a little nicer than before." He snickered. "You think with his granddaddy being a millionaire and all, the kid would try to look decent."

Travis took a swig of the whiskey. "He's looking around. Studying the place."

"Yeah. So?"

"It's like he's never seen the spot before."

"Well, maybe he hasn't. From what Simon said, the kid's been gone ten years or more. Things change."

Travis laughed. "Yeah. Right."

"Do you think he got the day wrong?"

"Dunno. Simon does stuff like this all the time. Likes to test people. Wonder if Rick knows?"

Monty shrugged. "He's at the craps table now. If it goes down like it's supposed to, Rick better get his butt over to the poker room. Can't rig a game if your inside man ain't in the mix."

JED LIKED VARSOUVIENNE. Better than Dennison's Exchange, where he'd spent the last several hours. He'd strolled through Arcade and Empire before that, casually checking them out. They all seemed to run a fairly clean game. He picked up a few of the more sophisticated cheaters at work, but not many were about tonight.

He nodded to a man who sauntered past. The stranger spoke a greeting to him and then seemed to think better of it. Jed wondered if he knew the man on the wanted poster.

Hell, he wasn't a Pinkerton. He really didn't know how to go about finding the criminal pictured on the wanted poster. He'd discovered from his trip through nearby towns that Stockton's Sheriff Bill had recently arrived from Kansas City, bringing a stack of placards with him.

Casual conversation in a saloon also led to information that most lawmen in California didn't care what happened back East. Still, Jed planned to keep his guard up. Sooner or later, he'd run into his double, or a lawman stalking the culprit. Men like that didn't become angels overnight. If the outlaw came to this area, he'd resort to old habits fast. Jed wished Cal Hart would stay the hell away from California and just terrorize the Midwest.

He ambled over to the buffet table. That was one perk of the gaming houses in Frisco. Free spreads of food to reel in customers. He'd even seen a massive version of it at Lucky Lil's when he stopped in ten days earlier.

He missed Lil. She had a sassy mouth on her, but then again, she was a smart woman. Maybe after his business with Simon was over, he would pay her a visit. Just to see if she'd break her famous rule again for him. He'd agreed he wouldn't frequent her establishment again, but he had a hankering to see Lil.

Jed munched on fruit and deviled eggs to start, then grabbed a hunk of fresh bread, brought out piping hot to the touch. He washed down a wedge of cheese with cold beer. He wasn't much of a drinker, but the drinks were pretty watered down. It paid to know facts like that.

Once he filled his belly, he was ready for a few hands of poker. He rubbed the case of his watch counter-clockwise. Funny, but he never could bring himself to rub it in the other direction.

He strolled into the poker room. Most of the seats were filled this time of night. The smoke from cigars and pipes hovered in the air. He spotted a man leaving and took his place. As he got closer, he saw the stranger he'd passed earlier at the same table. Maybe fate had led him to this particular spot, after all.

Jed pulled out the stool and nodded to the dealer.

"Minimum five dollar bets. Ante's two to start. Buy-in's twenty. Rick's the name. Can I get you chips, sir?"

He sat and brought out a hundred-dollar bill. Might as well start slow. Get a feel for the place and the players.

Rick exchanged his cash for chips.

The man on his left winked at him. He ignored it. Whether he thought he knew him or not, Jed focused now on the table in front of him. He liked the way Rick handled the cards. Some men had a nice touch, as this dealer did. Jed was also one of them.

It took more than touch, though. Lady Luck played a big part of it. Good math skills, too. Jed grinned, thinking of his eighth grade teacher. While other kids played chase or smoked behind the schoolhouse during the daily lunch break, the two of them had played high and low poker. Sometimes after school, too. He'd caught Seth Johnson's eye from the beginning. Both had a great memory for which cards had been played. It was one of the reasons Jed was so good now. That and Louis's tutelage during the war had made him the man he was today.

A damn fine gambler.

He sat on the dealer's right. Rick offered him the cut.

Jed rubbed his pocket watch counter-clockwise for luck, as those at the table anted up with two silver chips each.

"High poker, no wild cards, no pot limit. Here's your deal, gentlemen." Rick distributed the cards clockwise in a smooth manner to the four players seated at the table.

Jed waited to pick up his cards until all were dealt. It was habit, especially if he sat at a table of strangers. He knew cards, could categorize them in his mind quickly once he viewed them. With a glance Jed could make several combinations in his head from the cards he held.

Instead, he used the short time during the deal to study his opponents on the sly. The man next to him was big and burly. Held his cards close and evenly-spaced apart. Another picked up his cards one at a time, his eyes widening or narrowing with each one viewed. The third chewed nervously at his lip and looked around surreptitiously with the passing of each card.

All these tells could be used over time. Jed was a great observer of the game but especially the people who played it. They interested him. Fascinated him, actually. He could sit at a poker table until he turned a hundred, and never tire of the idiosyncrasies of his fellow players.

Jed had already named the men at the table. Clockwise they were Sneaky Pete, Wide-Eyed Willie, and Big Boy. Whether he learned their real names or not didn't matter. As he planned strategies in his mind, he wanted to have an easy way to refer to each player.

He lifted his cards and saw two red queens. A seven, eight, and jack rounded out his hand. Jed never rearranged cards in his hand. One of his many superstitions. Many players grouped together their straights or pairs, while most separated suits. Jed never touched the cards in his hand, other than to discard and gather up new ones.

Every man at the table had moved cards. Jed noticed where. It might mean nothing, but he was always quick to pick up on any little routine.

Sneaky Pete moistened his lips. "Five dollars." He threw a red chip into the pot.

Willie, eyes still wide, squeaked out, "Check."

"Ten." Big Boy called Pete's bet and raised it five.

In order for Jed to stay in this hand, he needed to match the five dollar call and the five dollar raise. His queens looked good so he did, tossing in two red chips to the center.

He preferred draw poker, in which the odds of getting a stronger hand increased with the chance of new cards.

Pete licked his lips again and nervously looked around. "Fold." He dropped his cards face down onto the table, now out seven dollars.

Willie quickly followed suit. "Ditto." He turned the cards down, only out his two-dollar ante.

Big Boy looked from his cards to Jed and back. "Raise you five." He added a red chip to the pot.

"Call and raise," Jed responded, dropping his two red chips along with those centered in the middle of the table.

Big Boy looked at his cards again and frowned. He

picked up a five-dollar chip and tossed it into the center of the table. "Call."

Jed fanned out his cards. "Two lovely ladies."

Big Boy snorted. "Pair of tens," he said, and laid his cards face up.

Jed didn't react, but he was surprised. Most players, if they had a poorer hand than his, would simply concede he'd won the pot without revealing what cards they'd held. Big Boy was an unusual player.

Over two hours, only he and Big Boy remained constant. Pete and Willie left within a half-hour of play. Six others came and went. Jed studied the habits of each carefully.

They'd also switched to draw poker. A player could request the change of the dealer. If the others present at the table agreed, the dealer made the switch. Big Boy had requested draw poker—jacks or better—almost an hour ago. His luck had gone from fair to poor in that space of time.

Jed, on the other hand, couldn't stop winning. He added close to fourteen hundred to the original one he began with. On a clear win streak, he'd pulled out an additional thousand from his pocket.

He found the newer players at his table more seasoned than the original participants. Consequently, the stakes rose more quickly. He didn't want to find himself tapped out, unable to bet more than what chips were before him, so he'd gotten more between hands from Rick.

"Lady Luck is smiling on you tonight, sir," the dealer said, a grin on his ruddy face.

Jed rubbed his thumb along his watch cover. "Might as well run with it while I can. She's a fickle female."

A small crowd gathered around their table. Fellow

players, who appreciated seeing a win streak unfold, congregated with girls from the Varsouvienne. One tried to get near Jed, rub his shoulders, play with his hair.

"Honey, we might get together later," he said to her over his shoulder. "But nothing, not even a good-looking woman, gets in my space—win or lose."

It was another of his superstitions. He didn't like to be distracted in any way from the game at hand. Many times the house would deliberately send over some looker to do just that. At those times, women were simply bothersome, like the flies a horse swatted away with his tail.

The girl gave him a pretty pout, but he turned his eyes back to the game. He also held his cards a little closer to the vest. With a crowd came cheating. The girl might have tried signaling what was in his hand to another player. He had learned that lesson long ago—the hard way.

Jed's exhilaration grew with each pot win. A few times he folded. A smart player respected the cards and didn't try to over-bet.

Then he got a doozy of a hand. He only drew one card after a round of heavy betting and found himself sitting on a queen-high straight flush. All those diamonds in a row winked at him. He fought to keep a smile from his face.

As the betting rounds continued, eventually every player folded except a confident Big Boy. It was obvious the player didn't see how he could be beat. The only hand that could do Jed in would be a royal flush. Even though Big Boy's bets were high, Jed doubted the gambler held the magic hand. A royal flush was so rare that many gamblers never saw it in their lifetimes.

Jed himself had only seen it once and never held it himself.

Excitement charged the air as Big Boy tossed a piece of paper into the pot that sat next to him on the table.

"This is a deed to the best whorehouse in town." His smile didn't reach his eyes as he looked at Jed. "Worth more than its weight in gold."

Rick picked up the paper and whistled. He looked to Jed. "Will you accept this as the gentleman's call, sir?" His eyes sparkled. "Being a native, I know the value. It's a bit unorthodox, but it would cover the bet. And much more."

Jed nodded. "I'll trust your advice, Rick."

"Then it's showdown," Rick announced to the gathering. "Your cards, sir?" He motioned to Big Boy, who revealed his cards and slapped the table.

"Four sweet eights. Ain't gonna beat them, Sonny Boy." He reached toward the pot with both arms, ready to rake in the mound of chips.

Jed placed a hand on Big Boy's beefy forearm. "Wait a minute."

"Get your hand off me," Big Boy growled.

Jed removed his hand and laid his cards face up on the table. "Queen-high straight flush."

Big Boy's mouth flew open then clamped quickly shut. He threw the stool back. "Damn!" he shouted, as he stomped away from the table, the crowd buzzing. The burly man had been cleaned out.

"Congratulations, sir," Rick told him.

"Was a good night, Rick." Jed scooped up a handful of hundred dollar chips and gave them to the dealer.

The dealer beamed at the incredibly generous tip. "I assume you're ready to cash in?"

Jed nodded. He stood and stretched. His back ached after such a long spell sitting. He reached for the watery beer on the table and drained the glass. Pats on the back came from strangers and playing partners alike.

"I'll meet you up front, sir," Rick hollered over the din. "We can arrange an escort to your hotel."

Jed didn't have one yet. Maybe Rick could recommend one to him. He spoke idly to several around him, listening to some replaying the last hand to their neighbors.

Winning was sweet.

He worked his way to the front of Varsouvienne. The balding manager, overweight by at least a hundred pounds, waddled over to him.

"A pleasure to have you play here tonight, sir. Might I inquire your name?"

"Stone. Jed Stone."

"We hope to see more of you, Mr. Stone. Good players make for good business. As long as you give us a chance to win back some of our money in the future, that is."

Rick touched his elbow. He handed Jed a large duffel bag that contained his winnings. "Two men will escort you home, sir. I know you wouldn't want to lose those winnings the hard way. The Square can be rough this time of night."

"Call me Jed."

"Jed," Rick repeated. "And here's your document. I kept it separate."

Jed opened the folded paper with mild curiosity.

It was the deed to Lucky Lil's.

8

Will Montgomery surveyed the room and his companions, wishing for better times to hit again. He'd experienced moderate success along the East coast in touring companies, doing everything from Shakespeare to Congreve. Still, there weren't many roles now for a man with his age and girth. Audiences preferred young men, even if they had to don gray wigs to make them look old enough to play Lear or Falstaff.

And damn that John Wilkes Booth. Monty looked a much older version of the pretty boy and presidential assassin. He couldn't begin to name the number of times in the last five years that directors had passed on him.

'*Got a bit of Booth's look about you,*' one finally admitted. '*Can't take a chance with the audience, Monty. Sorry.*'

So he'd come to California, desperate for work. Theater was all he knew. He'd also remembered his old friend, Gordon Fisher, had moved here years ago, long before the war broke out. Trailing after his old man, hoping to wring another hundred dollars out of him—that was Gordon.

Fair actor. A good drinking buddy. They'd picked up like there was no lost time between them. Gordon helped Monty get this recent gig. He didn't understand exactly what was involved, only that Gordon's friend needed someone who knew how to play poker and could act like a big spender.

He thought he'd done an excellent job last night. He'd actually been caught up in the thrill of the hands, the high stakes, the atmosphere charged with money.

And even though he knew he was destined to lose in the end, he'd done it with aplomb. He was that good.

Travis gulped his beer and complimented him. "Monty, you was incredible last night. Played it to the hilt."

"Cal wasn't bad either," Rick added. "He's a really decent player. I tested him a few times but he knew exactly when to fold." He shook his head in amazement. "He almost didn't need my help to win."

"The last hand was the best," Travis continued. "And when Monty stomped off, you coulda heard a pin drop."

Monty spoke up. "I think young Cal helped there. I could feel his eyes boring into my back as I stalked away."

"Exactly. He followed you out with narrowed eyes, just as if he was sure he'd made an enemy for life."

"Greetings, gentlemen."

Simon Morgan entered the suite, looking dapper in a light gray pinstripe coat and charcoal gray pants. He swept his pearl gray hat from his head with a flourish. Monty thought Morgan himself had a bit of the thespian in him.

"Glad you could make it." He seated himself on the

yellow brocaded settee, casually draping his arm over the sofa's high back. "I'd like to finalize our plans for this evening."

Monty started and saw his companions wore the same puzzled look he himself must mirror.

"Oh, don't look like such dolts, gentlemen. Nothing's changed. I just want to go over a few of the finer points. I want this operation to proceed like clockwork."

"But... but... it went down last night, Mr. Morgan." Travis shifted uncomfortably in his seat. "The kid walked away with the deed just like we planned."

Simon Morgan exploded. "What do you mean?" His face instantly flushed a bright red. A thin line of sweat broke out above his lip and along his forehead. Monty watched a vein throb in the man's temple. It looked as if it would explode at any second.

Morgan rose and backhanded the poor kid that had delivered the bad news. Travis touched a hand to his split lip but didn't speak. No one volunteered anymore information as Morgan paced like a caged tiger around the hotel suite. The group of assembled men watched him carefully.

Suddenly, a lock turned in the silence. All eyes flew to the door as Cal Fisher sauntered in.

"Ask him," Rick said, tersely. "He can explain everything."

LILY DISTRACTEDLY TOYED with her coal-black wig as she looked into the mirror. Her mother was worse. Lily had missed going downstairs the previous two evenings because of her concern. She couldn't afford to keep up that behavior. The house would suffer.

Lilian's health wasn't her only worry. It was the money that kept her awake nights after Lucky Lil's closed down. How could she pay off the mortgage now held by the bank? If she pinched tight, she would be able to make the first payment at the end of February —but just barely. It would leave no cushion at all in case an emergency arose.

Or if a coffin and funeral needed to be paid for.

Guilt surged through Lily. She shoved it aside. The house had nothing of real value to sell. The Aubussons were worn. The furniture, while of good quality, was badly in need of new upholstery. She could part with some of the Tiffany lamps, but she dare not take down the chandeliers. If she did, she might as well place a front-page ad in the *Chronicle* that Lucky Lil's had fallen upon hard times.

Lily refused to do so.

Then who should be let go? Not the girls. They were the main source of income. She wondered if she should broach a different split. Sixty-forty? Seventy-thirty? That was more common at other houses. But never Lucky Lil's.

Raymond? Ben? How could she do without either of them? She was sick with anxiety and fear. She also wanted Dr. Sewell to examine Lilian, but her mother had said to wait.

She stood, ready to escape the sickroom where she'd lingered the past few days. She went down the hall to the upper parlor, empty at the moment, and tried to sort out the swirling mess in her mind.

"May I speak to you, Miss Lil?"

The words pierced her concentration. Lily glanced up to see Sarah Jane, with the fresh look of the minister's daughter that she was, hesitantly standing in the doorway. The girl must be back from her mother's funeral. She'd been gone almost two weeks, but she drew in a steady clientele that would be delighted with her return.

Time to get back into character.

"Yes. Come in, *mon ami*. It's good to see you have returned."

Sarah Jane motioned behind her and Lily saw she had Gertie in tow. Gertie had stayed out of Lil's way the past two weeks, probably guilt-ridden over having broken the famous rule.

The two young women, both barely in their twenties, stood before her nervously.

"What is it?"

Sarah Jane cleared her throat. "I'd ask not to service a certain customer again, Miss Lil."

Lilian occasionally got that request but not often. Since posing as her mother, Lily hadn't received one at all. It wasn't often the girls came forth in this manner. They put up with a lot—unwashed bodies, blubbery stomachs, bony knees, sharp toenails—so nearly every time this happened, it was due to a man reminding a girl of her father or lost sweetheart.

The girls realized they were in a business that counted on keeping its customers satisfied for long-lasting success and accommodated whatever acts were requested. By the look on Sarah Jane's face, though, this patron had demanded—or done—something vile.

"Who and exactly what went on?" Lily asked gently but firmly. "Was it his look or the nature of the act itself?"

Some girls were more comfortable with unusual requests than others. Sarah Jane hadn't struck Lily as being shy in any manner before now.

The girl flushed at her question. "Maybe I shouldn't have come…"

Gertie blurted out, "You weren't downstairs that night." She lowered her voice. "It was the handsome one, Miss Lil. Imagine that. The one with the devil of a smile, and was he ever a wicked devil with our Sarah Jane. I been telling her she ought to come to you. She's been too ashamed, hiding out in her room and me sneaking food up to her since you thought she was gone to her mama's funeral."

The pit of Lily's stomach went cold. "Cal Fisher? The one who broke my rule?"

"Yes!" Gertie exclaimed. "He was so awful to Sarah Jane. He wasn't like that at all with me. Even though he was tired as all get out, he pleasured me. *Me!* That happens as often as men walk on the moon."

Lily waved a hand to shush Gertie. "How did he hurt you?" she asked the other girl. "I must know."

Reluctantly, the girl shed her dress. Lily saw fading bruises in a ring around her neck, evenly spaced, as if someone had tried to choke the life out of Sarah Jane. Her torso was marred with an assortment of marks, some which looked like bite marks. Lily spotted two burns which had likely come from a cigarette.

"He broke a few ribs, too," Gertie revealed.

"You may dress now." Lily seethed with rage.

She lay a hand on Sarah Jane's shoulder. "I will ban him from here, *cherie*. He will never enter this house again. You have my word."

She waved away the profuse thanks and added, "We will get the doctor to look at you. I want you to rest for another week."

It would hurt to have the girl laid up, but Lily couldn't have other men see what had been done to Sarah Jane. Rumors spread rapidly in this town. She wouldn't have her girls subjected to criminal behavior. Other houses might not care for the well-being of its girls, but Lucky Lil's was a cut above.

"Dr. Sewell will examine you tomorrow."

Lily sat long after the girls had gone. Men were all worthless. Pierre had wined and dined her in Paris, telling her she was the only woman in the universe. She would have given him her virginity if Lilian hadn't interrupted.

After a week passed with no word from him, Lily nearly had lost her mind, desperate to contact him. She had no idea where he lived, for Pierre had told her it would be unseemly for an unchaperoned young lady to visit him in his home. When she glimpsed a servant that had delivered Pierre's letters to her passing through the marketplace, Lily had bribed the man for her lover's address. She was certain Pierre would see her and want to work things out, despite her mother's misgivings about his motives.

As Lily arrived, ready to plead for Pierre's forgiveness, ready to give herself to her true love, she'd seen him leave on an outing—with his wife on his arm and two children skipping alongside them.

All his sweet kisses and promises, all her trust shattered instantly. How could a man proclaim love so freely and use women so badly? To Lily, all men were liars and users—from Pierre to Cal Fisher.

Lily became aware of noise from below, the sounds of voices and music wafting up. She glanced at the clock. She needed to go greet her patrons and move among them.

Within minutes, a small circle had gathered around her. One man lit her cigarette. Another fetched a drink. She remained amusing and light-hearted, but still simmered with anger. A local lawyer, a famous architect, even the mayor gathered around her. Why weren't these men at home with their wives?

The mayor brushed a finger playfully along her forearm. "You know, Lil, I think I come here as much for the food and conversation as I do your girls."

The men milling around all nodded in agreement.

"Then if you've had your fill of food and talk," she said lightly, "I will see to the rest." She got each man settled with a girl of their choice, keeping her social smile pasted on her face.

As she descended the steps, Raymond softly playing Schubert in the background, Lily saw Ben open the door. Cal Fisher walked through the archway. She flew down the remaining stairs and threw out a hand which fell flat against his chest. It was a wall of hard muscle. Lily fought the urge to sweep along its length, disgusted with herself.

"You are not to enter here again," she said, her voice low and smoky. "I won't cater to your kind. I've only banned two men in twenty years. You'll be the third."

She removed her hand and willed it not to tremble.

Cal withdrew a folded sheaf of papers from his coat pocket and handed them to her.

"You can't keep an owner from his property."

9

"I t's gotta be a woman."

Simon Morgan heard the laughter and became aware of his surroundings. Three tablemates leered at him as they held up their cards, waiting for his play.

"Sorry." He placed his cards face down on the table. "I believe I'm through for the night." He scooped up the few chips left in front of him and pocketed them.

"Hope she's worth the bundle you dropped tonight, Morgan."

Simon looked at the man. A virtual stranger stared back at him. He kept his temper in check. Usually, he knew every move, every blink of an eye his opponents made. Tonight was different.

Simon made his way to a small alcove where he could keep his eye on the door. He hadn't been able to focus on his game because of the god-awful mistake that had been made. *He* should now be the owner of Lucky Lil's.

He surveyed the room and signaled for a drink, receiving his usual brand of whiskey in less than a minute. It was close to midnight and most of the action now took place above stairs. The gaming room still had twenty or so men in attendance but conversation was more subdued.

Simon sipped his whiskey, trying to make sense of the situation. He closed his eyes and thought back on the revelations the morning had brought.

"Where's the deed?" Cal Fisher laughed heartily. "That's a good one."

Simon had stared steadily at his old running buddy. "I asked you where the deed to Lucky Lil's is."

Cal poured himself a drink. "So, are we ready for tonight?" He tossed back the liquor in one gulp. "I've visited Lil's already. The meat's sweet, that's for sure. It'll be fine to know the new owner."

Simon threw a hard punch that knocked Cal off his feet. Cal quickly jumped up. The other three men present restrained him from attacking their boss.

Monty looked at Cal hard, then turned to Simon. "That's not him."

"What do you mean?" He was in no mood for any more jokes.

"Exactly what I said. Cal and the man from last night are two different people."

Simon watched Rick and Travis study Cal, who now sat on the sofa, holding his jaw, cursing under his breath.

Monty continued. "I gave the kid credit. He was a good actor and an excellent poker player. This kid is neither."

Cal spoke up. "I am a good card player. Simon taught me himself."

Monty and Rick both shook their heads. Rick said, "The guy last night is a dead ringer for Cal."

Travis added, "No wonder he acted like he didn't know us. He didn't."

Then who was the man who now held the deed to Lucky Lil's? That's why he was here tonight.

Simon finished his drink. He didn't feel like another game of chance. He'd tried to sniff out any news, but Lil had been surrounded by a group of men, several of whom Simon didn't want to offend. Better try tomorrow.

He rose and set down his glass. Just then, he spotted Lil descending the stairs. Maybe now she was alone he would try to shake her down. She wasn't the invulnerable ice queen she once was. She had caught the gambling fever. Yes, it was time for a little talk with Lilian Frontiere.

As Simon started across the room, Ben answered the door. In walked Cal's twin. Simon was momentarily paralyzed.

The man at the door was Cal's height but his general build was tighter, more muscular. His hair was the dark blond of Cal's, thick and with a slight wave. The mustache was slightly darker. The skin on his face was lighter than Cal's, as if he hadn't spent much time outdoors.

But it was the eyes that did it. They were Cal's, penetrating, ice blue eyes—but they weren't. The stranger's eyes had a hint of acceptance in them, of a civility totally lacking in Cal Fisher.

Simon knew those eyes from somewhere in his past. But from where?

He watched the man pull a sheaf of papers from his pocket and assumed it was the deed to the house. The new owner quickly ushered Lil upstairs.

Damn! Where did he know the look-alike from?

JED GRABBED Lil's elbow before she fainted and escorted her upstairs to the parlor. He counted on it being vacant this time of night.

They passed a pretty brunette in the hall who gasped. He grinned, thinking maybe the girl thought Lil was servicing a customer herself. He tipped his hat to her and politely said, "Evening, ma'am."

The girl flattened herself against the wall. Jed wondered at her strange reaction, but he had more serious matters on his mind. He opened the parlor door and seated the still-stunned Madam Lil before returning to close the door.

"I thought you'd like some privacy, Lil. That's why I came when I did to let you know the unusual circumstances we find ourselves in."

Jed himself had reeled from the discovery last night when Rick handed him the deed. It was only from sheer exhaustion after the intense poker game that his body allowed him to sleep at all.

This morning he had seen an attorney, based on the recommendation of the same bank clerk who'd helped him open his account yesterday. He'd gone there as soon as the bank opened to deposit last night's enormous winnings in his safety deposit box and growing bank account.

The clerk steered him to Stanton McRidge's office. The lawyer guaranteed Jed his possession of the whorehouse deed was a legal transaction, though a highly unusual one. He'd asked three separate times if Jed was certain he wanted to keep the house instead of selling it. Jed had assured the attorney he would keep it for now, until he explored his options. Mr. McRidge would remain on retainer and help him with any other unforeseen situations that might arise.

His main goal in coming to Lucky Lil's tonight was to see why the deed had floated around so casually. Earlier in the evening, he visited several whorehouses.

From everything he'd gleaned, Lil's establishment was a cut above the rest.

Madam Lil was seated on the sofa, intently reading the documents, her lips moving imperceptibly. Jed idly wondered what Lil looked like under her heavy make-up.

He could still feel the heat from her palm on his chest. Being guilty of sexual feelings for an older women was new for him. Of course, Lil was an experienced, worldly woman. Her lush figure sang a siren's song to him.

Jed glanced at her. Her low-cut bodice revealed rounded, creamy flesh, unwrinkled by the passage of time. Long, slender fingers with perfectly polished ovals held the papers he'd presented to her. He wished that hot palm rested against his cheek.

He realized the woman didn't come with the house, but he'd always been one up for an adventure. Being in Lil's bed would certainly be an exhilarating one. Jed loved to learn, and he was certain Madam Lil had a few lessons to impart.

Lil shook her head. "I don't understand how this happened."

"How you were foolish enough to let your business go? Or how I was lucky enough to get it?"

Jed instantly regretted his quick retort when the hurt look sprang to her face, followed by a flush across her cheeks. He laid a hand on her arm to comfort her and apologize for his crassness.

She jerked away from him. "You might own Lucky Lil's, but you don't own me." She stood. "I will speak to my attorney first thing tomorrow."

"Of course. My lawyer is Stanton McRidge if that's of any help." He hesitated a moment. "Could we meet tomorrow and discuss things further?"

Lil agreed. "Come tomorrow night before I begin my hostessing obligations."

"I'll do that. Goodnight, Lil."

Jed left the parlor. As he walked down the hall, he had a nervous energy about him. Maybe Gertie was free. He paused at her door and listened. No activity came from within. He knocked lightly on the door and Gertie answered it almost immediately.

Before he could greet her, she slapped him hard across the cheek.

"You have some nerve." She slammed the door shut in his face.

Jed shrugged. Women.

10

Lily burst through the doors of Maximilian Fisher's study, Harold close behind her. She pulled off her gloves as she spoke and slapped them against her thigh.

"I've been robbed, Max. Robbed!"

Her friend wheeled around his chair and studied her with amusement. "Shall I give chase to the thief?"

"Max!"

Harold indicated a chair and Lily sat. The valet rolled Max closer to her and then took a seat himself.

Max sighed. "It's that bad, Harold?"

The servant nodded. "I've ordered fresh coffee and rolls brought around, sir. Margaret will be here with them momentarily."

Max took her hand and patted it. "Margaret's coffee cures all, Lily. Harold and I go through vast amounts of it when we make our most clever decisions."

Lily managed to smile at them both. As usual, Max was already having a calming effect upon her.

"And they're very clever indeed. At least according to the *Chronicle* and *Examiner*."

The two men chuckled. "Master Max makes all the financial decisions, Miss Lily. I simply write down his words."

"Then change them before you dash off notes to my solicitor or investment brokers," Max gruffly added. "Harold has saved me many times over from unwise business dealings. If there is a crisis to be solved, Harold will come through for you, my dear."

A gentle knock occurred, and Margaret rolled in the tea caddy.

"Got tea for Miss Lily and coffee for you two con-spirators," she said in her broad Irish brogue. She winked at Lily. "Try some of those lovely croissants, sweetie. They'll melt in your mouth."

The trio busied themselves with preparing their refreshments, and then Lily got down to business. "I'm more composed now. Thank you, Harold." She winked at the valet, who winked right back at her. "I received the most distressing news last night. A stranger showed up at our doorstep with the deed to Lucky Lil's."

Lily had decided not to mention Cal Fisher held the deed. She hoped Max would be able to help extricate her from this messy situation without having to know his great-grandson was involved.

Max steepled his fingers. "Surely it was a forgery."

He must have read the look on her face. "Why was the deed not in Lilian's possession in the first place?"

"*Maman* has been gambling, Max."

She waited for the looks of horror to cross their faces. Instead, both men calmly took a sip of the strong brew in their cups, each wearing the same bland expression as if she'd told them it might rain next Tuesday.

"She had to mortgage it due to her extreme losses. She dealt with a man named Tate at the—"

"Tate?" Max looked at Harold, who nodded sagely. "That explains a good deal right there. It's a toss-up *which* is more crooked—Tate or Lombard Street."

"Dishonest or not, I need to know how to get it back."

Max sighed. "You probably can't. Of course, you may see my attorney, then have him visit the new owner's attorney. I'm sure he's cunning enough to have obtained one. Then we could drag through a legal muckamuck for years. In the end, I'm sure the court would hold that the gentleman in question owns Lucky Lil's."

The thought of calling Cal Fisher a gentleman made Lily even angrier. What he had done to poor Sarah Jane flashed through her mind. What was worse was Sarah Jane seeing them together last night even though Lily had promised her the monster would never enter Lucky Lil's again. She might as well order up her penance of crow dinner right now and chow down.

Would he abuse the other girls that way? If he did, the girls would flee in droves—but where would they go?

And what would be her role now? Would she be expected to continue to supervise the house? Run the show at a salary? Would she be allowed to continue living there? And what about her mother? Even worse, would Cal Fisher move in?

Lily supposed her charade was over now. She wondered if Max would be willing to take them in.

"Don't look so glum, child. No need to mess with all the legal gobbledygook."

She raised tear-filled eyes to her friend. "What do you mean?"

"I'll just buy it back for you."

She threw her arms around him. "Oh, Max! I can't thank you enough. We'll repay you somehow. I promise."

"Enough, enough." He pushed her away and she hid her smile. "Explain exactly how it came to this."

Lily told him what she'd found in the books once she'd taken over a few months before, and how Lilian confided about running short one month.

"One thing led to another and *Maman* suddenly found herself in dire straits. She indulged me so, and I took it all for granted. No expense was spared on our trip to Europe. First-class accommodations on the ship and in every hotel. New gowns and hats by the dozens.

"Even my education before that. It must've cost a fortune."

Max and Harold exchanged a look and she felt they were judging her mother poorly.

"Don't do that. I was her only one. She simply wanted the best for me."

"Nothing to it, Lily. We'll simply contact my lawyer and do the same for this scoundrel's man."

"He's hired Stanton McRidge."

Harold chuckled. "How convenient. He represents Master Max, as well."

"At least we know the man's no fool." Max took a sip of coffee. "It will make everything more convenient in the long run. We'll offer this interloper good money for the house, and before you know it, he'll be out of your life. Mac can broker the deal."

She felt a surge of guilt, knowing it was Max's own flesh and blood they would banish, albeit for a price.

"Enough of business. Tell me how Lilian is."

Lily swallowed. "She finally saw Dr. Seward yesterday. He said that she needs a drier climate."

Max sat up. "Then maybe this fellow with the deed is a blessing in disguise. It would free you to—"

"*Maman* has refused to go. She said San Francisco is her true home. She won't leave, especially for sun-baked skin and hot dust for dinner."

Max laughed. "I can just hear her now." He patted Lily's knee. "Then you'll go to my lawyer tomorrow. I'll send a note around so he'll be expecting you. This will be settled in a day or two. Now, let's get down to business. Harold, please pass me that raspberry scone."

"I heard it calling your name for some time, Master Max." He handed it to his employer.

"Are we ready to talk about other matters?" Max settled back into his chair once again. "Did you hear where the Golden Gate Iron Works was destroyed by fire yesterday? And that General Colton's was burglarized?"

"No," Lily responded. "What's missing?"

Max rolled his eyes. "Well, the newspaper said it was a large amount of silverware stolen. Absolutely dreadful."

After a brief silence, the three all laughed aloud. Max said, "Never liked Colton. Pompous ass, in my opinion."

Lily left an hour later, eager to confront Cal Fisher.

DARKNESS SET in on the chilly February evening. Lily sat with her mother most of the afternoon, which Lilian had slept away. Now Ben slipped in with a supper tray for them both.

She touched her mother's shoulder gently. "*Maman*? Wake up, darling. Ben has brought you some broth and bread."

Lilian's eyes fluttered open and shut several times. "I don't want anything," she said disagreeably.

"You must eat," Lily replied sternly. "You need it to regain your strength."

She propped up the pillows and helped her mother ease onto them. She spooned a few bites of the chicken soup into Lilian before her mother turned her head away.

"No more. Just talk to me, *cherie*."

So she did, telling them of what had transpired last night and of her conversation this morning with Max.

"I can't believe I trusted that banker, Tate." Lilian's bitterness turned her mouth sour.

"Regardless of what he did, *Maman*, Max will buy back Lucky Lil's. Isn't that wonderful?"

Lilian shrugged. "*Pas mal.*" She shook her head. "Leave me. I want to be alone."

Hurt, Lily removed the tray and wiped her mother's mouth with a cloth. Lilian turned on her side and closed her eyes. Lily stepped out into the hall a moment with Ben.

"I'm so disappointed, Ben. She has no energy. She didn't even seem to care that much about what's gone on the last two days."

Ben laid a hand on her shoulder. "She is not getting any better, Miss Lily."

"But I'd hoped such good news would raise her spirits."

"Miz Lil's hanging on."

"For what?"

"She knows she's dying. She wants to see you settled."

Lily shrugged off Ben's warm hand. "That's ridiculous! No one's dying or going anywhere."

Ben studied her with sad eyes. "Gotta get moving. You eat something." He lumbered down the hall, a gentle giant.

She returned to the room and lifted the cover from her meal. Usually sea bass was her favorite, but she was too nervous to eat. She placed the silver cover back over the fish and went to the dressing table.

As she sat, she glanced back over her shoulder at her mother's still form on the bed. In her heart, she knew Ben's words were true. She wondered how long she had before her mother's death. Turning her thoughts to what she could control, she began the routine that had become second nature, changing herself into Lilian Frontiere, a self-assured, worldly madam of the best-known brothel in San Francisco.

Lily idly wondered what her true surname was. Lilian changed it soon after arriving in California. It was a new frontier and so she had named herself and her infant daughter accordingly. Her father had been killed in the riots that swept Paris in 1848. She had been born just before his death.

She wished her mother had spoken of him more often. She knew he had been intelligent and very political. Lilian said upon occasion that Lily was very like him. Her transformation now completed, she tried to calm her nerves. She loathed Cal Fisher. Yet, a growing excitement built inside her at the prospect of seeing him again.

Insanity. That was the only explanation. She was not a good judge of character when it came to men. Look how she fell for the married Pierre's sweet lies.

No, she must learn to watch her step if a man was involved in any business dealing.

Ben tapped lightly on the door and stuck his head in. "He's here."

Lily steeled herself for their showdown.

11

Jed fidgeted in the parlor. Why he was nervous escaped him. Facing Madam Lil was nothing compared to screaming Johnny Rebs coming at you from three sides, ready to blow your head off in the blink of an eye. He stood and glanced at himself in the gilded mirror, admiring the reflection.

The concierge at the Baldwin had recommended an excellent tailor who'd fashioned this gray pin-striped suit in two days. Jed immediately ordered three more when he saw the quality of work. He wanted to look the part of a prosperous businessman.

He also wanted to gain a certain reputation at the tables. That would lure Simon. Jed saw his nemesis the night before, when he broke the news to Lil that he held the deed to her house of ill repute.

As they'd spoken briefly downstairs, he'd felt eyes on him. Being a connoisseur himself in the art of studying an opponent, he'd casually glanced around, curious as to who would be scrutinizing him so closely.

Simon Morgan had examined him at length, a puzzled look on his handsome features. Jed saw him trying to figure out where he knew the new owner of

Lucky Lil's from. Hopefully, the addition of the mustache and different haircut would pass the test of recognition.

Jed would rather have kept the full beard once he engaged Simon's attention but he couldn't afford to resemble Cal Hart. The thought of swinging at the end of a rope made a lasting impression on him. At least with a mustache he appeared older than the clean-shaven kid Morgan took for a ride.

Glad he now had ample money to play with, Jed decided to hire an investigator to research Morgan's history and his flaws. He'd engaged Walker Thompson this afternoon for that very purpose. Thompson did occasional work for Stanton McRidge. Mac assured Jed Thompson's inquiries were always discreet. At the last minute, Jed asked for a report on Lilian Frontiere, as well. He still wasn't sure why.

At that moment the woman herself entered the parlor, wearing a lilac dress, her square bodice revealing an enticing amount of rounded breasts. She was flushed, a rosy hue that enhanced her cheekbones and amber eyes.

Jed would swear she'd found Ponce de Leon's fountain of youth. He fought to squash his growing attraction to her. Heck, she'd probably slap him harder than Gertie if he tried to pursue her. Besides, he never mixed work and pleasure.

At least he didn't think he would. Yet.

"It's a pleasure to see you again, Lil." He stood to greet her.

"Pleasure comes from counting my money after a good night," she snapped. "Not in seeing you again."

He stifled a grin. He'd always found feisty women a particular weakness of his. He looked at her lush mouth, painted a startling red, and wished he could cover it with his own right about now.

Instead, he said, "I hope you had time to think on what we talked about last night."

Lil smoothed the folds of her gown as she sat. "No thinking was necessary. I don't want you associated with me or Lucky Lil's. I'd like to buy it back."

Jed had expected this offer. Mac mentioned it when they'd spoken at his office early this afternoon. It wasn't strictly ethical, his being informed of Lil's intentions, but both he and Lil apparently had the same lawyer. He decided to string her along a bit.

"How? If you so desperately needed money that you'd mortgage the place to begin with, how do you have the funds to buy it back now?"

Lil patted her hair in an utterly feminine gesture. "I have a new investor who will meet your price."

"No."

She gave him an angry look. "What?"

"The answer's no. Lucky Lil's is not for sale. At any price."

Lil rose to her feet, her hands going to her small waist, balled into fists. "Every man has a price."

Jed grinned shamelessly. "Not me." He inspected his newly-buffed nails for a moment. "I look forward to working with you, Lil. You will stay on?"

Flustered, Lil replied, "I don't think you understand the kind of money we're talking about."

"No need. We aren't talking money."

Lil glared at him. "Be serious. Name your price. It will be deposited into your account within twenty-four hours."

He grew serious. "I told you. There'll be no sale."

Lil wore a look of astonishment. "Does that mean you're moving in and taking over immediately?"

Jed thought on it. He hated to give up the comforts of the Baldwin, but the idea intrigued him. He made a quick decision he hoped he wouldn't regret.

"Yes. I'll move in the day after tomorrow, in the afternoon. Save a couple of hours for me then. We'll go over the books. I'd like to see how Lucky Lil's can turn a profit."

Steely-eyed, she told him, "I'll have a room prepared. But do not touch my girls. I won't have it."

"Well, it's obvious Gertie won't have anything to do with me. She slapped me but good last night." He stood. "Don't worry. I will keep my hands off the girls. Any servicing needs done, I'll come to the expert."

Lil looked at him blankly. "Who?"

"Why *you*, Lil. Who else?"

LILY ROSE EARLY, heating water for a bath. She poured in a vial of strawberry scent she'd found in Paris, and remembered Cal asking about her that first night he'd come to Lucky Lil's. She pushed aside the memory of being held tightly by a strong stranger and climbed in.

The bath did wonders for her spirits but she still dressed with special care as Lilian. Cal Fisher was as sharp as any tool in the shed. She didn't want him to have an inkling of her true identity.

She waited for him in her own bedroom. She'd only spent rare moments here since her mother had taken ill. She'd had a desk brought in, along with all the accounting. Once a month, she spread out everything and dealt with financial matters. The rest of her time was spent next door with Lilian or downstairs playing hostess to their clients.

Lily idly wondered what it would be like to have

time once again to pick up a book of poetry or stroll along Market Street, looking in the windows of the dozens of retail shops. She also missed the theater. With both her mother and Max out of commission, she had no inclination to go.

Yet, she was so tired. Tired of the limiting life of the house. Of ministering to her mother, who'd become increasingly peevish this last week. Of never having anyone to talk to—*really* talk to. She did have tea twice a month with Max, but that wasn't the same as having a companion on a daily basis.

Sighing, she opened the ledger for the past month and became engrossed in the dollars and cents. Suddenly, a shadow loomed over the page and she glanced up. Cal Fisher stood next to her, closer than she would have liked, peering at the numbers.

"I see you've made an early start of it." He smiled apologetically. "Ben sent me up. I did knock. No response."

He looked around the room. "Very feminine. Tiny rosebuds on the wallpaper. White, wispy lace curtains. Plush carpet." He smoothed his hand along the satin bedspread. "Lots of throw pillows. Not the room of a working girl, I'd venture."

"Certainly not." She reached to the desk for a cigarette. Thank God a few were already rolled. Her shaking hands would easily betray her frayed nerves. What was it about this man that turned her into quivering jelly?

Cal lit it for her in a graceful gesture. Everything about him was as smooth as his ice-blue eyes, but his good manners didn't fool her. She'd seen his true colors that day at Max's house.

She cleared her throat. "This is my daughter's room."

"You have a child?"

Lily laughed, the sound deep in her throat. "Yes, I'm a mother. A rather *young* mother," she emphasized, knowing how Lilian hated others to think of her as old. "I had my baby when I was quite the *jeune fille* myself."

"And will I meet this daughter?" Cal's eyes glittered with mischief.

"Your thoughts of seducing my daughter are shameful, *monsieur*. Lily is visiting a friend back East at the moment. From her last letter, she is close to accepting a marriage proposal from a quite wealthy young banker."

She stood and took a long drag from the cigarette. "I would suggest that you move into here for now. This chamber is the largest one upstairs. If you like, it can be redecorated to more suit your taste."

Cal shrugged. "Leave the room the way it is for now. As long as I have a place to hang a few clothes, I'll be fine."

Lily thought of her wardrobe stuffed with gowns and capes and petticoats in every hue. Her drawers, too, held all kinds of wispy feminine garments. "I will need to remove a few of Lily's things. Would you like to look at the finances now?"

"Yes."

While he studied figures, she quietly went about clearing space for him. She made several trips between her room and her mother's, which would now house them both.

Cal seemed engrossed in the ledgers. Lily caught him frowning a time or two.

"Who's been in charge of the books the past few months?" he demanded.

Lily hesitated. "Why do you ask?"

Cal ran a hand through his thick hair. "They started out a total mess. Crooked columns, pieces of bills shoved in here and there. Huge amounts of cash withdrawn. Then everything assumes an order. Someone logical sat down and made amends for the shoddy bookkeeping up to this point."

She looked down her nose at him haughtily. "*I* have always kept the books until my daughter asked to be of help a few months ago, before she left on her trip."

He whistled. "Boy, she's got a head for business, Lil. She's organized. Made some wise decisions. She's balanced different accounts in a staggered fashion so that everyone is getting paid something. When did she leave?"

"Just a day or so before you showed up."

"Did she know you'd mortgaged the house?"

Lily nodded. "I shared it with her before she left."

"Well, I wish she were back. She could make things a hell of a lot easier for me. I've always been a whiz at math, but it's still going to take me hours to sort through these accounts."

"I'm sorry she didn't stay behind simply for your convenience, Mr. Fisher."

He gave her a blank look, which puzzled Lily. Surely, he would remember having introduced himself at Max's that day. And then it hit her. Cal Fisher had introduced himself to *Lily. Lilian* and Cal had never been formally introduced. He'd neglected to give his name during his brief, earlier stay.

"Just call me Jed. Jed Stone."

Lily wondered why he wanted to go by a different name. Maybe he was trying to make a new start, one where the Fisher name didn't follow him everywhere he went. It was common practice for many who moved

West to change their name for one reason or another. Even her own mother had chosen a new last name in her adopted land.

"All right. Jed. Anything else you need from me? I like to check on the girls while they eat. I sort out petty problems and small jealousies that tend to arise."

"I'll leave all that feminine nonsense to you. That leads me to one last thing. We haven't discussed your salary." He hesitated and then named a figure. Lily's happiness threatened to bubble over. It was more than generous, especially coming from such a scoundrel.

"If you think it fair," she said nonchalantly.

He glared at her. "You drive a hard bargain, Lil." He added another third to his offer and proclaimed, "That's it. If the house does well, say in six months' time, I'll see that you get a percentage of the take in addition to your salary."

She nodded. "As you wish."

Lily stood and exited her former bedroom, as the new owner of Lucky Lil's returned to the figures before him.

Maybe—just maybe—she would be able to pull off this charade a while longer.

12

Lily touched up her cosmetics before heading down to see the girls at dinner. Though distasteful, she wouldn't keep the change in ownership from them. Madam Lil was known for being open and honest with her girls.

Nervously, she smoothed her iced blue satin skirts and walked down the stairs, her stomach jumping like a toad from lily pads to the bank. She *would* get through this. One day at a time.

The chatter of the girls calmed her as she approached the kitchen. Their voices soothed her with the familiarity of life in the house. Lily opened the door and sailed in. As always, their talk died down in deference to her.

"*Mes amis*, I have news that may surprise you. We have been bought by a man named Jed Stone." Lily almost said Cal Fisher, but caught herself in time.

Immediately, questions sprang forth from several girls. She waved her hand to quieten them.

"No one is going anywhere. I will remain as hostess. You will continue to address any problems with me. *Monsieur* Stone has no interest in being serviced by you. This is simply an investment for him.

"He will be living with us. He wants to get an idea of the day-to-day events that make up our house, so please give him his due respect."

Lily then moved among them, all the while dreading what she would say to Gertie and Sarah Jane. Finally, she reached the two girls, in their usual place at the end. She motioned them to leave the table and come with her.

"I'll be blunt," she said as they entered the room off the kitchen. "I had promised to keep out the man who harmed you, Sarah Jane. I no longer can do so."

Gertie caught on instantly. "He's the new owner, isn't he? I saw him here last night."

A muffled sound came from Sarah Jane. Gertie put an arm about the girl and murmured to her softly. Lily ached at her loss of power.

"I have received full assurance from Mr. Stone that he will not touch any girl here. If he does so, please report it to me immediately. I will not tolerate what happened to you, Sarah Jane. He is very aware of that."

"I can look out for me and Sarah Jane," Gertie proclaimed. "Don't you worry none."

Lily smiled at Gertie's bravado. "Thank you. I'll count on you, Gertie."

They returned to the kitchen. Lily went upstairs to spend time with her mother before they opened for business.

JED SORTED the clutter on the bed into piles atop the pine desk. He'd been at it for several hours. His neck and back ached from bending. His eyes were dry, and he had a powerful thirst. He consulted his pocket watch, surprised that it was already after eight. Probably customers had arrived below, mingling with the girls, sipping drinks, maybe playing a few hands of poker or shooting craps before moving on to the upstairs activities.

He glanced in the floor-length mirror, satisfied with his appearance. He spotted his valise when he opened the door, and moved it into the bedroom, placing it on top of the bed. He looked around at the utterly feminine room, wondering what Lil's daughter looked like. Obviously, the girl never partook in life at the whorehouse, especially if she had traveled back East and was about to become Mrs. Young Banker.

The thought of Lil sashaying down the aisle to take her seat as mother of the bride caused Jed to smile. If she'd actually had the girl at sixteen or so and the daughter was now around eighteen, then Lil would only be in her mid-thirties. It mollified him to think there might only be a gap of ten years between them.

That soothed his conscience some because he'd had to force his attention time and again back to the numbers that danced on the page before him. Thoughts of Mouthy Madam Lil constantly interrupted him. He wished she would lay off the heavy cosmetics. Any fool could see a gorgeous woman lay underneath the layers of face powder and rouge and thick black eyeliner.

Jed decided he would definitely see what lay beneath both the makeup and the inviting gowns she wore. Lil had a figure that would stop traffic on Fifth Avenue. Just thinking about her made him hard.

He removed a few items from his bag and ran a comb through his hair for good measure. He even splashed on a hint of the new cologne his tailor had recommended. He straightened his tie and rubbed his pocket watch for good luck. Today was February seventh and seven was one of his lucky numbers. He was ready to see who frequented Lucky Lil's.

His place.

Jed spotted Lil immediately as he came down the stairs. She led a man on each arm to the gaming room, depositing them at neighboring tables and blowing them a kiss as she retreated. He joined her at the bottom of the stairs.

"Keep close to me," he said softly in her ear. "I'd like the scoop on as many customers as possible."

Lil raised a brow. "Lesson one—they're clients. Or patrons." Her gaze swept the room. "Take my arm."

He did as told and led her around the downstairs parlors and large gaming room while she provided him bits and pieces about those present.

"Wiry gray hair. Blue cravat. Assistant to the mayor. Red hair and freckles. Son of the owner of the Anglo-Californian Bank on California Street. Man throwing the dice left-handed is a big importer located on Front Street. A wife and mistress here and another wife in Hong Kong. The one with the whiskey in hand and wearing a sour look owns a department store on Market Street. Nine children with another on the way."

She continued to walk him through each man in the room and many of those who arrived in the next few hours. Politicians, theater owners, bankers, lawyers, shipping magnates—they all came to Lucky Lil's on a regular basis.

Lil was a charming hostess, making small talk that didn't seem trite at all. She knew a great deal about the men who frequented her place of business. Asked about their families, as well as their ventures and hobbies. She knew about financial transactions, arrivals of people and goods, billiards matches and regattas— more than Jed could've filed away in a year.

He could see why men were drawn here. Lil's personal touch brought them back again and again. It also didn't hurt that she had the prettiest gals around. He saw her pair up client after client with girls who looked fresh as blooming roses. Every time she remembered which man enjoyed a particular girl's charms.

What sent her under? Where had the large cash withdrawals disappeared? Why had Lil sacrificed everything she'd worked so hard for? Jed determined they would speak of this tomorrow, though he had a good idea where some of it had been spent. The dresses she'd removed from his room had been plentiful, expensively-cut, and in every fabric conceivable. He figured Lily Frontiere for a spoiled brat.

"Are you pleased?"

Jed loved her musical voice, the smoky tones smooth as black velvet.

He nodded. "Business seems good. I think most of the movers and shakers of San Francisco are present tonight. Do they come often?"

Lil shrugged. "Some yes. Some no. It depends what else goes on in the city. If it's a big night at the opera or theater, then many have a late supper with their wife or mistress and never make it here."

She tucked a wayward curl behind her ear, causing her silver earring to sway seductively. "If there are deals to be cut, they will come here to do so. It can be more private than an office, *n'est-ce pas*? Other times, they go to the Plaza and want to prove how important they are by gambling huge amounts of cash."

She smiled sweetly. "But they still come back.

They have for years." Lil looked at him earnestly. "I hope they will always want to come back."

Jed looked away, uncomfortable. He had a few ideas for changes. He was sure Lil would kick up a fuss.

Then his prickling set his body on fire. He immediately glanced toward the door and saw Simon Morgan entering. Jed stood close enough to Lil to feel her stiffen. He leaned a shoulder against her briefly to lend support. She straightened and painted on a social smile.

"Hello, Simon," she greeted the gambler as he approached them. "Have you met Jed Stone?" She tucked a hand into the crook of his arm. "Mr. Stone is the new owner of Lucky Lil's." She smiled up at him enticingly.

Jed almost burst out laughing. Lil had taken great pains all night to avoid mentioning the ownership of the house had transferred. Yet she flaunted it in this gambler's face, purring like a cat licking her bowl of cream.

He placed a hand atop hers and gave it a squeeze before offering his own to Simon. "Good to meet you. Have you been in the city long?"

The older man scowled at him. "Do you game, Stone? If you did, I'm sure you would've already heard of me. I've won several fortunes at tables in this fair city."

Lil snorted. "You just have gotten very good at cheating, Simon."

Jed saw the flare of anger in Morgan's eyes. For a moment, it was easy to see how such a handsome, affable man had been able to do what had been done to Sherry, as well as setting Louis up for the blame. He fingered the gun inside his pocket. He'd taken it when he'd escaped Stockton's mob and was never without it.

It took all his willpower not to casually remove it and aim it point blank at his sworn enemy. Only Lil's hand tightening imperceptibly on his arm helped him keep his senses.

Diffusing the tense moment, he said, "Maybe we'll have a go at each other some time."

Simon waved his hand broadly. "Why not here and now? I'd love to talk further over a hand of poker." He looked at Lil. "And maybe Lily could come down to watch. I bet I'd be pretty lucky if she were around to cheer me on."

"I'm afraid Lily's on holiday," Jed said smoothly. "And I will have to beg off. I don't think it above board for an owner to play at his own tables. Too much talk if I win." He narrowed his eyes as he looked at Simon. "And I tell you now, with fair warning, I *would* win."

He took a step away, tugging on Lil to accompany him. "I'm sure we'll run into one another soon."

As they moved across the room, Lil hissed up at him, "That is not a man to make an enemy of, Jed. From what you told me earlier, you know this."

She pulled away from him and studied his face intently. "Why are you playing some kind of cat and mouse game with him? Better yet, why didn't he know you?"

Jed smiled down at her and said pleasantly, "I'd like to try the buffet. I haven't had anything to eat since this morning and I'm famished."

He led her to the large display of food. "Shall I make a plate for you?" He smiled at her lazily. "Or would you like to eat off mine?"

Lil jerked a plate off the stack of fine china, looking ready to crack it over his head.

"I guess I'll make my own." Jed followed her along,

biting back his laughter. For an older, wiser woman, Lil could be stirred to act quite immaturely.

He liked that about her. A lot.

THEY CLOSED UP TOGETHER, seeing all their guests out. Jed pulled his pocket watch from his vest and frowned.

"I have two minutes past three. That will never do."

Lil laughed, a deep, throaty laugh, and took a drag from her cigarette. She pointed to the grandfather clock, which began striking three.

"I go by Tommy. So do my clients. They know he's as reliable as the swallows that return to Capistrano each year."

"Tommy?"

"A friend of mine won the clock in a bet. He thought it would look good there." Lil shook her head. "He was another one who always bothered me about my rule. With Tommy in plain sight, he knew he'd stay on my good side."

"Why Tommy?"

Lil studied it fondly. "When the clock was delivered, one of the girls said it was as tall and wide as her Uncle Tommy. The name stuck."

Jed ran a hand over the timepiece's smooth wood. He glanced around the empty rooms. "It's nice. Quiet."

"Yes. I love this time. The girls go quickly to bed, tired from their evening's work. Ben checks around outside and then locks up."

Lil began to walk as she spoke, extinguishing lights. He appreciatively watched the sway of her hips as he followed her from room to room.

"Tired?"

She tilted her head to one side. "Not really."

"Then may I make a suggestion?" She nodded. "Why don't we make a habit each night of unwinding after a long day? We can snack from the buffet while we count our proceeds for the night."

"Hmm." She considered his suggestion. "In the past, I have always done so the next day."

"Then perhaps we can make a small change in routine."

"All right. But, I have no way of knowing how much we made this evening. I have a good estimate, based on how many went upstairs and from what I saw at the tables."

"You mean the men don't pay before they go upstairs?"

"No. I settle up the next day with the girls, fifty-fifty."

Jed whistled. "They get a large split."

"*C'est vrai*, but they are prime. I don't keep anyone over twenty-five. That way the turnover is frequent enough to keep things from getting stale."

"I see." He moved to the buffet. "Then let's grab some fruit and cheese and simply visit a while."

He made up a plate and took it over to a coffee table, a rich mahogany polished to perfection. "Your furniture is beautiful," he complimented.

"Thank you. *Maman*... I mean... my *maman* had exquisite taste. I learned much from her."

"What did you do before you came to California, Lil?"

She got a faraway look in her eye. "I lived in Paris. No city is more beautiful than the City of Lights. The theater, the open markets. No place holds a candle to it."

"Then why did you leave?"

Her lips set in a tight smile. "Many reasons. Politics. Upheaval. It's a long story." She tilted her head so that it rested along the back of the burgundy sofa. Jed admired her profile. He more than admired her full lips, begging to be kissed.

He began to lean in closer to her. She must have sensed it. She opened her eyes and quickly popped her head upright.

"Still, San Francisco has a charm all of its own. I would not trade my time here. It's here I forged a successful business and raised a lovely daughter. My years in California have been well-spent."

Lil abruptly stood. "Maybe we can finish our conversation in the morning. I find I'm suddenly very tired."

Jed rose and before she could protest, bent and kissed her cheek. "Then good night to you, Lil."

She looked at him warily. "*Au revoir*, Jed Stone." She lifted her skirts and quickly left the room.

13

Jed rose shortly after nine and dressed to go downstairs. He didn't think any girls would be stirring yet, but he did smell coffee brewing. His stomach gurgled loudly as he made his way down the hall to the first floor.

The domestic staff was hard at work, polishing lamps, sweeping carpets, and cleaning the remnants of last night's buffet. They curtsied to him and continued their work. He shook his head at the gesture, feeling like a king.

A large fire burned in the kitchen hearth. An overweight, balding man stood enjoying a cup of coffee.

"Jed Stone." He thrust out his hand to the man.

"*Monsieur* Stone. Madam Lil said to expect you. *Café au lait*?" he asked, holding up his own mug to Jed.

"Yes, please."

"I am Manet Lambert, chef extraordinaire for Lucky Lil's." He poured the steaming coffee into a cup and briskly doctored it before he handed it over. "I take care of the girls, the staff, and the buffet for the clients."

"I had the buffet last night and a meal a few weeks

ago. Veal piccata, baby carrots in some delicious sauce, and angel food cake topped with fresh strawberries and cream. Definitely the best meal I've had in months."

Manet bowed his head. "I feed the girls well. Madam Lil wishes it so. Happy girls make happy patrons. Happiness starts at the stomach." Manet slapped his large belly. Jed found himself liking the overweight cook.

"I whip you up an omelet?"

He wasn't quite sure what that was. All he knew was the coffee was good and the veal had been better. He decided to trust the Frenchman. If the chef knew half about food what Louis had taught Jed about cards, he was in good hands.

"Prepare whatever you wish, Manet."

Soon, Jed feasted on eggs filled with mushrooms, green peppers, onions, cheese, and bacon.

"My compliments, Chef. This was outstanding."

The cook waved a hand. "No. It was nothing. I will make you a real breakfast tomorrow, *Monsieur* Jed. Until you've had my Liege waffles or *pain perdu,* you have not breakfasted well."

"I'll look forward to whatever you prepare."

"*Allo, Madame.*"

Jed turned to see Lil standing in the doorway. She wore a soft peach day gown of silk with an inlay of mint green. The cut of the gown made her waist look impossibly small. He longed to span it with his hands. For a start.

"*Bonjour, mon ami. Comment alley-vous aujourd'hui*"?

"*Je vais bien, Madame.*" Manet poured a cup of coffee and brought it to her. "You are up and about early."

"Mr. Stone and I have much business to go over, Manet." Lil walked to the door. "Shall we?"

Jed followed her out. "I have a few questions to ask and also a change or two that might streamline things."

Lil stiffened then shrugged nonchalantly. "It's your place now. Make whatever changes you see fit."

He took her arm and led her into one of the downstairs parlors that had already been cleaned. "I want your opinion on my ideas, Lil. I don't want you to feel shut out in any way. And please, call me Jed."

She set down her coffee cup and moved a china spittoon over by an inch before sitting on a camelback sofa of plush crimson velvet. "Then let's begin."

He leaned against a hand-carved liquor cabinet, closed for the time being. "Just some questions to clarify things for me. How much do the girls pay in rent?"

"Five dollars a week. Payable each Monday before three." He caught a gleam in her eye. "Three in the afternoon, that is."

He fought the grin that threatened to spread. "All the furnishings in their bedroom are supplied?"

"Yes." Lil herself pursed her lips, suppressing a smile. "Each room has a bed and wardrobe, plus a small table next to the bed, which contains a velvet perfumed box for personal items such as a comb or rouge pot. There is also a screen for discreet dressing and undressing. Hand-painted, I might add."

She eyed him carefully. "Don't look so glum. They were paid for long ago. They add a touch of class, I believe."

"And the clothes they wear? I've never seen better dressed women."

"The girls pay for their own wardrobes. I do encourage them to go to Annie Spencer, a dressmaker I have used for over fifteen years now. On their birthday, they may go to Annie and choose a pair of gloves. That is my gift to them."

"Then if the girls provide their own gowns, why is the Spencer account so large?"

Lil raised her chin a notch. "Because I have my dresses done there. My daughter's, as well."

"You two have incredibly expensive taste, Lil."

She frowned at him. "A woman must always look her best, Jed. It is obvious from what you say that you have never kept a woman before." She studied her nails.

He let the comment slide. "If you urge the girls to see Annie Spencer, you are bringing her quite a lot of business. I think we need to talk to her about this."

Lil looked puzzled. "Why?"

"You deserve a kickback from the trade you bring in." He saw the shock register on her face. "Don't get huffy, Lil. We'll ask for a small percentage. Say five percent. If she refuses, we'll just ask the girls to shop elsewhere. Believe me, this Annie Spencer will want to keep your business. It's a small price to pay."

"It seems so... vulgar."

"Darlin', that's the American way." He moved to sit next to her on the sofa. "Tell me about your monthly expenses."

"You saw the bills."

"I want to hear about them from you."

She settled against the cushions, ticking fingers off as she went. "First, the girls receive half of each transaction they complete. Then there's the kitchen and domestic staffs. A couple work nights, emptying spittoons, replenishing the buffet, refreshing drinks, bringing hot water or towels if they are requested.

"Ben and the other bouncers are on the payroll, as is Raymond. He plays the piano. I also have a string quartet that performs during his breaks."

She frowned, mentally going down a list. "There are payoffs to the police. Those vary from month to month. Of course, you have the licensing fees, too. Many times the mayor has waived that for me, if he's in a particularly good mood. Food and liquor add up to quite a bit, feeding the staff and supplying the buffet for our clients. Manet has been with me for years and his food alone can draw a crowd.

"The dealers at the gaming tables are a different matter. I don't pay them a regular salary. They work off a commission of the table take. They only work a night or so each week."

"They hold a regular job elsewhere?"

"Yes. They work in gaming hells around town. They work for me on their night off." She laughed. "Believe me, Jed, I have sought them out very carefully, on an individual basis. They are some of the best in the city. And if their table has a particularly good night, I allow them the option of a free night on the house, their choice of girl."

Lil scrunched up her face in thought. "I believe that's the biggest portion. Oh, wait. Doctor Seward comes twice a month."

Jed interrupted her. "What does he do?"

"He examines the girls for venereal disease. Once or twice, he's tried to clean up a crude attempt at abortion. He lectures them about their overuse of belladonna and laudanum.

"And," she added, becoming very still, "on a few occasions he's had to tend to a girl assaulted by a client."

His disgust rose at once. "You don't condone that here?"

She flushed. "I don't approve but it sometimes happens. Most times, it's too late to stop. I've only heard about it... after the fact." She stared at him intently.

"We'll have to think about stationing a man upstairs to patrol the hallway. His presence alone might cut down on this occasional, unacceptable behavior. Ben and I should command enough presence downstairs. Choose one man to keep and give the others a week's notice before we let them go."

He saw her wince. "I'll watch the domestics for a few days. We'll see how many work hard. If you've been in the habit of rising late, they would know when to look busy. We may be able to eliminate a few positions in this area, as well."

She sat silently examining her hands in her lap, so he decided to continue. "I've been to hurdy-gurdy houses where they charge a gold dollar a dance. The management issues a ticket to the customer once he's paid, and that's what he presents to the girl.

"We could do the same. Once a man decides to go upstairs for the night, he could purchase a metal token. That way the house would get its money up front. The girls could turn in their tokens the next day and settle up."

He looked at her. "Do you still feel comfortable with the fifty-fifty split?"

She raised large eyes to his. "Yes. We don't accept quick 'dates' like other houses, where a girl has a frequent turnover. Once a girl is booked, it's until three. She deserves half of the fee for her services."

"Then we'll keep that the same."

"Thank you."

"I do think we provide a very lavish buffet. Maybe you could work with Manet on cutting back some. I don't mean be miserly," he said, when he saw her mouth set hard, "just more reasonable. I don't expect clients to be charged for it as in other houses, but I don't think we should provide paté and boiled shrimp and maple salmon and veal every night."

Jed cleared his throat. "As for music—"

"Raymond must stay," Lil interjected. "He is family."

"That's fine. He adds quite an ambiance and he's very talented. But an entire string quartet? That's pretty extravagant. May we compromise with a single violinist or harpist?"

Lil nodded slightly. "I could agree to that."

"I also thought of one last thing."

"Only one thing?"

He sensed her smoldering under the good manners. "Yes. I've seen poker, craps, and faro at the tables. I'd like to add a few more games of chance."

"Such as?"

"Roulette. Rondo. And *Vingt-et-un*."

"Blackjack?"

"Yes, that's what they're calling it now. Would you be agreeable to those additions?"

"If we could find the right dealers, then I would have no objections."

"Don't worry. I'll handle that. I want talented, honest men. The games will be a more gradual change. I won't move on them until I'm ready."

He placed a hand on her knee. "I know this has all been very hard for you, Lil. I appreciate the way you've handled yourself." He lifted his hand and placed a swift kiss on her cheek as he rose.

"I've got to go to my bank and see my attorney. My

tailor, too. I won't be back until supper time. I'll see you then."

He took his leave, more intrigued than ever by the mysterious house madam. He couldn't wait to see what Thompson's report would hold.

14

Lily waited a full minute before she fled up the stairs to her room. Her mother's light snores permeated the room, for which she was grateful. Lilian had a rough night. Lily had sat up most of it with her. She had been too weary to go back to bed, cramped alongside her mother in the bed they now shared since Lucky Lil's new owner occupied her room.

She tore off the black wig ringed in curls and threw it on the floor. Jed Stone was dictating how everything in the house should be run. It infuriated her beyond words. She sat at the dressing table and creamed her face, roughly rubbing off the cosmetics that she wore most of each day now.

Finally, the image reflected back at her was the one she'd longed for. Impersonating her mother seemed such a challenge and adventure in the beginning. Now, she was tired of the charade.

Slipping off Lilian's revealing gown, she replaced it with one of her own, a robin's egg blue with a decent neckline that only hinted at the full breasts that lay beneath it. She hated the way men ogled her every night. Only the fact that she played Madam Lil made them keep their paws to themselves, but they feasted their eyes, nonetheless. She had even caught Jed Stone giving her bosom appreciative looks. He wouldn't like her temper if he pushed too hard.

And that kiss just now. *What had that been about?* One minute he looked at her as if she were a delicate morsel he'd love to devour in one bite. The next moment, he gave her a chaste kiss on the cheek. Even putting his hand on her knee was too forward, by far. Lily could still feel the heat of it where his fingers had rested.

Then she stopped and laughed aloud. *What should she expect?* He was a man. She was supposed to be a woman whom men bought. She displayed her wares in plain sight for all to see. She should be grateful he hadn't acted on his lustful urges.

What was she going to do?

Go to Max...

The solution echoed in her mind and she murmured it aloud. "Go to Max." Yes, she'd share with Max all that had happened. He would know what to do. Besides, Jed wouldn't be back for hours and hours. She could go as herself and still have plenty of time to return and transform herself into Madam Lil once again.

J ED SPENT the rest of his morning at the tailor's, trying on the suits he had ordered. He also chose several shirts and two pairs of shoes. He couldn't remember any time in his life when he'd owned more than a single pair of shoes, other than when Louis encouraged him to remove a pair of boots from a dead soldier who wouldn't be needing his anymore.

At the time his were in poor shape, stuffed with

cardboard and newspaper, so it hadn't taken much prodding. He slipped off the boots from the corpse and placed them on his own feet. He'd thought to keep his original pair as his ace in the hole. Instead, he'd returned less than five minutes later and put them on the soldier before his body was taken for burial. It hadn't seemed right, the man being barefoot and going to his grave.

He asked that his purchases be delivered to Lucky Lil's as he left for his luncheon appointment with Mac McBride. Jed rounded the corner and saw Mac coming from the other way. He waved and hurried across the street.

"Right on time, Jed." Mac shook his hand. You'll like this chop-house. Best cuts of meat in town."

The pair entered and immediately proceeded to their left. Every variety of beef known to man was on display.

"I'd recommend their eye of round," Mac told him. "The sirloin's good, too."

Both made their selections and saw the meat thrown on a section of fire that stretched over twelve feet in length. They watched while the steaks were grilled to perfection, ordering sides of baked potatoes and steamed vegetables while they waited.

Within minutes they were seated at a table on the right side of the chop-house, two mugs of cold beer accompanying the rest of their meal.

"How's life in the Big House?" asked Mac.

Jed smiled. "I suppose living with over two dozen of San Francisco's loveliest ladies isn't too hard a task."

"How do the books look?"

He frowned. "Lil kept them herself until a few months ago. They were a genteel mess. Bills and receipts stuffed here and there. Deposits not recorded.

Columns of numbers so crooked I didn't know at times if it was five dollars or five hundred dollars being added up."

"Will you be able to make any sense of them?"

"I'm starting to." He shook his head. "I need to meet Lil's daughter and thank her. That girl brought a semblance of order to years of hit-and-miss accounting."

"Lily's a pretty one. Last time I saw her, anyway."

The attorney's words piqued his curiosity. "What's she like?"

Mac leaned back in his chair. "Well, the last time I saw her was about six months ago. She was at the opera with Maximilian Fisher, just before he fell and broke his hip."

"*The* Maximilian Fisher?"

His friend nodded. "He took an interest in the girl years ago. She used to accompany him to cultural events about town. Museum openings. The theater. Max has been in a wheelchair since his accident. Doctors don't think he'll be up and walking anytime soon, according to gossip on the street."

"She's back East now. The daughter."

"Really? Didn't know that. Well, I'm sure you'll meet her when she returns. She's very close to her mother, by all accounts, even though she spent years at some fancy boarding school near Boston."

They finished their meal. Both refused dessert. Mac headed back to his office, while Jed stopped at the bank. He'd had a crazy notion and he hoped it paid off.

At his next stop, he traded the Stockton sheriff's bulky gun for a much smaller, sleeker model. The lawman had confiscated his gambler's gun, one that fit easily into his coat pocket, revealing no bulge. He'd never needed to use it before, but he liked going into a game prepared in every way. Besides, who knew when it might come in handy?

He then made his way to Walker Thompson's office. He was a bit early for their scheduled appointment but the secretary ushered him in anyway.

Thompson rose to greet him. "Mr. Stone, how are you? Please take a seat. Would you like coffee?"

"Coffee would be good. And please, call me Jed."

The detective nodded to his secretary. The men made small talk for a few minutes until she returned with a small tray and steaming cups of coffee.

"Thank you. And please close the door. We'll be tied up for a while."

Jed raised a brow. "Interesting findings?"

"I always learn interesting things, Jed." Thompson removed a file from his drawer and placed it on his desk top. "If you don't mind, I'll read you what I have. We can discuss it as we go. You'll receive one copy to take with you and I'll retain a copy for your file here. That way if anything gets misplaced—"

"You mean lost or stolen?" he interjected.

Thompson smiled. "Then we'll have another copy available."

The investigator opened the folder and began to read. "Lilian Frontiere, also known as Lilian Fremont, born Paris, 1825."

"My God! The woman is forty-five?"

"Yes. Amazingly well-preserved if you ask me. I saw her not two weeks ago and she looked mighty fine."

"Thank you for patronizing my new business."

Thompson chuckled. "Afraid I only played at the gaming tables. I had a client who chose to meet there. My wife keeps me quite happy at home."

He resumed his report. "Nothing else on her early background. Arrived in the city with a year-old daughter, father unknown. Earned close to fifty thousand her first year in California."

Jed whistled. "You've got to be kidding."

"No, actually several women did. They arrived amongst the hordes of men seeking their fortune and were very young, incredibly beautiful, and extremely talented at what they did. With gold coming off the fields as fast as it did, and their inflated prices, a handful of women made a killing. A few retired after that one year. They married or went back home.

"Our Madam Lil opened her own house the next year, just off the Financial District. Men flocked there, flush full of cash. Although Lil never went back to personally satisfying her customers, she had a long line of men who said they went because she liked men and she listened to them.

"Lost her first house in the Great Fire of Fifty-One. It swept away the entire business district, between fifteen hundred and two thousand structures. Volunteer fire companies worked with axes and crowbars to cut through wooden wharves. They saved the waterfront and dozens of ships at their moorings but more than twenty city blocks disappeared in the smoke and flames."

"And Lucky Lil's was one of them."

"She opened again the next year on Kearney, just south of Portsmouth Square, what we natives call the Plaza."

"And she's been there ever since."

"Right. For twenty years, Madam Lil has proven herself to be a charming, capable, and sometimes ruthless businesswoman." Thompson set the paper down and lit his pipe.

"Anything else?"

The detective puffed thoughtfully. "Yes."

Jed was intrigued by his answer.

"Daughter Lily had an English nanny. Pretty unusual for a whorehouse, I'd think. Sent the child to the Willett School outside of Boston at age thirteen when the nanny passed away unexpectedly. The girl remained there for several years without any visits home, due to war breaking out."

"Sounds pricey."

"It is," Thompson agreed. "Also, Madam Lil shut her house down for the first and only time for an extended period and took Lily on a European tour a while ago. That lasted close to a year."

"Her pocketbook must have taken quite a hit."

"Right again. Madam Lil found herself stretched pretty thin after their return and the start-up of her establishment once more. Yet she didn't run to her oldest and dearest friend—and supposed one-time lover—for help."

"Maximilian Fisher?" Jed inserted.

"You are good. Instead, she decided to solve the problem herself. By gambling."

He sat up. It was the last thing he would have expected from a woman with Lil's good sense. "What a fool."

"Funny, because Lil has a rule that no one in her house is allowed to gamble—not the girls, the musicians, even the domestics. It's something she's always felt strongly about.

"Anyway, she did fairly well to begin with. After all, not much gets by this gal."

He completed Thompson's thought since it was a story he knew all too well. "Then her luck took a turn for the worse. She didn't back off, but played more often, pushing the stakes higher and higher. Until not much was left."

"And she was forced to mortgage Lucky Lil's."

Jed toyed with his mustache. "That's the part that troubles me. If the bank held the title, how did the deed wind up in a high stakes poker game at Varsouvienne?"

"Albus Tate handled Lil's transaction. He's a known cheat and scoundrel, but his wife's father owns the bank he works at. If something dirty went down, I don't think the old man would call the cops on his own son-in-law. Especially when Tate's the father of six kids under the age of ten."

"This is great stuff, Walker."

"Got more. A little about Lil's daughter."

"Shoot."

"The daughter hasn't been seen much since returning from the European tour at age twenty. She'd be twenty-two now. She's an occasional suffragette. Attends meetings at Dashaway Hall. Lil never allowed her daughter to participate in any of the life at the house."

Thompson closed the folder. "That about wraps up Lil. Ready for Simon Morgan?

Jed nodded.

15

Lily threw open the doors to the study. Max and Harold sat huddled over a chessboard, both deep in thought.

"Just set luncheon over there, Margaret," Max said, not taking his eye from the game. "We're about to break."

"It's not luncheon."

The two men looked up.

"We're delighted to see you, Miss Lily," said Harold.

"No," corrected Max. "You're delighted to see her. I'm losing. I never want to see anyone when I'm losing."

"Then allow me to finish you off, Master Max." Harold moved his piece and sat back with a smile.

"Oh, bother." Max tried to counter the move and threw his hands up in the air in disgust.

Harold made one last move. "Checkmate."

"It's this damn hip. I haven't been able to concentrate since I broke it." He turned to Lily. "Pain racks my poor body day and night."

Harold removed the game board from the table.

"The hip has healed but he'll use any excuse when losing."

"I didn't lose, actually. Lily's arrival distracted me from my plan. Given proper time and a new strategy, I might have rallied and won the match."

"As you wish." Harold rolled the luncheon cart over that Margaret had eased into the room during their discussion. "Why don't you take my place, Miss Lily, and have lunch with Master Max? He's in far too poor a disposition to be an entertaining luncheon companion to me."

"Then we'll suit each other well. I'm in a foul mood and would love to punch someone."

"Better leave, Harold. You wouldn't want to become Lily's punching bag."

The corner of Harold's mouth turned up slightly. "I am far too well paid simply to be pummeled. I shall be supervising the silver polishing if anyone needs me." He crossed the room with immense dignity and closed the door.

Max lifted the cover from one of the plates. "Ah. Curried chicken." He took a bite. "And quite tasty."

Lily joined him in the meal. "Do you want to hear why I'm peeved or not?"

"I suppose it has to do with your new owner. He wants to make changes or some other such nonsense."

"That's exactly right." Lily buttered a roll. "Jed Stone let one night pass, observed the state of things, and then this morning hit me with a list of things to do and change."

"Such as?"

Lily explained in great detail all the alterations Jed was determined to carry out. By the time she completed her diatribe, Max had moved on to dessert.

"Are you quite through ranting and raving, my

dear?" He broke a sugar cookie in half and bit into a piece.

Lily waved her fork in the air. "I suppose I am. So, what do you think? What can I do?"

"What can you do to enact these new policies?"

She growled. "You are deliberately misunderstanding me, Max Fisher. I expected a little more support from you. And sympathy. Lots of sympathy."

She skipped her entrée. The cookies looked too inviting.

"I think all of Mr. Stone's ideas have some merit."

"Oh, you do?" Lily jammed the cookie into her mouth and chewed it angrily. "Max, why aren't you listening?"

He nibbled another bite thoughtfully. "I did, Lily. Everything is perfectly sound business practice. I'm surprised Lilian didn't implement these ideas years ago."

Lily started to protest but Max cut her off.

"Just try them a while. If they don't work, I'm sure your Mr. Stone will notice and make the proper adjustments."

"He's not *my* Mr. Stone. I just wish he'd go away."

"I don't believe that will happen any time soon. Come. Sit. Let's have us a nice visit and not think about the wicked Mr. Stone for an hour."

Max rattled on about a tobacco company that had been lost to fire and a Chinese boy that had been caught in the blaze. Lily listened half-heartedly, feeling very alone.

"Cigar?" Walker Thompson offered Jed one from a wooden box atop his desk.

"No, thank you." He wanted to focus his full attention on what Thompson had found out about his enemy.

The detective pushed aside the file on Lil and removed a second folder from his desk drawer.

"Simon Anthony Morgan, born 1822, Biloxi, Mississippi. Life-long gambler. Has never held a steady, paying job in his forty-eight years. Plied his trade in his twenties and thirties on the Mississippi, mostly fleecing young, wealthy Southern gentlemen that didn't know any better.

"Was a gun runner during the war for the South, although he isn't political. Did it strictly for profit. After Gettysburg, when it became obvious the Confederacy was a lost cause, he retired to the Bahamas—mostly to make sure he wouldn't be arrested in the aftermath. When he thought it safe, he returned to the United States, via Brazil."

Jed shifted in his chair. Nothing he could use so far. He doubted Uncle Sam was still interested in a two-bit blockade-runner at this point.

"Morgan made several trips to San Francisco after his close friend Gordon Fisher moved here. This was before the war. When Lee surrendered and Morgan returned to the States, he relocated permanently in San Francisco, with occasional forays to New Orleans, New York, and Denver."

"What do you know about this Gordon Fisher?"

Walker's eyes lit with a gleam. "Fisher was an actor many years ago on the East coast. He moved here in the mid-1850s. Followed his daddy out to the coast. Does the name Maximilian Fisher ring any bells?"

Jed sat up. "The same man who is friends with Lil and her daughter? A millionaire many times over?"

Thompson set aside his pipe. "The very one.

Gordon has held a job with Fisher Industries for years, but it's mostly an empty title. No work is tossed his way. Gordon Fisher lives for gambling halls, liquor, and most of all—women. Young, pretty women."

"Interesting. All the parties seem to be acquainted."

"What's more fascinating is that although Morgan never married, he took an interest in Calvin, Gordon's son. Took the boy under his wing when the kid got in a bit of a bind. Calvin Fisher worked with him on the Mississippi before the war. They ran monte scams. He was just a boy then."

Thompson inhaled deeply and then stubbed out the cigar. He closed the folder he'd read from. "Another tidbit I know since I've lived here so long. Simon fancied Lilian Frontiere for year,s but she's never given him the time of day. Rumor is he now has eyes for her daughter, Lily. He's also let it be known around town that he wants to take over management of Lucky Lil's."

"But I beat him to it."

Thompson pushed both folders over to Jed. "Simon Morgan had something to do with the deed being in that card game, Jed. I couldn't find the link. No one's saying anything but it was a feeling I got as I snooped around. What I can't understand is why you came into possession of it."

"It was a mistake. That much is obvious. I suppose Morgan's gunning for me now."

Walker frowned. "Anything involving Simon Morgan, I'd watch my back. He's never been formally charged with any wrongdoing here in town, but he usually has a thug or two in tow. Right now there are two men named Travis and Montgomery that seem to be his shadows.

"Rumor has it that Calvin Fisher's back in town, as

well. He'll hook up again with Morgan. I'm sure of it. Trouble gravitates to more trouble."

Jed thought back to what Simon and his bruisers had done to Sherry. "One more thing." He pulled out the gold locket he'd retrieved on his bank visit and placed it on the desk. Thompson picked it up and examined it carefully.

"Would there be any way to trace the owner?"

The detective grew thoughtful. "Maybe. It's of fairly good quality. I spotted the initials *CLF* on the back. The daguerreotype inside is quite old. Would I have any more to go on?"

He felt exposed suddenly. He placed the locket back in his pocket. "I'll let you know," he said cryptically. He scooped up the two folders and extended his hand.

"Thanks again. You were fast and thorough, just as Mac promised."

Thompson grinned. "And discreet. That's what I'm known for. If you have need of me again, you know where to find me."

Jed tipped his hat and exited the building. He decided to walk back to Lucky Lil's. Some of his best thinking went on when he sauntered from one place to the next, letting his thoughts toss around in his mind.

He wondered if he should even pursue his mother's identity. The locket was his only clue. Still, he thought about her from time to time and wished he had some answers.

It also bothered him that his father had walked out on her. Elmira said he'd done so just minutes before Jed was born. What kind of man deserted a wife as she was about to give birth to their child? Was the man in the daguerreotype his mother's father—or his own?

And did that kind of bad blood run through his veins?

That thought alone had held him back from asking Walker Thompson to investigate the wanted poster sitting inside his safety deposit box. Whoever Cal Hart was would have to wait until Jed's business with Simon Morgan ran its course. Then he would explore any connection he had with the murderer who shared his likeness.

He arrived at Lucky Lil's and saw Ben pulling away in a carriage. A young woman went into the brothel. He wondered whom Ben had been squiring around town. Jed entered the house to the smell of pot roast. Several of the girls were coming downstairs for dinner. Some gave him an interested glance, recognizing him from last night.

He hadn't made any formal announcement to them about his role. He'd hoped Lil would do so.

Gertie breezed by him, her nose so far in the air Jed was sure she had trouble seeing where she was going. He caught up to her and took her elbow.

"Gertie? Still mad at me?"

She looked at him with something he didn't comprehend. It was fear he saw in her eyes.

"Gertie?"

She pulled away from him and ran down the hall like the devil was after her. Jed had no clue what was going on.

But he intended to find out.

16

Lily had stayed later at Max's than she'd intended. She hurried up the stairs and into her mother's room. Lilian sat up in bed, her color good for once. She went to her and kissed both cheeks.

"*Ou etes-tu alle?*"

"I went to see Max, *Maman.*" She removed her hat and set it on the chair. "He asked after you. How do you feel?"

"*Je me porte tres bien, merci.*"

Lily noticed the longer her mother remained ill, the more she lapsed into French. Thank goodness Lilian insisted Lily learn both French and English from the cradle. It had made the trip to Paris much easier.

It also made Pierre think she was a native willing to play his games. He probably thought she toyed with him when she claimed to be a young American from abroad.

She brushed aside thoughts of him. "Are you hungry?"

Lilian shook her head. "*J'ai sommeil.*"

"Then let's settle you back into the pillows since you are sleepy. Dr. Seward said you need rest." She smoothed the covers over her. Lilian's eyes closed and her breathing evened out almost immediately.

Lily went to her dressing table to apply her cosmetics. She stared at the image before her. A stranger looked back. She had lost her true self these last few months.

What would she do after her mother died? Lilian wasted away more each day. The time to hide from this truth had passed. Her mother's death was but a matter of time. At first, Lily wanted to care for her mother the best she could and keep the house running. Then she had thoughts of selling Lucky Lil's and going on stage as she'd always wished. Her mother had adamantly opposed the idea in the past. She believed actresses nothing more than whores.

Now the house wasn't hers to sell—and acting had lost its appeal after so many months of play-acting in real life. But what would she do? She couldn't continue being Lilian. She had a little money of her own and the salary Jed Stone would pay her, but that wouldn't last for long.

She longed for a family, but what man in San Francisco would have her? Everyone knew who she was. No decent man would ever offer marriage. The first time he tried to take her into polite society, she would be ostracized. Lily fought the tears that began to build.

She was well-educated. Maybe she could be a governess to young children. That way she could be around children, even if they weren't her own. The situations weren't always stable, but unless she became a wife and mother, what else was she qualified for?

Lying flat on her back.

She shuddered at the thought. She had seen too many girls come and go, seen how this business aged them, how they contracted venereal diseases and became addicted to laudanum and tried to terminate unwanted pregnancies. She refused to be any man's plaything. She would rather work as a house servant and scrub floors than service a man.

A knock sounded at the door. "Lil?"

She recognized Jed's voice. Lily took a cleansing breath to calm herself. "I am at my *toilette*, Jed."

"We could chat while you apply all that war paint," he glibly replied through the door. "I'll admit I'm curious as to the woman under the cosmetics."

Lily's eyes widened at his remark. She fought the panic that caused her heart to skip a beat. How would her mother respond?

"I have not a stitch on, you rascal. You certainly may not be a witness to my personal grooming. Go away. We'll speak later, *mon ami*." She prayed she'd sounded playful enough to put Jed off without arousing his suspicions.

"Saucy little madam," she heard him say. She assumed he left after his remark. The carpeting in the hallway was too thick for her to hear his footsteps recede.

Lily raised a trembling hand. She found she couldn't keep it still enough to apply her thick eyeliner. She held her wrist with her other hand to stop its shaking and managed to apply the cosmetic and then dress. She admired the picture she cut in the floor-length mirror next to her wardrobe. The amber gown of satin pushed her breasts together and lifted them enticingly. It emphasized her narrow waist as it fell in sweeping folds to the floor.

She was Madam Lil, ready to face the night.

JED HUNG around the bottom of the stairs for a few minutes, hoping to talk to Lil before she entered the kitchen. He'd never get a private word in, with all the chatter the girls created. He gave up and decided to grab some of the roast and carrots that sang his name.

"*Monsieur* Jed," Manet called out. "Come, sit. It takes a man to do justice to this meal." The cook waved away two girls and made room for him at the long table.

Soon, Jed teased away with those gathered around, thoroughly enjoying himself. He had always relished the company of women. The only dark shadow cast was by Gertie and her friend, seated at the far end. It strengthened his determination to speak to Lil about whatever was going on.

Lily entered the kitchen, curious about the giggling. Before she spoke, she spent a minute observing the scene. Jed sat in the center of the table in the midst of some tale that had the girls in fits. She watched his easy banter with the assembled women, except for Gertie and Sarah Jane, who snubbed him from the far end of the table.

"Good evening, girls," Lily called out in her husky Madam Lil voice. "You seem in high spirits tonight."

The laughter died down as she made her way around the table, talking with clusters of girls about their day. She admired one's new hairstyle and another's lavender dress.

"The nails are too long," she gently chastised a third. "We don't want to mar your beauty, pet."

"Or the hairy backs of our clients," another girl called out playfully.

Lily flashed a disapproving look. The girl sheepishly dipped her head low. She surveyed the rest of the table, ready to say what must be said.

"*Attention*," she said brusquely. The chatter died down immediately. Lil commanded respect above all else. It had been one of the most appealing aspects of Lily's role-playing. As Lilian, she was always shown deference.

"I would like to introduce you to my business associate and good friend, Jed Stone." All eyes turned to Jed. Although Lily had no wish to be Jed's friend, she knew if it were thought so, it would benefit the house in this time of transition.

"Mr. Stone now owns Lucky Lil's. He has come up with an idea for a new system of payment. Hear him out."

Jed's eyes connected with hers before he stood. "Thank you, Lil."

As he spoke, she didn't bother to listen to his smooth words. Instead, she watched him as he charmed his audience. Jed had a way about him. Lily knew instinctively that it wouldn't matter if he addressed men or women. Both would be drawn to him. Men would be comfortable with him, while women would view him as a potential lover.

Lily objectively took stock of him for a moment. He stood a good two inches over six feet and was broad through the shoulders. He wore an aura of power, of strength, as easily as another man might wear a freshly-laundered shirt. His dark blonde hair fell across his brow boyishly.

But his eyes entranced Lily. Ever since she'd first seen them, they'd drawn her to him like a magnet. She was powerless when she looked into those azure eyes.

That's why she avoided them. She'd focus on his mustache or glimpse at him quickly as she spoke, fiddling with an inane task, doing everything she could not to stare into them. She knew if she really looked at him, she would fall harder than an elephant felled by a tusk hunter.

He finished speaking and smiled. *Blast!* Another thing Lily hoped to avoid. He didn't use it often but when he did, Jed's smile was all bright warmth. Why, she bet he could sweet-talk even a tough old bird like Max into a thousand dollar loan on his smile alone, with absolutely no collateral. It was simply magical, that smile.

He started toward her and Lily forced her own smile in return. "I see you have worked your charm with the girls."

"All but two," he said succinctly. "Can we talk?"

She nodded and led him to the upstairs parlor where they would not be interrupted. Lily settled on a plush sofa and fussed with the throw pillows, trying to relax.

Jed closed the doors and then gave her a low whistle. "Madam Lil, you are lovely tonight. That dress brings out the fawn in your eyes."

Lily was helpless to control the blush that sprang to her cheeks. "You are comparing me to a yearling?"

He cocked his head to one side. "I hadn't thought of it before, but you do look like a doe. There's a slight slant to your eyes' shape, and the warm brown color does favor a helpless doe."

Lily snorted as her mother might. "Helpless? You don't know me at all, Jed Stone. I came to California with nothing and built the finest sporting house in San Francisco. I don't think a helpless woman could accomplish that."

He smiled at her, a slow smile that spread across his face and her insides like a rising sun. "I didn't mean to imply you weak or inefficient, Lil. I meant it more as a compliment. Like you're vulnerable-looking."

She started to snap off a reply when he held up his hand. "Come on, Lil. Even the most delicate flowers stand tall after being beaten down in a storm."

Lily had little experience with men, much less receiving compliments from them, thanks to the years spent in her all-female boarding school. Her only practice had been in Paris, where flattering remarks reeked of insincerity and were liberally tossed about.

"Thank you," she said simply, a bit in awe of the admiring glance Jed gave her. She rearranged the folds of her gown casually and asked, "What did you wish to speak to me about?"

"It's Gertie." Jed shook his head, and Lily could see true puzzlement filled his features. "She's been colder than a witch's tit since I've come back. You know, after that first visit when we spent time downright pleasurable time together. And she's got a friend that shoots me looks which would maim most men."

Lily bit the inside of her cheek. The welts and bite marks that had covered Sarah Jane's body filled her memory. How could she be so easily persuaded by the man that stood in front of her? Did he truly not remember his previous, abominable conduct?

"Maybe you've behaved unseemly toward them," she suggested neutrally, wondering if he'd been drunk during the coupling and had no recollection of it or what he'd done to the girl. She had no desire to get into a shouting match with Jed, which she knew would be inevitable if she mentioned the episode from beforehand.

Jed ran a hand through his thick hair. "Beats me. I only spent the one night with Gertie. I've never even seen the other girl."

Lily narrowed her eyes and studied him. He genuinely thought he told the truth. Was he a sociopath? Did he suffer from blackouts, where previous events were erased? Her comfort level fell dramatically. She wondered if he could be trusted in her presence, much less with her girls. Max certainly didn't trust him and had banned him from his home.

"I have no answers, Jed."

He rubbed his jaw in thought. "Maybe you do have another answer, Lil. Where's the new girl?"

Lily frowned. "I haven't hired anyone new in close to three months." She pursued her lips tightly. "I would suppose when I do, you will want final approval."

Jed waved a hand in the air. "No, that's your area of expertise. I trust your judgment in those matters. I'm talking about the girl I saw Ben drop off this afternoon. I was curious, is all. From a distance, she was a real looker."

Lily swallowed her instant fear. He'd actually seen her return this afternoon. Much too close for comfort.

"I guess we'll have to ask Ben, won't we?" Lily prayed that she would find Ben first.

Jed offered her a hand. "Then let's go look for him now."

17

Lily's panic caused her heart to race irrationally. Lilian would be bored by such trivial conversation. But where was Ben?

A knock sounded at the parlor door. Lily sprang to her feet as Gertie popped her head in.

"Trouble, Madam Lil. Sally Mae and Lydia are arguing about that new banker again. You better step in before Sally Mae starts pulling hair like last time."

"Excuse me," Lily told Jed and fled the room, glad for Sally Mae's volatile temper for once. She even spotted Ben on the staircase. Thank God her luck was holding.

Lily grabbed his arm. "Jed saw me come in this afternoon as Lily. He knows you were driving. Be ready."

She hurried after Gertie and rounded the corner to find Lydia lying on the floor. Sally Mae sat on top of her, both fists full of Lydia's long, golden tresses.

"Enough!"

Lily strode into the room as girls scattered left and right. She grabbed her own fistful of Sally Mae's hair and yanked hard. The girl screamed. She did let go of Lydia.

"Into the kitchen. Now!"

Lily walked forcefully in front of them, fully expecting them to follow her. She slammed the swinging door back as she entered and crossed her arms, trying to keep her harsh breathing under control.

"Neither of you may service the handsome banker if he shows up when we open tonight," she said crisply, as the two girls came in and stood before her. "He's not worth the fuss you two have created. No man is."

Sally Mae opened her mouth to protest, but Lily gave her best withering Madam Lil look to the girl.

"Who started this?"

Lydia quickly looked at Sally Mae and then forced herself to stare at the ground. Sally Mae raised a hand.

"As I thought." Lily made sure to study the guilty party thoroughly before speaking. Lilian was known to take her time when disputes arose among the girls. "Sally Mae, you will work a full shift for no pay the next three nights. If your temper gets the best of you again, you will pack your bags and never work at my house again."

Sally Mae nodded sullenly and lowered her eyes.

"Lydia? You will be docked one night's salary."

The girl kept her eyes on the floor. "Yes, ma'am."

"I will not tolerate arguing of any kind at Lucky Lil's. You are fortunate to work here. Your rooms are clean. The meals are first-class. Your hours and number of clients are less than that of other houses. I can replace you in the snap of a finger. I will if I see behavior like this ever again."

Lily let the silence work for a moment before she said, "You may go."

Both girls walked slowly through the door. She began to shake as they left.

Would she really turn them out? She hoped it

wouldn't come to that. How she wished she had her mother's decisive strength.

Jed entered, an amused look on his face. "I saw the culprits leaving the scene with long faces. Thoroughly disciplined?"

Lily nodded, not trusting her voice to speak.

"I found Ben."

She swallowed. "And what did he say?"

Jed shook his head. "He said he met her this morning and found she was down on her luck. He thought we might have a place for her, be it upstairs or in the kitchen."

Lily tried to look puzzled. "I never saw her."

"Ben says she walked straight through the front door and out the back. I guess she didn't like what she saw and changed her mind." He sighed. "It's too bad. She was awfully pretty from a distance. Would've brought in some new clients, I bet."

"We do good business as it is," she replied smoothly.

THE STAIRS FILLED as clients made their way down and out the front door. Tommy had just chimed three o'clock. Lil's well-trained customers filed out in an orderly fashion. It surprised Jed how cooperative they were. Outside a line of hacks waited to take them to their homes.

He closed the front door and locked it. "Successful night."

"Most are."

Lil sat upon a velvet sofa and slipped off her shoes. She closed her eyes and rested her head on the back of the sofa. Jed looked at the long column of exposed flesh, from her neck to her breasts and grew hard.

Something about this woman did strange things to him. He wanted to scoop her into his arms and take her upstairs for what remained of the night. He might even break his own rule about sleeping with a woman in his bed.

If it were Lil.

"Lil?"

"Hmm?" She didn't open her eyes.

He sat next to her. Tonight she wore a scent of musk, dark and mysterious. He inhaled its potent aroma and leaned closer, moving to kiss her throat when she murmured, "I saw a man today that could have been your twin."

Jed broke out into a cold sweat. He immediately stood and shoved his hands into his pockets. "My twin, you say," he said casually, and moved away from her. Scrambled thoughts danced through his head. He could see the wanted poster, smell the stench of the Stockton cell, hear Hanging Hal plunk his gavel upon the bench in a death sentence.

Lil sat up and looked at him. "He was a dead ringer for you." She studied him. "Are you all right, Jed?"

Hell, no.

"Right as rain, darlin.' Just a little tired, is all. Where'd you run into this fellow?"

Lil frowned. "It might have been outside the bank. I don't remember now. It just surprised me. I called out, thinking it was you."

"But it wasn't," he finished. "How could you tell?"

Lil grew thoughtful. "I'm not sure. The face, the hair, the mustache—they all looked like you. Yet it wasn't you. He wasn't as polished, I suppose. Just a general impression I had. Why? Do you know this man?"

Jed sat again on the couch next to her and buried his head in his hands. He was tired of being alone. Tired of not sharing anything with anyone. Lil had become his one friend now that Louis was dead. He raised his head and saw the concern written across her face.

He had to tell someone.

"I almost hanged for that man's crimes," he said bluntly.

Surprise washed over Lily. "What?"

"I'm a gambler, Lil. Been one for a long time now. The riverboat trade had seen better days so I decided to head West." He smiled wistfully, a smile Lily had never seen on him before. It made him appealing and yet vulnerable.

"My friend Louis told me tales of San Francisco while we fought in the war."

"You were a soldier?" She remembered he made the claim once before.

"Yes. Another story for another night. Louis and I fought together. He'd lived here before the war. He made it sound so different. So cosmopolitan."

Jed stood and walked to the decanter and poured himself a stiff drink. He washed it down in one gulp.

"I'd had a little trouble and figured it was time to make a change, so I began moving this way. I'd made it all the way to Stockton when I stopped in the local saloon for a quick pick-up game. That's when it happened."

He poured himself another drink. Lily watched as this time he drank slowly, thoughtfully. He was silent until he'd finished.

"I was arrested and hauled off to jail. I protested

my innocence to the local sheriff. He showed me a wanted poster in return."

Jed walked swiftly to the sofa and sat, taking her hands in his. "It was my face staring back at me on the poster, Lil. Said my name was Cal Hart. I was wanted for murder. Robbery. Rape."

He flushed and dropped her hands, balling his own into fists. "Before I could sneeze, I'd been tried and convicted and sentenced to hang."

"What happened?"

He laughed, a harsh, bitter laugh. "I escaped. A lynch mob came for another man. I got away in the confusion. I was running the night I first came here."

Lily remembered the men who'd come looking for him. She wondered if they had searched for Jed or this Cal Hart.

The man she now knew must be Cal Fisher.

What would Max think of his great-grandson wanted by the law? And why did Jed and Cal favor each other so? Was that a coincidence? She'd read once where everyone had a twin somewhere in this world. Maybe this was the case, but doubts lingered.

"I don't know who showed up that night banging on your door. Can't say if they were looking for the man on the wanted poster or the escaped criminal. Or the real me."

He looked at her in shame. She laid a hand next to his cheek. "You have nothing to be embarrassed about, Jed. You aren't guilty of any crimes."

"How will I explain that if I'm arrested again? Cal Hart is wanted for crimes in Texas and throughout the Midwest. I can't believe my bad luck. From what you've seen, he's turned up in San Francisco, of all places." He looked at her earnestly. "I may not have been the best man I could be, Lil, but I don't deserve to die for his crimes."

Lily wanted to console him somehow. Before she thought it through, she brought her other hand up and framed his face. Then she kissed him.

Their lips were a perfect fit. His hands went around her waist and pulled her close. His mouth moved over hers, tasting her, gently at first, and then more hungrily. Lily's lips parted for his tongue, which sweetly thrust inside, searching.

She'd known, always known, that a kiss with the right man would fill her soul.

Jed Stone was that man.

She pushed her fingers into his thick hair, kneading his scalp. If she started purring like a cat, it wouldn't surprise her.

His hands squeezed her waist again, his thumbs circling upward and grazing her breasts. She murmured something against his mouth, not sure herself what she'd said. Jed responded by deepening the kiss, moving even closer to her. The heat he radiated filled her, possessed her, urged her on.

What was she doing?

She brought her hands back down to his chest and gently pushed him away. She must act naturally, not like an innocent. Whatever she said must make him stop. Now.

"You are a skilled lover, Jed Stone. But no more of this nonsense."

Jed's eyes blazed with aroused passion. "Give me one good reason why, Lil," he said huskily.

She cocked her head and shrugged her shoulders. "My daughter Lily arrives tomorrow morning for a short visit. I would not want her to find you in my bed."

18

"**Y**our daughter?" Jed echoed, his head still reeling from the kiss.

Lil smoothed the folds of her skirt. "I've mentioned Lily to you before. She arrives tomorrow morning."

"From back East."

"She's missed me and our beautiful bay. Since you now occupy her room, she'll sleep with me." Lil gave him a sly look. "I don't think my bed would accommodate the three of us."

He flushed. "Of course not." He stood and began pacing the room. "Is there another room I can move to?"

"No, we're full at the moment."

"Then I'll go to a hotel."

"No!"

Her vehemence surprised him. "I don't mind, Lil. And I remember all those clothes in her room. She'll probably bring ten trunks with her."

"Lily is not the frivolous girl you think," Lil said thoughtfully. "She has an entire wardrobe here. I expect she'll have packed very lightly."

"Are you sure?" he asked.

"I will enjoy sharing my room with her. It will give

us more opportunity to spend time together. After all," she said wryly, "I wouldn't want to inconvenience the new owner of Lucky Lil's."

She stood suddenly. "I need to get my beauty sleep, *mon ami*. I will see you tomorrow."

Jed watched her float out of the room. The sway of her hips only intensified his hunger for her.

That kiss.

Jed wished he'd been able to explore her mouth more. And much more than her mouth.

***

"PLEASE, *MAMAN*. ONE MORE BITE."

"*Non, ma petite*. Just give me the belladonna."

Lily put aside the bowl of warm beef broth and picked up the glass bottle and dropper. She disguised her worry with a smile. "Here it is. Open for me."

Lilian complied and almost immediately fell asleep. Lily then nervously began going through the wardrobe. She didn't know what to wear for her first meeting with Jed.

She had surprised herself by announcing her own visit last night. And once Jed had been gentlemanly enough to offer to leave, she knew she didn't want him to. Besides, it would be easier to care for her mother and continue her role-playing if she did so from one place.

After several minutes of debate, she decided on a daffodil yellow dress with tight sleeves and a bodice that flared into a full skirt. She had washed her hair very early and brushed it until it shone. For once she enjoyed sitting at the vanity, happy she dressed her own hair. She'd always thought brown hair ordinary but after wearing the dark wig for so long, she appreciated her own cinnamon hair, with its soft color and warm highlights.

Jed rarely rose before ten. She counted on that schedule today. Lily packed a small valise and slipped out and down the rear stairs. She walked around the chicken-house and out the back gate. Once she was several blocks away, she hailed a cab and gave the address to Lucky Lil's.

The driver looked at her oddly. "Only a few blocks, miss." He shrugged and took up her case, muttering away.

Lily didn't care if he thought her a spoiled young woman too good to walk a quarter of a mile or if he judged her poorly because she headed to a whore-house. She needed to be seen arriving. She hoped she'd timed things right.

She paid the driver and started up the walkway. Jed came bounding out the door and tipped his hat to her. He must have been watching for her arrival, brimming with curiosity.

"Good morning, miss. May I help you?"

He was wearing a dark blue suit and starched white shirt. His blue cravat was of good silk. Lily thought he was about the most handsome man she'd ever seen.

And then he smiled. *By Jiminy!* Did he have to snatch her breath away before she could call out a pleasant greeting?

She offered her hand to him. "Good day, sir. This is my home. And I don't have much to carry."

Jed took the suitcase from her. "I'll have Ben take this upstairs. I'm sure you'll want to see your mother."

"No, I doubt *Maman* is up yet. Are you one of our new bouncers?" she inquired lightly.

He replaced his hat. "No. My name is Jed Stone."

He looked about him. "It's a fine day. Since Lil won't be awake for a while, would you like to take a walk? I need to catch you up on what's been happening at Lucky Lil's."

Lily smiled. "I would enjoy that. I've missed San Francisco and this mild weather."

"Let me place your valise inside." He was only gone a moment before he came back and offered his arm.

"I am Lily Frontiere."

He grinned. "I know."

He led them down the path and out the gate. Lily asked about some of the local gossip. It surprised her that Jed had a ready answer for all her questions. She hadn't been aware how closely he read the various newspapers or listened to the nightly conversations of their clients.

As they passed a café he asked, "Would you like to stop for a cup of coffee?"

"That would be very nice."

They sat and placed their order with the waiter, who brought their drinks immediately. "Fresh pot. Enjoy."

Lily sweetened hers with sugar and milk. Jed left his black.

"I you're not a new bouncer, then who are you, Mr. Stone? A new chef? Surely Manet would not have left?"

He laughed. "No. It's more complicated than that."

Jed studied the young woman across from him. She was a natural beauty. It was obvious she was Lil's daughter, even though her hair wasn't the house madam's raven black. They favored each other closely and their gestures were very similar. If he hadn't known, he would have taken them for sisters.

He decided to be blunt. "I'm the new owner of Lucky Lil's." He watched a shadow cross her face. She sipped her coffee carefully before she responded.

"I was afraid it would come to this. *Maman* was in financial trouble before I left town."

"Yes, she told me about the gambling." Jed saw her look of surprise. "Your mother was not happy about the shift in owners, but we have become friends."

"I'm glad," Lily said softly. "She needs a friend."

"I hear she's friends with Maximilian Fisher."

He watched Lily's face light up with pleasure. "Oh, Max. He's the best of friends to both of us. *Maman* wrote me of his fall. He broke his hip. I must go to see him soon."

"Maybe I could escort you?" Jed offered.

"I... d-don't think that's possible," she stammered.

"Why not?"

"Max is... well, he's not quite a hermit, but he's not really open to meeting new people. I suppose at his age he doesn't have to be."

That piqued his curiosity. "How old is he?"

"Ninety."

He whistled. "I guess with his age and piles of money, he can set his own terms."

She grinned. "Max favors Mr. Thoreau's words." She paused and then quoted, "*If a man does not keep pace with his companions, perhaps it is because he hears a different drummer.*"

Jed finished the famous saying. "*Let him step to music which he hears, however measured or far away.*"

His companion rewarded him with a sweet smile. "Max has always marched to his own drummer. He's been like a father to me."

"And who was your father?"

"You are rather forthright, aren't you, Mr. Stone?"

"Call me Jed. We're living in the same house now."
He paused. "I've actually been staying in your room."

He waited for her tantrum, but was surprised when it didn't occur. In fact, everything about Lily Frontiere surprised him. She was articulate and charming. Even a bit playful. He'd pictured a younger version of Madam Lil, a pretty but street-smart girl. She was so much more.

And Jed already didn't want this vision of loveliness to return back East.

"I'll just share with *Maman*. Her room is quite large. We'll giggle like schoolgirls all night."

They finished their coffee and sat chatting pleasantly in the cool morning for another half-hour before Jed asked, "Are you ready to go back home? I'm sure Lil's up by now."

She nodded eagerly. "I have so much to share with her. I'm eager to tell her about my trip."

He paid for their coffee and they strolled back to Lucky Lil's. He asked, "How long will you be staying?"

Lily shrugged, her gesture very much like one Lil made. "I'm not certain of my plans."

"Well, it's a pleasure finally to meet you. I had a high opinion of you even before today."

"Oh, really?"

He loved the blush that came to her cheeks and could see her curiosity at his words. "I went through the accounts when I first took over the place. Lil was no seasoned bookkeeper, I'm afraid to say."

Lily laughed. "Things were a mess, weren't they?"

He gave her an admiring look. "You certainly set the books straight. I thought you were a professional bookkeeper."

She glowed at his compliment. "Thank you."

They entered the house, which was still quiet. It was close to noon.

"I think I'll go visit *Maman* now."

"It's good to have you here, Lily," he told her as she went up the stairs. She looked over her shoulder and gave him a shy smile before she turned down the hallway.

Hell's bells!

Jed thought he was smitten with Lil. But after one conversation with Lily, he was already halfway in love with her charming daughter.

A soft knock sounded at the door. He turned and opened it. A gentlemen in his late forties stood on the porch.

"I'm afraid we're not open for business, sir," Jed told him politely.

The man cleared his throat with an important harrumph. "I'm not a paying customer. I'm Dr. Seward. Who are you?"

"Jed Stone. The new owner of Lucky Lil's. I thought you only came every other week, Doctor."

"I do normally. Today I'm here to see Mrs. Frontiere."

"Why? What's wrong with her?"

Dr. Seward shook his head impatiently. "Don't you know anything, Mr. Stone? Lilian is close to dying."

19

"Lil? Dying? You have to be joking."

"I never joke about death, Mr. Stone. If you are the new owner of Lucky Lil's, I would think you would know about Lilian's condition. And when she passes, Lucky Lil's will be just another house. Her clients have come all these years for Lil. No Lilian— and this whorehouse will be a dime a dozen. Better adjust to a drop in income, sir."

"What's exactly wrong with her?"

Dr. Seward gave him a cutting glance. "I do not discuss the private medical condition of my patients." He harrumphed again for good measure and ascended the stairs.

Jed watched him go and noticed a slight wavering in the man's step. Was he drunk or was it his age? Was the physician confused about whom he had come to see? If the good doctor had seen Lil poured into her amber dress last night, he would realize the mistake he'd made. Last night's kiss would prove to any man that Lilian Frontiere was far from kissing this earth goodbye.

He would get to the bottom of this.

DR. SEWARD FINISHED HIS EXAMINATION. Lily hadn't realized her mother had sent for him. She would never have gallivanted around with Jed Stone otherwise.

The doctor patted his patient's hand. She seemed at peace. Lily wondered if this is what her mother would look like when death came calling for her.

The physician guided Lily close to the window.

"I'm afraid we're near the end, Lily," he said gently. "I would think a week. Possibly two."

Though his words were expected, they cut her to the bone. "What can we do for her?"

"Make her comfortable. Keep her company." He slipped a vial from his pocket and placed it in her hand. "If the belladonna isn't working, give her a few drops of this."

"What is it?"

"Morphine."

Lily flinched. "How much?"

"A couple of drops at the beginning. Once you start, though, she'll beg for more. If she has any business to take care of, finish it before you start the morphine. She'll be lucid off and on after that first dose."

He handed her his handkerchief. Only then did she realize tears had begun to fall.

"Send for me no matter what the hour if I'm needed."

"Thank you." Lily returned the cloth and he left the room, quietly shutting the door behind him. She turned to stare out the window.

"No tears."

The words caught her by surprise. She ran to the bed and stroked her mother's hair gently.

"We must do as he said. Bring me pen and paper."

She did as asked, putting them on the table next to the bed. Her mother struggled to sit up. Lily placed pillows behind Lilian for comfort.

"I will write both Max and my solicitor. I want you to go to the bank for me. See a Mr. Crowder when you arrive. He'll arrange everything."

"What is this about, *Maman*?"

Lilian frowned in pain. "A small account there. Not related to the house. The new owner is not entitled to any of it. Have Crowder withdraw the money for your new start."

"But—"

"No buts, *ma petite*. You cannot stay in this city. There's no life for you here. Perhaps New York. Or even Europe. It will give you a chance for a new life."

Lilian reached for the sheaf of papers. "Go now. I have some strength left. These things must be done, as Dr. Seward said. Crowder has always been a steady client and given me good advice. He will be discreet in the transaction. Trust whatever he says."

Lily slipped her reticule over her wrist and left the room. For the second time that day she used the back staircase to avoid Jed. She was in no mood to see him now. She walked to the small stable and was glad to find Ben there watering their horse.

"I must go to the bank at once."

The Indian nodded and rigged the carriage. Within minutes, she entered the bank and asked for Mr. Crowder. She briefly explained what needed to be done and why. Crowder took care of things in a quarter of an hour. He wished her well and promised his secrecy.

She crossed the lobby of the bank. As she reached its doors, Jed stepped in. She was outraged that he followed her there. Then she immediately noticed a

20

Jed's good manners forced him to move closer and take Lil's hand. Her weak grasp told him as much as her pale skin.

"It's nice to meet you, ma'am."

The woman laughed from deep in her chest. For a moment, Jed glimpsed the faded beauty that lay dormant in the sickly body. He still couldn't think of this shell as Lil.

"So, you won my house in a card game?" She gave him a look of disdain. "You're a gambler."

"I believe we both are."

"*Touché*. What do you think of Lucky Lil's?"

"The girls are top-drawer," Jed answered without hesitation. "Young, pretty, and they do their job well. The gaming room is a nice touch, too."

"And the food?" Her amber eyes bore into his.

"Manet's buffet is first-class. Raymond's a talented musician. There's not much to complain about."

Lil appraised him thoughtfully. "But, you have made changes." When he nodded, she said, "Tell me about them."

Jed described the voucher system and the cutbacks in bouncers and buffet. Lil nodded approvingly.

"You are astute, *Monsieur* Stone. Lucky Lil's will flourish under your hand." She smiled weakly. "You have questions of me. I will speak as long as I feel able."

"Who's played Lil since you've fallen ill?" It was the only question he had of her.

Lil dabbed a handkerchief to her mouth and coughed. The deep rattling in her chest frightened him.

"Would you like some water?" he asked.

"*Oui.*"

He poured from a pitcher sitting on the bedside table and handed it to her. Her hand shook so he brought it to her lips. After a sip, she frowned and pushed it away.

"Who is Lil?" She shook her head. "I look at her and see myself all those years ago. I wonder where time went. How I became what you see today." She took a deep breath.

"My daughter Lily stepped into my shoes several months ago when I became unwell."

Lily?

"She's good, *n'est-ce pas*? She always loved to act."

Jed reeled from the information. The demure Lily of this morning had disguised herself so thoroughly that she had deceived all of San Francisco. Even Simon Morgan. How could an innocent pull off such a ruse?

And then he thought of the kiss last night. It was Lily he'd kissed. Lily he'd been attracted to these past few weeks. Lily who'd haunted his dreams and caused him to burn when awake. No wonder he'd fallen under her spell so quickly this morning. He already wanted her.

She had assumed her mother's every gesture.

She'd worn her clothes, smoked her cigarettes, and taken over the house's management, even down to disciplining the girls.

And no one suspected.

She would make a fine poker player. Any woman who could pull off this would make mincemeat of her opponents. Jed had admired her figure and her humor, her compassion and her beauty. Now, he respected her brains.

He had wanted to know what Lil looked like under her heavy cosmetics. He'd discovered that this morning—fresh, beautiful, and untouched.

Thank God he was a card player, and a damn fine one at that. Otherwise, he'd blurt out to Lilian Frontiere how taken he was with her daughter. One face-to-face meeting with the real Lil had his senses spinning.

Jed nodded. "She has men eating from her hand."

"Then the secret will be safe for now?"

"Yes. In fact," he mused, "let's keep it our secret."

Lil studied him carefully. "*Pour maintenant.*" She closed her eyes. "I tire, Jed Stone. Leave me to rest."

He watched as she fell into a light sleep. He went to raise the covers around her and spotted a sheet of paper next to her. He hesitated before he reached for it, but Lilian intrigued him. As he lifted it he read:

MON CHER MAXIMILIAN —

I die soon but will go happy, my memories of you and your gentle touch to sustain
me. Take care of my Lily, won't you?
Maybe you can help her, mon ami doux, to start a new life away from this place.

*She will never be accepted by society here. Give her a way to escape and build new
      dreams.
      Je t'aime. Toujours.
      Your Lilian*

HE READ the letter a second time, knowing from the wobbly letters just how much effort it had taken for Lil to write it. She would worry about her only child until the end.

Jed realized it was up to him to protect Lily.

LILY CHANGED her mind about running to Max. What would she tell him anyway?

"Max, your great-grandson is a wanted outlaw who viciously beat one of my girls and is rude to me. And by the way, the fellow that could pass for his twin and who now owns Lucky Lil's kissed me, but he thinks I'm my mother."

That would be just the thing to tell a ninety-year-old man. He'd probably have a heart attack on the spot.

So, Lily did what she knew any red-blooded American woman did in times of trouble. She decided to buy a new hat. She rationalized it by telling herself that Jed was paying her—or rather, Lil—a good salary. She hadn't shopped for a new hat in over a year. Lilian said it did a soul good to purchase a stylish hat every now and then.

She had Ben stop at Annie Spencer's shop. She could trust Annie and her prices. She remembered how Jed wanted to take a cut from the business

Madam Lil sent Annie's way. Well, he'd have to be the one to address the issue. She had no desire to break that news to Annie.

As she entered the shop, Lily stopped dead in her tracks. Simon Morgan was there, accompanied by a girl barely in her teens. It was obvious by her dress that she was a tart. The girl was busy trying on hats herself.

She turned to slip out the door but he saw her.

"Why, if it isn't Miss Lily."

She turned her head and gave a curt nod.

"I haven't seen you in several months, my dear." He eyed her appraisingly. "Pale yellow. The color of winter's early morning sun. I've never seen a woman do justice to that color until now."

Though she had taken special pains to look her best today, she suddenly felt dirty. His complimentary words might speak of admiration, but the look in his eyes told of things she didn't understand and had no desire to unravel.

"I really must go, Mr. Morgan."

"Simon. Mr. Morgan was my father. I've missed you, Lily. Perhaps if I stopped by tonight, you'd come downstairs for once and spend a little time in conversation with me."

Lily thought she'd rather die than be in his company a moment longer. But, business was business. Innocent Lily would not be present tonight. She needed her Madam Lil clothes. She could handle any man when she was Lilian Frontiere. Why did words fail her now?

She tried to pull herself together. She managed worse than Simon on any given night. Besides, he spent big at the tables. They needed his business. She would encourage him to visit, no matter what her personal feelings were.

"I know you have a fondness for our tables and Manet's buffet. I'll arrange for a twenty-dollar gold piece to be waiting for you in the gaming room if you do come by."

Simon laughed harshly at the bargain she dangled before him. "Your mother would rather I frequent other places, but I think I will stop in. Just to see you." He gave her arm a squeeze. "And that free gold piece." He returned to his companion.

"That looks lovely on you," he cooed to the girl.

Lily stumbled from the store. Ben asked no questions and drove her straight home. First Cal Fisher. Now Simon Morgan. Did she wear some advertisement that attracted the wrong men?

She leaped from the carriage as it stopped, ready to hide in her mother's room before tonight's clients came through the door. She would transform herself into Madam Lil. The clothes would become her armor against the hostile world.

She entered the house and ran smack into its owner. Flustered, she apologized. "I'm so sorry, Mr. Stone."

"Jed." He gave her an amused look. "You were just the person I wanted to see."

"I was?" She hated that her voice squeaked like a naïve schoolgirl. "What did you need?"

"I've worked every night since I won the deed to Lucky Lil's. I think it's time I took a night off."

Lily looked at him blankly. "So, why did you need me?"

He smiled his killer smile. The one that caused her toes to curl up and made her knees go weak. The smile that was as sweet as summer rain and wider than a rainbow.

"I wanted your company, Lily. I have tickets to the opera tonight. Would you care to go with me?"

21

———

S imon Morgan slipped on a midnight blue waistcoat and studied himself in the oval mirror. He smoothed a hand through his hair, still thick and full at forty-eight, no hint of gray. He couldn't say the same for the rest of him. Age was catching up. Years of long nights drinking and partaking of fine cuisine on the riverboats had taken their toll. He watched his weight carefully now, and still he'd ballooned up in the last five years. He dressed to disguise his flaws.

The picture he cut tonight satisfied him. He looked forward to seeing Lily. By God, he still wanted her and Lucky Lil's so badly, it was a physical pain. It felt much like the constant heartburn that seemed to plague him daily.

He slipped his money clip into his pocket. He was ready for a good game of poker tonight. He felt a winning streak coming on. If only Lily would hang on his arm and give him adoring gazes, life would be complete.

He stepped into the hall and saw Gordon Fisher staggering his way.

"About time you showed your surly mug." He

slapped Gordon on the back. "Heard you were on a real bender."

Gordon's flushed face indicated the drinking spree hadn't ended. "Thought we could go paint this town red."

They walked down the hall and followed the staircase to the hotel's lobby. Simon hated the shabby carpeting and cheap furniture. His bad run of luck forced him to move here to cut down on his lavish lifestyle. Things hadn't gone well at the tables in over a year, ever since he'd hit it big while in New Orleans.

But his bones said his luck would change now.

"Let's head over to Lil's for a while. Big surprise waiting there for you."

Gordon looked at him sleepily. "I've done it with every whore in that place. Why don't we go to—"

"No," Simon interrupted. "I really want you to see someone there. Jed Stone's his name."

Gordon sneezed. "Who the hell is Jed Stone?"

"The new owner at Lil's." The words came out bitterly.

"I thought you were planning to take over Lil's place. Albus Tate and you cut some kind of deal, didn't you? Cal told me something about it." Gordon rubbed his bloodshot eyes. "Having a little trouble remembering things lately."

He thought how Gordon had let himself go in the last couple of years. Too much booze, too many women, and what money he wheedled from Max was spent with nothing to show for it.

Simon hailed a cab and helped his friend climb inside. Before he could start up a conversation, Gordon's snores filled the carriage. He leaned back and stared out the window. The rain an hour before washed the streets and brought a clean, balmy tang to the night air.

The driver pulled up at Lucky Lil's. Simon shook Gordon awake and paid the fare. He could hear Raymond's fingers tinkling the keyboard as they approached the door. Ben opened it and as usual, said nothing. Simon often wondered about the big Indian's connection with Lil. Whatever it was, it ran deep. Ben had always worked the door at Lucky Lil's, even before the big fire destroyed her first house.

He maneuvered Gordon inside and signaled for drinks. They came quickly, accompanied by a twenty-dollar gold piece.

His friend lapped the first one down like lemonade and called for another. "I like that Lil never waters down a drink."

Simon strained his neck looking for Lily, a huge waste of time. The girl never mixed with Lil's clientele. The only reason he even knew what she looked like were the few times he'd seen her coming out of a side entrance. She always stepped into a waiting carriage and was gone like the wind.

He began to arrive at Lucky Lil's early on opening nights of a new opera or play, hoping to catch a glimpse of Lily before she was whisked away. Twice, he timed it right and exchanged paltry words with her. He began wanting her more as time passed. That feeling grew stronger the past few months when she'd been rumored to be visiting back East. After seeing her today at the milliner's shop, now more than ever, he wanted her. Tonight.

He moved with Gordon into a small alcove fitted with two chairs and a table and sat, his drink in his hand. Before he spoke, he watched Gordon's eyes bug out.

"That damn whippersnapper," Gordon growled. "Told me he was tapped out just yesterday. Look at that suit he has on. It's as fine as something Max would wear."

Gordon half-rose but Simon pulled him down. "Just watch," he advised his friend.

Jed Stone worked the room like a pro. Simon had heard about Jed's infrequent visits to Portsmouth Square. The dealers said he was on a big win streak. He only played afternoons, spending his nights hosting at Lil's. Once, Simon spotted him in a high stakes poker game. The minute Simon took a chair, Stone cashed in and left.

He's taunting me, Simon thought.

"Who the hell does he think he is?" Gordon asked. "He's strolling around like he owns the place."

"He does."

Gordon screwed up his face. "What do you mean?"

"I mean that's Jed Stone."

"My God." Gordon stared at the man. "He's the spitting image of my Cal."

"That's what I thought when I first met him. They look alike, sound alike. They could pass as twins."

Gordon turned white as a sheet. "I'm outta here." He stumbled to his feet and rushed out before Simon moved.

Tommy chimed the hour. The room grew quiet. His eyes followed Jed Stone, who paused at the foot of the staircase. Stone looked up, smiling. Simon saw why.

Lily Frontiere floated down in pink chiffon, off the shoulder, exposing creamy flesh and a proper amount of bosom. She was absolutely radiant. Simon knew he and every man in the room ached at such innocent beauty.

She reached the bottom of the stairs as the chimes ended. Jed Stone offered her his arm. They went out the front door. At once, the noise level revved up. It was business as usual at Lucky Lil's. A sour taste lingered in his mouth. He started for the door.

Maybe his luck hadn't changed after all.

LILY THOUGHT she must be Cinderella going to the ball. Her gown had come from Paris two years ago, but no handsome prince awaited her at the foot of the stairs then.

Tonight was different. Jed stood at the bottom with an admiring smile. He was decked out in a suit of fine black wool and a silk waistcoat. His cravat of maroon and gray softened the look of the suit. He escorted her from the house to a waiting carriage.

"You look lovely tonight." He smiled again.

Waves of pleasure rippled through her. He handed her up and then waited while she situated the gown about her before he climbed in and sat on the opposite seat.

She wished he'd sat next to her. At least she wouldn't have to keep looking away from his direct stare. He seemed amused about something.

"I understand you attend the opera frequently with Max."

She nodded. "Max has a box. He can't use it anymore since he's confined to the house. I wonder," she mused, "if we could sit there tonight?"

"We can check with the house manager. If you're known as a frequent guest of his, I'm sure management wouldn't refuse you." Jed looked into her eyes. "I don't think any man could refuse you tonight, Lily. You are simply stunning."

She flushed, embarrassed by the compliment. Lilian had always pushed good manners, though, so she thanked him and turned to watch the passing scenery in order to avoid locking eyes with him.

"I hope your banker won't mind my accompanying you."

"What?" Lily drew a blank. What banker?

A corner of his mouth turned up. Jed tried to suppress a grin. This was more fun than he'd anticipated.

"I thought Lil told me you were very serious about a banker back East. She thought you might marry this young scion."

He watched the dawning realization on her face as he kept his poker face in place.

"Oh, you mean Charles," she said quickly, too quickly. "Yes, we have seen rather much of each other lately. But marriage? I don't know what *Maman* was thinking."

"Then that would be a premature announcement?"

"I doubt that announcement will ever be made," Lily said firmly.

"Good." He relaxed against the plush velvet seat. "I would hate to see you leave so quickly, especially when we're just getting to know one other."

She turned pink again to his delight. He couldn't remember the last time he'd made a girl blush, much less twice in the same minute. Lily turned to look out the window again and Jed studied her at his leisure. He couldn't find one thing he didn't like about her.

Funny. He liked the real Lil, as well. He ached for Lily, knowing how she'd led a double life for months now. It must hurt her a great deal to watch her mother lie dying, not to mention trying to save the house at the same time. He knew he'd upset the apple cart when he walked in that night with the deed to Lucky Lil's.

Then, it hit him. As he inhaled the fresh scent of strawberries inside the coach, he realized it was Lily who'd aided him during his first visit to Lucky Lil's. She'd been the girl he'd grabbed in the hallway. She'd sneaked him into her mother's room and then confronted the men who searched for him.

He remembered how he remained in the wardrobe for a good half hour before she let him out. She must have donned her Madam Lil make-up and clothes. His admiration for her grew even more. A beauty who thought fast on her feet.

What man wouldn't fall in love with her?

Jed fought the feelings that stirred in him. He didn't want to be in love. Didn't have time for it. He told himself all he felt for Lily was lust, pure and simple. Knowing what he did now, he'd have to tamp down his desire for her. She had to be a virgin, and he had no experience deflowering one of those.

No, give him an experienced girl that could show him a good time and leave him in peace. He'd wake up the next day in his own bed. Alone. Grateful that was the way things were.

But that didn't mean he couldn't enjoy her company tonight.

22

It had been the most wonderful week of her life. Lily couldn't remember when she'd had more fun or felt more carefree. She looked out the window at the cloudy day. San Francisco was experiencing an early spring and she'd been out in it almost every afternoon as herself. It was so refreshing to wear her own clothes and go without the heavy wig and thick cosmetics. She'd spent more time being Lily this week than she had in the past six months.

All because of Jed.

Every day he made some kind of plans with her. He used the excuse that he was new to the area. As a native, she could show him the town. He took her to eat in Chinatown and for afternoon tea. They went to a matinee performance of *Macbeth* and to the sea front at Golden Gate. The clear day allowed them to see the peaks of the Farallone Islands from the beach. Jed thoughtfully had Manet pack them a picnic lunch. The hours flew by.

But Cinderella had to return to the whorehouse in time to make herself up as Madam Lil. Jed took his hosting duties seriously and insisted they arrive in time for the evening's clientele.

So she did double duty, transforming herself into Lilian each night. It bothered her that she envied her own mother. Jed was so charming to Madam Lil, bantering and sharing business ideas. She'd come to cherish the time they spent after hours, when Tommy chimed three and their patrons left for the evening. She and Jed would sit and talk an hour or two before they retired for the night.

He was always up at ten, though, which didn't allow her all the sleep she needed. He looked like he'd stepped off the bandbox each morning. She was afraid her lack of beauty sleep would soon show. Still, she loved the hours as herself, so she rose each day by the same hour.

Her mother seemed to be doing better, which only added to her spirits. When she'd been reluctant to leave her once, Lilian encouraged her to go.

"You don't get out enough. If this Jed Stone doesn't mind squiring you around, let him. Enjoy yourself, pet."

She'd rarely gone anywhere in the city without Max or her mother. It was fun being out and about with someone near her own age. Jed was good company and now her friend.

She wished it could go beyond friendship.

Lily picked up her hat from the dresser and placed it upon her head. She fiddled until it pleased her and then grabbed her shawl and slipped from the room. Jed said to meet him downstairs at noon. She didn't know where they were going.

He met her in the hall. "I was coming to your room."

"Oh, I'm glad you didn't. *Maman* is still asleep. I wouldn't want to disturb her."

"Lil? She wouldn't have minded."

Lily frowned. "I don't know about that. *Maman* is cranky without enough rest." She started down the stairs.

"Yes, I've noticed."

When had she acted cranky?

She opened her mouth to ask him about it and realized she couldn't. "Well, you have been keeping late hours. She used to go to bed at a quarter past three. Three-thirty at the latest. I think you two must stay up and talk the night away."

He smiled. "Lil is an interesting woman. I'll be honest with you, Lily. I'm quite attracted to your mother."

Lily's eyes widened. "But *Maman* is forty-five! She's much too old for you."

He shrugged. "I'm comfortable around older women. Lil is beautiful, witty, and has a good business head."

Lily wanted to strangle him. "Surely, you shouldn't mix business with pleasure?" she asked sweetly.

"I don't know. What if the business *is* pleasure?"

Jed took her hand and tucked it through his arm. "Enough talk. I shouldn't have said anything."

He was right about that. Jealousy ate Lily alive within seconds. She wanted Jed interested in *her*. She wanted him to find *her* beautiful and intelligent and funny. He already did. He just didn't know it.

But as much as she was tempted to tell him, she couldn't.

They rode in the cart to the outskirts of the city. She forced herself to remain calm and pleasant. *How could you be jealous of yourself?* Well, she would be so charming and vivacious today that Jed couldn't help but be fascinated by her.

"Where are we going?"

He handled the reins easily as he answered. "I thought we'd go to Cliff House."

She broke out into a smile. "I've never been there, but I've always wanted to go."

"My friend Mac told me about it. Said it's set on the edge of some cliffs."

"I've seen a painting of it. It rises sharply from the ocean. Lots of people take Saturday half-holidays there."

"Well, today's Saturday. I guess we'll see."

They took the Point Lobos Road, which was already heavy with traffic. They chatted away until they reached the hotel.

"Let's see if their restaurant is any good."

She thought the food incredibly rich and artfully displayed. Cliff House itself was beautiful, a low, rambling building that faced west. After luncheon they walked down to Seal Rock, which was close to the hotel. The sun broke through the clouds and brought a delicious warmth.

"Let's rest here a moment." He led her onto a wide, shady piazza with chairs for lounging. It gave a perfect view to watch the lazy seals basking in the sun on top of the large rocks.

"Watch that one." Jed pointed to a seal that sneakily sidled up to a sleeping one and barked loudly next to his ear before slapping the seal soundly. The two got into a barking match that could be heard over the roar of the waves.

Lily found herself mesmerized by their interaction.

Jed found himself spellbound by Lily. He watched her as she looked at the seals at play, a dozen emotions flitting across her face. He discovered several different women all in one. She laughed at the seals' antics. She frowned when their play became rough. Smiled wistfully at them as if she wished she could be frolicking with them herself.

It moved Jed like nothing ever had. He placed his palm against her cheek and turned her face toward him. Before he could stop himself, he kissed her.

She tasted like the strawberries she often smelled of, only sweeter and softer. Her mouth, lush as any fruit, yielded to him easily. His kiss was tender at first, that of a considerate lover. Then she made one of those womanly sighs from the back of her throat. He lost his head.

He brought an arm about her. He drew her close to him until her breasts brushed against his chest. His tongue sought hers, massaging it slowly, lovingly. He was drowning in an abyss of sheer pleasure. It was the sweetest kiss of his life.

Lily did what came naturally, what woman always did when enthralled with man. Her senses screamed from every direction. The waves crashed with intensity. The smell of male filled her nostrils. Her nipples swelled and ached as they brushed the front of Jed's coat.

She dropped the hat she'd held. It fluttered to the pavilion floor. Her hands moved to touch Jed. She had to touch him, feel him, be a part of him. Her palms flattened against his chest and slid upwards around his neck. She pulled him closer to her. Her fingers toyed with the back of his hair.

"Mommy! Mommy! They shouldn't do that."

Jed stepped away from Lily, taking his heat and her pleasure away. She opened her eyes to a little girl of about five standing in front of them.

"Come away, Claire. Now."

The child gave them a sour look and hurried back

to her mother's side. Lily's eyes met those of the disapproving mother. She blushed to her roots. She'd behaved like a brazen hussy in a public place, no better than a girl from Lucky Lil's. No, actually, Lil's girls would have shown more restraint. They never practiced any part of their trade in full view of an audience.

Jed leaned down and scooped her hat from the ground and placed it gently on her head.

"Let's go," he whispered, and took her hand in his. She tried to pull away, but he held it firmly. She decided not to cause a further scene and followed him back down the path to their carriage.

What was she doing kissing Jed Stone on the piazza at Seal Rock with half of San Francisco in attendance?

Her fading pleasure turned to humiliation. She would never place herself in this kind of situation again. He was a gambler, a charmer, a ne'er-do-well. For all she knew, he'd swindled someone more deserving out of the deed to their house. He'd tried to ingratiate himself with Lil—and now he did the same with her daughter. He was a fickle two-timer.

Who really, really knew how to kiss.

Better than Pierre. Better than the boys at the dances back East. Well, she was no easy tart. She'd set the record straight with him. What had happened was a huge mistake on her part. It wouldn't happen again.

He handed her into the cart and climbed up beside her. She was aware of his very nearness, his muscled thigh brushing against hers, burning her through her layers of clothing.

Jed turned to her. "I'm sorry, Lily," he said softly. "That won't ever happen again."

23

Jed lathered his face and picked up the shaving blade. As he stroked along his cheek, he thought again of his mistake. Kissing Lily. She was an innocent girl. Well, maybe not a girl. More of a woman-child, ripe for the picking, but not for the likes of him. She had education and poise, and deserved much better than a rambling gambler and whorehouse owner.

Lil had done the right thing to keep her only daughter away from the house life. Boarding school back East and going to cultural events with Maximilian Fisher had made a real lady out of Lily. Once Lil passed on, Jed and probably Max would see that Lily had enough money to get away from San Francisco and start a new life.

He read women well, and Lily was all for settling down and having babies. That was the last thing he wanted. True, having ownership of Lucky Lil's might cause him to stay in one place for a while, but eventually he'd get itchy feet. Doc Seward was right. The clients came to Lucky Lil's for Lil herself. Once she died, Jed could see selling it off and moving on before business dried up.

Besides, there was no point in staying if he couldn't be around Lily.

"Ouch!"

He nicked himself. He finished his shave, rinsed the cream away, and held a handkerchief to the cut. That's what daydreaming about Lily Frontiere would get him—nothing but pain.

They'd spent an awkward week avoiding each other. No more carefree outings. The odd thing was that his time spent with Lily posing as Madam Lil had been terrific. He'd spent hours in her company each night, enjoying every minute. He was glad Lily didn't know he knew she impersonated her mother. It enabled him to enjoy being with her.

As Jed dressed he glanced out the window, surprised to see Lily headed down the sidewalk. Ben awaited her. If she were off on errands or to see Max, this might be a good time for him to visit Madam Lil. She had intrigued him plenty but with the situation, he hadn't returned for a visit. Lily's absence made now a perfect time.

He knocked lightly at her door, unsure with Lil's condition if she'd be awake or asleep. He heard a muffled voice call out and he entered the sickroom.

"Hello, Lil. I hope I'm not disturbing you."

Lil looked alone and very ill amidst the pillows on the bed. He hoped vanity had kept her from a mirror.

She lifted a hand and waved him over, giving him a weak smile. "You have come to visit me again, Jed Stone?"

He took a seat next to the bed. "I haven't had an opportunity before now. Since Lily isn't aware that I know about her deception, I can't very well barge in here."

"And you were busy squiring my daughter around town."

He started to answer quickly until he caught the glint in her eyes.

"Are you amused or upset that I escorted your daughter about?"

Lilian sighed. "I'm grateful, truth be told. Lily has no friends here. She's led a sheltered life. Of course she had friends at her school and she made a few while we were in Paris."

"When was that?"

It took her a moment to answer. Jed realized that conversation tired her. He would leave soon.

"We left close to two years ago, and spent almost eight months there."

He watched the sadness rest like a shadow upon her.

"Did you both enjoy your visit there?"

Lil shrugged. "It was the same, yet it was not. I suppose I should have expected that. I loved showing Lily Paris, though. To hear and think in French again was a luxury. And yet..." Her voice trailed off.

He sat up expectantly. "What happened?"

Lil closed her eyes. He thought she'd fallen asleep. Then she spoke, choosing her words carefully.

"Lily loved the scenery and the people. The food and the openness of society. She did not," Lil added quietly, "enjoy the attentions of a certain man."

A surge of anger rushed through him. Before he could analyze his surprise at it, he asked, "Who was this man? What did he do to her?"

The house madam looked at him thoughtfully. "He hurt her terribly. Not physically. But my Lily's heart broke over Pierre." She began to cry softly.

Jed pulled out a handkerchief and wiped her tears.

"You are a kind man, Jed Stone."

He smiled wryly. "That's not always the case, Lil."

She placed a hand over his. "I know men, Jed. It's what I have always done. That's why I tell you what I do now."

Lil swallowed, gripping his hand weakly. "I need someone to look after my *jeune fille*. Max won't be here much longer than I. I have to know she'll be safe."

Her eyes never wavered from his. "She thinks she doesn't like men. Pierre was a typical Parisian—carefree, sensual, animated. He made her feel attractive and adored. But he wanted her and said anything it took to have her."

Jed's anger rumbled low in the pit of his belly. "Did he try—" but he couldn't finish the thought.

"No. One night I found out he would take things beyond flirtation. I intervened before Lily gave herself to him. Oh, she was angry and said things she later regretted, but what hurt the most was when she went to him later."

A single tear cascaded down Lil's cheek. "She still loved him and was ready to have a life with him. She saw him leaving on an outing with his wife and children. That did her in. My Lily has never trusted a man with her heart since then."

His frustration simmered just below the surface. A worldly man taking advantage of a young girl swept up in her first experience abroad, with all the romantic feelings that would accompany such a time. It was criminal. That it had been done to Lily was unthinkable.

Lil finished, her exhaustion evident. "She feels men are good only as clients. I want more for her, though. I hope you can help." She moaned and said, "I want the drops."

"Where?" Jed looked at the bottles on the table.

"Those. The clear vial."

He picked it up. "How many?"

"I don't know. I've only had the belladonna until now. I have put off the morphine. Dr. Seward said once I started it, I would be... how do you say... slipping in and out of things." Lil grimaced. "The pain is too terrible. I must have some relief."

"Then let's start with two drops."

He knew a little about narcotics from tending to Elmira during her illness. The doctor had recommended two drops of morphine at the beginning. By the end, his foster mother had consumed five times that amount.

He placed the dropper on her tongue and squeezed off the two drops. At first he'd put the medicine in Elmira's water, but he'd soon learned she couldn't drink much by that point. Directly on the tongue gave her an instant relief. He wished for Lil to be soothed now.

Jed settled her in the bed, fluffing the pillows and drawing the quilt around her snugly. She slept almost immediately, worn out from their talk. Yet he was glad of what he'd learned from her.

It told him just how hurt Lily was.

❧

JED WATCHED for Lily's return from his window. When he saw Ben pull up a little past noon, he went downstairs to meet her.

She opened the door and swept off her hat, turning to close the door behind her.

"Lily?"

She jumped. It was evident she hadn't seen him

before, and by the look on her face didn't want to see him now.

"I have things to do. If you'll excuse me."

"No." He quickly closed the distance between them and took her elbow. He pulled her into one of the downstairs parlors and backed her up to a loveseat.

"Sit," he commanded. When she didn't, he took a seat and yanked her down beside him.

"You are insufferable! Don't think because you own this house that you own me."

"Lily, all I'm trying to do is apologize to you for the other day. You haven't given me ten seconds in the last week. I decided to take them for myself."

She blushed and stammered, "There's nothing to apologize for. I—"

"You were a perfectly wonderful companion and I was a cad. I had a weak moment and took advantage of you. I'd like to say I'm sorry."

Her defensive pose seemed to soften. "Jed, I—"

"Would you accompany me to the Mercantile Library's Ball on the twenty-fourth?"

Lily's mouth dropped. "The Mercantile Ball? Everyone in San Francisco will be there. How did you get tickets?"

"Mac McRidge helped me out a bit. Now will you forgive me?"

Before she could answer, he sensed movement under his feet. He glanced up as the chandelier began to sway lazily. The divan began to vibrate beneath them.

"What the hell?"

Lily smiled almost cheerfully. She leaned around him and began counting aloud. "One, two, three..."

Confused, Jed gripped the arm of the loveseat. By the time Lily reached eight, the tremors had stopped.

"Twelve-fifteen," she announced happily.

"What on God's green earth—"

"Actually," she interrupted, "it's *inside* God's green earth." She giggled. "You haven't been in California long, Jed. Welcome to your first earthquake."

"That was an earthquake?" Jed's heart still raced as he looked at a few pictures that sat askew on the wall. Other than that, no evidence showed what just took place.

"Relax," she advised him. "These happen from time to time. Max always likes me to note the time and duration of each quake. We compare notes afterward."

He shook his head. "I hope that never happens again."

"I'll go."

"Go where?"

"Did the quake addle your brain?" she teased. "To the ball, of course."

"There's also a concert two days later that is a part of the tickets. Are you interested in that, too?"

Lily beamed. "I think that sounds lovely."

"Then I'll check with Lil to see if it's all right. I hate to strand her by herself two nights so closely together. On second thought," he mused, "why don't we go to the ball together, and I can give you and Lil the concert tickets. It would do you both good to get out together. I'd love to see the two prettiest gals in San Francisco, side-by-side."

24

Lily readied herself for the ball the *Examiner* called "the party of the century." At least she had a Parisian gown worthy of the affair. It had been a long time since she accompanied Max to the Grand or Wade's Opera House. She'd forgotten the fun of dressing up, with elegant gloves and silk wraps and outrageous hats.

Jed offered to take her to an early supper at Martin's but she didn't know if she'd be able to eat anything in her excitement. She took a deep breath, slowly exhaling. It did seem to calm her.

She lifted the satin ball gown over her head and watched in the mirror as the mint green folds fell about her. Lily winced, remembering how much the crafty Parisian dressmaker charged. The amount would easily have kept Lucky Lil's running for two months. She had learned much in the past year about finances.

Still, she couldn't help but preen a little in front of her mirror. She doubted she'd ever looked as good as she did tonight. Her hair was perfectly coiffed, her cheeks rosy and glowing in the candlelight of the room.

She had worn the gown once before, which caused her to question the wisdom in wearing it again. Pierre had fawned over her, flirting outrageously, admiring her, whispering sweet *bon mots* in her ear.

She'd been ready to give herself to him that night. Fortunately, her mother had interrupted their rendezvous.

Could she anticipate such a liaison with Jed tonight? There would be no Lilian to break in this time. Did she want Jed as much as she had Pierre?

More. Much more.

Lily had fought her feelings for some time but she could hide from them no longer. She was in love with Jed Stone.

"Lily?"

Her mother's voice interrupted dangerous thoughts. "*Oui, Maman?*"

"*Venir ici.*"

Lily went to the bed and took her mother's icy hands in hers. She rubbed them, trying to bring warmth.

"You look lovely, my sweet. I wish your father could see you now. He would be so proud." Lilian smiled faintly, as if seeing her husband from long ago.

"But you are here to see me. I hope I make you proud." She kissed her mother's brow, wishing fervently the sickness would disappear like the fog that burned off the bay each day.

"Every minute. Now go. Leave me to my rest."

Lily checked her mirror once more, and then took the matching wrap for the dress and brought it around her shoulders. She swallowed her nervousness and left the room.

The house was springing to life. The girls had eaten and dressed for their clients. Raymond was warming up at the piano. Manet fussed over that night's buffet, making last-minute adjustments to its arrangement.

Gertie came over. Of all the girls, she liked Gertie best. Most thought her aloof and rarely spoke to her. Gertie tried to make conversation each time they met.

"You look a sight, Miss Lily. I hear you're going to a real ball."

"Yes, with Mr. Stone."

Gertie frowned. "I ain't never gonna figure that one out. Sweet as a lamb, and then all surly and mean to Sarah Jane. At least he hasn't touched her since."

Lily lay an arm on Gertie's shoulder. "There are things you don't understand just now, Gertie. Don't worry. I'll be fine."

The young girl smiled brightly at Lily. "Well, gal, all I understand is Cinderella don't have nothing on you. You look a sight prettier than any fairy tale."

"Thank you, Gertie."

Just then Jed walked into the room. Gertie hustled off. Lily turned and faced him. His admiring glance told her all she needed to know. Choosing to wear the dress again was the right decision. No thoughts of Pierre would linger tonight with a man like Jed giving her such approving looks.

"Pretty as a picture," he said as he offered her his arm. "It looks like the Frontiere women share the looks in this family."

Lily tried to swallow the fears his words brought. She'd never really thought about it much before, when Max escorted her and *Maman* to the opera or theater, but how many of Lilian's clients had seen her there and thought she looked like a younger version of the best-known madam in the Bay area? Did they think Lily was in the trade?

Lilian had taken such pains to keep her daughter separate from the sporting life. When they went out together, they always used the staircase next to Lilian's room. Lily had never been paraded downstairs. She'd had little to no contact with her mother's establishment.

It was only the few times she'd run into Simon Morgan that she'd been bothered before. But, tonight —out in society with the owner of Lucky Lil's—how many heads would turn her way?

She knew if she were to enjoy this evening, she must push all troubling thoughts away. She planted a smile on her face and looked at Jed. The smile's stiffness relaxed as she looked at her escort in his formal attire. He led her to the waiting carriage.

She barely remembered the ride to the ball. She found herself looking at Jed and nodding, smiling, shaking her head politely, but she didn't follow much of his conversation. He was too handsome for his own good. Every time Lily had a coherent thought, one look at Jed Stone scrambled it.

He helped her up the stairs and checked her wrap before they entered the ballroom itself. It looked like a fairy wonderland. Between the lovely gowns and glittering gems on San Francisco's choice society, she felt like a poor relation sneaking in for a glimpse.

"Impressive," Jed murmured close to her ear, sending new chills through her. He raised a hand and waved. "There's my attorney, Stanton McRidge. We're at his table."

They crossed the room, where Jed presented her to the lawyer, calling him Mac.

Graciously, he took her hand and expressed his pleasure in being introduced. She smiled at him gratefully. His gentlemanly behavior put her immediately at ease.

"And this is my wife, Sylvia." She was a petite brunette, her eyes full of sparkle. Lily liked her on sight.

"Thank goodness you arrived. If I have to hear Mac drone on about one more deal he's cut, I'll lose my mind." She offered her hand to Jed in introduction. "I'm sure you have enough sense to ask Miss Frontiere to dance, Mr. Stone. That might give my husband the idea for how tonight's actually supposed to be spent."

"What? Dance at a ball?" Mac said in amazement. "That's news to me."

Sylvia laid a hand on her husband's arm. "I believe it's about time you escorted me out on the floor."

"Your devoted servant, my dear. Excuse us." McRidge led his wife to the middle of the floor.

"Champagne?"

Lily turned and saw Jed taking two flutes from a passing waiter. "Yes, please." She sipped the liquid as the bubbles tickled her nose.

He set down his glass. "Care to dance?"

"I thought you'd never ask."

Her feet glided easily along the polished hardwood floor. Jed was an accomplished dancer. They danced to three tunes before she became out of breath.

Reading her mind, he asked, "Would you like to go to the table? I think it might be cooler there than among all these dancers."

She was maddeningly aware of his warm palm on her back as he led her to the table and seated her.

Sylvia Stanton leaned over. "Would you care to accompany me to the retiring room?"

Lily was more than willing. They excused themselves and slipped along the edges of the crowd.

"I so adore your gown, Miss Frontiere. Is it from Paris?"

She nodded. "It's a couple of years old but I love it."

"Even Mac commented on how attractive it is. If Mac noticed, you have to be doing something right."

They entered a large room full of women patting their hair and powdering their noses. She and Sylvia joined them in their primping.

"He's quite a catch. Mr. Stone. He's awfully handsome. Mac hasn't known him long but he thinks the world of him."

Lily blushed and looked down, digging through her reticule. "He's really just an acquaintance. A business associate of my mother's."

Sylvia grinned. "If he were my escort, dear, I'd make sure he became more than a passing acquaintance."

JED WATCHED LILY APPROACH. An explosion of butterflies flooded his stomach. He thought he was going to be sick for a moment, but the giddiness floated away.

"How about another dance?" he asked her, surprised at how smooth his voice sounded.

He led her back onto the dance floor. A waltz began, and he swept Lily into his arms and across the floor. She was light on her feet and made him feel like a true gentleman, hobnobbing with the elite of the Bay area.

As he twirled her around the dance floor, he caught sight of Simon Morgan watching them. Instinctively, he pulled Lily a fraction closer, wanting to protect her from spotting the gambler. He knew that would put a damper on her evening.

The waltz ended to the shouts of "Again!" The orchestra leader complied, sending couples whirling in motion a second time with the seductive strains of Strauss. Jed held Lily even closer, drinking in the scent of fresh strawberries which always seemed a part of her. Every step he made, she matched. It was if they moved as one.

He decided at that moment that he wanted her. He couldn't—no, wouldn't—let another man have her. Wanderlust be dammed. He'd sell Lucky Lil's, go straight, give up gambling. Whatever it took. He had to have her and take care of her. Lily belonged in his arms, no others.

Yet in the back of his mind he wondered how to get her to confess her impersonation of Lil and end her ruse.

25

Jed readied himself for the evening. Since he'd come to his decision about Lily last night, he had to take care of Simon Morgan. Revenge could be a nasty business. He didn't want Lily involved in it. He'd waited long enough to avenge Louis's death.

He wanted to admit his feelings to Lily now. They were still so new to him. It amazed him how in the space of a few weeks he'd become a different person. If anyone had told him even a month ago he'd consider quitting the gaming life, he'd have thought them drunk, crazy, or both.

Lily had changed everything for him. He'd never pictured a future. He always lived in the here and now. After Elmira died he drifted from one job to another, never finding what he wanted. When war came, he'd found himself drafted without funds to pay for a replacement.

War caused a man to live from one minute to the next. It was a jinx to think what might lie ahead beyond the curve in the road, much less where your regiment would bed down for the night. When Louis saved him from certain death one afternoon, Jed had been afraid to think about any tomorrows.

The Frenchman gradually restored Jed's faith in living. They had been more than fellow soldiers, more than men who craved the turn of a card. Their bond ran deeply, as if they were brothers born of the same mother. Of course, Louis had his flaws. He often got into trouble with his commanding officers. When they would rail against him, his friend simply shrugged and reminded them that he was a French citizen, doing them a favor by fighting in their war.

It still amused him that Louis, who hated the sight of blood and would do anything to avoid a fight, volunteered to serve in the Union army. It was there the Frenchman learned to drink hard liquor, something he'd avoided his first thirty years.

That was Louis's fatal flaw, not being able to stop before disaster hit. In fact, he ran a gambit of emotions when drinking. He started out slightly tipsy as a clown. By his third drink he became foul-tempered. By the sixth he was lovable and cuddly. After ten, he passed out. Upon awakening, he would lose bits of his memory. Once, he had trouble remembering who Jed was.

Still, they were amiable companions, sticking close to one another after the war. Jed never had a friend before Louis. He kept to himself and observed others. It had served him well in his gambling. Louis broke through his wall of reserve and refused to leave.

He wondered what Louis would say about Jed giving up gambling for a woman. For falling in love like he'd never thought possible. For wanting to be respectable and fit into polite society. And if he could have a sweet baby girl with Lily's looks to rock to sleep, it would be icing on the cake. He had money now. Lots of it. What he needed was a new occupation. Mac McRidge could help. His newfound friend would have an idea on how to help Jed become legitimate.

It might take leaving San Francisco. That would be a pity. He'd come to love the mix of people and foods and things to do—but he wanted a fresh start with Lily. He wondered idly if she might like the flair of New Orleans.

Tonight was the night for total honesty. He hadn't thought it through yet, but somehow he would make Lily confess about portraying Lilian these past few months. With that out of the way, there would be no barriers between them. Jed would tell her how much he loved her.

He found it odd in a way that he had such a need for truth. Maybe because it played such a small role in his life up until now. He'd never known about his real parents. From what Elmira had told him of the night he was born, his father wasn't truthful with his mother. What little the midwife heard convinced her that Jed's mother had never even been married to his father. The poor girl hadn't known it until just before she died in childbirth.

Elmira described his mother as fragile and naïve. That his father took advantage of such an innocent and her trust brought shame to him. A scoundrel's blood coursed through his veins. Knowing that steered him away from any serious commitment with a woman. He enjoyed their company, but he never wanted more beyond a casual, fleeting affair.

He also saw through his various jobs and travels how employers hid truth from their workers. His commanding officers had hidden reality from their own soldiers. Everywhere he looked, Jed saw little value placed upon the truth.

That was why he insisted upon it now. His relationship with Lily started in deception on her part. He had discovered the true Lily beneath her Lilian veneer. If their love was going to have any chance—if Jed were truly to change and become a new person, thanks to this remarkable woman who had entered his life—then he wanted nothing to hinder it. His gut told him a lasting love must be built upon the solid rock of honesty. He wanted no obstructions, no confines. He needed them both to lay their souls bare before one another. It called for a fresh start.

He wouldn't trick her into confessing. Not after what his father did to his mother. Yet, somehow he needed her to trust him. He wanted her to share the burden she'd carried these past several months. He longed to assure her that they could do anything together. Deciding to push Lily would be risky, but then again he'd been a risk-taker most of his life. He rubbed his pocket watch for good measure.

JED BIDED HIS TIME PATIENTLY, waiting until Tommy struck three. The clients filed out as girls blew kisses and called for them to come again. He'd grown used to the ritual. The house and its inhabitants had become home.

Elmira never provided much of a home life for Jed. At least she'd taken him in. He might've grown up in an orphanage if not for her generosity. Jed made sure that in each town he visited, he contributed a few dollars to the local orphanage. In San Francisco, he'd given money already to the Protestant Orphan Asylum on Laguna and the Roman Catholic Orphan Asylum in the southern part of the city. He'd been one of the lucky ones. Maybe those dollars would make a difference in one child's life.

The girls headed toward their rooms, ready to sleep after a long night's work. It was time to have a little talk with Madam Lil. He strolled over and locked the front door as Lily doused lights and emptied a few ashtrays.

"Leave that, Lil. The help can do it in the morning."

"If you insist," she replied.

Jed loved how Lily spoke in a slight accent, how she pitched her voice just a little huskier when she was Lil. She was a clever, talented woman. And she had the sweetest lips he'd ever tasted.

"It was a good night's take," he said, as he draped his long frame onto the sofa and placed booted feet on the coffee table in front of him. Lily sat on the sofa, not too closely, but not too far away. Jed suppressed a grin.

"Yes. It was a good night. Every girl's card was filled and the gaming room had an excellent run."

He rested an arm casually against the back of the sofa. His fingers barely brushed Lily's shoulder. She threw him a look with raised brows, as if Madam Lil were curious about his gesture.

"I've been thinking, Lil." Jed rubbed a thumb along her shoulder as he spoke. "We've grown close. I want to show you how I appreciate your friendship. You've taken a difficult situation and made it quite pleasant."

He watched a blush rise in her cheeks. She held her ground, though. Didn't move as he continued the touches.

"You need show me no special appreciation, Jed. You pay me quite a nice salary as it is."

"You deserve a raise. Consider it done. A twenty-five percent increase, effectively immediately."

Lily tried to still her heart. The increase in money was wonderful, but what Jed's fingers were doing was not. They brought rolls of sensual chills through her, coupled with hot anger. After their wonderful night at the ball, she had assumed things might be different between them. Now he was flirting—and with her mother, at that!

He took a curl and slowly twirled it around his finger. She was ready to scream for him to stop.

"Perhaps we might go upstairs together. Are you game, Lil?"

All the tender feelings she'd had for him fled. Her first impression had been right, even if he wasn't vulgar as Cal Fisher. Jed Stone was a typical, no good, two-timing gambler. She tensed, ready to tell him off, but he dropped the curl and moved away from her.

"If you're not up for it, I'm sure someone else is. Maybe Gertie or Lydia. Or that sweet Sarah Jane."

Lily panicked. She couldn't have Sarah Jane service Jed. The girl was still terrified of him. Or at least whom she thought Jed was. She'd do whatever it took to protect Sarah Jane. Even if it meant suffer Jed Stone's attentions. He was no better than a snake in the grass. All men were the same. So much for her daydreams of happily-ever-after starring Jed in the role of her Prince Charming.

Why had she thought that he was different? How could she believe he'd come to sweep her off her feet? Why think he'd take her away from all the madness that had become her life? He must have had a good laugh at her expense, toying with her affections.

It was obvious from what he'd said that he was ready for a good roll in the hay with her mother. Any gentleman who harbored true feelings for a lady would never, ever, make such a proposition to another woman—yet alone the girl's mother.

It served her right to be forced to make this sacrifice.

Lily knew in that moment she'd never escape from her fate. She'd been destined to work in the house. Once Lilian died, it would be the only thing left for her to do. Jed Stone was experienced. She might as well learn from the best if she wanted to become the best.

But the thought scared her to death. All the feelings he aroused in her—feelings that confused her, excited her, drove all other thoughts from her mind—would now lie trampled under what had once been her heart. The very man she loved would turn her heart to stone.

And what if she couldn't pull it off? Despite being raised in a whorehouse, she was woefully unprepared. Of course, she had watched the flirting, the coquettish looks that passed from the girls to their clients these past few months. She practiced those very looks for hours in the mirror, perfecting each smile, every gesture, until she could pass without question as Lilian. The house madam of Lucky Lil's was a woman of charm, one totally at ease with the opposite sex. Lily had drawn upon every ounce of talent she possessed until her performance as Madam Lil was flawless.

But, to extend her little drama to the boudoir? She only knew the bare rudiments of the act. Did the girls remove all their clothes at once, or a few at a time? Did they undress the client or would he do that himself?

She wasn't ignorant of the male body. She'd seen enough good art to know how Jed would be made. But there was a big difference between a sculpture in stone created by an artist long ago, and a living, breathing, naked male by her side.

And how did she go about it all? She'd heard the springs singing merrily in rhythm since she was a toddler. Who began that dance? Did you talk during it? Did you kiss? She'd heard some of the girls speak in hushed tones over the years, but what knowledge she'd pieced together from these random conversations abandoned her now.

Most importantly, would Jed know she was a virgin?

Lily donned her best Madam Lil bored gaze and answered him. "All right. If you insist. But let's go to your room. By now, Lily is fast asleep in mine."

She rose, her nails digging into her palms. She wouldn't crumple or burst into tears. She looked steadily at Jed. He seemed surprised by her answer.

He studied her carefully before saying, "On second thought, Lil, it might be smarter to keep business and pleasure separate. We've been successful up until now. I'd hate to tinker with a good thing."

He stood. "I'll see you tomorrow. I know ladies your age need to get their beauty sleep."

Lily watched him leave, relief turning her knees to jelly. She waited a moment before leaving, not wanting to see him again. As she went to her room, bitter tears began to fall. She thought of his charm and that winning smile. His smile alone had likely acquired more ladies' hearts than the number of winning poker hands he'd secured.

She undressed in the dark, throwing her clothes onto the chair. She lit a candle and creamed her face to remove all traces of Madam Lil. As she scrubbed harder, the hurt grew deeper. By trying to bed her mother, Jed lost all the good qualities he'd displayed since they met. The magical outings had been spoiled. If he were the last man on earth, she would reject any further overtures.

Yet despite her resolve, she crawled into bed next to her mother, hot tears soaking the pillow because she was crazy about the cad.

And then Lilian reached out a hand to stroke her hair. The gesture made her cry all the more.

"What troubles you, pet?" Lilian rasped.

"Oh, *Maman*, I've done a foolish thing." She hiccupped as she tried to choke back the tears. "I've fallen in love again with the wrong man. Why do I have such poor taste?"

Lilian wrapped a bony arm about her in comfort. "Who is this man?" Her words came out somewhat slurred but Lily ignored that and rushed ahead.

"It's Jed. The new house owner. And I hate it because he thinks I'm you. I've been jealous of you. Every time he's shown an interest in me, it was really you. *You* are the one who's witty and charming. Not me. I hate myself and I've hated you and now I hate him!"

She buried her face into the pillow again.

"Lily."

She raised her head quickly, hearing the pain in her mother's voice. "Oh, *Maman*. I'm so sorry."

She struck a match and lit the candle next to the bed. Her mother looked so small and feeble, her face racked with pain. Guilt flooded her for thinking only of herself.

"Lily," her mother began again, but no words came out. She could see her mother trying to concentrate, her brow furrowing. Her eyes were unfocused, though, and Lily doubted she'd even understood what she'd told her.

"Go to sleep, *Maman*." She held her mother in her arms, stroking her hair, gentle humming a soft lullaby to her. After a few more attempts to speak, Lilian fell into a restless sleep.

It was a long time before sleep came to Lily.

JED TOSSED and turned in the bed. No matter which way he faced, he could not get comfortable. Nor could he turn off the screeching bell in his brain that let him know what a huge mistake he'd made. His plan totally backfired.

He'd almost choked when Lily accepted his invitation to go upstairs. Why, she was supposed to fall into his arms and confess her deception. He would comfort her and let her know that she was the one he really loved, not Lilian. She in turn would admit her undying love for him, and they would go share their good news with Lilian, who would bestow her blessings upon them.

Instead, Lily must think him a true bounder, first wining and dining her, and then becoming a predator around her mother. After this fiasco, Lily would hate him. What irony. He was finally ready to commit to one woman, but after the way he'd behaved, she would never have him. He could hear Louis chuckling in his grave over the turn of events.

Jed finally fell asleep before dawn and awakened at his usual time to a splitting headache. He shaved and dressed, and decided a cup of Manet's rich French-blend coffee might make the headache flee. Louis always said the right cup of coffee was second only to a night of love.

He slipped down the stairs quietly and opened the door of the kitchen. Manet frowned at him.

"*Monsieur* Jed, why the long face?" The chef clucked his tongue sympathetically. "No need to answer. It must be a woman. It's written all over you."

His eyes widened. He better learn to keep his poker face on. He couldn't believe his misery was so obvious.

"Could I have some coffee, Manet?"

The cook smiled at him. "One cup of *café au lait* coming up. Would you like eggs and toast? Waffles?"

"No, coffee's fine. I'm not hungry this morning."

Manet shot him a surprised glance, but busied himself readying the beverage.

"Is Lil up this morning?" he asked casually, warming up to ask about Lily.

"No, *Monsieur* Jed. Only Miss Lily. She left the house about a quarter-hour ago."

"Did she say where she was going?"

The chef shrugged. "No. And she looked in no mood to be asked." Suddenly, he narrowed his eyes at Jed. "Hmm," he murmured sagely. "I suppose you won't tell me about it."

He tamped down the defensive feeling that sprang to the surface. "No." He left it at that and finished the last swig of coffee before excusing himself.

It was time for another talk with the real Madam Lil.

Jed tapped on her door and got no answer. Aware of her condition, he decided to slip inside and check on her. Lil stirred slightly. He walked closer, saddened to see how gaunt she had become in their short acquaintance. She was so pale, almost white, with dark circles that went halfway down her cheeks. Her hair, which had probably been her pride, lay limp against the pillow.

"*Ma cherie*?" Lilian's eyes fluttered open.

"No. It's Jed Stone."

Her lips turned up in a thin smile. "Ah, Jed Stone," she echoed. "You have never seen me at my best. I was beautiful once. Not anymore."

He took a chair and slipped his hand over hers. "You still are lovely, Lil. And you'll live on through Lily."

That brought an attempt at a bigger smile. "My darling girl. She is a beauty." Then she frowned. "Why did you hurt my Lily? She cried a river of tears last night."

"I made a huge mistake." He squeezed the dying madam's hand. "But I'll fix it. What I came to tell you is I love her."

"You think you love my daughter?"

"I know I love her. I haven't been the man she deserves, but once I clear up some unfinished business, I plan to change. No more gambling. I'll put down roots."

"Change? All men make rash promises when they want a woman. What makes you so different, Jed Stone?"

"I'm crazy for Lily," he blurted out. "I admire her strength of character. How she's tried so hard to keep the house from falling down. How she's cared for you and all the girls and never takes a moment for herself. How she's smart and funny and good at keeping the books. How she jumps in headfirst and drinks up a new situation like an innocent child. How I know I'll go through life unhappy and unsatisfied unless I can love her and protect her. That's how I'm different from all the rest."

He sat back, surprised at the emotion that rushed out in the tumble of words. It was all true, though. There was nothing about Lily he didn't love.

Lilian gestured toward the table. Immediately, Jed picked up the clear vial.

"Two?"

"Three."

He gave her the drops and she sank into the pillows.

"They make me slur my words," she told him. "When I want to say something, I can't. I think the words. I hear them in my head. But they won't come out."

Jed brushed back a lock of hair off her face. "That's all right, Lil. You don't have to talk."

"I want to. I need to tell you that I approve. I think my Lily will be well matched with you. But there's one thing I would ask of you."

"Name it."

"You must pass Maximilian Fisher's muster."

26

Jed climbed the steps to Fisher House. He took in the incredible view, wondering how much Maximilian Fisher paid for such beauty. San Francisco lay before him in all her glory. He looked ahead at the imposing house and threw back his shoulders.

He wasn't sure if he'd be seen. Once Lil made this the condition of his marrying Lily, he wanted it out of the way. He had a lot of apologizing to do. The sooner he started, the better his chances at acceptance were. If he could tell Lily he had the stamp of approval from both her mother and the millionaire, his case would be stronger.

He fingered the letter inside his pocket. Lil had called for ink and paper. She struggled to write a few lines before the morphine kicked in. Scrawling her shaky signature on it, she allowed Jed to fold and seal it. He did so without looking at its contents.

Now, he wondered if that had been wise.

He'd put on his best suit and set out for Fisher House. He had no appointment but he didn't think the reclusive Maximilian Fisher had a full schedule at his advanced age. With his soft spot for Lily, Jed knew he stood a better chance of getting in the door if he admitted his business involved her.

The polished brass knocker gleamed on the oak door. He steadied his nerves and rapped on the door.

Poker face, he told himself.

A tall butler opened the door and looked down on him. The man had to be a good three inches taller than Jed.

"May I help you, sir?" he inquired in a polite British tone, yet Jed caught the disdain in the servant's voice.

"Yes. I don't have an appointment, but I would like to see Mr. Maximilian Fisher if he isn't otherwise engaged." He could be as formal as the next guy.

The butler shot him the best *Go to hell* look Jed had ever received. "Mr. Fisher won't see visitors. Especially you. Good day, sir." The butler shut the door before Jed could open his mouth.

He did not like being caught off-guard. He could understand the old geezer not seeing people but why not him in particular? Anxiously, he knocked on the door again.

It opened quickly. "Mr. Fisher is still not seeing visitors."

"I feel sure Mr. Fisher would like to have a word with me. It's about Lily Frontiere."

The servant gave him a wary glance. "What concern is Miss Lily to you?"

He could feel the heat of the man's contempt and was puzzled how he earned it in the space of twenty seconds. He pulled out the envelope from his suit coat.

"I have a letter Lily's mother has written to Mr. Fisher. This should explain everything."

"Let me see that." The butler plucked it from Jed's

hand. He studied the writing on the front. "Come this way."

He opened the door wider to admit Jed into a large, airy receiving hall. "I will give this to Master Max. It will be up to him if he wishes to see you or not."

Jed spent the minutes studying his surroundings, admiring several paintings, and scared to sit on a chair simply because he hadn't been invited to do so.

The butler returned after ten minutes. "Follow me."

He wondered if all the rich had such snooty servants. The man looked at him like he was lower than dirt. Jed stole a quick glance in a mirror they passed to see if he'd sprouted horns on the trip over.

When they reached a set of doors, the retainer stopped. "Do not upset him. State your business quickly and quietly. Do not raise your voice. If he chooses to discuss things with you, he will. If not, you are to leave immediately."

"All right." He wondered if people taken before the Grand Inquisition had been so well advised.

The butler knocked gently on the door before opening it. "Mr. Fisher, sir."

He spied Maximilian Fisher in his wheelchair. The opened letter sat in his lap. He wore a puzzled expression. Jed wished he would have read the letter that Lil penned.

"Come in. Harold, close the door."

The butler did as requested, but stayed in the room. Jed supposed the servant would act as a guard dog. If anything happened to upset his employer, he would give Jed the boot. He looked like he could do it, too.

"Come closer."

Jed crossed the room to stand before the old man. Lily had told him that Max was ninety. It was obvious he'd seen many suns rise. He tried to look at ease under such close scrutiny.

"How do you do, sir? I'm Jed Stone."

At that, the bushy eyebrows lifted. He cut his eyes to the butler and back. "Have a seat, Mr. Stone. I'd like to ask you a few questions."

He sat opposite the millionaire, letting his game experience take over. Many times he'd sat across from a powerful opponent who wanted to win at any cost. Jed wouldn't let a man like Maximilian Fisher intimidate him. Not with his future happiness at stake.

"Tell me about your background."

He decided nothing but total candor would do the trick. The old man's eyes were quick. He hadn't inherited his millions but made them, probably from the ground up. Even at an advanced age, Jed doubted much got passed him. And with every moment in his presence, Jed found himself admiring the old man. Liking him.

"Very humble, sir. I was born in New York City in 1845. I did fairly well in school. I could've done better but I excelled at math. I've worked in a boot factory and a brewery. Did a hitch at sea. Poured drinks and kept the books at a pub. Fought in the war. And I've been a gambler."

Fisher eyed him speculatively. "You've had a hard time finding what suits you, Mr. Stone."

He shrugged. "I've tried a lot of things. I've made some money. I know a gambler and a rambler isn't whom you would have chosen for Lily, but I'm willing to settle down and make the necessary changes."

He sat taller and continued. "I came here to win your approval, Mr. Fisher. I haven't been long in San

Francisco, but I'm a good man. I'll be a better one if Lily will have me."

Fisher spent a long moment before saying, "You mentioned New York. I'm very familiar with it. What were your parents' names, young man?"

He kept the poker face in place but he answered honestly again. "I don't like to talk much about that, sir." He collected his thoughts, knowing he owed the old man an answer. "I don't know their names," he revealed.

"Why not?" Fisher's face held no judgment in it, only curiosity.

"Because my father fetched a midwife and then walked out while my mother was still in labor. He never came back. Elmira Stone had never met either of them before she was summoned. My mother died immediately after I was born."

Jed ran a hand through his hair. "All I have of hers is the gold locket she wore, with her initials engraved on the back. Elmira was a hard woman, but she actually pitied me. That's why she didn't take me to the orphanage."

He didn't know why he'd divulged so much to a total stranger, but if it would convince the old man to agree to the match, he'd done the right thing.

"You say you'll change for my Lily. What do you plan to do?"

"I haven't a clue, sir. I have earned a considerable amount of money gambling. I thought I'd talk it over with Mac McRidge, my attorney. He's become a good friend. I know he'll have some career and investment advice for me."

Max snorted. "Knowing Mac, he'll have plenty of ideas, especially for a man with money." The old man blew his nose loudly into a handkerchief. "He's my legal advisor, too."

Jed took pride in knowing he had chosen the same lawyer as a millionaire. If Mac pleased Max Fisher, that might be a point in his favor.

"I'll want to hear it from Lily's lips that she'll have you. If she agrees to the match, I won't oppose it."

Jed rose, a smile on his face, and extended his hand. "Thank you, sir. I promise to make her happy. As soon as she's speaking to me again, that is."

The old man and the butler both chuckled.

"Miss Lily is a spitfire," the retainer said. "She is stubborn, sir, but she doesn't hold a grudge for long."

"I hope you're right," he replied. "Thank you again for seeing me, Mr. Fisher."

Max gave him a genuine smile. "Come back again with Lily if you can. Harold, please see Mr. Stone out."

"Yes, sir."

The two men started toward the door.

"And Harold?"

The butler gave his employer a knowing look. "You would like me to send for Mister Gordon?"

"You're damn right, Harold. The sooner the better."

As he left the Fisher estate, Jed wondered who Mr. Gordon could be.

27

Gordon Fisher's nerves were already frayed. He didn't need a confrontation with his grandfather to shred them further. The messenger roused him from a less than satisfying sleep to come to Fisher House at once. Gordon needed a couple of drinks and a woman in that order. He rarely started a day off without a drink or two. The minute he left Max's, he'd stop by for a few rounds. Maybe Simon would like to grab a steak and a few beers before he went out gambling tonight.

He rubbed his eyes, still matted with sleep, and tried to straighten his tie. He'd dressed hurriedly. He didn't know why a command from the old man made him nervous.

But it always did.

He pulled a comb from his pocket and ran it through his sparse hair. Why, Max had more hair than he did these days. What did his grandfather want? He'd left Gordon alone for a long time. However, Max still let him come into the office and stay a few hours on rare occasions. Still paid him a generous wage.

Then where did it all go?

He reached automatically for the silver hip flask

for the third time, remembering again that he'd forgotten to slip it into his pocket in his rush to get down to the waiting carriage. A man didn't keep Max Fisher waiting.

The carriage stopped. Gordon's stomach gurgled noisily. He wondered when he'd last eaten. Years of alcohol had dulled his taste for food. He ate when he thought about it, but that didn't happen often. At least he'd go to Max without liquor on his breath. That was a plus.

Wearily, he climbed from the coach and placed his hat on his head, already dreading the eighty steps leading up to Fisher House. By the time he reached the top, his breath came in gasping spurts. He decided to forego knocking, and rest on the front porch. He'd catch his breath and calm down.

No such luck. Harold immediately opened the door.

"Master Max saw the carriage arrive. May I take your hat?"

Gordon sighed. So much for collecting himself. He handed his hat to Harold. "Do you know what this is about?"

The butler looked down upon him. "I haven't a clue, Mister Gordon."

"Right." Harold knew everything that happened at Fisher House before it happened. He was closer to Max than sardines in a tin can. It must be bad if Harold wouldn't give him a clue. Gordon fought the queasiness. God, he needed a drink.

They went upstairs to the library. Gordon hadn't seen another room in the house for ten years. He regretted quarreling and moving out to his own place. He rarely saw Max when he'd lived here. All he could afford nowadays was a couple of rented rooms with infrequent maid service.

Harold knocked on the door and opened it. "Mister Gordon's here, sir." He ushered Gordon in and closed the door behind them.

Damn. If Harold was staying, this was a big deal. Might as well put up a good front. He clasped his hands behind his back to still their trembling. Oh, God, he wished he could have a drink!

He summoned what remained of his former acting skills and put a smile on his face. "Afternoon, Max." He crossed the large room as steadily as he could. "So, what's the summons for?"

His grandfather stared him down until he wanted to hide in a dark closet. "My God, Gordon! What have you been doing? Your eyes are so bloodshot I can't even see what color they are. You're sallow as a fish gone bad and you don't smell much better."

"You look good, too, Max."

Gordon had learned not to argue with the family patriarch. Better to deflect the bad comments and learn what the business at hand was. Max didn't keep him waiting.

As he took a seat the old man glared at him. "Why in the hell does Jed Stone look exactly like my no-good, only great-grandson?"

Max sure didn't pull any punches. The likeness had shaken Gordon, too. He'd thought the man *was* Cal. It stirred memories that he wasn't up to facing. That's why he'd fled Lucky Lil's and put it out of his mind. Until now.

"They could be twins, Gordon. *Twins!* He was born the same place in the same year. Start talking, boy— and don't stop until I know all the facts."

"I'll admit there's a likeness between them."

"You've seen him?"

He nodded grudgingly. "At Lil's the other night. Thought he was Cal for a minute."

"Jed Stone is more refined. Speaks more assuredly and is more comfortable in a decent set of clothes. Called me 'sir' more times than I could count. You're right. He's definitely not Cal."

His curiosity rose. "Under what circumstances did you come to meet Jed Stone?"

"That's neither here nor there," Max snapped. "Quit avoiding the topic, Gordon. You've always been good at that."

"What else do you need to know? They look alike. Everyone has a double somewhere. How should I know?"

He began to play with the bottom button on his vest, buttoning and unbuttoning it over and over. "What do you care? You got the heir you wanted."

Max narrowed his eyes and leaned forward in the wheelchair. "Yes, I have an heir. Not necessarily one I wanted. Cal is no better than you or Crenshaw. The lot of you has caused me nothing but trouble. Maybe I should claim Mr. Stone is your son and leave my fortune to him instead. I don't know a court in California that wouldn't think him related after putting the two of them side by side. Maybe that way my money would be put to good use."

His words shook Gordon to the core. Max had threatened to disinherit him a thousand times. He'd recently warned Cal never to come back to Fisher House. Gordon supposed that was all talk. He hoped his grandfather would do what society considered the right thing and leave him *some* money. Max was heavily into philanthropy, giving away reams of cash, and he figured the old man would will a neat bundle to all his worthy causes.

But Gordon always assumed he would be taken care of, probably through a trust managed by Stanton McRidge. He deserved some of the immense fortune Max had stockpiled over the years. He was tired of being kept on a chain like a small dog, a few crumbs thrown his way every now and then if he performed the right trick for polite company.

He tried to keep the loathing out of his voice as he questioned Max's wisdom. "You'd leave your fortune to a complete stranger? A gambler and whorehouse owner?"

"As if a second-rate actor and his wastrel son are any better? At least Mr. Stone is polite. I know Mac McRidge would vouch for his character."

Gordon stood. "You're going to do what you want, Max. You washed your hands of us and started a new life here in California. I'm sure you were fit to be tied when I showed up with Cal, trying to make amends for all the wrongs you placed at my doorstep. I don't care what happens to your money when you kick the bucket. If you don't leave it to Jed Stone, it'll just go to some charitable cause. Cal and I will never see a dime of it."

He crossed the room, anger boiling inside of him. Things never changed between them. It seemed the most he could hope for was if Max *did* leave his money to Jed Stone. Maybe then he could find someone who'd swear the old man had been incompetent when he did so. Who would leave millions to a whorehouse owner he'd just met? Gordon figured it was a lawsuit waiting to happen.

"I guess you know about the gold locket."

He froze in his steps and willed himself to turn around. "What locket? What are you talking about?"

"The locket Mr. Stone has that was his mother's. Her initials are engraved on the back."

He became lightheaded. No, it couldn't be. Women all across America wore gold lockets. It couldn't be Cara Lee's. It couldn't.

But what if it were?

He hadn't the money nor the inclination to buy Cara Lee a wedding ring for the mock ceremony they'd gone through. Instead of a gold band, he presented her with a locket that Max had given his wife Geraldine. It had been passed down to Crenshaw's wife after that. Gordon played up the fact that it was a family heirloom. He'd actually taken the time to have her initials engraved on the back. When he'd left with Cal bundled in his arms that day, he didn't give a thought to reclaiming the necklace. When Max asked him about it later, he said he buried it with his wife.

"You're not making much sense, Max. I think I'll excuse myself and leave. No, Harold, don't see me out. I don't think my grandfather should be left alone now."

He hurried down the steps, stumbling as he missed one. He clung to the banister for a moment. He needed to see Monty. Monty was from the old days. Monty remembered things. Monty would know what to make of all this.

The next twenty minutes blurred. Gordon forced his mind to go blank. He was afraid to think about the past. The carriage arrived at Monty's hotel. He walked through the lobby and up a flight of stairs. At the third door on the left, he banged loudly, as if his life depended upon it.

Monty opened the door. "Gordon? What the hell?

You're knocking loud enough to wake the dead." His friend studied him a moment. "You're white as a sheet. You could *be* the dead. Come in. Sit down."

Monty took Gordon's arm and brought him into the small room, where he seated him in the only chair. "You look like you could use a brandy." He poured a shot glass to the brim.

Gordon reached for it hungrily. He drained the glass in seconds and held it out again. Monty took the cue and refilled it. He drank the second glass more slowly. He set it down, his hands shaking badly.

Monty sat on the narrow bed. "What's troubling you?"

"It's Cara Lee."

Monty gave him a raised brow. "You mean Mrs. Gordon Fisher?"

"Exactly." He tried to stop his hands from shaking and failed. He placed them between his knees and clamped his legs together tightly. "Max ran into a man that's the spitting image of Cal. I've seen him, too. I think... oh my God, Monty... I think..."

"That Cara Lee... had two babies that day," Monty finished, his voice wavering. "I've seen him, too, Gordon. I think that's precisely what happened."

"When? Do you really think he's Cal's twin?"

Monty nodded sagely. "Remember how Simon told you he had a deal he needed help on?"

He nodded. "He never gave me any details."

"Well, it involved a scam surrounding the deed to some whorehouse. A place called Lucky Lil's." Monty cracked his knuckles as he spoke. "Cal was to come in and win the deed at Varsouvienne's one night. Everything was staged. We had players, the dealer in our pocket, the works.

"I was in there a night early, just checking out the

lay of the land. You know how I like to be prepared for a role."

Gordon cringed. In their acting days, Monty did everything from shaving his head bald to moving south for a couple of months in order to pick up a realistic Southern accent. He went to great lengths to be in character. No wonder he'd gone to the gambling hall beforehand.

"As I sat talking with another of Simon's men who was part of the scheme, in strolls Cal, cool as a cucumber and itching to play. I thought somehow Simon changed things, that we hadn't gotten word. I rounded up Rick, the dealer, and it all came down as planned.

"Trouble hit when we met up the next day. Simon began going over the plan again like the scam was still on. We tried to explain how things happened early. After watching and listening to Cal talk when he arrived, I realized another man walked off with the deed. I'd only met Cal in passing, just so I'd know what he looked like. The man who came in to the gaming hall that night was a dead ringer for your boy."

Gordon closed his eyes. At the time he'd thought it would be easy to walk out on Cara Lee after their son was born. He'd gotten the heir Max wanted with little effort on his part. Yet within days, guilt burdened his conscience. Hell, he hadn't even known he *had* a conscience.

The feelings became so overpowering that he'd gone back to find Cara Lee. Even though the midwife told him she wouldn't survive the birth, he half expected her to be waiting for his return, ready to throw her arms around him and forgive all the hurt and pain he'd caused. Instead, after he'd tracked down that bossy midwife, she'd told him to go rot in hell because his wife had died only minutes after he'd abandoned her.

He pretended for a long time it didn't matter. As time passed, the shame wore a heavy hole in his normally cavalier conscience. Women came and went. Gordon never found lasting happiness with any of them. The years wore on and the acting jobs dried up. He ruined his good looks with hard living. The choice he'd made to abandon Cara Lee to certain death and walk away with their newborn son led to the start of his heavy drinking. He realized his life was one lined with regrets.

Now, the ghosts from the past haunted him in full measure. What was he supposed to do?

"I don't want anyone to know about this, Monty."

"Too late," a voice from the doorway softly said.

28

Jed rubbed his pocket watch for luck as he crossed the street. He'd been to the bank and Mac's office after he left Fisher House and was now on his way home. A small boy stepped in front of him and held up a bunch of flowers.

"Would you like to buy some flowers, sir?"

His eye quickly scanned the bouquet. Twenty-two flowers in all. One of his lucky numbers. It was a sign.

"Yes, I would, young man." He gave the boy a smile and pulled out his money clip. The boy's eyes grew round at the bill he presented. Jed took the flowers from him and said over his shoulder, "Keep the change."

He walked with a spring in his step. Mac had told him of several real estate development opportunities. He hadn't gone into much detail since he was taking Sylvia to the concert tonight and wanted to get out of the office early, but Jed had a better idea now of the direction he might take. He would scout some of the properties Mac mentioned, starting tomorrow. He liked the idea of seeing things built on property he'd purchased, maybe even owning a few buildings. He'd make certain they weren't like the rat trap he and

Elmira had lived in. Their landlord had been the fattest rat of all. Jed intended to be very different.

He entered the house and glanced at Tommy. The girls would be at supper. Lily would already be there as Madam Lil, asking about problems and recommending new hairdos. She had a gift with people. She'd given him a gift—a chance at a different kind of life.

If he could convince her to take a chance with him.

He stuck the flowers in an empty vase. He'd worry about them later. Right now, he wanted to see Lily.

As he started to push open the swinging kitchen door, it opened from the other side. Lily came through, decked out in full Madam Lil make-up and wardrobe. Even knowing she was under all of that, Jed still would've had a hard time guessing her true identity. Lily had down the walk, the gestures, the accent, and even the tilt of the head that was so Lilian Frontiere.

Lil had told him that she regretted he'd never seen her before she became ill. He actually had, through Lily.

When she recognized him, Lily gave him a cool stare. "I didn't know you'd come home."

"Can we talk upstairs?" Jed realized his mistake by the look in her eye. "I meant in the upstairs parlor."

"If you wish." Her tone would freeze raindrops in July. He followed her up the stairs, enjoying the view each step of the way. She turned and went into the parlor. He closed the doors behind them.

He had envisioned a thousand ways of trying to tell Lily how much he loved her as he'd walked home this afternoon. Yet all the pretty words in the world wouldn't melt the fortress of ice she surrounded herself with. He decided to advance full-force, as an army assault. Some fireworks might be all it took for Lily to thaw. His lips could do the talking in more ways than the spoken word.

As she turned, Jed caught her in his arms, bringing her tightly against him. "I love you," he said simply and bent close for a kiss.

Jed's move caught Lily off-balance. She wanted to protest, to push him away, but before she could think —even act—his lips were on hers. Like magic, they nudged all thoughts from her mind. All she felt were sensations. His hands warm along her back. Butter-flies multiplying in her stomach. His stubble rubbing against her skin.

She tried to sigh in relief, in pleasure, but he swal-lowed the sound as he took her mouth, greedily, hun-grily, possessing her with a heat that threatened to explode. Lily drowned in fire, in that musky scent she associated with Jed, in waves of desire.

"I love you," he murmured against her mouth.

The declaration brought her to her senses. He didn't love her. He loved Madam Lil, an experienced, beautiful, older woman that Lily could never be. She broke the kiss and struggled in his arms, trying to free herself.

"No." He looked down at her tenderly. "I won't let you go anywhere but here." He kissed her again very gently, quick butterfly kisses that covered her face.

She had to escape.

"I love you," he said a third time. "And I know."

She began to cry, silent tears that sprang quickly and cascaded down her cheeks. Her mind raced like a greyhound, the world blurring around her. Her care-fully applied cosmetics would run soon. It would be over.

She had to tell him who she was. The ruse had run

its course. He had to be told it was all an illusion. The Lil he wanted to make love with didn't exist any longer.

"Jed..." Her voice broke. She swallowed hard. "Jed, I must confess—"

"I said I already know. I've known for a while now." He smiled down at her. "Aren't you even listening to me?" He kissed at the tears. Lily was moved beyond words.

And then it hit her.

"You know what?" she demanded in a low tone.

"I know it's Lily I hold in my arms and Lily that I love more than life itself."

He knew. *He knew?*

Her anger erupted. He'd known she was masquerading as her mother? What kind of twisted game did he play? Jed Stone was no better than Cal Fisher. She squirmed in his arms, trying to escape his hold. She hated him, more than she hated Simon or Pierre or any other man.

"Oh, Lily, my girl. My sweet, sweet girl," he crooned softly.

She writhed until she freed a hand and struck out, hoping to claw him and draw blood. He grabbed her wrist and then the other one and spun them both around. Jed pushed her against the door, his hands encircling her wrists, trapping them away from her body. Lily felt exposed. And scared.

Then he leaned his body against hers. Rock-solid muscle surrounded her, pinning her breasts against his chest. His eyes glittered with a fiery tenderness that frightened her, then excited her.

Was she crazy? Living in a fantasy? Or had Jed actually said he knew it was she. That he loved *her*, not Lilian.

Her eyes met his and reflected her dawning understanding. Then he kissed her tenderly. The assault on her mouth was gentler than before, but just as deadly. It went on and on until she was mindless. She melted into Jed, eager for him, wanting his kiss, his touch. She pressed her body close to his as he nuzzled her neck.

When he pulled away, she tried to follow and did, wrapping her arms around his neck and drawing him close. He kissed her again until she ached for something she didn't understand that she wanted. All she knew was she had to stay next to him or it would be worse than death.

"Come here, Lily," he said huskily against her ear. He took her hand and led her to the sofa.

"I have something for you." He reached into his pocket and lifted out a gold locket strung on a slender gold chain.

"It's beautiful," she said dumbly, wondering how it related to what had gone on.

Jed unfastened the clasp and placed the pendant around her neck. "This belonged to my mother. I want you to wear it, so you'll always be reminded of my love for you."

Lily stared down at the heart-shaped locket and lifted it in her fingers with wonder.

"You know what I've done all these months? How I've paraded around in suggestive clothes and run a brothel? How—"

"You did everything in your power to save the house and your mother. I know it all, Lily. I've met Lil and Max both and I have their approval. I told them how I love your strength and commitment and character and your beauty and brains and that I won't last another day without you in my arms."

Jed hugged her tightly to him. "I want you as my

wife, Lily. I want you more than anything in this world. I'll give up gambling, I'll sell the house. I'll do whatever you wish. Just say you'll be mine."

Say you'll be mine. Were those the sweetest words ever spoken? Certainly to Lily they were.

She took Jed's face in her hands. "I would be honored to marry you, Jed Stone." She kissed him lightly, brushing her lips against his, sealing the commitment between them.

"Max will be glad to hear I've soothed the savage beast," he said lightly, but she could hear the emotion underneath his words.

"You like Max?"

Jed smiled, that smile she'd fallen in love with, the one that showered warmth upon her. "He's a crusty old guy but I do like him. A lot. And if I didn't adore you so much, I would have to think about falling in love with your mother."

She blinked back tears. "*Maman* is a wonderful lady."

"And she loves you very much."

Jed pulled her against him. Lily rested her cheek against his chest. His steady heartbeat pounded just below her ear, reassuring her in an odd way. She stayed that way several minutes, basking in the glow of first love. How she could have thought she loved Pierre amazed her. It was nothing compared to her feelings for Jed.

"Would you like us to go visit Lil?" he asked.

Lily sat up and rubbed her eyes. Her hand had black all over it. "I must be a mess!" she cried, thinking how her tears had caused the heavy eyeliner to smear.

Jed smiled at her. "You're a beautiful mess." He kissed her soundly. "And you're my mess." He kissed her again. Then he stood and reached for her hand, pulling her up against him.

After another lingering kiss, he whispered, "Let's go see Lil. I want her to share in our happiness."

He tucked her hand possessively through his arm. Lily floated by his side down the hallway to her mother's room. She was loved, actually loved, by a remarkable man. He even said he'd give up gambling for her. She must be inside a lovely dream. If she were, she wished she'd never awaken. Her lips still tingled from his touch. A delicious warmth filled her.

They reached Lilian's room. She quietly turned the knob and stepped inside. It was already dark on this late February afternoon. Jed moved near the bed and lit a lamp. Suddenly, he placed his hands on her shoulders.

"Let's go, Lily," he said quietly, and began guiding her from the room.

"Go? But I thought you wanted to see *Maman*. Is she asleep?"

His face remained a blank, but his eyes clouded over. "I'm sorry."

She knew why at once. She broke from him and ran to her mother. She knelt next to the bed, her mouth trembling.

Lilian's eyes stared vacantly back at her.

29

Lily didn't know how Jed pulled it off, but he arranged for her mother's funeral to be held at Grace Church Episcopal. The imposing stone building had several stained-glass windows which muted the light inside. Masses of fresh flowers in a rainbow of colors filled the cathedral. The wooden pews themselves were packed.

Most of those gathered were men, those who set policies and trends in San Francisco. The tremendous turnout touched Lily. She realized it wouldn't have happened for most women in this occupation. For so many clients to attend spoke to Lilian's remarkable way with people.

Also present was everyone connected with Lucky Lil's—the girls, the domestics, Raymond, Manet, Ben. Several house madams from rival establishments also came to pay their last respects, dressed in refined and austere black.

Lily wished Max could be here, but he never left home nowadays. Those wishing to pay a call upon her after the graveside services would be directed to Fisher House. Max had insisted.

She sat with Jed on one side and Harold on her

other. The funeral service was to be brief. Jed would give the eulogy. She knew she couldn't deliver it herself.

The last strains of *Amazing Grace* died from the pipe organ. Jed rose and went to the pulpit. He pulled a sheet of paper from his pocket and placed it in front of him.

"Most of you here were fortunate to know Lilian Frontiere much longer than I did, but in our short acquaintance, I found her to be a genteel woman. Lilian left the political upheaval of Paris to make a new life for herself and her daughter, Lily, in California. She became an astute businesswoman and contributor to the arts in San Francisco. More importantly, though, Lilian gave the gift of herself. When you spoke, she listened. All who entered her house felt welcomed and comforted. She was a graceful woman full of graciousness and soothing charm. Lilian Frontiere was a good mother, a successful businesswoman, and a faithful friend. Her death is all of San Francisco's loss."

Jed stepped down and returned to his seat. His words had been short but to the point. He took her hand and gave it a quick squeeze before helping Lily to her feet. They walked past ornate displays of flowers artfully arranged until they reached the closed casket at the front of the church. Lilian would never wish to be seen in her present state. She would want those around her to remember her as she had been—beautiful, vital, and vibrantly alive.

She paused in front of the mahogany coffin and rested her hand upon the smooth, polished wood. She buried not only her mother but her best friend. She fought the painful tears. Then, she let them fall. She had every right to weep.

Jed placed an arm around her and led her back to

their seats. Thank God he'd come into her life. She didn't know how she could have coped the last few days without his strength to lean on. She only wished her mother would have lived long enough to see them married.

One by one, the entire congregation filed past the casket to pay their respects. She recognized every man in the line, thanks to having worked downstairs these last few months. Her time as Madam Lil had given her a tremendous respect for her mother—for what she built, how she always conducted herself as a lady, and how she'd done her absolute best in raising her daughter.

Jed appreciated the mass that turned out for Lil's funeral. The numbers present only confirmed how special Lilian Frontiere had been. He couldn't imagine any other madam in California would command this kind of crowd, much less be mourned as sorrowfully as she would.

Jed spotted Simon Morgan as he filed toward the coffin. Behind him was a man Jed had seen with Simon at Lucky Lil's once before. Then his breath caught in his throat. He thought he would suffocate.

Standing in the aisle next to him was the man from the wanted poster.

He gripped Lily's hand tightly, fighting to stay calm.

The man passed before the coffin and then in front of them. Their eyes met for a fraction of a second. The stranger who shared his face gave Jed an eerie grin before moving on.

Jed glanced at Lily to see what she made of all of this. Her head was bowed as she sobbed quietly into her handkerchief. He realized she hadn't seen the man at all.

He fought turning around to watch the wanted outlaw walk back down the aisle. In the brief time he'd seen him, the similarities had been uncanny—the way his hair fell across his brow, his stance, his arms swinging at his side. And yet this lookalike hadn't seemed surprised to see Jed. It was as if he already knew of his double's existence.

He'd been only one man back from Simon Morgan when he went to pay his respects. Jed knew with certainty this man was involved with Simon. If that were the case, then the danger was even closer than he'd imagined. He marveled at how Simon hadn't yet recognized him, even though Jed knew how different he looked from New Orleans a year ago.

The addition of the mustache, the change of his part—they both altered his appearance remarkably. Yet someone with Simon's playing skills would have catalogued Jed's looks, his accent, his gestures. He probably lived on borrowed time before Simon remembered him. Especially with this man around him, it could trigger the gambler's memory at any moment.

That made it imperative for Jed to make a move on Simon soon. He'd give it a day or two, since Lucky Lil's would be closed anyway. He'd come to San Francisco to exact revenge on Simon. He'd put it off due to his attraction to Lil and his discovery that she was actually Lily.

Now, he'd better steam ahead. The gambler's actions had cost Jed his best friend. He had to make Simon Morgan pay for Louis' death.

SIMON ROLLED the wine around his mouth, enjoying the taste. Cal bounced around the room like a giddy schoolgirl. Gordon looked as dead as Lil must've been in her coffin. Rumor had it she'd been poisoned by a former lover or was shot by an angry client who claimed he'd been gypped.

What a waste. Lilian Frontiere dead. Yet, that sweet morsel Lily still haunted the place. He wondered if she kept out of Jed Stone's way. Probably so, until now. Lil had always been protective of the girl, but with her gone from the picture, the vultures would make their moves. Lily was fresh meat on the market.

And Simon wanted a taste of her.

He knew Lily would have nowhere to go. Jed Stone owned Lucky Lil's and all its contents. Lily might have a few jewels from Lilian and her fancy Parisian clothing, but it was a piddling inheritance. He wondered if she would accept an offer of his protection. He could tell her it was a way to leave the house of ill repute until she decided what her future held. He doubted she was ready to jump in and spread her legs for a living, as coddled and cosseted by Lilian as she had been.

"Did you see him? Did you see him get a look at me?" Cal took a swig from his whiskey glass. "I swear he went whiter than a ghost when he laid eyes on me."

Cal drained the contents of the shot glass and wiped his mouth with the back of his hand. "I'm glad I knew he'd be there. It was spooky, though. Almost like looking into a mirror. I wish we could have gone over to Max's after the burial and shaken him up a little more. Damn, I want to get my hands on that deed."

"Shut up," Gordon growled.

Simon looked at Gordon, his hands clasped in his lap. His eyes filled with something between pity and remorse.

"What the hell's the matter with you?" Cal glared at his father. "Have a drink. You don't look so good."

He poured a tumbler full and handed it to Gordon. "Drink up, old man. Maybe it'll put a little color back in your face."

Simon had learned to sense when people were at their weakest. Gordon Fisher was at the end of his rope. He took a twenty dollar gold piece from his pocket, money he could ill afford to part with, but he flipped the coin to Cal.

"Go have a little fun tonight, Cal. I'll keep your daddy company."

Cal broke out in a big smile. "Hey, with this I could invite that luscious Lily out on the town. Think she'd care to celebrate her poor mama's demise?"

Gordon's penetrating glance hushed his son's words. "Stay away from Fisher House, son. And stay away from Lucky Lil's and Jed Stone. He's bad news."

Cal shrugged. "Don't worry about me none. I can always find some action up on the Square." He tossed the coin into the air and caught it, pocketing it in a swift movement and heading out the door.

Simon was glad to be rid of him. Cal tended to get on his nerves. Still, he did serve a limited purpose at times. He looked over at Gordon, who'd buried his face in his hands. Time to go to work. Gordon Fisher had a little secret. He'd only come in on the tail end of it but Gordon didn't know that. Simon was ready to hear the whole of it.

"So, Gordon." He poured himself another glass of wine and offered one to his friend. Gordon shook his head and slumped morosely on the sofa.

"Let's talk about this thing with Monty. I want the full story."

"It's all in the past, Simon. Let it stay buried with the dead."

"I think the past is walking around ready to bite

you in the ass, my friend. That dead ringer for Cal sure isn't going to let sleeping dogs lie."

Gordon sighed. "He may be uneasy about seeing Cal, but he doesn't know they're related."

Related?

He decided to venture a guess and pressed his friend. "Why wouldn't you want to introduce two brothers to each other?"

Gordon broke down. The sobs almost unnerved Simon. They were gut-wrenching, torn from raw emotion and deep pain. He didn't know exactly what to do, so he went over and clapped Gordon on the back hard.

"Shake it off, man. Pull yourself together."

Gordon wiped his eyes with his sleeve. "How was I supposed to know it was twins? I only needed an heir to show Max. When I left with Cal, I thought that she'd be dead within minutes. I didn't know. Oh, God. I didn't know there was another baby."

Simon put it together in a blink of an eye. Knowing how Max had wanted Gordon to quit the acting business and join his company, how he'd wanted Gordon to settle down and have an heir, Simon figured out Gordon must've knocked up some sweet young thing and then taken off with the baby the minute he was born. How ironic that another child came after he left.

How interesting to learn that Jed Stone could stand to inherit millions when his great-granddaddy, Maximilian Fisher, died.

If Max learned of their connection.

"But you left her anyway, didn't you?"

Gordon began crying again. "The midwife said Cara Lee wouldn't make it. I was just doing what was best for the boy."

"Running him to his rich granddaddy and finding a wet nurse to care for him?" He patted him on the back. "Of course, Gordon. You did what you thought was right."

Gordon Fisher had been a drunk when Simon met him years ago. He wondered if his drinking began when he walked out on his wife. Or if the chit who'd given birth to the twins had even been his wife.

And Jed Stone hadn't a clue that Gordon was his father or that he was a twin to Cal. He sure didn't know Maximilian Fisher could be his key to life on Easy Street. But where had he crossed paths with Jed Stone in the past? It was on the tip of his tongue but he still couldn't place him or the circumstances.

Simon wondered how he could use the information Gordon had spilled to his benefit.

Suddenly, Gordon Fisher produced a small pistol from his pocket and placed it to his temple. He pulled the trigger, and Simon watched his body slump to the floor.

Cal left the shabby hotel in a hurry. The money Simon gave him burned a hole in his pocket. It was early to hit Portsmouth Square. The heavy drinking and games of chance wouldn't be in full swing for several hours. He was hungry, too. He might as well eat before looking for some action. Too bad Lucky Lil's was shut down tonight. He could use a good poke with the lovely Sarah Jane.

He walked through the financial district, teeming with men returning to their jobs from their mid-day luncheon break, pausing to hunt for a cheap place to eat.

"Good day, Mr. Stone."

Cal watched a stranger approach him and then realized the man thought he was Jed Stone. By his dress and glasses perched near the end of his nose, Cal took him for a clerk. How did that card sharp know a respectable type?

"I see you're coming to do a little business, sir."

Cal casually looked to his right and saw they stood in front of a bank.

Holy Mother of God.

This must be Stone's bank. With the money the

man had won at gaming tables across the city, he'd probably deposited a pile inside. Cal's greediness went into overdrive.

He clapped the man on the back. "Yessir, I need to make a hefty withdrawal." He grinned at the bank clerk. "I know you're the one to help me."

"Certainly, Mr. Stone." The fellow held the door open for him and they entered the cool confines of the bank.

Truth be told, banks gave him the jimjams. He robbed a few on his own before he hooked up with the Landrey gang. The last time out some old busybody started giving him what for. Cal clubbed the scrawny woman with the butt of his gun. She'd plopped down quicker than a tossed sack of flour, which prompted one of the male customers to come after him. Cal shot that man and then the woman for good measure. The entire robbery netted just under four hundred dollars, not even worth his time. Ever since then, he tried to steer clear of banks.

But this was too sweet an opportunity to pass up.

He followed the bank employee over to the counter. He leaned against it as the man readied himself, fiddling with the drawer and stacks of paper on his side of the divided counter.

"Hurry up, would you? I haven't got all day."

The man paused and gave him an odd look. "Of course, sir. Almost ready."

Cal looked around the bank's interior. A single customer waited at the far end. A lone guard paced the length of the room. He wondered idly how easily a place like this could be robbed. Hell, he didn't need to worry about that. He was about to collect the sweetest paycheck of his life. If he played his cards right.

"You wish to make a large withdrawal, Mr. Stone?"

"That's right, sonny."

"May I see your passbook, please?"

He went through the motions of searching his pockets for the item. "I seemed to have walked out without it. That won't be a problem, will it?" His tone conveyed that he was an important customer, not one to be kept waiting.

"Of course not, Mr. Stone." The clerk pulled a slip of paper from under the counter. "If you'll just sign here, we can use this blank withdrawal slip. You'll need to be sure and note the amount you removed in your passbook, though."

"How much do I have in there now?"

"One moment." The clerk consulted a file and quoted him a figure, a nice, round figure that was music to his ears. Yet it didn't come close to what he knew Jed Stone had won since he'd hit San Francisco.

Did he have more than one bank that housed his money?

"I was hoping to take more than that."

"Then I suppose you'll need into your safety deposit box?" the clerk asked helpfully.

"You're absolutely right."

Cal smiled, thinking this would be the easiest payday ever gotten. Like picking money off a tree. He didn't want to tip the clerk off in any way as to his identity, so he'd leave a couple of hundred in this account. The real pay-off would be in that box.

"Mr. Stone?"

He came floating back down to earth. The man handed him a fountain pen. He dipped it into the inkwell. He doubted the bank clerk would even look at the signature. After all, he'd been the one who'd recognized him as Jed Stone. Besides, who ever looked at signatures anyway?

Quickly, he scrawled *Jed Stone* on the page and pushed it back across. "Leave two hundred in the account. I'm pulling the rest out."

The clerk frowned at him. "Will you be traveling, sir? I could put part of it in bills and the rest in a cashier's check."

"Cash is what I want," he snapped. "It's my money, right?"

The clerk colored beet red. "Yes, sir." He busied himself with the transaction. "I'll need to see the manager, sir. We'll have to get into the safe. I don't have that much cash in my drawer."

"Sure. Whatever."

The clerk scurried off. Cal tried to calm his thumping heart. He was actually going to get away with it.

"Jed. What are you doing here? I thought you'd be with Lily."

He looked up and saw a well-dressed man crossing the lobby. Nice suit, clean-shaven, well-manicured hands. Had to be a banker or lawyer.

"Had to do a little business, you know," Cal said easily. "Lily understands these things. She's with Max." That thought soured as he spoke it. He should be the one comforting the dotty old man now that his whore was dead. Or even comforting the luscious Lily in her time of sorrow.

Not that slick Jed Stone. Still, he had to thank the gambler for making it easy enough for him to stroll in and help himself to all this cash.

"I am sorry to hear about Lilian. I spoke briefly to Lily after the funeral but I had to make a court date. Wouldn't you know it? The other party never showed."

So, he was a lawyer. Maybe he was Jed Stone's lawyer. Cal felt a fine sheen of perspiration spring across his forehead. He might be able to fool a bank clerk, but how could he trick someone who really knew Stone?

"Mr. Stone?"

He saw the clerk coming toward him. "I have the cash you requested. I'll just place it in this envelope. Would you like me to hold it while you check your box?"

Cal reached across and slipped the manila envelope from the man's hands. "No, I'll just add a little to it. Keep it all together, you know."

"Is this about the property we spoke of, Jed? I didn't think you were ready to close on the transaction so fast. And I definitely don't want you walking around with that much cash."

Cal tucked the envelope into his coat pocket. "Nope, this is another deal. Doesn't involve you. Well, gotta go. Good seeing you."

He motioned to the clerk, who came from behind the counter and led him down a flight of stairs. How was he supposed to get into this security box if he didn't have the key? Hell, he didn't even know the number.

"I'm afraid my key is with my passbook."

The shorter man scrutinized him, a look of disdain crossing his features. "Very well, sir. I'll have to gain access to the master. Please wait here."

In the minutes the man was gone, Cal's mood went from elation to paranoia. What if the clerk was onto him?

Finally, the man returned. "This is highly unusual, Mr. Stone. Mr. Larkin is most unhappy. He wanted me to send you home to retrieve your key. I explained to him what a good customer you were, though, so he's granted us a little leeway for the time being."

"Good."

Since he didn't have a key, he didn't need to fake going to Stone's box. The little clerk went right to it, inserting the master and turning both locks for him.

"Let me know when you're through, and I'll lock it back up." He placed the long, slender box upon a table.

Cal waited for the man to exit before he sat. His hands shook as he lifted the lid. Inside were stacks and stacks of bills, all high denominations. Cal took them all out and placed them upon the table. The deed to Lucky Lil's followed. The only other item was a folded piece of paper.

He reached in and took it out, unfolding it slowly. His own face stared back at him. It was a wanted poster describing a few of his many misdeeds. How had Stone gotten hold of that? Quickly, he slipped it inside his shirt.

Seeing the poster and knowing he was robbing Jed Stone blind, Cal needed to get out of town fast. Maybe even out of California. With all the money he now had, he could go just about anywhere. He hated the East coast. Europe would be too snooty for his tastes. This kind of money would go a long way down in Mexico or maybe even South America. The sooner he left, the better. Confronted with the proof of a price on his head, he realized this windfall was a godsend.

He jammed as much as he could inside the envelope and the rest in every pocket he had. He folded the deed to the whorehouse and slipped it up his sleeve. He'd think what to do with that later. Cal returned the box to its slot. Cold sweat had broken out along his back and neck. A tiny trickle slowly skated down, sending shivers along his spine.

Why couldn't he be like his father? The actor in

Gordon would handle this situation smoothly, despite whatever amount of liquor he'd consumed. For a swift moment, Cal wondered if he should share the fortune with his father.

The answer was no.

Simon Morgan had been more of a father to him than Gordon, but even Simon was drying up now. He'd gone through a massive losing streak. Cal didn't see any money coming his way through Simon. Better to cut his ties with the both of them and get while the getting was good.

He returned to the main lobby to tell the clerk he was done. Before he could speak, the clerk surprised him once again.

"Oh, Mr. Stone. Good news. The wire transfer you expected tomorrow is actually coming in today. Mr. Larkin just received a telegram relating the details."

Wire transfer? Cal wondered how much could be at stake. Maybe he should just count his lucky stars and head on out. Then greed caused him to ask, "Do you remember how much is involved?"

The clerk beamed. "Just over thirty thousand, sir."

His thoughts whirled. He already had enough to live on for years stuffed inside his pockets. Should he risk staying around for more? Why not? The real Jed Stone, the one who'd stolen Lucky Lil's from him, would still be comforting the grieving Lily. He wouldn't head off to a bank today.

"I guess I can wait. When is it supposed to arrive?"

The clerk consulted his pocket watch. "Probably within the hour. Surely, no later than an hour and a half."

Thirty thousand in ninety minutes? He could definitely wait.

"Would you come with me, sir? Mr. Larkin needs you to sign a few papers. You can wait in his office. He just left for an appointment."

Cal smiled. "That'll be just fine."

31

Lily looked out the carriage window as they exited Lone Mountain cemetery. The huge wooden cross on the summit of the singular mountain loomed large above the graves it guarded. It comforted her knowing she could see the cross from almost anywhere in the city. The cemetery also looked out over the bay. Her mother would rest peacefully near the water she'd come to love.

Jed took her hand and draped an arm about her, pulling her close. She rested her head against his shoulder. Her hand moved to play with the locket he'd given her. She hadn't taken it off since she'd received it. It reassured her that Jed wasn't going anywhere.

"Ready to face the crowd at Max's?"

She nodded. "What a wonderful turnout in *Maman's* honor."

"Lil would've been pleased at the tribute."

They fell silent for the ride back to Fisher House. Lily was glad she'd closed the graveside service to the public. Only she, Jed, and Ben had been in attendance. Now she readied herself to deal with the parade of mourners.

Ben slowed the horses and stopped them at the

foot of the path leading up to Fisher House. Jed handed her down and they began climbing the stairs to the top.

Once inside, she was swept up into the crowd convened in the receiving hall and downstairs parlor. She went from group to group, both giving and receiving condolences. After an hour she was exhausted, her face pained by the smile worn since she'd arrived.

She caught Jed watching her with concern. He signaled Harold. Within ten minutes, the men had graciously cleared out the many guests.

The butler came to her. "Master Max is waiting for you and Mister Jed in the library. I'll bring fresh coffee."

"Thank you, Harold. Everything was wonderful. Please give my compliments to Margaret."

Jed took her elbow and led her up the grand staircase to Max's retreat. He sat by the window, a faraway look in his eyes. She hadn't seen him since Lilian's death. The millionaire seemed to have aged a decade. Max never seemed old to her, but today every one of his ninety years showed in his lined face.

"Mr. Fisher?" Jed called out, making him aware of their presence.

Max turned and smiled weakly at them. Lily ached when she observed that the gleam in his eye was missing. Jed hurried over and wheeled Max's chair near the fire. That small gesture meant the world to her. She went to them and sat on a settee next to Max's chair. Jed joined her.

"Did everything go well, my dear? Harold told me how many attended the service at Grace Episcopal. I'd surmise Lilian would have been delighted."

Lily smiled at her dear friend. "The service was

lovely. Jed handled all the arrangements—the obituary, the priest, the music. He even gave the eulogy."

She took his hand and he threaded his fingers through hers. The light in his eyes glowed with his love for her. She pushed down an ache deep within her, wishing her mother could have seen her so happy, so in love with this man. Maybe Lilian did see her, watching from a cloud upon high.

Max cleared his throat. "I know I appreciate your young fellow coming to give me the news personally."

She forced herself to turn away from Jed's gaze to look at Max. "He insisted on coming, Max. I think Jed's quite taken with you." She smiled mischievously. "I wonder if it's a case of two like minds coming together."

Harold rolled in a cart filled with coffee, fruit, and sandwiches. "Just a little something to refresh you. I didn't see you eat a bite, Miss Lily. You need to keep up your strength." He placed a cloth napkin across her lap. "Mister Jed, will you see to her while I fix Master Max a plate?"

"Of course, Harold."

Jed winked at Lily, glad to have something to do. All day he'd been a caged tiger while he visited with a good number of San Francisco's finest gentlemen, oozing charm and listening attentively, studying those who'd come to pay tribute to Lilian Frontiere.

Yet in the back of his mind, all he could see was his lookalike, the man who'd wrenched his guts loose until they flopped around inside him like a bird with a broken wing.

He filled Lily's plate while she protested. "I can't eat all of that, Jed. Honestly."

"You've eaten two bites of toast in two days. You will eat this, Lily, and enjoy every bite."

He caught Harold suppressing a grin beneath his stern exterior. Max simply tossed up his napkin in delight.

"You've met your match, my girl."

Suddenly, Max motioned for quiet. His eyes misted with tears. Jed assumed he was feeling the loss of Lil again.

Max smiled at him then. He started to speak but his voice broke. Lily looked at Jed questioningly.

"Is something wrong, sir?" Jed asked, as he slipped the china teacup from the old man's trembling hands. "Would you like us to leave? I know it's been a long day for you."

Max turned to Harold. "It's as I feared," he told the trusted retainer. "If I had any doubts at all, this confirms my suspicions." He leaned close to Lily and lifted her gold locket between two fingers, handling it lovingly, a sadness permeating his face.

Jed watched as the butler put a comforting arm around his employer. "I know it's a shock after Mrs. Lilian's death, but all will be well, Master Max. You have the power. It's not too late to repair Mister Gordon's damage."

Gordon? That was the name the millionaire used the first time Jed visited him. He'd told Harold to summon Gordon as Jed had left. Who was this mysterious Mr. Gordon?

The old man straightened and patted his butler's hand. "Of course, Harold. I can right a few wrongs this day."

He looked at Jed with tears streaming down his wrinkled cheeks. "Would you remove the locket from Lily so that I may examine it?"

Jed did as asked, unfastening the clasp and handing the necklace to Max. He glanced uncertainly at Lily, who seemed as puzzled as he did by what was taking place.

The old man turned the locket in his gnarled hands, stroking the necklace fondly. He stared at the picture within for a moment before handing it to Harold. The butler squinted at the tiny picture. His mouth set in a harsh line. He returned the jewelry to his employer.

"Oh, where to start?" Max asked aloud. "I know you both think me mad but not in the sense you think. I'm madder than hell at my grandson, Gordon Fisher."

Jed looked to Lily, a deep frown etched on her brow. Then her jaw dropped. All color drained from her face.

"Lily?" Jed asked uncertainly.

"I think Lily is beginning to understand the magnitude of the situation," Max replied.

"You don't mean... that they are... he's not... then that would explain..."

Max nodded wearily. "Yes, that's exactly what I think," he answered cryptically. "I want him to know. For your sake. And his." He looked at Jed again, a benevolent smile on his lips.

Jed looked at those gathered around him. "Will someone tell me what on earth is going on?"

The old man held a hand up. "Long ago, I married my dearest love and gifted her with a simple gold locket. She was so proud of it and wore it always, until she died a year later in childbirth."

Max shook his head. "I'm afraid a part of me always blamed my son for my beloved's death. I shuttled him off to the care of nannies and servants, while I threw what heart I had left into making money. I'm sure it was my ignoring Crenshaw that made him become the selfish weakling he was.

"When Crenshaw married, I passed the locket to his wife. Rebecca was a greedy, unethical woman who took her own life when my grandson Gordon turned ten. I held the locket in trust for him until he married.

"Gordon brought a sweet girl named Cara Lee to my home in New York. Gordon asked for the locket, to give to her. They had eloped and he wanted his wife to wear it."

A sick rush of fear and loathing coursed through Jed. The back of his mother's locket was engraved with *CLF. Cara Lee Fisher.* He looked to Max in confusion.

"Less than a year later, Gordon brought a baby to me. His son. Cara Lee had died in childbirth and he needed help raising the boy. Gordon was an irresponsible actor, a foolish man full of pride and arrogance. When I asked about the locket, he said he buried it with Cara Lee, wanting her to have something of him as she lay in a cold grave.

"My great-grandson, Cal Fisher—Gordon's boy— is identical to you, Jed. We are on poor terms. I've banned him from my home."

Max laid a hand gently on Jed's arm. "I'm afraid Gordon didn't tell me the truth. I fear he abandoned Cara Lee and took her son from her, all to get himself back into my good graces as far as his inheritance was concerned."

Jed said woodenly, "And what he didn't know is that Cara Lee gave birth to another son after he left. *Me.*"

Waves of bitterness filled Jed. His eyes blurred with tears. His father *had* abandoned his mother. Left her to die. And she had struggled alone, giving birth to this monster's second son, after he had treated her so cruelly.

"I couldn't be more pleased, Jed. You will make

Lily a fine husband. I will be proud to announce to the world that you are indeed my great-grandson."

Jed stood. He needed air. He had to think. He rushed from the room, oblivious to the others' cries, running down the stairs and flinging open the door.

Stanton McRidge approached the front porch. Jed rammed into him and Mac gripped his arm tightly.

"Jed! Whatever's wrong with you, you better snap out of it. There's a man that could be your twin cleaning out your accounts down at the bank. If you want to have any money left to your name, you'd better come with me."

32

Jed swung open the cab's door before it came to a complete stop. Mac stopped him from vaulting out.

"Hold up, Jed. You barely listened to a word I said on the way over. God knows why, when that man is robbing you blind. Wait here until I see how things have progressed."

Mac glared at him like a schoolmaster who'd caught a kid smoking during recess, before he turned and walked into the bank's entrance. He got the message to stay still. He tried to collect his thoughts. Although Mac didn't know who was in there, Jed certainly did. It was his twin brother, Cal Fisher. The sketched face from the wanted poster.

The door opened and Mac motioned him in. Jed entered the lobby and spotted Cleveland Armstrong, the gangly clerk who'd helped him set up his account. Although close in age, Jed saw the bank employee as an unworldly, much younger brother. They'd chatted on several occasions when he did his banking. He even gave Cleveland a few pointers on how to play cards.

The bank clerk stood next to Mac. He broke out in

a huge grin and beckoned a third, husky man over. The two men came up to where he stood with Mac.

The clerk declared, "This is Mr. Stone."

The stranger nodded briskly at him. "Detective Robinson, sir. Seems like we have a bit of a problem here."

Armstrong couldn't contain his excitement. "A man came in a while ago and I called him Mr. Stone. He looks like you, sir. But he doesn't have your good manners. Nor your impeccable taste in attire."

The policeman gave the eager clerk a look that silenced him. "Fellow claimed to be you, Mr. Stone. Didn't have his passbook on him but he wanted to make a large withdrawal. Mr. Armstrong here had him sign for it, and immediately recognized it wasn't your signature."

"When Mr. McRidge came in and spoke to him, I could tell he also knew something just wasn't right. I told him it wasn't you."

The detective glared at the clerk, who shrugged and clamped his lips together tightly. "Seems he also got into your safety deposit box, Mr. Stone. Mr. Armstrong found a way to keep him here in the bank president's office."

"Waiting for a large wire transfer," the young man added quickly. "Avarice was written all over his face when I told him you had some money coming in a day early. I knew that would hold him until we could rouse you, Mr. Stone." He grinned sheepishly at the exasperated detective. "Sorry."

"We'll arrest him for impersonation and theft, naturally. We do need to confirm your identity, Mr. Stone. For the record."

Jed mustered a pleasant smile, even though he itched to confront Cal Fisher. The man almost caused him to lose his life. He remained composed, though, and offered, "Will my passbook be good enough, Cleveland? I never leave home without it." He removed it from his pocket and handed it over for inspection.

The bank clerk took it and studied it carefully before nodding. "Talking to him lets me know this is Mr. Stone, Detective. His passbook is icing on the cake."

"If you would please sign your name on a piece of paper, Mr. Stone? Just to make things official."

Jed complied, writing his name across the page.

Armstrong adjusted his spectacles. "See, he's a lefty, same as me, like I told you. That other fellow wrote with his right hand. And none too neatly, I might add. His penmanship is atrocious."

Detective Robinson shook his head. Jed could tell his patience had worn thin with the overzealous clerk. "That's all I need for now, sir. If you'll go down to the station, we can write out the complaint. Shouldn't take too long."

"Could I stick around and see this man?"

Robinson nodded and moved across the lobby. He entered a closed office. Moments later, they heard a muffled shout and the door flew open. Cal Fisher came barreling across the room. He stopped dead in his tracks.

"Hell's bells! I might've known you was here!"

"You're damned right I'm here!" Jed roared. "If you think you're going to add stealing my money to your long list of misdeeds, you've got another think coming, Cal Fisher."

"Like you know anything about me, little brother. You come prancing into town wearing your fancy suits, flashing cash around. You don't know squat about me or the hell I've gone through. Be glad you didn't grow up the way I had to."

Detective Robinson came up but Jed waved him off. "I know a lot more about you than you do about me. None of it's good. You were brought up knowing your father. I didn't even have a name. I was raised in poverty by a woman who never had time for me. You had Max all these years and treated him so shabbily he never wants to see you again.

"And I've seen the wanted poster, Cal. I know what a sorry scoundrel you really are."

His twin's eyes widened. He slammed a fist in Jed's direction but he expected it. Cal wouldn't want the law in San Francisco to know of his criminal past. He avoided the blow and came around quickly, managing a solid punch of his own. Cal grunted and clutched his mid-section.

The policeman signaled Jed to stay put. While Cal gasped for air, Robinson cuffed his hands and searched his pockets and beyond. He removed stacks of cash, as well as a gun and the folded deed, placing it all on the counter for the clerk to handle.

"Ain't never had any luck," Cal mouthed. "It's not fair. You get all the money and the whorehouse and that sweet morsel, Lily. I'll be damned."

A single page floated to the ground and fell at Jed's feet. Jed reached for it and handed it to Robinson.

"Cal Hart, hmm? Wanted in several states for murder, robbery, and rape?"

Cal looked up sullenly. "Wasn't none of it my idea. Stupid Landrey gang. Said we'd make us some fast money. Have us a little fun. Well, it was hard work with nothing to show for it." He glared daggers at Jed. "He's the one who's got it all. I never got a break in my life. Never."

Jed thought Cal must have squandered away every opportunity he'd been given. He was glad he'd never known this brother. He hadn't missed out on much. He was embarrassed they were related. No wonder Max had ordered Cal banned from Fisher House.

Robinson grabbed hold of Cal's arm. "Come along, Cal Hart Fisher. And enjoy the light while you can, son. It's the last you'll see for a long, long time."

Jed turned and shook hands with Cleveland Armstrong. "I have you to thank, Cleveland."

The clerk beamed. "Just doing my job, sir."

"I will put in a good word with your boss. And Mac?" He turned to his friend. "Do you think we could work out some kind of reward for Mr. Armstrong?"

Mac grinned. "That can easily be arranged, Jed."

Cleveland broke into a huge smile. "I would appreciate that, Mr. Stone."

"We'll be in touch."

He and Mac followed the policeman and his prisoner out to the curb.

"Meet me at the station," the detective told them. "We'll get this straightened out as soon as we can."

JED REELED from the day's revelations. *He was Maximilian Fisher's great-grandson.* Not some anonymous orphan, although knowing the little he did about Gordon Fisher, he wondered if he and his twin brother were even legitimate. He longed to meet his father face-to-face. He had so many questions. What had his mother been like? Who were her people? How did she meet Gordon?

And why did his father walk out on her?

He hoped he could get a few answers from Gordon Fisher before he strangled him.

"Jed?"

He turned and looked at Mac. The attorney had proved a good friend to him, never more so than today.

"We've reached Fisher House. Would you like me to go in with you?"

He shook his head. "Go home to Sylvia, Mac. I'll come by your office in the morning and sort out the rest of the mess."

His friend hesitated. "Are you sure?"

Jed nodded. "Yes. I think I need some time alone with Max. And Lily."

He opened the carriage door and stepped down, motioning the driver to move on. He watched the cab pull away and turned to climb the steps to Fisher House.

Suddenly, a blur caught his eyes. Before he even recognized her, Lily threw herself from the last few steps into his arms, almost toppling him in the process.

"Oh, Jed, I was so worried." She clung to him tightly, burying her face in his chest. "You rushed out so quickly after Max told you that you were his great-grandson."

Jed loved everything about her at that moment—the strawberry scent rising off her warm skin, the tremor in her voice that told him how much she cared about him, the quick beating of her heart against his.

She raised a tear-stained face and met his eyes. "Jed?" she whispered. "Where have you been?"

"Let's go see Max," he said quietly. He put an arm around her and began up the long flight of stairs.

Harold greeted them. "Good evening, Mister Jed.

We've been concerned about you." He ushered them into the foyer. "Master Max is anxiously awaiting you both in the library."

The last hours had turned Jed's world upside down. Now, though, he was safe again, back at Fisher House. As they went to join Max, he finally relaxed.

Max greeted them as they entered. "Brandy?" he asked.

Jed nodded, hoping that might still the trembling in his legs that he'd just noticed. He and Lily joined his great-grandfather by the fire, while Harold poured out a drink for the men. He brought coffee for Lily.

"Drink up," Max encouraged him. "We need to clear up the mess of the past."

"And the future?" Jed questioned before he downed the drink. He settled back in the chair and steepled his fingers. He needed to let them know what had transpired. Lily placed a hand on his arm and squeezed reassuringly.

"Mac met me earlier on my way out of Fisher House." He looked steadily at Max. "Seems my twin brother decided to help himself to all the money in my bank accounts."

Max shook his head in disgust. "That boy was rotten from the get-go. I fear he learned his lack of morals from his father. You seemed to have taken your good sense and manners from Cara Lee."

The unexpected words hit Jed hard. Without warning, tears stung his eyes. Suddenly, all the hate that had snarled inside him unwound. He wiped at the tears that slid down his cheeks, embarrassed at their release.

His great-grandfather leaned over and patted his knee. "Would you like to hear about your mother, Jed?"

He nodded, the raging loneliness he'd fought his entire life filling him with the desire to learn more about the woman who died giving life to him.

"Ah, Cara Lee. Dainty thing. Stood just over five feet. Round blue eyes like you'd find in a China doll. Smooth, porcelain skin, and cheeks that flushed bright red at the least little bit of attention. Hair the color of sun on wheat that fell to her waist. Couldn't have been more than seventeen when I first set eyes on her."

Max took a sip of the amber liquid and replaced it on the table. "She radiated goodness and innocence. She absolutely adored Gordon. At least, she did when we met. I only saw her twice before they left New York so Gordon could chase his dream of fame on the stage. I don't know how things were between them in the end."

"But it didn't matter, did it? He left her during childbirth. Took away her son and left her to die." Jed heard his bitterness echoed in the words. Lily slipped her hand around his in a show of comfort.

"Yes. Gordon was always selfish and cruel. It appears even I didn't know to what lengths he might go." Max looked at him sadly. "If it helps ease you in any way, he's a total drunk. Gordon's guilt at what he did may have caused it. He's been muddled ever since Cara Lee's death."

"Where is he now?"

"In San Francisco, but he looks very little like the man pictured in the locket. Gordon's is a life gone to waste."

"I want to meet him."

Max gazed intently at him. "Would it really accomplish anything? You have a full life now, Jed. Do you need him—or do you just want to vent your hate upon him?"

He thought a moment. It was not that he wanted a father. He'd done fine without one all these years. If he could have his curiosity appeased, he would settle for that, but he doubted Gordon would shoot straight with him. The man had lied and covered those lies for many years.

"I guess not." He hesitated a moment but decided to press on. "What can you tell me about my twin brother?"

Max rubbed his eyes wearily. "I gave him too much. Cal expected the world would fall at his feet and give him whatever he wanted because of his good looks. He's a rude and arrogant man. It all came to a head years ago when Gordon couldn't control him anymore and let a gambler named Simon Morgan take Cal under his wing. What a mistake."

Jed knew Morgan had been involved. "You said you'd banned him from Fisher House."

Max nodded. "Not long ago, Cal showed up after years of no contact. I had no idea where the boy was all that time. Came to me wanting money for some cockamamie scheme. When I refused, he became belligerent. Threatened me. I knew then that I'd finally had enough.

"There's no love lost between us. I ordered him out. Poor Lily had come for a visit and heard us arguing. I'd never shared with her or Lilian anything about my past or the sorry family I'd produced. They're not something I'm proud of, you know."

"And Lily met Cal?"

"Briefly, in the hallway," Lily inserted, her nose wrinkling in disgust.

Max chuckled. "I felt I had to explain to her, so I did. In fact, she thought *you* were Cal when you showed up with the deed to Lucky Lil's. Apparently, the few words they exchanged previously weren't pleasant. When she thought Cal was the new owner, Lily was furious."

Jed tried to remember the night he showed up with the deed to Lucky Lil's. Lily had been hostile. He'd written it off to her having lost control of her own house, not animosity directed solely at him.

"My Lily swallowed her pride and asked me for a loan so she could buy back the place. I agreed but you refused to sell. She complained to me about all the changes, too.

"Yet," Max said, his gaze level and steady, "she never once told me it was my great-grandson who'd bought the house. She figured out you were two different men."

Lily nodded. "It became clear as mud to me, but I didn't share what I knew with Max. If I had told him of the strong resemblance, he might have pieced things together."

Harold interrupted. "You could have knocked me over with a feather the day Mister Jed showed up with a letter from your mother, Miss Lily. I thought he was his brother at first. After he and Master Max spoke, though, we knew somehow there had to be two of them. We sent for Mister Gordon but he was of little help."

Jed turned to Max. "There's something unpleasant you need to know, Max. I told you before that Cal impersonated me at my bank. The police arrested him after he withdrew most everything in my account, as well as the items in my safety deposit box. Mac McRidge happened to be in the bank and spoke with him."

Max sat up straight. "Of course, Mac knew the minute he spoke to Cal. You two are different as night and day. It wouldn't take a smart attorney to figure that out."

"Before Mac could act on his suspicions, a bank clerk confronted him, since he'd overheard their conversation. Said it couldn't be Mr. Stone because he signed everything with his right hand. I'm left-handed. The same clerk commented to me before on how the both of us were southpaws.

"The clerk even pulled the signature card and showed Mac. The two signatures looked nothing alike. Mac had the clerk hold the impostor there and send for the police. He came directly to Fisher House looking for me, knowing I'd come back here after the funeral."

Max rubbed his temples, as if trying to assimilate all the information. "Cal has been taken into custody?"

He swallowed. "It's worse than forgery and theft. When the authorities searched Cal, not only did he have my property on him, but they found a wanted poster. Of him."

He stood and began to pace, the story tumbling out. "When I came West to California, I was arrested for murder, robbery, and rape. I swore to the sheriff I was innocent of these crimes. He gave me a wanted poster with my likeness on it."

Lily blurted out, "But it was Cal, wasn't it?"

"Yes. The name on the poster read Cal Hart. Still, I was tried and convicted and sentenced to hang. I escaped from jail and fled to San Francisco. I've lived in fear of being arrested again and wanted desperately to find the man from the poster."

He sat down again, exhausted from the swift turn

of events. "Little did I know I would find my own twin brother." He laid his head in his hands.

Max wheeled over to him. "Look at me, my boy."

Jed raised his gaze to Max's understanding one.

"Since my Geraldine died, I've wanted someone to share my life. Crenshaw, Gordon, and Cal were all terrible disappointments. They took after Geraldine's brother. He had a weakness, a sickness. No matter what I did, nothing worked." He took Jed's hand in his.

"You are my blood, Jed. Forget the past. Let us look to the future. Get to know one another. You have me and you have dearest Lily. She's been the light of my life. I would like nothing better than to see you united together.

"You had my approval for a match even before I was certain you were my great-grandson. You have it still."

His words moved Jed as nothing else. He clasped the old man's hand tightly and kissed the weathered cheek. Surprised at his action, he sat back in the chair.

Max looked pleased as punch. He told Jed, "It's been a long day for us all. Why don't you and Lily go home?"

Home. The word called to him sweetly. He rose and offered Lily his hand.

"We'll stop by tomorrow, Max. Who knows?" He grinned at Lily. "By the next time you see us, we may just be Mr. and Mrs. Stone." Lily blushed at his words.

Harold shook his head. "Don't deny us the pleasure of planning a wedding, Mister Jed."

He laughed. "Then you'll definitely see us tomorrow, Harold. I don't want to wait too long."

"Make it early, Mister Jed. A good number of arrangements will need to be made."

"As long as you can pull it together for the day after tomorrow, we'll be fine," he replied.

He thought of Lily's response to his kisses. They'd been from the heart. The passion that lay behind them had him ready for more. Much more. Lily wasn't experienced in the ways of love, but she had a sensual side to her, ready to bloom under the right man.

He still wanted to be that man for her. And the sooner, the better.

33

They arrived at Lucky Lil's a little before seven. The place was in total darkness. It hit Lily there was no trade tonight. Jed had given the girls the night off after this morning's funeral. She heard some talk among the girls about attending a show at the Adelphi or Alhambra since they so rarely had time off. She doubted any of them would be home.

It would be just her and Jed. She smiled.

They entered as Tommy chimed the hour. Silence blanketed the downstairs rooms. Jed lit a lamp and its warm glow spread across the foyer. She sat on a sofa and pulled off her gloves, tossing them behind her with abandon.

His eyebrows raised and he sat next to her, draping an arm about her shoulders. A sweet rush of love for this amazing man swam through her veins. He lifted a strand of her hair and rubbed the silky tress between his fingers. He stroked his thumb across her cheek. Instinctively, she turned toward it. As she gazed at him, she knew that despite the lingering sadness of her mother's death, today was the beginning of the rest of their lives. Together. Forever.

He pushed his hands into her hair and leaned

close to her. "I love you with all my heart, Lily Frontiere. I want to be with you always."

Jed pressed his mouth softly to hers. Her lips parted and his tongue glided slowly along the insides of her mouth. Her hands went to his chest and moved up its muscled expanse. His mouth grew more insistent on hers, his tongue more possessive with each stroke.

Gradually, he leaned her back onto the sofa, pressing hot kisses along her jaw. A fire ignited inside her, followed by a low drum cadence that spoke of some urgent, unfulfilled need burning inside her. When he touched her breast with his palm, the fire blazed higher. The heat of his hand radiated through her dress as he slowly massaged it.

"Touch me," she cried. She could sense his mouth turning upward in a smile as he kissed her neck.

"I am, Lily."

"No, I mean..." She could feel the blush rising up her neck. "I mean... without my gown."

He stilled. "Are you sure?" he asked, his voice so low she barely heard it.

Lily raised her hands to frame his face. "I've never been more certain of anything."

He placed his hands over hers, turning them to kiss each open palm. Hot shivers ran along her with each kiss. Then he pulled her to her feet and swept her into his arms, causing her heart to leap. He took the stairs slowly. With each step, another kiss quickened her pulse and confirmed his love to her.

They reached his room and he sat upon the bed, keeping her close to him, his arms around her. As he slipped each button through its hole, he kissed her, quick butterfly kisses on her cheeks, her eyes, her brow. He reached the last one, sliding the dress off her shoulders to her waist.

Lily moved to the edge of the bed and worked the dress over her hips, letting it pool at her feet. Jed wrapped his arms around her from behind, his lips trailing hot kisses along her nape and shoulders. He pushed aside the chemise and it, too, fell to her waist. His hands moved to her breasts, encircling them, stroking them, making an ache throb throughout her.

He moved aside to lay her across the bed again, his mouth going to her breast. The shock of his tongue against her nipple brought quick delight, and even more as he flicked it around and around. She took his head and held him closer to her, wanting even more of him. He suckled her until she almost screamed, the pleasure was so great.

Finally, he left her breasts and trailed a line of scorching kisses downward. He nuzzled her belly as the throb now centered between her legs, an insistent drumbeat pulsing stronger and stronger. Jed tenderly removed her chemise, petticoats, and stockings and lay down beside her, stroking her belly as he kissed her deeply.

His hand wandered to the inside of her thighs, smoothing the tender flesh in loving strokes. Lily thought she should be embarrassed at such familiarity, but it fled as he kissed her senseless.

Then he touched her most private of places. His caresses became more intimate while the throbbing raged out of control.

He pushed a finger slowly into her. She arched her back instinctively and moaned softly. When he repeated the motion, she met him without hesitation. He continued stroking her with his fingers as he unbuttoned his shirt and loosened his tie. Gradually he increased the speed and pressure until she writhed beneath his hand, mindless to all but that incredible sensation. She cried out her pleasure and somehow understood her body was ready for him.

Jed pulled away from her, unthreading his tie and slipping off his coat and shirt while she was still dazed. He lit a candle and as he unbuttoned his pants, she drank in the perfection of his body. He was flawless, magnificent in every way.

And he was hers.

Rejoining her on the bed, he kissed her soundly, intimately touching her again. "I hope you want me as much as I want you," he told her, his voice husky and low, causing shivers of pleasures to ripple through her.

"I'll always want you," she told him softly.

He looked at her tenderly. "I've never wanted a woman more than you, Lily. But I know that's because I've never been in love. Until now. With you."

He kissed her deeply and entered her quickly. She flinched at the unexpected, sharp pain and a small whimper escaped her lips.

"It's all right, love. It only hurts once. And never again. The rest will be magic. I promise."

She saw the truth in his eyes and knew she would always trust whatever Jed told her.

Gradually, he began to move within her.

Lily clung to his shoulders, wrapping her arms tightly around his neck. His bare chest was hard and masculine, the hair tickling her breasts, teasing her along the way. The throbbing that had become such a part of her intensified, as the fire he began now blazed out of control. With each thrust she met him, her hips raising without thought, his mouth hard on hers.

Then waves of pleasure erupted, carrying her to a place she'd never known existed, never dreamed of going because she hadn't known it was there. She cried out as Jed did the same and they clung to one another, spent. As he lay atop her, she rejoiced in his hard body against her soft one, his heart racing as fast as hers.

He brushed soft kisses along her temple and in her hair before he rolled to his side, taking her along with him. They lay in each others' arms, drowsy, flush with love. Her worries of not knowing what to do with a man were all for naught. She enjoyed every minute of their coupling, and now knew she was meant to love one man—Jed Stone.

After some minutes, Lily felt her body begin to cool slightly. Jed reached down and brought the covers over them, but continued to cradle her in his arms.

"I don't ever want to let you go," he murmured against her hair.

"Then don't," she told him in a whisper.

34

Simon slipped on his hat and hurried down the steps of the police station. He reeked of stale liquor and his own fear. He needed a drink and turned toward the Square, ready to stop at the first place he crossed. He'd spent the last seven hours in custody before the police ascertained he hadn't killed Gordon Fisher.

Despite his protests, they locked him away with men no better than vermin. The holding cell crawled with cockroaches and the freshly-arrested, drunk on cheap alcohol and the readily-available opium.

As a man crudely propositioned him, an overweight sergeant bellowed out Simon's name. He scrambled to the unlocked cell door. He gave a brief interview again regarding Gordon's state of mind, the depression and drinking, the unrest shown in recent days. He didn't provide any specifics, stating although he and Fisher were friends, the man had been very private in his affairs.

But Simon knew good, old-fashioned guilt—with a splash of regret mixed in—killed Gordon Fisher. Jed Stone was Gordon's son, the twin to Cal. And the Lucky Lil's owner had no idea he was Maximilian

Fisher's great-grandson and heir. The millionaire had probably figured it out by now. He was a cagey old bird, according to Gordon.

But would Max tell his great-grandson they were family?

Simon counted on it. He'd finally remembered where he'd encountered the elusive Jed Stone before, despite the fact Stone went by a different name then. It bothered him for weeks, nagging him like a bad head cold. Stone was the young riverboat gambler who accused him of cheating over a year ago. Of course, Simon *was* cheating. He rarely had a poker hand good enough to win. Rather than fold and cut his losses, he always tried to help his hand along.

Stone pulled him from the lounge and told him to straighten up his act or he'd expose him. Simon knew the ship's captain was ornery enough to put him off at the next port or maybe simply toss him into the Mississippi.

He had agreed to play in a more honorable fashion. It had cost him a fortune. The game went from incredibly competitive to overwhelmingly intense and lasted close to thirty hours.

At the end, he lost literally everything he had, thousands he'd claimed through bilking and blackmail and cheating at cards. He was totally ruined. But he made sure he paid the young arrogant bastard back. Simon hit him in his weakest spot, then ran like hell out of New Orleans.

He was amazed how different Stone looked now. He'd changed his center part to a side one and had grown a thick mustache, aging him by several years. The alterations radically transformed his appearance, so much that Simon hadn't recognized Stone all these months later.

Except for those ice-blue eyes. It was Stone's eyes that always bothered him. And now he remembered it all.

Funny how the changes the whorehouse owner made turned him into Cal's spitting image. There was a passing resemblance before, but now with his altered appearance, the likeness was uncanny. Stone turning up in San Francisco was no coincidence. Especially since he'd met Simon socially and hadn't claimed a previous acquaintance. He knew the man was bent on revenge. Stone was a sly one, playing his cards close to the vest. Stone hadn't given any inkling of his plans. But Simon felt in his bones that Jed Stone was gunning for him.

He would have to hit him in his soft spot again.

Lily.

Simon had hoped to offer Lily Frontiere sanctuary after her mother's death. The funeral let him know that she and Stone had a close bond. Now all he had to do was put two and two together in order to make the killing of a lifetime. The girl was the key to everything.

Even if the old man hadn't told Stone about them being blood kin, Max would pay a handsome sum for Lily's return. The girl was like a granddaughter to him. Stone would pressure the old man to get his lady love back.

So, how to do it?

Simon was desperate enough to act on the crazy scheme. With less than a hundred dollars to his name and bills run up all over town, he couldn't even return to his hotel. He already owed them two months' back rent. They would probably charge him for removing Gordon's body and blood from the room.

He would get a meal in him and a drink. Then he'd put his plan into action.

JED AWOKE to Lily's curves molded against his chest. He'd never wanted a woman staying overnight in his bed before, but Lily was no ordinary woman. Despite her inexperience, she proved to be full of passion. The heat of desire flickered within him. He reached out and smoothed her hair.

She stirred, snuggling closer to him. Jed's arms went around her automatically, drawing her close. He held a true miracle in his arms, one who gave him a reason to be a better man. Maybe he should let go of his bitterness toward Simon Morgan, and look to his future with this woman instead.

Lily murmured something into his neck. He kissed the top of her head, content to have her rest in his arms all day and into the night.

She tilted back her head to look at him, a sweet smile on her face. "Good morning," she whispered.

Just the lilt of her voice made him go hard. He touched his mouth lightly to hers in reply.

"This is a nice way to wake up." Her eyes gleamed with mischief. "And I can think of something even nicer."

Her hand looped around his neck and pulled his lips back to hers. The kiss started slow, full of heat and honey. Lily was in full control. Jed let her take command. Obviously, she was a fast learner because she aroused a hunger in him more quickly than he'd ever known.

He rolled them over and entered her slowly. He made love to her gently, aware that she might be tender after last night. He'd always satisfied women before, but he'd done it without much thought. Now each kiss, each stroke, was done with her pleasure in mind. He listened for her reactions, both with his ears and his body, sensitive to every move she made.

When he was spent, he cuddled with her in his arms, moved by the experience. Louis once told Jed that when he found the right woman, it would be like heaven raining tears upon their coupling.

The Frenchman had been right.

"Lily."

She loved how husky his voice seemed just now, low and tender. "Yes?"

"I know Lilian just passed, but I want us married. I was serious last night."

Her mother never stood on formalities. If Lily voiced they should wait a year for the mourning period to be completed, Lilian would probably rise from her grave and forbid it.

"I know *Maman* would want us to be happy. If you want, I'll marry you today."

He chuckled. "I don't know if that'll do. Harold mentioned something about planning a wedding."

She giggled. "Harold would make a lovely bridesmaid."

Jed kissed her soundly. "You are a babbling fool." He kissed her again, softly, and her bones melted at his touch.

He grew serious. "I spoke to Mac about some investments. Some business ventures. Real estate and whatnot. I want to give you a life away from the house, Lily."

She looked at him questioningly. "Are you going to sell Lucky Lil's?"

"I know this is no life for us as a couple. For raising

a family."

Her insides quivered in excitement. She'd always dreamed of a place away from the house—its odd hours, the lack of privacy, the business always greedily sucking the marrow from their lives.

"So, will you sell?"

"It's ours to sell, love. Not mine. I'll do whatever you wish, but I think we should close shop for good. There'll never be anyone like Lil again. Let Lucky Lil's go down as a fond place in people's memories."

She realized what a thoughtful gesture that would be. It would also cost Jed a good deal of money to give up such a lucrative trade. The house was on good real estate. He could auction it and the services of the girls to the highest bidder and make a nice sum.

Instead, he gave her the choice. It would be hard to see everyone go, but somehow she ventured Jed would see everyone taken care of before he shut down the place.

She wrapped her arms around him. "I think that is very sweet of you, Jed Stone."

He playfully bit her earlobe. "Not nearly as sweet as you." He kissed her cheek and then climbed out of bed. "I think I'll go tell Max that there has to be a wedding at Fisher House by tomorrow. Surely Harold can pull together some flowers and music with a day's notice. I'll bet Max has a judge that can come to the house on short notice."

She grinned. "I already have a dress to wear, but I do think I should buy a new hat."

"Women," Jed proclaimed. He picked up her chemise from the floor and pulled it over her head. "It's only mid-morning and I know none of the girls will be up, but I do think you should get dressed before heading out to shop."

He helped her into her gown and buttoned it up as she protested. "I'll just have to take it off and put on a fresh one. It's a mass of wrinkles."

"Let's keep up appearances. Just for today."

She returned to her mother's room, a little sad despite the happiness in her heart. She brushed out her hair and washed before she donned a new gown. She sensed rather than heard Jed leave, and went to the window to see him walking jauntily down the sidewalk, whistling as he went. He turned to wave at her as if he'd known she'd be watching him.

Lily blew him a kiss, which he caught and slipped into his pocket. She couldn't believe her good luck. She removed the dress from her wardrobe that she intended for her wedding. The pale pink satin had a rounded neck and tight bodice that skimmed her body in perfection. It was the last dress she'd had made in Paris and she'd never worn it before. After the fiasco with Pierre, she hadn't attended any more balls in the brief time they remained in Paris.

Still, Lily loved the dress. It would make a wonderful wedding gown—as long as she had the right hat to accompany it. A quick trip to Annie Spencer's shop would be the answer. Annie always had the right accessory—a fashionable hat, a whimsical fan, slender gloves in a pastel shade. Lily knew she would find what she was looking for.

She slipped down the side staircase, intending to see if Ben could drive her. The day was lovely, though, so she decided to walk. The shop was less than half a mile and her mood so light, she might actually float most of the way.

Lily turned to go up the street and stopped dead in her tracks.

Simon Morgan stood in her way.

35

"Why, good morning, Lily. Don't you look especially lovely today?"

Lily gathered her shawl about her tightly. Simon Morgan always made her nervous. Here they were on a street in broad daylight and she still felt jumpy in his presence.

"I am so sorry about Lilian's passing. She was a dear soul."

"Thank you," she said curtly. "If you'll excuse me, I have business with Annie Spencer to attend to."

"Oh, I don't mean to keep you, my dear. I was just headed up to the house to see Jed."

She frowned. Why would Simon wish to speak with Jed? "He's not home at the moment. Could I give him a message?"

Simon looked disappointed. "I'm sorry to hear that. It's just as well I dashed off a note to him in case I didn't catch him. It's in regard to some unfinished business."

He withdrew an envelope from his coat pocket. "Perhaps you could leave this where he'll find it the minute he arrives home?"

She took the offered letter. "Yes, I'll see that he gets

it. Good day." She hurried back inside the house, eager to escape the eyes that undressed her with each glance.

As she turned the sealed envelope in her hands, a dozen questions flooding her mind. Jed had asked several questions about Simon when he first arrived in town. She guessed Simon had cheated Jed at cards. She doubted they had any dealings to speak of, certainly not of a personal nature, as Simon would like her to believe.

More than anything, Lily wished to read the letter. Her curiosity was overwhelming. Yet Jed would share with her anything Simon had to say. For all she knew, he might be offering to take Lucky Lil's off Jed's hands with Lilian's death. Simon had never been shy about letting it be known how badly he wanted to run the house.

She glanced out the front window, searching the walkway for any sight of Simon. Relief washed over her when she didn't spy him. She placed the letter on the front table where mail was deposited and decided to set out for Annie's shop again.

The earlier sunshine hid behind a set of clouds that had blown in. She hesitated a moment, almost turning back to find Ben, then decided that an encounter with Simon Morgan wouldn't spoil her hat-shopping expedition. She would do her business and return home as soon as she could. Perhaps by then Jed would be waiting for her. She had wicked thoughts of what they might do to pass the time until tomorrow's vows.

As she passed a group of buildings closely set together, a shiver ran along her spine. She shrugged it off. No thoughts of Simon would ruin her good mood. She crossed alongside a narrow alley between the buildings when a hissing cat ran out in front of her, frightening her.

She paused to collect herself and was roughly grabbed from behind, forced into the alleyway by strong hands pulling her along. She opened her mouth to scream when a sweet, sickly smell surrounded her. Something clung to her nose and mouth. She struggled as her head began to swim. It was as if she were being dragged down into a dark pool.

All went black.

JED HURRIED FROM HIS CAB, eager to reach Mac's office. He was pleased at the quick arrangements Max and Harold had thrown together. As he left, the pair had been thick as thieves, planning a noon wedding at Fisher House to be followed by a luncheon catered by Margaret. Max reiterated how happy he was at their plans.

Jed entered the law office and was greeted by Mac himself in the reception room.

"Come on in, Jed. Coffee?"

"No, thanks. Any news on Cal Fisher?"

They sat in the leather chairs that faced Mac's desk. The attorney picked up a newspaper and hesitated a moment before setting it down.

"The police telegraphed three different states to verify the crimes listed on the wanted poster. All are willing to have Cal extradited to stand trial for the criminal acts cited on the handbill."

Mac shook his head. "That young man will surely hang."

Jed thought how close he came to hanging for

Cal's crimes. He decided to keep quiet about that. He had the future to look forward to, Lily at his side.

"Let's turn to more pleasant thoughts, Mac. Lily and I are getting married tomorrow."

His friend broke into a wide smile. "That's wonderful news, Jed."

"We'd like you and Sylvia to stand up for us if you would. It'll be at Fisher House tomorrow at noon. Max is arranging for a Judge Barrett to perform the ceremony."

"We'd be honored." Mac called in his secretary. "Send a messenger to Mrs. McRidge that we'll be attending a wedding tomorrow at noon. And clear my calendar for that afternoon, as well."

As the secretary left, Mac confided, "Women like to have advance notice about these things. You'll learn. Sylvia will probably need a new hat and gloves for the occasion."

"Where do you think Lily is right now?"

The two men enjoyed a laugh, Mac wiping his eyes with the back of his hand. "So, do you think you'll stay in San Francisco?"

Jed grew contemplative. "I'm not sure. The first thing to do is close Lucky Lil's. It wouldn't be the same without Lil herself running the place. I think it's best if that chapter of Lily's life ends here and now."

Mac nodded in approval. "I agree. Lil could never be replaced and a change of scenery will be good for Lily."

"My thoughts exactly. I don't know how comfortable or accepted Lily would be here in polite society. Of course, I'm still interested in the real estate dealings we discussed."

"I have contacts in Denver and St. Louis. Sylvia's family comes from Philadelphia. Think about any of those places and I could set you up with the right people."

"We will, Mac. Thanks for your support." He stood. "I really want to get back home now."

"Jed." Mac paused, a shadow crossing his face. An uneasy feeling trickled through Jed, his gambler's instinct honing in.

"You said you'd been to Max's this morning. Did either of you read this morning's paper?"

"No. I got there early. Max had it open next to his breakfast tray but he didn't mention seeing anything of importance. Why?"

Mac picked up the newspaper from his desk. It was folded back about halfway through a section. "It's Gordon."

Jed's stomach rolled over. He took the paper from Mac's hand and located the article. He skimmed it quickly and then sat while he read it through more slowly.

"I assume the police will be contacting Max. I think I'll head over there now," Mac said.

A dull ache filled him. The story said the wound was self-inflicted. He wondered if Gordon finally pieced the story together like the rest of them. Was he depressed—or had he simply been too much of a coward to face the music?

Jed would never know.

Mac placed a hand on his shoulder. "Don't let this change your plans with Lily tomorrow. I'm sure Max will hold a memorial service later in the week. If I were you, I wouldn't feel any obligation to attend."

"I'll think about it."

He didn't want this small cloud on the horizon to dim the bright future that was his for the taking. He would dispel any demons and make sweet love to Lily all afternoon. That would keep the world at bay.

He caught a cab back to Lucky Lil's, his mood improving as he entered the doorway. Gertie was coming down the stairs. As she saw him, she turned and started back up.

"Gertie. I need to see you and Sarah Jane in the upstairs parlor. Now."

She looked over her shoulder defiantly, but he knew she'd answer the summons. Gertie was one of the best workers in the house.

Jed gave it five minutes before he ascended the stairs. Both women waited nervously on a sofa. Gertie tossed him an angry glance. Sarah Jane sat wringing her hands, her eyes focused on her lap.

He shut the door and took a seat directly across from them.

"I need to explain something to you both, in private." He hesitated and then decided to plunge ahead.

"I have a twin brother that, until yesterday, I was totally unaware existed."

Both women looked at him in wonder. He saw understanding dawn in Gertie's eyes first.

"I visited Lucky Lil's and was fortunate enough to have Gertie entertain me that evening. I did not enter the house again until I won the deed in a card game."

Gertie took Sarah Jane's hand in hers. "Then you mean the devil who tortured Sarah Jane wasn't you."

"That's right. I never understood why Sarah Jane was so frightened of me, or why you, Gertie, acted the way you did. I now know it was my brother Cal who did the damage. I am so sorry for whatever he did to you."

Sarah Jane blinked back tears. She tried to speak

but nothing came out. Gertie wrapped a friendly arm about her.

Finally, Sarah Jane managed, "Will he be coming back?"

"No," Jed reassured her. "He was arrested yesterday for impersonating me. The authorities found he has a long list of crimes he committed in other states. I'd say we've seen the last of Cal Fisher."

He continued. "I do have something I want to share with you both. I'll be talking to the other girls at dinner about it. I'm shutting down Lucky Lil's."

Sarah Jane burst into tears. "I won't have nowhere to go. This has been the best place to me. Ever."

Gertie comforted her friend, but Jed saw that she also had tears in her eyes. He regretted these two young girls had fallen into such a life. Then an idea came to him.

"I want to make sure everyone has a place to go before we close for good, but I may have a job for the two of you." He wondered how they would take his offer.

"Lily and I are getting married tomorrow. We don't know where we'll go, but we'll need a couple of people to run our household. Would you consider working for us?"

The two looked at each other in surprise. "You mean we'd do your cleaning and dusting and stuff?" Gertie asked.

"Yes," he replied. "I'm sorry. I guess you feel that's beneath you."

"No, Mr. Stone. Sarah Jane and I'd do anything to leave the life." Gertie flushed. "Not that Madam Lil and you ain't been good to us. But we both kinda fell into this. We didn't have a way to leave. I mean, what do you tell a prospective employer in a fancy house? That you've been spreading your legs at the best place in town? With my luck, I'd have wound up looking for work at the house of a former client."

"So, you would be interested?"

Sarah Jane nodded. "I would. I used to do all the cooking and cleaning before my mama died. I was good with babies, too. Maybe if you and Miss Lily have a baby, I could help take care of her. Or him." She gave him a shy smile.

Jed returned her smile. "Then it's settled. I wish I could take in all the girls but I can't. Let's keep this between us for now. And if you change your minds, I'll understand."

"You kidding?" Gertie asked. "This is an answered prayer, Mr. Stone." She pulled Sarah Jane to her feet. Both girls thanked him again and left the room, their steps lighthearted. It gave him a good feeling.

He left and went to Lily's room. He was disappointed she wasn't there. He walked down the hallway to his room, sure he'd find her. Still, no Lily.

"How long does it take to buy a damn hat?"

Restless, he wandered back downstairs to check the morning's post. He picked up the stack and flipped through it. The letter on bottom got his attention. Only his name was scrawled across the envelope, no address evident. He wondered if it had been hand-delivered while he was out.

He tore it open and removed the single sheet of paper inside. As he read, his temples began to pound fiercely.

"Dear God," he muttered and shoved it deep into his pocket before flying out the door.

CHAPTER36

Lily swallowed. *Why was her mouth so dry?* She fought to open her eyes but a heavy weight had settled upon her lids. She decided to leave them closed for now. Her head ached painfully, as if she'd had too much to drink. A flash of pain flickered across her temple, forcing her eyes open.

The room was dark and dank. A smell like rotten eggs permeated the air. She started to push back a lock of hair but found she couldn't. What was wrong?

A door slammed in the distance. A baby started crying. She heard a woman's voice curse loudly, answered by a man's rougher reply. The walls were paper-thin.

Where was she?

She tried to move her hands again and realized they were tightly restrained behind her. She tried to pull her wrists apart, but whatever bound them was snug. She had no sensation as she wiggled her fingers.

Panic set in. She was strapped to a chair, her feet apart and bound to the chair's legs. Whoever placed her here wanted to be sure she would remain. Through a fog, Lily remembered her trip to Annie Spencer's. But, she'd never arrived there.

Simon.

A shudder ran through her. She thought she would be sick as she caught a whiff of the smell coming from her collar. It was faintly medicinal and caused her throat to catch. It must have knocked her senseless before.

A rat appeared from the shadows, studying her carefully. Lily tensed, fearful of being bitten but helpless to move. The rodent might climb up her skirts. She glared back at it, willing the rodent to go away.

As it began to inch more closely to her, the door scraped suddenly. The rat scampered across the room and out of sight. A bigger rat entered the room. Simon closed the door and lit a small kerosene lamp.

"Well, my dear, I see that you are awake."

"Are you mad?"

Simon flashed a wicked grin. "Mad as in angry—or mad as in insane?" He shrugged. "Probably a little of both."

He sat on the lumpy bed, the only furniture besides the chair in the small room.

She licked her parched lips nervously. "Why am I here?"

"You are, quite simply, my ticket to freedom. I'm down on my luck and need some quick cash. A lot of it. You, my dear, will guarantee me a new and prosperous future."

"I don't understand."

"You've been kidnapped, Lily. Your Mr. Stone is probably showing the ransom letter to his dear great-grandfather now. Maximilian Fisher should be willing to part with some of his vast fortune to see you returned."

Kidnapped? He was holding her for money?

"You're crazy," Lily blurted out. "You won't get away with this."

He examined his nails carefully. "Oh, Lily, if you only knew what I have gotten away with in the past. Theft here and there, a little blackmail thrown in, simply an array of misdeeds. Why, I even snookered Jed Stone."

"Jed?" She hated how faint her voice sounded. She needed to sound stronger, be braver. "What did you try to pull on Jed?"

"He had the audacity to call me out as a cheat."

Lily looked at him disdainfully. "You *are* a cheat of the worst kind."

He waved away her accusation. "That's beside the point. Gamblers should respect a better code of conduct when amongst their own."

"Honor among thieves?"

Simon smiled. "*Touché*. After he threatened to expose me and we returned to our table, Mr. Stone broke me during the longest game I've ever sat in. He and his friend, Louis. Fortunately, Louis was caught soon after in a compromising position with a dead woman, and no recollection of how he killed her."

She read it in his face. "*You* killed her."

"Clever Lily. Maybe you do have some of Lil's street smarts after all. Yes, I framed Jed's bosom buddy. A Frenchman who drank too much and passed out when he did. I told Stone I could alibi Louis. The chit was a mere dance hall girl. The police would've washed their hands of the matter."

"But you didn't, did you?"

The shadows flickering along Simon's face revealed the evil within him. "I told Stone I would exonerate his good friend. For a price. The exact amount he walked away with in the card game. The fool never hesitated, so willing to sacrifice money for friendship.

"Unfortunately for his jailed companion, I remembered an out of town engagement and left immediately for the West coast after our little transaction."

Lily could see it all—Jed proclaiming his friend's innocence, no money, no alibi, Simon vanished. A trial and execution. No wonder he'd come after Simon. Then something occurred to her.

"Why didn't you know him? Surely, you realized he'd come for revenge?"

"He changed his name. Altered his appearance. I didn't recognize him except for his eyes. It took a good while before I figured it out. I'd known his brother years ago when he was quite young. Once I realized there were two of them, it took a little time and thought, but I made the connection.

"That's where you come in. Maximilian Fisher will pay a hefty sum to see you returned unharmed. With his own great-grandson at his elbow, begging him to act, it's a done deal. I'll get the money and never return to San Francisco again."

"How? How will you get the money?"

"I'm going to have Jed Stone bring it to me." He gave her an urbane smile. "Then I'm going to kill him."

Jed went straight to Fisher House. When Harold answered his knock, he almost knocked the butler down.

"Is Mac still here?"

"Why, yes, Mister Jed. He and Master Max—"

"Come on," Jed commanded and raced up the

stairs. He pushed through the library doors, Harold steps behind him.

Before they could greet him, he threw out, "Lily's been taken. Kidnapped. Simon Morgan is behind it."

Both men wore stunned expressions. Mac recovered first. "How do you know?"

Jed yanked the letter from his pocket and handed it to Mac. The lawyer read it and passed it to Max. Harold hovered over his employer's shoulder.

Mac frowned. "Where was this?"

"Waiting for me at Lucky Lil's with the rest of the mail. It had to have been hand-delivered, though. No address on the envelope. Only my name."

Max cleared his throat. "Why Simon Morgan? The note is unsigned."

He collapsed onto a chair. "I came to California to punish him. He cost me everything I owned and the life of my dearest friend. I also know his writing. I've received a letter from him before. It's not a script easy to forget."

"But... why Lily?" Max's voice broke. Jed watched his great-grandfather's trembling hands and labored breathing, realizing how helpless the older man seemed at that moment.

He set his jaw. "She's my weakest point. Morgan hit me once before the same way. And probably," he looked at Max, "because he's figured out our connection. I saw him with Gordon before. Again with Cal at Lil's funeral. If I can't pay his demand, he would guess I would come to you."

"We can't contact the police," Mac interrupted. "The threat was obvious what he would do to Lily if we did. Will you let me speak to Walker Thompson?"

Jed remembered the private investigator's discretion. "Do it. I'm going to see Cal. Meet me back here."

He laid a hand on Max's shoulder. The millionaire looked every one of his ninety years. "We'll get her back, Max. She means the world to me. Morgan won't win again."

Jed returned to his waiting cab and ordered it downtown to the police station where Cal was being held. He asked for Detective Robinson, the arresting officer, at the desk. He hoped he could pull this off.

The husky detective greeted him. "What can I do for you, Mr. Stone? Got any other brothers I need to lock up?" he asked jokingly.

He calmed himself, not wanting his nervousness to show. *Play it like a poker game*, he told himself.

"No, sir, but could I speak to the one you have in custody?"

Robinson looked puzzled. "Why? From what you told me in our interview, it's not like you're on friendly terms."

He shrugged. "I need to tell him about our father. I've just heard myself." He briefly explained about Gordon's suicide yesterday.

Detective Robinson whistled. "You don't say? We had a Simon Morgan in here, questioning him about it all. Mr. Fisher killed himself in Mr. Morgan's hotel room. I guess it is a small world."

Jed knew Simon had taken Lily elsewhere. He was counting on Cal telling him. If he could get his twin to talk.

"Can we have a few minutes alone?"

The policeman nodded. "Sure thing, Mr. Stone. He's not due to be transferred out for another couple of hours."

"Thank you."

He led Jed to a small room with a minimum of furniture. Jed assumed those arrested were interrogated or met with their attorneys here. After several minutes they brought in Cal, hands cuffed and leg irons on.

"Sit right here, Fisher. Your brother's got some news for you." Robinson left, closing the door behind him.

Cal glared at him. "What the hell do you want now?"

"Gordon's dead."

His brother went white. "Dead?" he echoed.

"He shot himself."

Cal scratched his head. "If that don't beat all." He studied Jed for a moment. "The way's paved clear now, ain't it, little brother? Dear old Daddy dead. Me with one foot in the grave. Did you come here to gloat? All those Fisher millions lined up waiting to be spent by you once Max kicks the bucket."

Jed could have all the money in the world but without Lily, it would mean nothing.

"I'm not interested in Max's money. I want to find Simon Morgan."

His twin looked dazed. "Simon? What do you want with him? He's been a sorry-ass friend to my daddy and me."

"I just want to talk to him. That's all."

Cal thrust out his chin. "Talk all you like. I don't give a rat's ass. I'm stuck in here and not doing you or nobody any favors. You got your good looks, the best whorehouse in town, and the sweetest piece of meat this side of the Mississippi. You don't get squat from me."

"Even if you knew Lily were in trouble?" It was a card he had to chance playing. He didn't think Cal would help him but he had to try.

"What do you mean, trouble?" Cal's eyes lit up. "You mean the sweet thing threw you over for Simon?"

He started laughing. "That's funny. I never figured it out. The ladies always wanted a piece of Simon. Me? I never saw it."

Jed decided he wouldn't clarify the conclusion Cal jumped to. "Where might I find them?"

Cal chuckled. "That might be fun, throwing a little misfortune Simon's way. Sure. Why the hell not?" He stretched out his legs straight in front of him.

"If he's not at his hotel, he's at my daddy's place. Or if he really wanted to lay low, he'll head over to my room on Crawford. Not too fancy a place." Cal snickered. "Miss Lily might even feel the bedbugs biting there."

Jed stood. "What's the address?"

Cal smiled widely. "You can figure that one out on your own."

36

Jed hurried from the police station. He handed the cabby another twenty for good faith, thankful the man had driven him all over and waited each time as he'd promised.

"Crawford Street," he said and climbed into the cab.

The driver squinted at him over his humped shoulder and shook his head. "I grew up near there, mister. It ain't for your likes. Nothing good comes outta Crawford Street."

He held his temper but his voice betrayed the emotion boiling beneath the surface. "It's life or death, man. Will you drive me or not?"

The driver pulled his cap lower over his eyes. "Sit back, sir. We'll be there quick as I can." He snapped the reins and the horses took off at a brisk clip.

Jed leaned back, his thoughts a jumble. He'd found a father, although be it a sorry one, only to lose him before they could speak. He'd discovered a twin brother so full of hatred that he was better off never having spoken to him.

And he'd finally met up with love, only to be on the verge of losing her to a nightmare from his past.

He must find Lily. Even discovering that Max was his blood kin would be worthless without her beside him. If he didn't save Lily, he would lose himself to an abyss he could never climb from. He must rise above the hand he'd been dealt, a legacy of deceit and lies.

The carriage stopped and the driver turned around. "Crawford runs three blocks, sir. Didn't say exactly where you wanted to go."

"Do you know of any rooms for rent?"

The cabby screwed up his face in thought. "Just Old Man Goddard's place, up there. That's if'n he's still alive." He pointed to a shabby building of peeling paint.

Jed pulled out a roll of cash and peeled several bills off. He gave them to the driver.

"You remember the precinct we just left?"

The man nodded and flicked the toothpick from his mouth. "I'm to go back there?"

He nodded. "Get a Detective Robinson to come here with you in a hurry. Bring him personally. I'll be in there," he said, indicating the building the driver had pointed to.

Jed jumped from the cab and steeled himself for the confrontation that lay ahead.

"I'VE GOT to leave for awhile. I have a few things to arrange before you can be returned."

Simon's eyes caused Lily to doubt his words. If he did lure Jed here, she would be a witness to her fiancé's murder. She suspected the gambler would leave no loose ends behind.

He leaned over and ran a finger along her cheek and down her throat. Lily ceased breathing. The sensual gesture revolted her. She fought the terror that rose.

Simon spread his fingers wide along her throat, caressing her, a smile playing upon his cruel lips. His hand slipped lower and touched her breast, skimming the nipple. Lily immediately let out a scream. Simon quickly stifled it with his large hand. He pulled a wrinkled handkerchief from his pocket and wadded it into a ball before removing his hand and stuffing the cloth into her mouth.

"Not that anyone here would be interested in your cries, my dear. People on Crawford Street keep to themselves. I just don't want you to be a nuisance to the tenants in the building."

He tore a long strip from the dirty bed sheet, using it to secure the gag in her mouth. He ran his hand along her jaw and down to her breast again before he twisted the nipple roughly. Lily's protest came out muffled.

He leered at her as he rose. "It might take old Max and Jed a while to pull together that much cash." He leaned close, his breath sour. She fought the urge to turn away and stared at him, her courage beginning to ebb.

"I've always fancied you, Lily." He placed a hand upon her shoulder and squeezed hard. "Fancy Lily—a fancy lady. Maybe when I'm done with you, I'll sell you to one of the local bordellos. Add a little more cash to my stash."

He chuckled, an eerie sound that pierced her soul. "Maybe I'll even want Mr. Stone to watch while we have our fun."

Lily struggled to keep calm as the vile image played in her mind. She sat still as a mouse spied by a cat, willing herself not to be sick.

Simon doused the lantern and slipped out the door.

She'd die before allowing Simon Morgan to lay another finger on her. Lily looked around the darkened room for anything that might help her escape. She strained against the chair, seeing if she could move it and scooted it a little bit along the floor.

That small movement gave her a ray of hope.

JED APPROACHED THE BUILDING, praying it was the right place. His hand went automatically to his coat pocket where his pistol lay ready.

His gut said he would find his nemesis here. His gambler's sixth sense had kicked in. Everything moved in slow motion as he ascended the steps of the ramshackle building. He was attuned to the slightest noise as he entered.

Where first?

He studied the interior. It was late afternoon, the sun long hidden behind clouds. No windows were evident in the darkened hallway. His hunch said Lily would be upstairs. He went with it, slowly moving up the staircase, the hairs on the back of his neck standing at attention.

Loud voices mixed with softer ones. A hungry baby wailed in the distance. A slap popped flesh and a woman cried out. A door closed and someone started down the stairs. It was a small boy of five or six. He took one look at Jed and swore softly. Elmira would've blackened Jed's eye if he'd uttered such an epithet at that young age.

The boy eyed him. He came to a decision and

raced by Jed, awarding a swift kick to Jed's shin as he passed.

Jed howled his own curse before he realized the child must have had an unpleasant encounter with Cal.

He was definitely in the right place.

He moved silently up the stairs and turned at the landing, continuing his journey upward. A door opened. A young woman stepped into the hallway. When she realized someone was there, he saw the look of panic that crossed her face in the dim light.

"I'm not him," he said quietly, holding his hands out, away from his body. "It's my twin brother you know. I'm just here to find him. I don't want to hurt you."

He moved a step up but the girl, no more than fifteen, took one back. Jed saw her greasy hair, the tattered clothes and faded looks, despite her young years. Maybe an offer of money would buy the information he needed.

"I can pay you. I just need to find Cal Fisher's room." He withdrew his money clip and took a few bills from it. He placed the money three stairs ahead and then backed down two more.

He gestured toward it. "It's for you. All I need to know is which room is his."

The girl sized him up. Apparently, she didn't find him as much a threat as the young boy had. She scampered over and whipped the bills in her hand and down her dress front within three seconds. Her movements were smooth, much like the pickpocket she probably was.

She eased back toward her door. Before she disappeared inside, she pointed down the hall. "Last on the left." The door closed quietly. Jed heard a lock thrown into place.

Pay dirt.

He cautiously made his way to Cal's room. The stench of unwashed bodies, spoiled food, and alcohol mixed with rodent droppings. He had lived in many such places before the war. Louis had helped him to find a different way.

Lily would help him find a better one.

He placed an ear against the thin door, straining to hear Simon's movements. As thin as the walls were, he was surprised he couldn't hear the man's breathing.

Then he did hear a noise. A scraping sound, close to the door. Then a loud thump and a moan.

Jed broke through the door.

37

Lily lay on the floor, tied to a chair. Jed entered with gun raised, scanning the room cautiously. No Simon. He tucked the gun into his pocket and shut the door before pulling her and the chair upright.

Her tear-stained face had never looked sweeter. He untied the strip of cloth from behind her head and eased the dirty handkerchief from her parched lips. She gulped air.

"Slowly, sweetheart. Deep breaths." He had calmed injured soldiers at the front, young boys so fearful they gasped for air. He gave the same advice to those shot. "Breathe in, breathe out. You're fine. I'm here now."

Fresh tears flooded her eyes. She tried to speak but his lips silenced her effort. He gave her a chaste kiss, one to quieten yet reassure her. Jed cradled her face.

"I'm going to loosen these restraints, Lily. Keep still for me."

She nodded and gave him a weak smile. He pulled out his pocketknife and leaned around her to cut the bonds. Her strawberry scent mingled with something medicinal. Probably whatever Morgan used to render her unconscious and get her here.

Fresh anger welled inside him. Jed thought of what Simon Morgan did to poor Sherry, how he knew it had been Simon who'd killed the girl and blamed it on Louis. To think Lily... no, he wouldn't think of it. He couldn't.

He sliced through the tightly coiled rope. It fell to the floor. He began to massage Lily's wrists. She gave a little cry of pain. Her circulation had been cut off.

"It'll sting for a while but you'll be all right." He started to bend to free her feet, when she threw her arms around him tightly.

He slipped his arms about her waist and brought her close. He rubbed her back tenderly and pulled away just enough for his mouth to meet hers.

This time it was no modest kiss. As he sought her lips with his own, Jed willed new life and courage into Lily. He kissed her deeply, hungrily, searching for answers that he didn't know if she could give him.

Lily returned Jed's kiss greedily, her tongue mating with his, becoming entwined as one. She wanted him as close as he could get but it still wasn't enough. She needed him deep inside her so she would know she was his, alive in his arms, free of Simon.

"Simon," she gasped into his mouth, pulling away, the terror coursing through her veins. "We have to get out of here! He'll come back. He's going to kill you. He..."

Jed took her hands in his and gave her that Jed smile, that brilliant, sunshine smile. She knew in that moment all was well.

He released her hands and cut the rope that bound her ankles and helped her to stand. Her knees gave out and she collapsed against him.

"I'm fine, I'll be fine," she murmured. It was important to her to stand on her own and she did. She felt some small victory within her.

More calmly, she told Jed, "He said he sent you a ransom note. That you would convince Max to pay it. He told me that he would lure you here and then kill you. After..." her voice faded at the thought of her being sold to a house of ill repute.

Jed wrapped an arm around her. "You're safe now. Simon Morgan will pay for this."

"He... he said he'd hurt you before. He caused your friend to be arrested and swindled you out of a fortune."

"Hush," he said against her hair as he stroked it. Lily luxuriated in the movement. "It was a long time ago. It only matters that you're safe now." Jed took her chin in his hand and tilted her face up to his. "I'd rather have you than all the money in the world."

He kissed her gently again, his passion restrained, yet she sensed it bubbling under the surface.

"Where is he now?" Jed's voice was taut with urgency.

"I don't know. He went out. He had things to do. I tried to get the chair to the door but the rickety thing tilted over."

He touched her cheek gently. "That would explain this new bruise cropping up." He brushed his fingers across it carefully before he looked at her intently.

"He... he didn't hurt you, did he? Beyond securing you to the chair?"

She saw the worry in his eyes. "No. He wanted to get the money and hurt you. He seemed so desperate."

"He is. He's gambled down to nothing. Cal's been arrested and his friend Gordon Fisher shot himself in Morgan's room. The police interrogated Morgan about his role in the death. Maybe that's what set him off. I don't know."

She hesitated. "I'm sorry about your father." She wasn't that sorry. Any man who'd abandon his wife and steal their child was no less than a monster in her eyes.

"I'm not," Jed said quietly. "He was never a father to me. And besides, I've found you and Max."

He steadied her. "Let's go downstairs. I've sent for a detective. He should arrive soon. We can give him the details and let him stick around to arrest Morgan."

Simon Morgan behind bars was Lily's fondest wish at the moment. Jed tossed the chair aside and pulled open the door, which barely hung on a few hinges. She stepped into the dimly lit hallway. The smells that assaulted her made her glad she'd missed them on the way in. Old urine and spilt beer mixed with human sweat and worse. She grieved for the poverty of the place.

She grabbed onto a wobbly banister for support then thought better of it. She trusted her quivering legs more than the railing in this decrepit building. Jed placed a hand on her shoulder, and Lily turned toward him.

A scream froze in her throat as Simon Morgan came from the murky shadows, a gun raised in his hand. He slammed it down on the back of Jed's head. Jed's knees buckled and he went tumbling down the staircase to the landing below.

Simon raced past her to reach Jed first. He turned him over. "Damn bastard!" Simon roared. He gave a swift kick to Jed's temple. Jed grunted and went rock still.

"No!" Lily screamed, scrambling down the stairs. She saw a trickle of blood course down Jed's face. He lay motionless on the ground, his right arm bent at an odd angle behind him.

She fell to her knees, but Simon grabbed her arm and yanked her to her feet. "It wasn't supposed to go this way," he bellowed. "How did he find us? The fool shouldn't be here. And he couldn't have all the money yet. It's too soon."

He pocketed the gun that he'd used to cold-cock Jed and bent, one hand wrapped firmly around her wrist, the other searching Jed's pockets. He found Jed's money clip and slipped it inside his coat.

"Well, now, what have we here?" He pulled out a gun. She recoiled as Simon snapped it open, checking to see if it was loaded.

"I see Mr. Stone came prepared after all." He held the cold steel alongside her temple. Her pulse throbbed rapidly against the metal. She tensed, waiting for Simon to pull the trigger.

Movement stirred above her. She glanced up to see a few shadowy figures on the landing above them.

"Help me." Her words came out in a desperate whisper. Those watching scrambled from view.

"Help? On Crawford Street?" Simon's tone was amused. "Think again, Lily. People here mind their own business."

His arm snaked around her waist, clutching her tightly. He caressed her temple with the gun itself, sliding it slowly down her face, along her jawline, and down to the valley between her breasts.

Lily froze, unbelieving that no one came to her aid, that no one would go for help. She would be assaulted and murdered here and only dull eyes would watch from afar.

She glanced down at Jed, wondering how badly he was injured, or if he was even alive.

He wasn't there.

She cut her eyes quickly to a shadow that flickered nearby. It was Jed, rising on shaky legs. He must have come to and was trying to slip behind Simon. He was unsteady on his feet despite his stealth. She had to buy him some time.

Or they'd both wind up dead.

Simon ran the gun down her body and back up again. She decided to shock him with brazenness.

"Why don't you put the gun down and try that with your hand, Simon?" she purred in her best Madam Lil voice.

Instantly, he stilled the gun, his body taut. "What?"

If the situation hadn't been so dangerous, she would have laughed aloud at his confusion.

"I know you've always wanted to. *Maman* was right."

His grip tightened on her. "What did Lil say?"

"She always thought you had fine hands. Lover's hands, I think she called them. She once said she wished you would caress her the way you did a winning hand."

She fought the urge to see where Jed was. Lily prayed he'd recovered his senses and would end this nightmare. She didn't know how much longer she could stand Simon's touch as he brought his arm holding the gun around her. Now, she was wrapped in the cocoon of his arms. She stifled the urge to fight, to try and escape this prison.

Then she was free. The pistol slid across the uneven wooden floor. She leaped for the gun. She fell hard on both knees but her hands wrapped around it. She rolled to her side as Jed slammed Simon against the wall. He punched Simon's gut twice, both punishing blows. The gambler fell to the floor with a thud.

She rushed the gun to Jed. Before she could ask if he was all right, she remembered this was Jed's gun. Simon had one, too. She heard the sound of it cock, followed by a loud explosion and a high, girlish scream. As the wafting smoke dissipated, Lily saw Simon cradled a bloody hand.

Jed placed his gun inside his coat pocket and reached down to pick up Simon's weapon. She looked at him in amazement.

A sheepish grin on his face, he merely shrugged. "The war taught me to have quick reactions."

Lily realized Jed had aimed and fired upon Simon before the older man had gotten off his shot.

Noise below distracted her, as someone rushed up the darkened stairs, gun drawn in hand.

"Police. Move away." The man reached their landing and spotted Simon on the ground, moaning and cursing. His eyes met Jed's. "You seem to have the situation in hand, Mr. Stone."

"This is Simon Morgan, Detective Robinson. He abducted Miss Frontiere and demanded a ransom. In our struggle to retain possession of her," and he flashed a wicked look Lily's way, "my gun went off, injuring Mr. Morgan. I'll make whatever statement is necessary, Detective. After I get my arm looked at."

She noticed that while Jed's left hand, which held Simon's gun, seemed fine, his right arm hung unnaturally by his side. She reached out and touched it, but he flinched and pulled away.

"It's a little tender, Lily. I don't think it can take being smothered in kisses," he said lightly.

She gave him a coy look. "How about the rest of you?" Without waiting, she flung her arms around his neck and began covering him in kisses.

JED STOOD beside Lily in front of Judge Barrett, amazed that she wanted to be married on schedule. She didn't seem any worse for the trauma she'd undergone. He loved that about her—her resiliency, her intelligence, and lest he forget—the sweet curves that belonged next to him. Forever.

"Do you have the ring?" the magistrate asked.

Mac handed over the wedding band and Jed faced his one true love. She held out a steady hand. He was the nervous one. He slid the ring onto her finger with his left hand, while he let her rest her hand atop the cast his right now wore. The dammed thing proved a little inconvenient in bed last night.

But only a little.

"By the authority invested in me by the State of California, I now pronounce you husband and wife. You may kiss your bride, Mr. Stone."

Tears stung his eyes at the depth of love he saw on Lily's face. He leaned close and whispered, "I may not be able to give you the moon and the stars, my love, but you have the gift of my heart."

Her beaming smile was the reply he needed as his lips met hers and sealed their vows. Their kiss tasted of a sacred promise.

Louis had been right. Life would never be the same.

EPILOGUE

"M r. Stone!"

Jed turned as six-year-old Sebastian flew down the pathway. He screeched to a halt and held out his hand to Jed. Jed took it and then leaned down and hugged the boy.

"Thank you," Sebastian said, his voice full of exuberance. "I'll write you and everything."

With that, the boy turned and ran back to the couple awaiting him at the top of the hill. Sebastian took one of their hands in each of his as they began to walk away. Only the boy's new mother looked back and smiled shyly at Jed.

"Another dream fulfilled," he said to himself.

It was close to five. Cleveland Armstrong could handle anything else that came up. Jed decided he could go home.

Home.

Was there ever a sweeter word created? Pictures of his large, rambling house and those within filled his mind as he increased his pace. Once he'd never thought to own a home, much less the family that now came with it.

He thought how Sebastian, too, would have a place

to call his own. The boy was one of countless orphans that Jed had placed with loving parents since he arrived in Denver. Thanks to Mac's connections and his own investments, Jed dabbled in real estate and the stock market. His gambler's luck had paid off handsomely. He need never work again.

His dream of helping orphans like himself took shape over the last year, thanks to Lily's help. She wormed out of him how he always found the nearest orphan asylum and donated to its coffers when he passed through a town.

"Money's not enough, Jed," she'd boldly proclaimed. "Those children need parents."

And so a vision had been born. Jed used his charm, coupled with business and social connections, to find homes for children who had none. With Lily, he created a charitable foundation to raise funds for this process. It was satisfying work, something he took immense pride in.

He opened the gate and whistled as he went up the walkway. Lily would be pleased he was home early. Maybe she would show him how pleased before tonight's benefit.

As he opened the door, thoughts of romantic seduction fled. Chaos reigned at the Stone household, as usual.

"Master Louis, down from that chair. Chairs are to be sat in, not jumped upon."

Jed swept his two-year-old son into his arms as he entered the room. Louis rewarded him with a wet kiss.

"Papa! Play horsey. Max wants horsey now!"

He scooped his other two-year-old into his free hand. "Well, hello to you, too, Max. How about a greeting?"

Max beamed at him, the Stone smile working its usual magic.

Harold interrupted, looking like he needed a minute to himself. "I'll tell Miss Lily you've arrived."

Louis scrambled after the butler, deciding a month earlier to appoint himself Harold's shadow. The poor man hadn't taken a step by himself since then if Louis were awake.

Max immediately reclaimed Jed's attention.

"Papa. Go horsey now!"

"Oh, all right."

He retreated to his knees as Max climbed atop his back, holding tightly onto his collar. He lumbered around the room, throwing in a few bucks for good measure. Max looped fingers into his hair to hold on for the duration of the ride, squealing with delight.

"Max? Max? Maxine Stone, will you look at me?"

Both Jed and his daughter turned to see Lily in the doorway, hands on her hips, trying her best to hide a smile. She crossed to them and picked up the girl.

"Max, you will tear every hair from your papa's head if you continue to ride him and use his hair to hold on. You wouldn't want Papa bald now, would you?"

The little girl looked at her father with saucer eyes and then began to laugh. "Papa bald. Papa look funny."

Lily smiled again at him and Jed's insides melted like butter. They always did when around his children. Louis was his spitting image and had Jed's personality, to boot. Max, on the other hand, was a smaller version of Lily and quite a handful. Still, both twins caused him to thank his lucky stars every night. He was blessed with riches, and his children were the largest part of his fortune.

Except for Lily. He looked at her, seeing everything he would want in a woman. She was wise beyond her years, and had regained her hourglass figure after a difficult pregnancy. Her sense of humor made him appreciate her every day.

They had needed each other and come to trust one another totally as they built a life together. Maximilian Fisher might be gone from it, but the old man lived on in spirit through Maxine. In fact, Jed sometimes wondered if it really wasn't Max inside his great, great-granddaughter, encouraging her to do some of the outrageous things she did. Jed hoped Harold would stay beyond when the twins someday left home. *He* would need Harold to look after him then.

Lily placed her daughter back on the ground. "Run along, sweet. Harold says your dinner is ready."

"Papa come?"

Lily shot him a look.

"Can I help it if she's wrapped me around her finger?"

"I'm not going to answer that," his wife told him. She looked back at Max. "Daddy needs to change clothes, love. We're going out tonight. Remember I showed you my pretty new ball gown?"

Max's face fell. Lily amended with, "He'll be ready in time to come share some of your dessert. Now, run along."

Max thought it over a moment then asked, "Cookies?"

Lily smiled. "You can have cookies only if you eat some of your carrots and peas."

"Two cookies?" Max pleaded.

Lily nodded and Max shot out of the room. She turned to Jed. "She's a master at manipulation, you know."

He wrapped his arms around his wife. "Did she get that from Max—or me?" He kissed her lightly.

She pressed herself against him and replied, "Maybe she got it from me."

"Whatever you say." Jed kissed her again, the pleasure of holding her close washing over him anew. He would never get enough of his wife. Never.

"You said something about my needing to change clothes?" he asked playfully.

Lily grinned as she undid his tie slowly. "I thought you might want to get into something more comfortable."

"I thought that was your line."

She raised an eyebrow. "My line, your line. Does it matter?"

He bent and slipped an arm behind her knees and swept her into his arms. He carried her up the staircase and to their room.

"Would you open the door?" he murmured against her lips, not wanting to take even a hand away for a moment.

"With pleasure," she replied.

As Lily opened the door, Jed thought how she'd opened his life to so many new things, but most of all, love.

He was grinning as he shut the door with his foot.

ALSO BY ALEXA ASTON

THE HOLLYWOOD NAME GAME

Hollywood Heartbreaker

Hollywood Flirt

Hollywood Player

Hollywood Double

Hollywood Enigma

Lawmen of the West

Runaway Hearts

Blind Faith

Love and the Lawman

Ballad Beauty

DUKES OF DISTINCTION:

Duke of Renown

Duke of Charm

Duke of Disrepute

Duke of Arrogance

Duke of Honor

MEDIEVAL RUNAWAY WIVES:

Song of the Heart

A Promise of Tomorrow

Destined for Love

SOLDIERS AND SOULMATES:

To Heal an Earl

To Tame a Rogue

To Trust a Duke

To Save a Love

To Win a Widow

THE ST. CLAIRS:

Devoted to the Duke

Midnight with the Marquess

Embracing the Earl

Defending the Duke

Suddenly a St. Clair

THE KING'S COUSINS:

God of the Seas

The Pawn

The Heir

The Bastard

THE KNIGHTS OF HONOR:

Rise of de Wolfe

Word of Honor

Marked by Honor

Code of Honor

Journey to Honor

Heart of Honor

Bold in Honor

Love and Honor

Gift of Honor

Path to Honor

Return to Honor

Season of Honor

NOVELLAS:

Diana

Derek

Thea

The Lyon's Lady Love

ABOUT THE AUTHOR

A native Texan and former history teacher, award-winning and internationally bestselling author Alexa Aston lives with her husband in a Dallas suburb, where she eats her fair share of dark chocolate and plots out stories while she walks every morning. She enjoys travel, sports, and binge-watching—and never misses an episode of *Survivor*.

Alexa brings her characters to life in steamy historicals, contemporary romances, and romantic suspense novels that resonate with passion, intensity, and heart.

Kᴇᴇᴘ ᴜᴘ ᴡɪᴛʜ Aʟᴇxᴀ
Visit her website
Newsletter Sign-Up

Mᴏʀᴇ ᴡᴀʏs ᴛᴏ ᴄᴏɴɴᴇᴄᴛ ᴡɪᴛʜ Aʟᴇxᴀ

www.ingramcontent.com/pod-product-compliance
Lightning Source LLC
Chambersburg PA
CBHW011932050726
47590CB00011B/3245

The Necromancer; Or, The Tale of the Black Forest

by Karl Friedrich Kahlert

Published by NRM Books.

ISBN: 978-1-965179-43-7

CREDITS
Cover Art by: Nathan Reese Maher

COPYRIGHT

The Necromancer; Or, The Tale of the Black Forest cover and layout are protected under the copyright laws of the United States of America. Any reproductions or unauthorized use of the contents herein including, but not limited to, artwork and text is prohibited without written permission from the publisher. The Necromancer; Or, The Tale of the Black Forest published herein is part of the public domain.

The Necromancer; Or, The Tale of the Black Forest

by Karl Friedrich Kahlert

Published by NRM Books.

ISBN: 978-1-965179-43-7

CREDITS
Cover Art by: Nathan Reese Maher

COPYRIGHT

The Necromancer; Or, The Tale of the Black Forest cover and layout are protected under the copyright laws of the United States of America. Any reproductions or unauthorized use of the contents herein including, but not limited to, artwork and text is prohibited without written permission from the publisher. The Necromancer; Or, The Tale of the Black Forest published herein is part of the public domain.

AF254296

The Necromancer; Or, The Tale of the Black Forest

by Karl Friedrich Kahlert

Published 1794

PART I

THE hurricane was howling, the hailstones beating against the windows, the hoarse croaking of the raven bidding adieu to autumn, and the weather-cock's dismal creaking joined with the mournful dirge of the solitary owl;- such was the evening when Herman and Elfrid, who had been united by the strongest bonds of friendship from their youthful days, were seated by the cheering fireside. Thirty long years had elapsed since they were separated by different employments; Herman having been called to distant countries, whilst Elfrid (leaving the University where their mutual friendship had begun) hastened home to his parents, to ease the burden of their old age, and to cheer the tempestuous evening of his dear progenitor's

Part I

life.

On his journey homewards, he rambled over some of the most charming parts of Germany; yet he sought in vain after pleasure, separated as he was from the dear companion of his youthful days. At length he found in the circle of his family, what he had been seeking in vain abroad. The pleasure which his venerable parents felt, in again beholding the offspring of their mutual love, soothed the disquiet of his mind; the joy sparkling in their eyes at the sight of the supporter of their declining years, tinged his cheeks with the rosy hue of contentment, and filled his soul with inward bliss. After ten years of congenial happiness, his aged father died, closing a well I spent life in his seventy-second year. The guardian angel of virtue carried his unspotted soul to the cheerful mansion of everlasting peace; the gentle smile of a good conscience sat still on his wan lips, when his sainted spirit arrived in heaven, hailed by millions of holy angels.

Twelve years longer Elfrid soothed the sorrows of his mother, and supported her under the heavy load of ever-increasing infirmities, until she was re-united to the dear companion of all her earthly joys and cares. He dropped a tear of filial affection on her tomb, and now directed all his care and tenderness towards the promoting his only sister's happiness; who as well as himself remained unmarried; and some years after, in order to disperse the clouds of gloomy fancies, the usual companions of bachelors, he determined on taking a journey, and left the care of his house to his maiden sister.

He was so fortunate as to meet on his journey with many friends of his earlier days, companions of his academical studies; at length he also traced out his dear Herman, the most beloved among his youthful friends.

He found his worthy friend a favourite of fortune, blest in the lap of sweet contentment and unmixed happiness.-A loving wife crowned the favours which fortune had so abundantly blessed him with; providence had also surrounded him with a circle of promising children, two of whom were happily married, and had blessed him with two granddaughters and three grandsons-Heaven's greatest blessings smiled upon him wherever he went, contentment and joy sat upon his reverend brow, and peace of mind had taken her abode within his heart.

"Good God!" exclaimed he, as soon as he could find words to give vent to the rapture of his soul," do I then behold, once more before I die, the dear companion of my youthful days? Heaven be praised for that unexpected happiness! Now all my wishes are fulfilled

-Oh, Elfrid! The separation from thee, the

Part I

apprehension of seeing thee no more, was the only bitterness mixed in the cup of bliss which providence has kindly administered to thy friend. Thou art alive-I have nothing else to wish than that my end may be as happy as this hour."

After the first ecstasy of meeting was over, Elfrid related how anxiously he had ever been inquiring after his dear friend; told him how many letters he had written to get information of his abode, and was going to chide him for his negligence, when Herman fetched a letter from an old acquaintance of his, who had written to him, that "Elfrid had left the service of the Muses, enlisted under the banners of Mars during the Seven Years' War, and had fallen a victim to his martial spirit." Elfrid was satisfied with this explanation.

"Brother," he exclaimed, "let us forget our age and live together, as long as I can remain with thee, as if the thirty years since we have seen each other had never passed, and be as merry as we have been in our youthful days."

Herman's cheek glowed with pleasure, and he squeezed Elfrid's hand. Six days passed in mutual joy. Herman resided at a country seat, situated on the banks of the Elbe, and enclosed by an ancient forest, which made it a pleasant abode to Elfrid, who was passionately fond of hunting. Every morning they rambled through the woods, and the two friends pursued the fleet game with almost juvenile ardour, till the dinner bell summoned them to a substantial meal and a bottle of old Rhenish wine. When the cloth was removed, the goblet went cheerfully round, and the two happy friends drank and talked of the achievements of their younger days, and what had happened during their separation. Thus days rolled on like hours, and Elfrid did not yet think of departing.

The gloominess of the weather, on the day when this narrative opens, gave their conversation a serious turn. They began to discourse on the calamities of war; of the dangers they had formerly undergone, and of the many distresses and sufferings they had experienced in the early part of their lives. As night advanced, the tempest grew more furious, the flame in the chimney was wafted to and fro, and began to die away by degrees, when Herman fed it with dry wood, stirred the ashes, and it began again to blaze.

"Brother," said Elfrid, "brother, dost thou believe in apparitions? Dost thou believe in spirits?

Herman, smiling, shook his head. "I also," Elfrid went on, " do not believe in apparitions; yet, when travelling through Germany, I have met with adventures which I still am unable to unriddle."

Part I

Upon Herman's requesting an explanation, Elfrid began as follows: "The great fair was just beginning when I arrived at F; the bustle of the buyers and vendors, the meeting with a number of dear friends, and the many different amusements, promised to afford me a great deal of pleasure, and I resolved to stop a few weeks at that town.

"The inn where I had taken lodging was crowded with travellers: an aged hoary man amongst them was particularly noticed by every one, on account of his remarkable appearance. His looks were reverend; his dress, though very plain, was costly; he appeared to be a rich nobleman, and occupied the best apartments. A coach and six, with four servants richly dressed, carried him frequently out; he was seen at all the public places, was present at all amusements, yet, what raised my curiosity, he was constantly alone and in profound meditation. I often remarked, that wherever he was, he did not take the least notice of what was doing around him, and, as if a prey to grief and inward sufferings, seemed to be insensible of all the objects that surrounded him. He was also continually alone when in his apart- ment, the door of which was always bolted. He rode out as soon as dinner was over, and commonly returned very late at night.

"I questioned the landlord about this strange man, but he shrugged up his shoulders and could tell me nothing. But,' exclaimed I peevishly, you certainly know where he comes from, could not you ask his servants?" The servants,' answered he, are as mute as their master. He is supposed to be an English lord, that is all I know.'

"I was of the same opinion when I first saw him; having met, on my travels, with many Englishmen who had behaved in the same sullen and reserved manner. His melancholy mood I fancied to be the effect of the spleen, and I did not trouble myself any more about him.

"I had not been above three days at F when I lost my purse. At first I fancied I had dropped it some- where in a shop, or my pocket had been picked in the street, and determined to be more careful in future; but, in spite of all my precaution and care, I suffered a second loss the next day, missing a diamond ring, with a miniature picture of my deceased mother; I was sure that the preceding night I had pulled that ring from my finger and put it on the table when I went to bed; I questioned the waiters, but they appeared to be offended at my inquiries-in short, the ring was gone.

"A few days after, I went to the play; I had a snuff- box, of very little value, in the right pocket of my coat; a gentleman who was sitting by me, at the left, begged me to give him a pinch of snuff, but I could not find my

Part I

box. That insignificant theft made me smile. I was only glad that I had left my purse at home.

"The play was over, and a boy with a lighted torch went before me to an adjacent tavern; I wanted to see what hour it was, but my watch was also gone. Cursed misfortune!' exclaimed I. The boy reminded me of his money, I gave it him, and entered the supper room. An acquaintance of mine took notice of the paleness of my countenance, inquiring whether I was ill; I denied it, and took my seat at the table. I hurried down my supper without noticing my neighbour, and determined to depart the next morning, being persuaded that some cunning rogues had singled me out to try their skill with me at the expense of my property. As I was pushing back my chair, somebody close by me asked me what o'clock it was. I did not answer, because that question, by reminding me of my loss, had vexed me, and was going to leave the room.

"Sir, what o'clock is it?' exclaimed somebody once more, tapping me on the shoulder. I do not know,' I replied, without looking back, and paid my bill.-' Have you no watch with you?' exclaimed the same person again. Now I turned round in great vexation, and, guess my surprise, the troublesome inquirer was my neighbour at the inn, the very same gentleman who had excited my curiosity so much some days ago.

"He stared me in the face, as if expecting an answer.

"Sir,' said I now, 'my watch–'

"Has been stolen,' interrupted he quickly, 'I have caught the thief, there it is.' So saying, he put my watch into my hand. I was stunned with amazement, and could not help wishing to know the thief, that I might recover the other things I had lost, for I was sure that the same person who had robbed me of my watch, had also pilfered what I had lost before; but, ere I could signify my wish, the mysterious gentleman had vanished.

"I went home, struck with astonishment, but the Stranger was not yet arrived. At length he came, as usual, at midnight; I rushed out of the door when I heard him coming up stairs, made a respectful bow, and begged him to give me leave to ask a question; but he passed me hastily, without taking notice of me, absorbed in melancholy thoughts, took the candle from the servant, and bolted his door.

"All my attempts of speaking with him were fruitless. When at home, his door was bolted, in the hall he took no notice of me, and in public places he shunned me. Vexed at this rude behaviour, I would not make another attempt to get acquainted with that queer fellow.

Part I

"Meanwhile three days more elapsed, and that Strange accident had made me forget my departure; but now I renewed my resolution of setting off as soon as possible, and determined to leave F- the next day. I put every- thing in order, had my trunks packed, and was obliged to find out a banker who would take a bill on a person at Leipzig, which I had brought with me.

"Towards evening I met with a reasonable man; joyfully now did I put my hand into my pocket to take the pocket-book out of it, but I could not find it. For God's sake,' exclaimed the merchant, when he saw me pale and trembling, "what is the matter with you? Nothing, nothing at all," stammered I, rushing out of the house.

"A faint ray of hope was still glimmering within my soul; I fancied I had left all the remainder of my little fortune at the inn, though I was certain that I had taken the pocket-book with me. I arrived, trembling, at my lodging, and was hardly able to unlock my door; I entered slowly, as if I wanted to avoid the terrible blow that threatened me; I minutely searched the room, but alas all my property was gone.

"I could not believe the reality of my misfortune; I emptied my trunk more than ten times, and more than a hundred times did I search every corner of the room, thinking it impossible that the bill and the pocket-book should not be there, however I could find neither of them.

"It grew late, and I was still sitting on my trunk, half-distracted; at length I resolved to go next morning to some of my acquaintance, and endeavour to get some money advanced. That terrible evening was followed by a more terrible night; morning dawned and I still could not sleep-my pride revolted against the thought of borrowing money, but the idea of want staring me in the face, got the better of it, and I went. Every one whom I applied to was sorry for what had happened to me, railed against the villain who had robbed me; but nobody would lend me money-the scarcity of cash, the backwardness of debtors; these and a thouasnd other obstacles prevented my friends from assisting me. I went home in a melancholy mood, and did not know what to do. It struck one, the dinner was on table, but I could not eat. I was standing in my room with a down- cast look, and musing on my distress, and I cannot tell how long I had been in that desponding situation, when a gentle knock at my door roused me suddenly from my reverie: I exclaimed in an agony, Come in! The door opened, and I was thunderstruck when I beheld the unknown gentleman before me. I ran almost frantic with joy towards the stranger, clasped him in my arms, and exclaimed, 'Have you, have you found it?

Part I

"I have not!' answered he.

"No!' groaned I. 'Gracious heaven! how unhappy am I."

"Patience, young man,' he replied, although the thief may have made his escape, yet I am here.'

"I gazed at him with astonishment. He took his pocket-book, opened it, and gave me two papers. There, take them,' said he, 'there is as much as you may want at present, the mail will set off to-morrow, for your native country, I wish you a happy journey.'

"Then he laid the papers on my table, and hastened out of the room; a strange sensation fixed me to the floor, and fettered my tongue, I neither could thank my benefactor, nor inquire how I was to repay him. I felt veneration for this singular man, admired his humanity, and yet I could not help feeling some inward sensations of horror; I was for a considerable time as motionless as a statue. Having recovered from my amazement, I went to the table, took up the papers, and saw, with astonishment, that each of them was a draft for a hundred dollars payable at F. It grieved me to be obliged to accept a present from a stranger. But what could I do? How could I get access to him? Perhaps (thought I) he will send his direction, but I waited in vain for it. He got into his carriage and drove away.

"I also left the house and returned late, the stranger was not yet come home; however, I determined to await his return, and as soon as he should enter the house, hasten to his apartment, and insist upon his taking a bond for his money, and if he refused, force him to resume his present. This resolution, however, I could not execute, for he did not return.

"Night being far advanced, I laid myself down upon a couch and began to doze. Nodding, I heard a noise at my door; I got up, and all was silent. I fancied the noise I had heard was the effect of those early dreams which sometimes amuse our fancy when sleep is coming on, but soon after I heard the same noise again. I once more got up from my couch, and all was silent again. Listening attentively, I heard the same noise repeated; it grew now louder and louder, and resembled the tapping of somebody who could not find the latch. I was going to open the door, but before I got to the middle of the room saw it move on its hinges. I stopped, the door opened slowly, and now I could distinguish my visitor. It was a strange figure, tall and emaciated, clad in a white garment. As it entered the room, it advanced towards me with slow and solemn steps; I staggered back, and a chilly terror trembled through my frame. The apparition moved towards the table in awful silence. It took up my watch, looked at it, gave a hollow groan, and laid it down again. I was thunderstruck. The phantom now moved slowly back, and I looked at its face as it was passing the table where the candle stood. Merciful heaven! how was I chilled with horror when I beheld the features of my deceased mother! My knees shook, a cold sweat bedewed my face, and my strength forsook me.

"Meanwhile the apparition had come to the door without having turned its face; it opened the latch gently, and, when on the threshold turned round, staring me in the face with a ghastly look, and lifting up its emaciated hand, thrice made a threatening gesture and disappeared.

"I fell senseless back upon my couch, and when I could recollect myself again, I fancied I had been haunted by a bad dream. The clock struck one as I was going to look at my watch.

Vexed that the stranger did not come home, I went to bed and slept till it was broad day. When the waiter brought my breakfast, I asked whether my neighbour was come home. He said no. Then I asked if he had left F? The waiter answered, 'It may be, he always pays his bill after dinner, he carries no trunks with him, and none of his servants lodge in our house."

"I went with the waiter to the apartment which the Stranger had occupied. The key was in the lock, we walked in, all was empty. "I returned to my room, took up the drafts he had given me, and would have destroyed them, if I thus could have disencumbered myself of the obligation which I owed him. It suddenly came in my mind that they perhaps might be fictitious, or the name of the merchant who was to pay the money not known. This thought afforded me pleasure, though I could expect nothing but misery if it should prove true.

"I hastened to the host and shewed him my drafts, under the pretext of wanting to know the direction of the merchant. He described the house and the street where he lived. I was frightened and went that same morning to the merchant. He looked slightly at the paper but very seriously at me, and his eyes seemed to denote astonishment and pity. I expected joyfully that the bills would be protested; however, I was mistaken. He opened, sighing, his drawers, and counted down two hundred dollars, still looking at me with astonishment. I put the money in my pocket, and being convinced that he pitied me for being obliged to that stranger, I took the liberty of asking him by whom he was to be repaid; upon which he appeared disconcerted, shrugged his shoulders, muttered some unintelligible words, and left me suddenly. I went away under the greatest apprehen- sions, and the weather being fine, was tempted to walk to a public garden. The beautiful morning had assembled there a great number of foreigners, and of the inhabitants of F- ; I went into a remote bower, and ordered some chocolate. Retired from the noisy bustle of company, I could now muse on the strange accidents which I had experienced during my short stay at F. I also recollected my dream, and reflected on it more seriously than before. Though I was very much tempted to deem it something more than a delusion of fancy, yet I was still disinclined to ascribe that strange incident to a super- natural cause, being strongly prepossessed against the belief in apparitions, and found myself bewildered in a maze of irksome fancies. I struggled hard with my imagination, striving to forget what had made me so uneasy; but all was in vain; the dream, or rather the apparition, continually returned to my remembrance, in defiance of my reasoning, and the horrid spectre hovered still before my eyes.

"Tired and wearied with the struggle between reason and fancy, I endeavoured to ease my soul of her heavy load, by a loud exclamation, and, without recollecting where I was, I suddenly broke out in the words, 'No, it was a deluding dream?

"It was no dream!' exclaimed a well-known voice on a sudden. I looked up. Imagine my surprise at beholding the mysterious stranger standing before me !

"Young man,' said he, without giving me time to utter a single word, 'young man, do you wish for an explanation of the apparition of last night?' I gazed at him in dumb silence. 'If you wish to have unfolded that incident,' he resumed, after a short pause, 'then await me this evening by ten o'clock, at the town gate, next to the inn.' The stranger pronounced these words with a friendly, courteous mien, made me a bow, and disappeared amid the crowd.

"The waiter brought the chocolate, but I could not swallow a single drop. In vain did I now roam all over the garden in hopes of meeting the stranger; in vain ask all my acquaintance and the waiters, describing minutely the stranger to every one; nobody had seen him.

"I hastened home, awed and terror-struck. I entered my apartment; the door of my chamber seemed to be in constant motion, and the figure of my mother haunted me without intermission. I could not get rid of the gloomy reflection on her threatening looks, and left the house. I now rambled about in great uneasiness from the coffee-house to the promenade, from thence to the museum, from the museum to the tavern, from the tavern to the exhibition of wild beasts, and at last to the playhouse, but I could nowhere find tranquillity.

"It was growing dark when I left the playhouse, my soul was disturbed by strange sensations, and I was consulting with myself whether I should go or not. Doubt and apprehension suspended my resolution for a considerable time, and overwhelmed me with agony.

"Shall I go or not? Prudence asked, What hast thou to apprehend? I could give no answer, and fears and doubts still continued keeping up a most distressing conflict. Curiosity on a sudden raised her bewitching voice, driving away every doubt, and bidding defiance to the wise counsels of prudence. Thy departure is fixed, to-morrow thou art going to leave this town;' thus the charming seducer whispered in my ear; ' and to-day thou canst get rid of every teasing doubt. Thou wilt repent it if thou refusest to go. Courage, man, courage, don't be such a coward as to fear an old man; and thus my pride added, thou canst inform thyself how to pay the notes.'"

I was determined to go. I will repair to the place of rendezvous,' said I, and was instantly disencumbered of a load of uneasiness. I returned to my apartment with composure, called for a light, and began to write some letters. Having continued that occupation till eight o'clock, I went down stairs to amuse myself a little, and spent two hours at the table d'hôte. When supper was over, the landlord desired to speak to me in private. As soon as we were retired to another room, he said, 'I bring you happy tidings.' I listened attentively. 'You have lost several things during your residence in our town?" —' I have,' replied I, with surprise. 'Your loss has given me great uneasiness, on account of the reputation of my house.'-' To the point,' exclaimed I, with impatience. You have lost a purse, a snuff-box, a ring, and a pocket-book.'-' You know exactly what I have lost,' answered I with amazement.

"You will find every article in your room.' I staggered back. An unknown person brought all your things an hour ago.'-' An unknown person! Was it that strange gentleman? But it cannot be him, you know.'-'Whom do you mean?'-' My neighbour.'

"The landlord shook his head smiling, he was called away, and hastening to my room, I found everything as the landlord had told me. The bill of exchange was in the pocket book, and I was lost in dumb amazement, not doubting that this was a new trick of my unknown benefactor. But why did he not wait till ten o'clock?' said I to myself, why not return my things at our appointed meeting? Has he doubted my coming, or been obliged to depart suddenly?' The last was the most likely proposition, but at the same time the most disagreeable to me, as it would deprive me of the means of returning him his money, and paying my debt now I had recovered my property. But how could I be certain that he really was departed, since all his proceedings had been so strange and eccentric? How could a gentleman like him, a pattern of honesty, a

Part I

friend to human nature, how could he be guilty of transgressing the first duty of an honest man? How could it be possible that he would break his word? He had appointed me to meet him at ten o'clock, and the landlord had not said anything to the contrary.

"I went down to the supper room, requesting a few minutes' hearing of the landlord, and asked him if the unknown person, who had brought my lost property, had left no message for me. He replied in the negative, adding, that the messenger merely said, 'there are the things Mr. Elfrid has lost,' and without giving him time to question him any farther as to by whom he had been sent, he went away.

"I looked at my watch, it wanted fifteen minutes to ten, I fetched my hat and great coat and walked slowly towards the town gate. The night was exceedingly fine, the moon shone bright, and was surrounded with millions of sparkling stars. It struck ten when I stood on the appointed spot, I took every passenger for the stranger, ran towards several of them, and began to speak, but I was always disappointed. It was now forty-five minutes past ten, and I began to get tired, and to conclude that my apprehension that the stranger had been obliged to depart suddenly was correct.

"I will wait till it strikes eleven!' said I to myself, ' and then return home, if he should not be here.' The bell of the adjacent steeple tolled eleven, and the stranger was not yet come.

"I will stay fifteen minutes longer, and then return to the inn.' These fifteen minutes likewise expired without his making his appearance. The stillness of midnight surrounded me. I proceeded on my return.

"I had not gone ten steps, when the stranger came walking towards me with hasty paces; nobody could be more rejoiced than I was, and, forgetting entirely that had waited so long, I ran towards him. He shook me heartily by the hand, and said, 'I am sorry that I have kept you waiting so long.'

"'I would readily have waited still longer,' replied I, ' if I had been sure of seeing you at last, for I was anxious to obey your commands, and to get rid of my doubts.'

"'That you shall,' said he; follow me.'

"He began to walk so fast that I hardly could keep up with him; he uttered not a word; we arrived at the gate and it was opened at his command; our way led straight through the suburbs, at the bottom of which a solitary house was standing; my conductor knocked at the door; we were let in the house appeared to be empty and deserted, and we saw no living soul except an old decrepid man, who had

opened the door. The Stranger ordered a light;
a lamp was brought, and he walked without
stopping, through a dark passage till we came
to a door, leading into a garden, in the back of
which was a small pleasure-house; my
conductor opened the door, and we entered a
small damp room.

"Now we are on the spot,' said he, after
having carefully secured the door, tell me what
you want to know.'

"First of all, I wanted to give him a brief
account of the recovery of my effects, and then
began to ask him, if he had been my
benefactor. However, he prevented me from
doing it, exclaiming, 'I know it all, I beg you
will concentrate all you want to know into one
question.'

"I mused awhile, but I was not able to bring
all my wishes to one point, and it is very likely
that the presence of that extraordinary man,
had greatly contributed to my perplexity. I
found it impossible to make the question he
had ordered me to do.

"Seeing my distress, he said, 'Well, then,
inquire after the name of the friend who has
taken so much care of you.'

"That was the very question which I was
most eager to ask. I had wished to propose, but
I would not venture to do it for fear of

offending the stranger; with great joy I replied that is what I wish to know.

"Well then,' replied he, 'you shall get personally acquainted with that friend of yours.' ' Then I do not know him yet personally?' resumed I, 'I thought it was you, sir.' The stranger shook his head. I am only his deputy,' was his answer, and,' added he, after a short pause, only through the third hand.'

"I gazed at him with amazement, but he seemed to take no notice of it, and began to make preparations for introducing my friend in a most mysterious manner. He strewed sand on the floor, and drew two circles with an ebony wand, placing me in one and himself in the other.

"How will this end? thought I.

"The stranger was now standing opposite to me, in a solemn posture; he folded his hand upon his breast, his looks being lifted up to heaven. Silent and motion- less like a statue was he standing there. A chilly sensation of horror penetrated me, I did not dare fetch breath.

"The stranger remained in that posture for a quarter of an hour, my fear was swallowed up in dumb amazement, and my heart began soon to fail me from fear and awful expectations. At length my conductor broke his mysterious

Part I

silence; I heard his voice, but I could not understand what he said, the words he pronounced seemed to belong to a foreign language. The lamp afforded but a faint light, and I could not well distinguish the objects around me. All was silent as the grave. My conductor whispered only now and then some mysterious words, drawing figures in the sand with his ebony wand.

"Now I heard the clock strike twelve, with the last Stroke the stranger began to turn himself round about, within the circle, with an astonishing velocity, pronouncing the christian and surname of my deceased mother. I Staggered back thrilled with chilly horror. On a sudden I heard a noise under ground, like the distant rolling of thunder. The stranger pronounced the name of my mother a second time, and in a more solemn and tre- mendous voice than at first. A flash of lightning hissed through the room, and the voice of thunder grew louder and louder beneath my feet. Now he pronounced the name of my mother a third time, still louder and more tremendous. At once the whole pleasure-house appeared to be surrounded with fire. The ground began to shake under me, and I sank suddenly down. The ghost of my mother hovered before my eyes, with a grim, ghastly look; a chilly sweat bedewed my face and my senses forsook me.

"A violent shaking roused me at length from my stupefaction.

"The shaking did not cease, and I felt as if I was tossed to and fro: at the same time I heard a terrible creaking and whizzing not far off. As soon as I had recovered my recollection, I perceived that I was sitting in a coach, driving onward with an incredible velocity, and found myself closely confined. Something was snoring by my side, but I could not distinguish what it was, being surrounded with impenetrable darkness."

"You cannot imagine what I suffered in that terrible situation. I was seized with anxiety and apprehension, creating the most tormenting sensations, which cannot be described.

"The road my human or supernatural coachman had taken seemed to be very uneven, or, perhaps, he did not know the road, for I felt every moment the most violent jolts, which increased my anxiety still more, by the additional apprehension of being overturned. My bones, which already had been hurt very much by my falling down in the pleasure-house, seemed to be quite dislocated. I had been in that state of agony about half an hour, when a most violent jolt overturned the coach. A voice roared, Jesu Maria!' Methought I felt the freezing hand of death upon my heart, and lost the power of recollection.

At length I was roused from that state of insensibility, by the most excruciating pains. I opened my eyes; two men, each of them

Part I

holding a horse by the bridle, were standing by me; a countryman, with a lanthorn, was in their company, and the broken coach was lying on the ground at a small distance. They wanted to raise me up, but being pierced by terrible pains, I entreated them, for God's sake, not to touch me. My leg was fractured in two places: the horsemen promised to ride to a neighbouring town for assistance, and disappeared; the countryman remained with me and endeavoured to comfort me.

"I waited half an hour and nobody appeared; the night was cold: I waited an hour and no assistance came; one fainting fit followed the other. At length I heard the rolling of a coach, the countryman went with his lanthorn into the middle of the road, and saw a coach and four; the honest man begged the driver to stop, and related my misfortune. An old reverend man got out of the vehicle, lifted me, with the assistance of the good peasant, into the coach, and ordered the coachman to drive slowly onward.

"With the dawn of the morning we came to a village. My kind deliverer was the lord of it. Having been carried to the castle, a surgeon was sent for, meanwhile the old nobleman endeavoured, by his kind conversation, to make me forget part of my pains.

"The surgeon arrived a little while after, my wounds were dressed, and I was carried to bed. At first my deliverer would not leave me, and visited me afterwards three times a day. May heaven reward him for his generous and humane behaviour.'

"As soon as I had related to him all that had happened to me, he sent some of his people to look after the coach; but it could be found no where.

"After nine weeks' confinement I was recovered so far that I could return to F, the benevolent nobleman accompanied me thither, and my landlord was rejoiced to see me. Inquiring after the mysterious stranger I was told, that he had been seen no more since I had left the inn. My deliverer stayed three days with me, and then we parted in a most affectionate manner. The next day I set out for my own country, where I happily arrived without any farther accident."

Here Elfrid concluded his wonderful tale, which he, as he added, never had been able to unfold, though he had taken the greatest pains to come at the bottom of it. He looked at his friend, eager to hear what he would say to those extraordinary adventures; but Herman was lost in profound meditation for many minutes, at length he began: "Brother, thy tale is very wonderful, so wonderful, that I should not have believed it, if I had not met, on my travels, with adventures, which seem to have some connexion with thine."

Part I

Elfrid had apprehended that Herman would laugh at his story, as many of his friends had done; he was there- fore very much astonished at Herman's words, and besought him to give a short account of the adventures he had hinted at. Herman promised to give a full account of whatever had happened to him, partly by way of narration and partly in writing; however, he begged him to wait till to-morrow, that he might be able to arrange the necessary papers. Elfrid very readily consented to it. The next morning was uncommonly fine, yet Herman's guest had no inclination for a hunting party. As soon as breakfast was over he reminded his friend of his promise, asking whether he had found the papers he had been mentioning. Herman said he had, telling his friend at the same time, that he intended to relate only that part of those adventures in which he had been personally concerned, the remainder he would give him in writing, but not before his departure, lest ghosts and necromancers might deprive him of the pleasure of making his dear visitor as comfortable and happy as possible. Elfrid having consented to it, the two friends took their places by the fire-side, lighted their pipes, and Herman began as follows:

"Thou knowest, brother, that I, having finished my studies, was appointed governor to the young Baron de R- to conduct him on his travels. On our re- turn from Italy we took our way through Switzerland and Germany, and met, on this last tour, with the most remarkable adventure of our whole journey.

'Being arrived at the skirts of the Black Forest, our postillion missed his way, as it began to grow dark, and at length, did not know what direction he should take. Our fright was not little, when he apprised us of his distress, being desirous to get out of that dreadful forest as soon as possible, on account of the many instances of robberies and murders committed within its precincts, which the postillion had enlarged upon on the road; we therefore exhorted the fellow to go on, whatever might be the consequence. He did so, and after half an hour we came to an open spot.

"'Now we are safe!' exclaimed the postillion joyfully, ' and, if I am not mistaken, not far from a village.'

He was right. We soon heard the welcome barking of dogs not far off, and a little while after we saw lights.

"We entered a large village, but the inn was very indifferent, and the landlord was amazed at the uncommon sight of gentlemen. His whole stock of eatables consisted in some smoaked puddings, and a coarse sort of bread; he told us that neither wine nor beer could be got within the distance of many leagues and even our postillion could not drink his brandy.

Part I

We asked him where the lord of the village resided; he answered that he never lived there, because the castle had not been habitable for many years. I enquired the reason of it.

"'At present,' repled the host, 'I dare not give you an account of it, to-morrow you shall know everything; but, very likely, this night will make you guess the reason.'

"The Baron and I entreated him to satisfy our curi- osity, but he shook his head and left the room.

"Pinched by hunger we took up with our scanty supper, and then asked the landlord to show us to our beds, but, alas! there was not one bed unoccupied in the whole house, and we were obliged to rest our weary limbs upon a bed of clean straw in the middle of the room.

The Baron soon began to snore, but I could not get a wink of sleep. Now the watchman announced the hour of midnight with a hoarse voice, and on a sudden I heard the trampling of horses and the sound of horns. The noise came nearer, and methought I heard a number of horsemen rushing by, and sounding their horns as if a large hunting party were passing through the village; the troop darted like lightning through the street close by the windows of the inn. The Baron started up, asking me with a fearful voice,' What is this ? '—' I don't know,' replied I abruptly. I listened attentively, and the troop had not been far from our inn, when on a sudden all was again as silent as the grave; the Baron began to snore as before, and I to muse on that strange incident.

"I could not think it possible that any body would go a hunting in so large a company, at that unseasonable hour, and was much inclined to think all had been a deluding dream, when I suddenly recollected the mysterious words of our landlord, I cannot but confess that I was seized with horror. I was just falling asleep when the voice of the watchman, crying one o'clock, roused me from my slumber. No sooner had he finished his round than the former noise was heard again at a small distance. I started up and ran to the window, but before I could open it the whole troop had rushed by like a hurricane. A little while after all was silent again, yet in vain did I beseech the god of slumber to take me in his arms.

"The Baron had heard nothing the second time, snoring quietly by my side whilst I was ardently wishing for the morning, in order to satisfy my curiosity. I was too impatient to await the landlord's account of the castle, and when the watchman was crying two o'clock I hastened to the window, and began to converse with him.

"'Watchman,' exclaimed I, what did that

noise at twelve and one o'clock mean?' 'Your honour,' replied he, 'is certainly a stranger, for there's not a child in our village that does not know what that noise means; it is sometimes heard every night for several weeks, afterwards every thing is quiet again for a considerable time.'

"But,' said I, who is that person that goes a hunting at night?'

"That I can't tell you at present,' answered the watchman, 'ask your landlord, he will tell you all the particulars, I am here on my duty, and under the pro- tection of Providence, but I dare not speak of what I hear and see.'

"With these words he went away :-I wrapped myself up in my cloak, and sitting down by the window on a chair, expected, with anxious impatience, the rising of the sun. At length the eastern sky began to be em- broidered with purple streaks, the crowing of the cocks sounded through the village, and the watchman announced the approach of day. The Baron awoke.

"You are very early,' said he, rubbing his eyes, ' pray tell me, what noise was it I heard in the night?

"I myself am impatient to know it,' replied I, 'I wish the landlord would rise and unfold that mystery; the troop has rushed by again at one o'clock with the same terrible noise.' 66

While I was talking thus, I heard the trampling of horses, and looking out of the window, saw an officer with a servant. They alighted at the inn, knocked at the door, and entered the room. The officer, a lively young man, wore a Danish uniform, and was on the recruiting business; he had missed his way like ourselves, and we soon got acquainted with him. When the Baron related the nightly adventure, the officer at first thought he was joking, but when I most seriously affirmed every circumstance, he showed an ardent desire to get acquainted with those nocturnal sportsmen.

"That honour you can easily have,' said the Baron, 'if you will stay here the ensuing night, we will give you company.'

"Bravo!' exclaimed the officer, perhaps the gentlemen will be so polite to invite us to their sport, and then we may be so fortunate as to get a haunch of venison.'

"Now the landlord entered the room. 'Well,' said he, bidding us a good morning, 'have you heard any- thing to night, gentlemen?'

"More than I liked,' answered I; 'who are those sportsmen that go a hunting at midnight.'

Part I

"Why,' replied he,' we don't talk of it: I would not tell you anything about it last night, for fear your curiosity might expose you to some misfortune; yet, having promised you yesterday to tell you as much of it as I know, I will be as good as my word.' C

"After having paused awhile, he began thus, in a confidential tone: Close by our village is a very large building, where formerly the Lord of this village used to reside. One of the former masters of the castle was a very wicked and irreligious man, who found great delight in tormenting the poor peasants; every body trembled when he appeared. He trampled with his feet upon his own children, confined them in dark dungeons, where they were often kept for many days without a morsel of bread. He used to call his tenants dogs, and to treat them as such-in short, he was cruelty itself.

"'Hunting was his only amusement, and he always kept a vast number of deer, which were the ruin of the peasants' little property, and reduced them to the utmost poverty; no one dared to drive them from his fields, and if he did, he was confined in a damp dungeon, under ground, for many weeks. When that wicked man wanted to hunt, then the whole village was called together to serve him instead of dogs; if any one was not alert enough, then he would hunt him instead of the deer, till he fell down expiring under the lashes of his whip.

"'One time after he had roved about from morning till night, he fell from his horse and broke his neck. He was buried in his garden. But now he was terribly punished for his wickedness, having had no rest in his grave to the present day. At certain times of the year he is doomed to appear in the village, at twelve o'clock at night, and to make his entry into the castle with his infernal crew, but as soon as the clock strikes one he is plunged back again into the lake of fire burning with brimstone. Nobody can inhabit the castle! Many who have been so fool-hardy to attempt it have lost their lives; whoever ventures to look out of the window when the infernal hosts are passing by gets a swollen face as a punishment for his curiosity. We are now used to that nocturnal sport, and do not care for those infernal spirits, but many strangers have fallen ill through fright.'

"Here the landlord finished his tale, and seemed to be pleased with out astonishment; however, his pleasure was soon damped when the Lieutenant broke out in a roar- ing laughter.

"Laugh as long as you please,' said he ; Stay here till night if you have courage, and then we shall see if you will laugh.'

"'That I will,' replied the officer, 'I will not

only Stay in your house, but I will also spend the coming night at that dreadful castle. I dare say, gentlemen,' added he, you will keep me company.'

"The Baron, being a man of honor, thought it a great disgrace to betray the least want of courage in the presence of the soldier; he therefore promised to accompany him thither I made several objections, representing to the officer the danger we should run, not knowing who those spirits might be; however, he silenced all my remonstrances: 'I am a soldier,' said he, ' and all ghosts and hobgoblins have ever been kept at a respectful distance by a martial dress.'

"At length I was obliged to take a part in the expedition, if I would not desert the Baron. The landlord, who had all that time been staring at us in dumb amazement, lifted up his hands when I had consented to go to the castle, and entreated us, for God's sake, to desist from our undertaking: If you go,' added he, then all of you will be dead before to-morrow morning: for heaven's sake, dear gentlemen, do not run into the very mouth of the devil thus wantonly !'

"However, the raillery of the Lieutenant put him soon so much out of temper, that he left us in great wrath, swearing in the height of his anger, that the devil would make us smart for our fool-hardiness and unbelief.

Gentlemen,' began now the officer, 'pray let us take a walk to that terrible place, where we are going to spend the night, and reconnoitre it before dinner,' — Approving of that proposal, we went all three to that residence of terror.

"We approached and beheld the gothic remains of a half decayed castle, the gate was open and we entered the fabric. The arched walls, overgrown with moss and ivy, echoed to the sound of our footsteps; a long narrow passage led to a spacious court-yard, paved with stones; now we espied a spiral stair-case of stone, and ascended it in dumb silence. A second long and narrow passage, which received a faint glimmering of light through several small windows, strongly guarded by iron bars, led us to a back door; the chilly damps of the long confined air rushed from the aperture when the Lieutenant had pushed it open; the apartment to which it led bore the gloomy appearance of a prison-the remains of half- decayed tapestry, covered with cobwebs, gave the room a dark dreary appearance; pieces of broken furniture were scattered about on the floor, a lamp hung in the middle from an iron chain fastened to the arched ceiling.

"Just as we were going to leave this abode of gloom and horror, I perceived a little door in the remotest corner of the room, it was likewise unbolted, and we entered a second room, which bore the same gloomy aspect with the former apartment, being covered with half-

Part I

rotten remains of broken furniture; another door led us at length into a spacious hall, where the cheering light of the day hailed us at last, many of the arched windows being either open or broken to pieces; the fresh air, the beautiful view meeting our eye from every side, chased at once from our countenance the solemn awe.

"Here," exclaimed the Lieutenant, 'here we will meet the airy Lords of this Manor; Let us try, gentlemen, whether we cannot fit a table and some seats among the rotten relics of furniture.'

"We succeeded in our attempt, dragged a round massy table in the middle of the hall, supported it by four worm-eaten poles, then we fetched some pieces of wood from the adjacent apartments, placing them upon large stones round the table, and thus secured a resting place for the night.

"Now we rambled through several apartments on the other side of the hall, and meeting with nothing worthy of our notice, except the traces of desolation, we returned by the way we had entered that gloomy mansion.

"We descended into the court-yard and made there likewise our observations: spurred on by curiosity, we entered through a ruinous side building, a garden, which still bore some marks of former grandeur; broken statues of marble were here and there lying on the ground. We cleared with our sabres a way through brambles and nettles to a grove of beech trees; it likewise was hardly penetrable.

"Having worked our way for more than half an hour, with much toil and difficulty, through a thicket of thistles and brambles, we arrived at length wearied and fatigued at an open spot; in the middle of it we beheld a statue, bearing in one hand an urn of black marble- we approached and read the following inscription on the pedestal :-

"HIC JACET GODOFREDUS HAUSSINGERUS, PECCATOR.

(Here lieth Godfrey Haussinger, a Sinner.)

"A little lower down we perceived a cross engraved in the stone, and under it

A.D. 1603.

"We stared at each other in dumb amazement, and being already too much fatigued, we did not like to work our way farther into the garden, and returned.

"Gentlemen,' began the officer, as we were going back, 'what do you think of the inscription on that tomb?'

"I think," replied I, 'it strongly corroborates

Part I

what the landlord has told us.'

"My companions smiled, and we came again into the court-yard, looking around we observed and arched wall opposite the stair-case; as we came nearer we saw a flight of steps leading to a cellar, which was shut up by a massy iron door, strongly secured by an enormous padlock.

Having now examined every corner we returned to our inn.

"The landlord, who was ignorant of what we had been about, was struck with horror and amazement when we related where we had been, and did his utmost to persuade us to desist from our design; however, when he saw he was spending his breath in vain, he kept his peace, and mentioned not a single word more about it during the whole day-we did the same-for the Lieu- tenant's conversation amused us so well, that evening stole upon us unawares.

"Our dinner was better than our scanty supper on the preceding day, because the Lieutenant had brought with him an ample provision of ham and cold beef; some bottles of excellent wine, which he was also provided with, raised our spirits, and increased his and the Baron's courage, in such a manner, that they expected the approach of night with the greatest impatience-they were constantly looking at their watches, and as soon as the clock had struck nine, thought it high time to go to the castle.

"We called the landlord to pay our bill, and the poor fellow tried once more to persuade us not to go to the castle he entreated us not to expose our lives thus daringly to certain danger, and at last fell on his knees; --but when we left the room, without taking notice of his entreaties and ardent prayers, he lamented before hand our untimely death, gave us a lamp, and bolted the door, fetching a deep sigh.

"The Lieutenant's servant walked before us, carrying the lighted lamp in his hand, and a portmanteau stocked H with provisions under his arm, and we kept close to his heels, armed with sabres and pistols.

"It was autumn, and of course very dark. We arrived at the castle; the faint glimmering of the lamp spread a kind of awful twilight around us as we were walking through the lofty arches of the vaulted passage leading to the court-yard. Having fired our pistols and loaded them again with bullets, we ascended the staircase; the doors leading to the hall we left open, that we might have a view of the court-yard, and sat cheerfully down down to supper; a bottle of wine we had taken with us to keep us alert, was handed round: however, we missed our aim, for every one of us began

Part I

to grow drowsy soon after we had finished our meal-we rose and walked about in order to avoid falling asleep, but we were soon tired of it, the ground being so very uneven, and returned to our seats. I recollected now, very fortunately, that I had put the fables of Gellert in my pocket. I took the book out, and began to read to the company; then I gave it to the Baron, and he was relieved by the Lieu- tenant-thus we were enabled to resist the powerful charms of sleep.

"Now it struck eleven. All around us was buried in awful silence, which only now and then was interrupted by the creaking of our feeble chairs; the Lieutenant wound up his watch and put it before him on the table.

"'One hour more,' began now the officer, and we shall be in another world.' Then he awoke his servant, who was fast asleep, and the Baron began again to read to us. When the Lieutenant's turn came for the second time, he looked at his watch and exclaimed, 'three quarters past eleven, we must be on our guard.'

"He got up and went to the window, I followed him, impenetrable darkness surrounded us, no star could be seen; awful silence was still all around, interrupted only by the snoring John, and the creaking of the wood; the pale light of our lamp produced a horrid glimmering in the spacious dreary hall; the

Baron, leaning his head upon his arm, struggled to forget every object around him, and the officer uttered not a single word.

"Now we heard a clock toll twelve at a great dis- tance, and I walked softly back to my seat, the Lieutenant did the same, taking up one of his pistols, and rubbing the lock with his handkerchief. We looked at each other, and every one of us strove in vain to hide the horror he was struggling against. The watchman cried the hour, the crowing of the cocks told us midnight was set in, and still all around us was as silent as the grave. The Baron laid the book upon the table, and the Lieutenant was going to raise a loud laughter, asking us where the spirits might be, when suddenly the trampling of horses and the sound of horns was heard-we all were fixed to our seats, staring at each other with a ghastly look; now the noise seemed to be under our window; the Lieutenant ran towards it, with a cocked pistol in his hand, but he was too late.

"All was quiet again, and an awful stillness swayed around the castle: however, a few seconds after we heard suddenly a most tremendous noise in the court- yard, which was followed by a terrible trampling and a gingling of spurs on the stair-case, as if a great number of people in boots was coming up. The noise came nearer and nearer, my feet began to fail, my teeth to chatter in my mouth, and my hair to rise like bristles, while every sense was lost in anxious bodings; at length the noise grew fainter and fainter, and soon we could hear it no more, and midnight stillness resumed her awful sway.

"A long pause of dumb astonishment ensued, until at last the Lieutenant, who had recovered his spirits first, exclaimed, Shall we go down?' I shook my head without uttering a word, and the Baron was likewise silent. Then I will go alone,' said the Lieutenant, snatched up a brace of pistols, drew his sabre, and hurried down. He returned a few minutes after, exclaiming, 'It is surprising; I cannot see the least traces of either men or horses.'

"Now he retook his seat, casting down his looks in a pensive manner-his servant was still snoring — the Baron began again to read, and I fell fast asleep. At once I was roused by the report of a pistol, I and honest John started up at the same moment, and we heard once more the trampling of horses and the sound of horns, but it soon died away at a distance, and the Lieutenant entered the hall with the Baron.

"They also had not been able to resist the leaden wand of sleep, but the same noise in the court-yard we had heard at twelve o'clock had soon roused them from their slumber. 'As soon as we heard the noise,' said the Baron, 'we hastened to the outer room, our pistols cocked, but before we could reach it the noise was under the window of the castle; the Lieutenant knocked through one of the windows in the room close to the hall, and sent a bullet after the troop, which was rushing by like an hurricane ; however, he was prevented by the darkness of the night from distinguishing any thing except some white horses.

"'The spirits are afraid of us,' exclaimed the Lieutenant now, but come, let us return to our inn, we shall rest more comfortable on a bed of clean straw than on this damp ground.' We all consented to it, and left the gloomy abode of those nocturnal sportsmen. We knocked a good while at the door of the inn before it was opened : and at last the landlord appeared, stammering, lost in wonder, 'God be praised that you are still alive, how did you escape?'

"The Lieutenant silenced him by some hasty lies, and promised to give him a full account of the whole adventure after he should have rested a little.

"'Gentlemen,' said he, as soon as he got up in the morning, 'next night I will go once more to the haunted castle, and spend the night in the court-yard, will you keep me company?' "The Baron looked at me as if he wished me to refuse the proposal; I did so. 'We cannot,' said I, 'stay here a day longer, and such an undertaking would, besides, be too dangerous for only four people.'

"'Ol' exclaimed the Lieutenant, 'if that is all

you have to say against it, then I will soon make you easy. We will take a dozen stout fellows from the village with us, they will not hesitate to accompany us if we give them a couple of dollars and a good dram; it will be devilish good fun, and to-morrow, with the first dawn of day, I will depart with you.'

"The Baron consented to the proposal, and I myself did not dislike it; in short, we remained, and sent our postillion through the village to publish, that all young fellows who would go with us to the castle next night, should have sixpence each, and as much brandy as they could drink.'

"In less than half an hour the whole village was as- sembled round the door of the inn. We selected fifteen of the stoutest, ordered them to provide themselves with proper arms, and to appear by ten o'clock at night at the inn. Our landlord, who beheld these preparations in dumb amazement, believed firmly that we must be arch necromancers, and his fancy having been fired by the wonderful account of our nocturnal adventure, which the Lieutenant had given him, he was himself not unwilling to go with us to the castle, and to bid defiance to the infernal hosts. However, as soon as it grew dark, his courage died away, and he wished success to our under- taking, telling us, he could not leave his house.

"Our little army was assembled before ten

o'clock, armed with scythes, poles, hay forks and flails. We ordered the landlord to give a dram to every one; took some tables, benches, lamps, and a small cask of brandy with us, and marched in triumph towards the castle.

"We pitched our camp in the court-yard, not far from the entrance, the peasants placed themselves round the brandy cask, lighted their pipes, and expected with pleasure the appearance of the airy gentlemen.

"Another advantage we reaped from that honest company was, that we had no need to keep sleep at a distance by reading, for the merriment of our little army soon rose to the highest pitch, and these jovial fellows, being heated by the contents of our little cask, challenged his satanic majesty and all his infernal hosts amid peals of roaring laughter.

"It was now past eleven o'clock, and the noise began to abate, some of our gentlemen were nodding, and some snoring, we were therefore obliged to beg those who had not yet yielded to the powerful charms of sleep, to give us a song, which they instantly did in so vociferous a manner, that our hearing organs were most painfully affected the sleepers started up when they heard that terrible noise, and joined the jovial songsters with all their might. Thus we chased away the god of sleep, who seemed not in the least to relish the disharmonious notes of our jolly companions.

Part I

"Now the Lieutenant beckoned to the blithesome crew, and the clamorous noise was suddenly hushed in awful silence. It struck twelve o'clock, and the sound of horns and the trampling of horses was heard at a distance. The peasants listened, their mouths wide open, and gazed at each other struck with chilly terror. No sound was heard, except the palpitating of their hearts, and here and there the chattering of teeth-all of them moved their lips as if praying ardently. The noise came nearer and nearer, and now it seemed to be in the castle. Again everything was silent, but in an instant the former noise Struck once more our listening ears, and the infernal hosts rushed by like lightning-the Lieutenant, the Baron, and I darted through the passage leading to the gate, but the airy gentlemen were already out of sight, and we could see nothing, save a faint glimmering of some white horses. The mingled noise of their horns and of the trampling of their horses soon died away; the stillness of midnight swayed all around, and we returned to the court-yard.

"Our valiant crew was still fixed to the ground, seized with horror and astonishment. None of them were able to distinguish whether we were ghosts or their fellow-adventurers; however, they recovered their spirits by degrees, and prepared to leave the residence of the infernal sportsmen.

"We left the castle, fully convinced that

these nocturnal ramblers must be beings who were afraid of us, discharged our courageous troop and went to rest.

"I awoke with the first ray of the morning sun, and roused the Baron and the Lieutenant; the latter seemed not to be inclined to fulfil his promise, being desirous to try his fortune once more, and to hide himself either in the court-yard, or before the gate. When he saw that we would not stay any longer, he postponed the execution of his design to a future time, and followed our example.

"We left our inn at six o'clock, the morning was gloomy and rainy, the wind swept furiously over the heath, and drove the black clouds still closer and closer together; after a few minutes we entered the Black Forest. Looking out of the coach I saw the Lieutenant and his servant turn to the left towards a brook, where we beheld an odd incident. A reverend old man was sitting there, and reading in a large book; bewildered in profound meditation, he seemed to take no notice of the howling storm; and not to be sensible of the rain rushing down in large drops upon his uncovered head, the tempest was sporting with his reverend grey locks, and the rain beating in his face, yet he did not stir. His long brown robe seemed to denote a traveller from the East-a long staff and a black wallet were lying by his side.

Part I

"I got out of the coach to view that strange being a little closer, and to speak to him, but before I could accost him, the Lieutenant exclaimed, 'Greybeard, what art thou reading?'

"The old man appeared to take no notice of his question, and went on reading as if nobody had been there.

"What art thou reading?' exclaimed the Lieutenant once more, alighting and looking over his shoulder at the book.

"The old man answered not a word, but still continued to read. I also was now standing behind him, and look- ing at the book, its leaves were of yellow parchment, the characters large and of different colours.

"The Baron was close at my heels, and the Lieutenant being provoked by the man's obstinate silence, shook him now violently by the shoulder, thundering in his ears, Greybeard, what art thou reading?'

"Now the old man lifted his reverend head slowly up, stared at us with angry looks, and then said, with a solemn awful voice,

"Wisdom !"

"What language is it?'

OLD MAN.(Reading again)—"The

language of wisdom." ""What dost thou call wisdom?'

OLD MAN." All that thou dost not comprehend."

LIEUTENANT.—"If thou knowest what other people can- not comprehend, then I should like to ask thee a question."

OLD MAN. (Staring again at him)—" What question?"

LIEUTENANT.-" There is a castle not far from the next village, where every night a numerous troop of spirits make their entry; I and these two gentlemen have watched there these two nights."

OLD MAN. (Interrupting him)—" And art not a bit wiser for□t, for thou seemest not to be fit to converse with spirits."

LIEUTENANT.- But thou-?"

OLD MAN. "I understand the language of Wisdom."

"The Lieutenant bit his lips, shaking his head with a contemptuous smile. Now the Baron accosted the old man, who again was immersed in profound meditation.

BARON." Well, then, if thy book contains

such a treasure of wisdom, then tell us why that castle is haunted by spirits, and for what reason they go their nightly rounds ? "

OLD MAN.-"That the spirits must tell thee themselves."

BARON.- What does then thy book contain ?"

OLD MAN." The ways and means of forcing them to a confession."

BARON." But why hast thou not forced them long ago to confess every thing?"

OLD MAN.-"Because I never cared for it."

BARON. (Laughing)-" But if we should entreat thee to do it, and pull our purses, would'st thou not do us that favour?"

OLD MAN. (Frowning)-" Vile mortal, can wisdom be bought with gold and silver?"

BARON.- "How can one then purchase it?"
OLD MAN." With nothing-hast thou courage ? "

BARON." Else we could not have watched in the dreadful castle."

OLD MAN." Then spend another night in it. I will be there a quarter before twelve o'clock-now leave me."

"We gazed at each other with doubtful looks. The old man resumed his reading, and seemed to take no further notice of us, who were still standing behind him lost in silent wonder. At length the Lieutenant mounted his horse, and we went back to our coach. 'Well,' said the officer, as we were getting in our carriage, well, gentlemen, will you return with me?'

"In vain did I make objections, the expectation of the two hot-headed young men was strained too much; it was impossible to subdue the eager curiosity of the young Baron, and the presence of the Lieutenant made me apprehend that all reasoning would not only be spent in vain, but at the same time make me contemptible; I therefore was forced to go back with them, and to embark in an enterprise, which, being not only useless, but also very dangerous, would plunge me in great distress.

"Our host was highly rejoiced and struck with astonishment, when he saw us come back with the intention (as he believed) to engage once more with the nightly sports- Our valiant companions of the preceding night had given a wonderful account of our adventure, relating how horribly the ghosts had looked, how courageously men they had encountered the infernal crew, and how the strange conjurors at last had banished the tremendous host from

Part I

the castle for ever.

"The whole village assembled, therefore, as soon as our return was known, gazing at us as supernatural beings, and consulting us about several matters. The Lieutenant had his fun with the simplicity of those honest people and the day was spent merrily.

"It was already dark, and the villagers had not yet left the inn; they unanimously intreated us to take them along with us to the castle. We were obliged to disavow our design, to feign sleepiness, and to order a bed of straw to be got ready.

"At ten o'clock we stole silently to the castle without a light; the Lieutenant's servant lighted our lamp in the courtyard, and we went to the hall, where we had spent the first night, waiting with impatience for the last quarter before midnight.

The Lieutenant did not believe the old man would be as good as his word; I joyfully seconded his opinion, and should have been glad if we had not waited for him; but the Baron, who, from his juvenile days, had been fond of every thing bearing the aspect of mysteriousness, was quite charmed with the reverend appearance of the old man, and maintained, upon his honour, that he certainly would stick to his appointment. "The Lieutenant began to discourse with the Baron on apparitions and necromancers, maintaining by experience and reasoning, that all was either deceit or the effects of a deluded fancy; yet the Baron would not relinquish his opinion, adding, that one ought not to speak lightly of those matters, and that the old man certainly would prove the truth of his assertion. We were still conjecturing who that strange wanderer might be, when we saw by our watches that there were but sixteen minutes wanting to twelve; as soon as it was three quarters after eleven we heard the sound of gentle steps in the passage.

"Our greybeard,' said the Lieutenant, is a man of honour,' and took up the lamp to meet the old man.

"Now he entered the hall, his black wallet on his back, and beckoned in a solemn manner to follow him. We did so, and he led us through the apartments and the vaulted passage down stairs. We followed him through the court-yard to the iron gate of the cellar without uttering a word; there he stopped, turning towards us, and eyeing us awhile with a ghastly look; after an awful pause of expectation, he said with a low trembling voice, 'Don't utter a word as you value your lives.' Then he went down the two first steps; taking from his bosom an enormous key which had been suspended round his neck by an iron chain, and opened, without the least difficulty, the monstrous padlock, the door flew open,

Part I

and the old man took the lamp from the Lieutenant, leading us down a large staircase of stone; we descended into a spacious cellar, vaulted with hewn stone, and beheld all around large iron doors, secured by strong padlocks; our hoary leader went slowly towards an iron folding door, opposite to the Staircase, and opened it likewise with his key; it flew suddenly open, and we beheld with horror a black vault, which received a faint light from a lamp suspended to the ceiling by an iron chain.

"The old man entered, uncovering his reverend head, and we did the same, standing by his side in trembling expectation, awed by the solemnity that reigned around us; a dreadful chilliness seized us, we felt the grasp of the icy fangs of horror, being in a burying vault surrounded by rotten coffins. Skulls and mouldered bones rattled beneath our feet, the grisly phantom of death stared in our faces from every side, with a grim, ghastly aspect. In the centre of the vault we beheld a black marble coffin, supported by a pedestal of stone, over it was sus- pended to the ceiling a lamp spreading a dismal, dying glimmering around. The air was heavy and of a musty smell, we could hardly respire, the objects around seemed to be wrapped in a blueish mist. The hollow sound of our footsteps re-echoed through the dreary abode of horror as we walked nigher.

"The old man stopped at a small distance from the marble coffin, beckoning to us to come nigher; we moved slowly on, and he made a sign not to advance farther than he could reach with extended arms. The Lieutenant placed himself at his right, I took my station at his left, and the Baron opposite to him.

"He put the lamp on the ground before him, taking his book, an ebony wand, and a box of white plate out of his wallet. Out of the latter he strewed a reddish sand around him, drew a circle with his wand, and folded his hands across the breast, then he pronounced, amid terrible convulsions, some mysterious words, opened the book and began to read, whilst his face was distorted in a ghastly manner; his convulsions grew more horrible as he went on reading; all his limbs seemed to be contracted by a convulsive fit. His eyebrows shrunk up, his fore- head was covered with wrinkles, and large drops of sweat were running down his cheeks-at once he threw down his book, gazing with a staring look, and his hands lifted up at the marble coffin.

"We soon perceived that midnight had set in; the trampling of horses and the sound of horns was heard, the Necromancer did not move a limb, still staring at the coffin with a haggard look. Now the noise was on the staircase of the cellar and still he was motionless, his eyes being immoveably directed towards the coffin. But now the noise was in the cellar, he brandished his wand and all around was buried in awful silence. He pronounced again three times an unintelligible word with a horrible thundering voice. A flash of lightning hissed suddenly through the dreary vault, licking the damp walls, and a hollow clap of thunder roared through the subterraneous abode of chilly horror. The light in the lamp was now extinguished, silence and darkness swayed all around; soon after we heard a gentle rustling just before us, and a faint glimmering was spreading through the gloomy vault. It grew lighter and lighter, and we soon perceived rays of dazzling lights hooting from the marble coffin, the lid of which began to rise higher and higher; at once the whole vault was illuminated, and a grisly human figure rose slow and awful from the coffin. The phantom, which was wrapped up in a shroud, bore a dying aspect, it trembled violently as it rose and emitted a hollow groan, looking around with chilly horror. Now the spectre descended from the pedestal, and moved with trembling steps and haggard looks towards the circle where we were standing.

"Who dares,' groaned it, in a faltering hollow accent; who dares to disturb the rest of the dead?'

"And who art thou?' replied our leader, with a threatening frowning aspect, 'who art thou, that thou darest to disturb the stillness of this castle, and the nocturnal slumber of those that inhabit its environs ? '

"The phantom shuddered back, groaning in a most lamentable accent, 'Not I, not I, my cursed husband disturbs the peace around and mine.'

OLD MAN. -"For what reason?" --

GHOST.-"I was assassinated, and he who judges men has thrown my sins upon the murderer." I comprehend thee, unhappy spirit, be- take thyself again to rest; by my power, which every spirit dreads, he shall disturb thee no more-begone-"

"The phantom bowed respectfully, staggered towards the pedestal, climbed up, got into the coffin, and dis- appeared; the lid sunk slowly down, and the light which had illuminated the dismal mansion of mortality died away by degrees. A flash of lightning hissed again through the vault, licking the damp walls, the hollow sound of thunder roared through the subterraneous abode of horror, the lamp began again to burn, and the awful silence of the grave swayed all around.

"The old man took up his wallet and his book, beck- oning us to follow him. We returned to the adjoining vault, through which we had entered that abode of awful dread; it was as lonesome as we had left it; our leader

Part I

locked the iron folding-door carefully; then he took out of his wallet a large piece of parchment on which a number of strange characters were written, a piece of black sealing wax, and a monstrous iron seal. Having made several crosses over those things with his ebony wand, he fixed the parchment above the lock, and sealed it hastily on the four corners.

"This done, he went into the middle of the cellar assigning us our places; then he strewed sand on the ground, drew a circle with his wand, and began again to read in his book amid horrible convulsions. He brandished his wand, pronouncing three times with a most tremendous voice the same word he had made use of in the burying vault. A flash of lightning hissed through the cellar, a clap of thunder shook the subter- raneous fabric, all the doors save that which had been sealed up were suddenly forced open with a thundering noise, the lamp was extinguished, and a blue light reflected in a grisly manner from the staircase against the damp wall; woful groans, lamentations, and the dismal clashing of chains resounded through the spacious caverns. The noise seemed to come from the staircase-gentle steps were heard a numerous troop seemed to be descending into the cellar; the lamentations and the woful groans advanced nearer, and louder resounded the clashing of chains.

"Horrid to behold did now a second phantom appear before our gazing looks, staggering slowly towards us, and leaving a numerous retinue on the staircase; the garment of the spectre was stained with blood, the skull fractured, the eyes like two portentous comets!

"'Who art thou?' roared our leader with a thundering voice, and the dreary cavern echoed to the sound.

"The phantom answered with a hollow, dismal voice, 'A damned soul!'

OLD MAN." What business hast thou in this castle?"

GHOST." I want to be redeemed from hell."

OLD MAN. How canst thou be redeemed?"

--

GHOST.-" By the forgiveness of my wife."

OLD MAN.-"How darest thou claim it, reprobate villain? Return to thy damned companions in hell. Respect this seal, respect these characters."

"Here the old man pointed at the door of the vault which had been sealed up: the phantom staggered towards it, but suddenly shuddered back and sunk groan- ing on the ground; a flash of lightning illuminated the cellar, and a tremendous peal of thunder resounded through the lofty vault; all the

Part I

doors were shut again with a terrible noise, a frightful howling filled our ears, and horrid phantoms hovered before our eyes; flashes of lightning hissed through the vault and roaring claps of thunder threatened to overturn the whole fabric.

The lightning ceased by degrees, and the roaring of the thunder died away, a blue flame was still glimmering on the staircase, but it soon died away, and we were surrounded with darkness; groans and dreadful Jamentations resounded still through the winding caverns, but soon all around was hushed in profound silence. After a short pause of horrid stillness, the trampling of horses and the sound of horns was heard again; yet that noise died also away before we recovered our recollection.

When our astonishment began to subside, we per- ceived that we were standing in a dark cellar, without knowing whether any one of us was missing. A disagreeable sulphurous odour affected our smelling organs, and bereft us almost of the power of respiration; not a whisper interrupted the dead midnight silence which surrounded us. At length, somebody took me by the hand, I shuddered back, my imagination being still the wrestling place of horrid wild phantoms, and my soul divining a thousand dreadful thoughts.

"It is I,' said the Lieutenant, and I felt at once as if a heavy load had been taken from my breast. Now the Baron began also to speak, 'Where are you?' whispered he, are you still alive?'

"We groped about in the dark, and at last found him leaning against the wall.

"'How shall we get out of this cursed residence of horror?' exclaimed the Lieutenant. 'Come, let us try whether we can find the staircase; It must be just opposite to us, if I am not mistaken.' Then he began to walk on, and we groped after him, tumbling now and then over loose stones.

"I have found the staircase,' cried our fellow adventurer, at last, after a long fruitless search, I feel the first step.'

A ray of joy beamed through our hearts as we were climbing up, but alas! it was soon most cruelly damped; the cellar door was locked up, and the blood congealed in our veins when the Lieutenant told it us. We exerted all our strength to force it open, but in vain, it was bolted on the outside. The Lieutenant called as loud as he could for his servant, whom he had left snoring in the hall; we joined our voices with his, calling with all our might' John! John!'

"The hollow echo repeated in a tremendous accent, John! John! but no human footstep would gladden our desponding hearts. Frantic with black despair did we now begin to knock at the massy door till the blood was running down from our hands, and to cry John, John, till our voices grew hoarse-the hollow echo still repeated in an awful tremendous accent our knocking and crying, but no human footstep was heard. The fellow sleeps and cannot hear us,' said the Lieutenant, at length with a faint voice, 'let us sit down and watch him when he shall come down.'

"'We did So, but I had no hope that the servant would come, yet I concealed my apprehension within my breast. The Lieutenant dissembled to be easy, and began to con- verse on what we had seen and heard; however his broken accent, the faltering of his speech, and his low voice, betrayed the anxiety of his mind. The Baron and I spoke little, and when we had been sitting about an hour not one uttered a word more; all was silent around us. Nothing interrupted the death-like stillness of the night, except the violent beating of our hearts.

"At length the Lieutenant asked if we were asleep; however, the anxiety of our minds and the dreadful apprehensions which assailed us, drove far away even the idea of sleep. We sat some hours in the dreadful situation, and it was now about five o'clock in the moining when the Lieutenant exclaimed, 'I fear we wait in vain for my servant, he cannot sleep so fast that he should not hear us! But where can he be?' Then he began again to knock violently against the massy iron door, but all was in vain. No human footsteps were heard, we remained some hours on the staircase, but all our waiting and listening was fruitless, no cheering sound of human footsteps would gladden our desponding hearts.

"I will not torment you by vain apprehensions,' began the Lieutenant at length, 'however, we seem to be doomed to destruction, yet let us try if we cannot escape some way or other, come down with me into the cellar, there we shall have a better chance to espy an outlet than here.'

"We descended, with trembling knees, without saying a word, and groped along in the dark a good while, knocking our heads against the damp wall, and the iron doors. Alas! our search seemed to be in vain, and the grim spectre of a lingering death stared us grisly in the face, my feet could support me no longer, and I dropped down wearied with anxiety.

"Now I began to reproach myself for having plunged into the gulph of destruction not only myself but also him who had been entrusted to my care. The apprehension of being famished in that infernal abode, thrilled my soul with horror and black despair; at first I heard the Baron and the Lieutenant still groping about; neither of them uttered a word; the hollow sound of their footsteps re-echoed horribly through the vault—at length the sound of the Baron's footsteps died away at a distance, and only one of my companions in destruction remained with me.

"Where are you?' exclaimed the Lieutenant.

"'Here I am,' replied I, 'but where is the Baron?' 'The Lieutenant called him, and I did the same, but we received no answer. At once a sudden hollow noise struck our ears, and at the same time a faint glimmering of light darted from a remote corner of our dungeon. I started up, half frantic with joy, and we pursued the gladdening ray of light; it seemed to come from an opening in the wall. No words can express the rapture we felt when we beheld one of the iron doors half open; we went through it with hasty steps, and entered a long vaulted passage. A faint dawn of light hailed our joyful looks at a great distance from below. We descended a declivity, the farther we went the more the light increased, at length we reached the end of the avenue, and perceived some steps leading into a spacious apartment, at the entrance of which some boards on the floor had given way. We descended the steps, and, who can paint the horror which rushed upon us, when we beheld the Baron lying lifeless in the deep vault, upon some mouldering straw? I leaped down without a moment's hesitation, the Lieutenant did the same, and now we began to shake the Baron till we at length perceived signs of returning life. We continued our endeavours to recall his senses, he breathed, gave a hollow groan, and opened his eyes : his fainting fit had been the effect of sudden terror, and he had not received the least hurt.

"He now told us that he had met in the dark with a long narrow passage which he had pursued, in a kind of insensibility, till he had staggered down from an elevated spot, when the boards suddenly gave way, dragging him along into the deep vault.

"Looking around we perceived that we were in a spacious cavern, which appeared to have been formerly a kind of stable. High over our heads were two large round holes, grated with strong iron bars, through which the daylight was admitted, and after a closer examination we espied a gloomy outlet in a remote corner, shut up by a wooden door, which we forced open without diffi-culty. We now ascended through a dark passage, higher and higher, till we at length with rapture beheld an outlet which opened into the garden; we were obliged to cut our way with our sabres, through the underwood and the entangled weeds, and soon came to the court-yard. Tears of joy sparkled in our eyes, rays of unspeakable rapture beamed through our hearts, and we praised God for our unexpected deliverance from the grisly jaws of a lingering death.

Part I

"The dreary desolated court-yard appeared to us a paradise, the dazzling splendour of the bright morning sun, and the pure air which we now inhaled, filled our hearts with the strongest sensations of bliss. We con- gratulated each other on our resurrection from the dreary abode of mortality, where we were doomed to be en- tombed alive, and shook each other by the hand half frantic with joy.

"We went now to the hall in search of the Lieutenant's servant; the table and everything was in the same condition we had left them, but John was not there. We went through the whole gloomy fabric shouting and hallooing, discharging our pistols, but no sound was heard except the hollow echo repeating our shouts and the reports of our pistols all over the dreary building.

"Very likely he is returned to the inn,' said the Lieutenant, 'and we shall find him there.'

"We left that dangerous abode of black horror, praising God again and again for our deliverance.

"As we entered the inn we beheld the landlord sur- rounded by a number of villagers, who were come to inquire whether we were returned from the castle. They were very much surprised when we entered the room, and, respectfully taking off their hats, told us, that the uproar at the village last night

72

had been more tremendous than ever. Every one was impatient to know the particulars of our adventure, but the Lieutenant having then no inclination of amusing himself with their simplicity, gave them a short answer, and asked the landlord where his servant was.

"I have not seen him since yesterday,' replied he.

"It is impossible,' resumed the Lieutenant; 'where are the horses?'

"They are in the stable,' replied the landlord, 'I have just been looking after them.'

"The Lieutenant gave us an apprehensive look, and begged the gaping peasants to look after him, all over the village and the adjacent places: they all were very willing to do it, and left the inn.

"It was nine o'clock when we entered the inn, and it struck twelve when our honest villagers returned, with the disagreeable news that they could find poor John nowhere.

"The Lieutenant thought it not prudent to remain any longer at that fatal place; the Baron likewise wished to depart and I too was impatient to be gone. As soon as we had finished our scanty dinner, we departed a second time; the tears started from our landlord's eyes, and from those of the good

Part I

villagers, when we bade them farewell, after having made them a small present, and they saw us depart with regret.

"The Lieutenant knew the ways through the Black Forest pretty well, he rode by our chaise leading his servant's horse with one hand, and we reached without any farther accident the limits of that dreadful forest. We parted company at the close of the second day, bidding each other a tender adieu.

"I thank you, gentlemen,' said the Lieutenant, as we were getting into our chaise at the door of the inn. 'I thank you for your kind and faithful assistance in the most dreadful adventure of my life; if I should be so fortunate to get at the bottom of the mystery which hangs over that castle, as I shall endeavour to do, I will take the first opportunity to apprise you of my success. Farewell, remember now and then the 20th of September, 1750, and do not forget your friend.'

"The postillion smacked his whip, and we went different roads. On the fifth day we arrived, without any further accident, at the castle of Baron R-, the father of my pupil.

"And here," added Herman," my narration is finished. A letter which the Baron wrote me, and a manuscript sent me by the Lieutenant, contains everything that has happened afterwards. But these papers you shall not get before your departure."

Though Elfrid's curiosity had been spurred very much, yet he could not but consent to his friend's proposal, and spent a fortnight more with him in uninterrupted pleasure.

The days rolled swiftly on, shortened by the conversation of his friend, by hunting and other diversions, and he at length was obliged to bid his host adieu. Before he parted with his Elfrid, he gave him the above-mentioned manuscript, assuring him that he would have given it him sooner, if he had been able to find it amongst a great many papers. He added, that he had searched for it in vain several days, and would have given him the continuation and conclusion of those mysterious adventures, by way of narration, if he could not have found the manuscript, but he had fortunately traced it out the day before his departure amongst a number of old musty papers. Herman cleaned it from the dust and gave it to his friend, saying to him, "Take, brother, take here the continuation of my tale, and if thou thinkest the publication of it will amuse and benefit the world thou art welcome to publish it."

Then they parted, alas! for ever. Herman's wish was accomplished, he had seen once more the faithful friend of his younger days, and soon after went to that better world where

Part I

good men will meet again the friends of their
bosom, never to part again. Elfrid, too, is
awaiting the solemn morn of resurrection in
his grave, and he, before he died, set down in
writing the foregoing narration. Now let us see
what the writings which his friend had given
him contain.

END OF THE FIRST PART

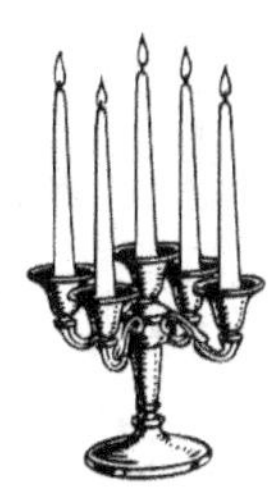

PART II

CHAPTER I

BARON R— TO MR.
HERMAN

"B- Nov. 11, 1772.

DEAR FRIEND,-It is with the greatest
pleasure I am going to communicate to you a
remarkable incident I met with this summer,
when at Pyrmont. I would have given you the
following account some time ago, if it had not
been for some papers which I was obliged to
wait for; they are arrived at last, and here I
send them, beseeching you to remit them to me
as soon as you shall have perused them.

"I had been three weeks at Pyrmont, when I
one time went to the promenade on a very
beautiful evening, there I happened to meet a
gentleman whose features interested me very
much though they were unknown to me.
Walking slowly on I soon saw him come after
me, he passed me with hasty steps, and
turning suddenly stared me in the face; I did
the same, being surprised that I also had
attracted the notice of the stranger. He went
on, but soon after turned round once more,
directing his steps towards me and staring
again at me. I stopped and did the same. He
moved his lips as if he wanted to speak to me,
just when I was going to ask him whether he

77

wanted something; however, we both remained silent, pursuing our walk. That pantomime we repeated several times, neither of us uttering a word, at length it began to grow dark and I went to my lodgings.

"The next morning I awoke with the first ray of the sun, and went again to the promenade, to inhale the salubrious breeze of the morning air, and to hail the rising king of the day under the canopy of heaven. I was no sooner seated on a bench beneath a majestic beech-tree, admiring the greatness of the Creator so Striking in the beautiful scenes of a fine summer's morning, when I once more beheld the stranger who had interested me so much the preceding evening. He came nearer, saluted me, and took a seat on the bench where I was sitting. We both admired, in profound silence, the beautiful scene around for a quarter of an hour. Every object which surrounded us pronounced the greatness of God: numbers of feathered songsters hailed the rising sun; diamonds and rubies sparkled on the leaves of the trees, loaded with the pearly drops of dew. Now the sun darted his warming cheerful rays all around, and the Stranger looked at me with an inquisitive eye. Sir,' he at length began, 'you will excuse me if I should be mistaken. I think I have had, some years past, the pleasure of being in your company somewhere or other.'

"It is possible,' replied I, 'that I have had that

honour. Will you favour me with your name ?'

"'My name is B- and I am Major in the service of the King of Denmark.'

"'B- ! I think I remember that name, yet I cannot recollect where I have had the honour of seeing you.'

"'Perhaps I may,' replied he, 'if you will be so kind to favour me with your name.'

"'My name is R—.' 'Did not you return from your travels to Germany in the year 1750?'

"I replied in the affirmative.

"Then I am not mistaken,' said he smiling, 'don't you remember the adventure at the Haunted Castle on the skirts of the Black Forest, and that villanous Necromancer?'

"I was struck with amazement, 'How,' exclaimed I, 'is it you? Do I not dream?'

"'Yes, dear friend, it is I,' he replied, 'you are not mistaken. How strangely and how unexpectedly do friends meet sometimes in this world! I am at present governor to a young prince who is on his travels. We are here incognito, yet I could not resist the ardent desire of making myself known to you. Did you never wish to get some further intelligence of the mystery of that terrible castle and its strange inhabitants? With the greatest pleasure I would have communicated to you what came to my knowledge since we parted, had I but known the place of your residence; I travelled on purpose to your native town as soon as I had finished my recruiting business, but I was told you had been sent by your prince to England on affairs of state."

"'Your kindness deserves my warmest acknowledg- ment, and I am very sorry that I had the misfortune of being absent when you intended to do me the honour of seeing me.'

"'Your absence vexed me very much,' he replied, 'because it not only deprived me of the pleasure of seeing once more an old friend, but also prevented me from performing the promise I had given you when we parted. This happy meeting affords me, therefore, the greatest pleasure, and if you will favour me with your company, at my apartments, I can give you a satisfactory account of several accidents which happened before and after our adventure at the castle, and which are nearly connected with what we have encountered.'

"I accepted his kind invitation, and went with him to breakfast in his apartments. On the way he inquired after you, and was rejoiced to hear that you are well and happy, blessed with the love of a dear and virtuous wife. He particularly seemed to be pleased with my little narrative of your matrimonial bliss-I forbore to inquire after the reason of it, fearing to renew the pains, which perhaps the recent loss of a dear beloved object might have inflicted upon him, and gave our conversation another turn until we arrived at his apartments.

"After we had breakfasted we seated ourselves by the window, and he began a tale which took an unexpected and a most wonderful turn, but the accidents were so various and many, that he only could give me a short sketch, which being interspersed with many episodes, was rather confused. He was himself sensible of the defects of his narrative, and promised to send me a written account of those wonderful accidents as soon as he should have finished his travels.

"I spent five happy days in his company, and then we parted reluctantly. Two months after he sent me the enclosed continuation of his adventures, which will Strike you with astonishment.

"Major B sends you his best wishes, he longs ardently to see you once more.

"Farewell, and remember "

Your faithful,

R—

CHAPTER II

ADVENTURES OF LIEUT. B-

"I was lost in profound meditation after I had parted with my companions; all the horrid scenes of the ad- venture at the castle hovered before my imagination; I fancied myself at the inn, in the ruinous hall, and then in the cellar, still beholding the Necromancer and the phantoms, seeing the flashes of lightning, and hearing the roaring of the thunder, and the hollow voices of the spectres. My fancy renewed all the horrors which had rushed upon me when shut up in the cellar, as well as the joy I felt when we had the good fortune to find an outlet from our infernal dungeon; my restless fancy painted all these pictures with the strongest colours, painted them so grisly, that I sent up to heaven the most fervent thanksgiving for my delivery from that infernal abode.

"These horrid dreams vanished at length, giving room to contemplations of a more serious cast. I was every moment reminded of the unhappy fate of my faithful John, and felt an ardent desire to get at the bottom of those mysterious events, that I might be enabled to deliver my poor servant from the clutches of the spirits, or, at least, revenge his death. I was however sensible, that I alone should not be equal to it; the peasants of the village I did not think fit for assisting me in my enterprise, and the whole undertaking too hazardous without the assistance and the counsel of an experienced and resolute man. I therefore was determined to search for such a man, and, aided by his counsel and assistance, once more to encounter those nocturnal sportsmen.

"This resolution was the result of my meditations on the first morning after my separation from my companions, and I burned with impatient desire to rid myself of that load of uncertainty which lay heavy upon my mind. At length I arrived at the place of my destination, and resumed my recruiting business, assisted by two old serjeants.

"I hastened to return to the skirts of the Black Forest, and went to F, while there I met with Prussian, Austrian, Hessian, and Swedish recruiting officers, and now and then with an old acquaintance of mine.

"Amongst others I got acquainted with an old Austrian officer, who was highly respected by every one; when he said anything, which happened not often, then everybody listened with the greatest attention, and when, now and then, a quarrel arose, everything was soon settled by his interference.

"A man who thus powerfully could influence a set of people who admit no law but that of superiority soon engaged my admiration in the highest degree, and I concluded he would be the fittest person to assist me in the execution of my design, to unfold the mystery of the Haunted Castle, if I could but gain his confidence ; yet I was sensible that it would be no easy task to ingratiate myself so far with him that he should not refuse believing a tale like mine, which bore such glaring marks of fiction. I apprehended a veteran of so much experience, and so serious a turn of mind, would laugh at my narrative, and treat it as a nursery tale.

"I was the more inclined to fear this apprehension might prove true, when I learned by experience that his curiosity was always guided by cool and just reasoning. His cheerfulness never exceeded the limits of moderated seriousness, and his smile was nothing more than an almost imperceptible unfolding of the wrinkles, which contracted his reverend brow; his mirth bore the resem-blance of his carriage, and whoever knew him, trembled at his anger, though none of his acquaintances had ever experienced the least mark of passion in his countenance, and much less had he ever betrayed a symptom of un-bridled wrath.

"I let slip no opportunity of doing him some little services, and thus endeavoured to gain his favour; how- ever, he appeared to take no notice of my unremitted zeal to please him; I treated him with marks of the highest veneration, whenever I was in his company, but he seemed not to regard it. All my most anxious endeavours to win that strange man over to my interest proved abortive, and, at last, I gave over every hope of engaging his attention.

"Chance befriended me, at length, unexpectedly, and I got by accident what I already had despaired to attain by the most indefatigable endeavours.

"The inn where one of the recruiting officers lodged was reported to be haunted; many strange stories circulated on account of that report, which the then owner of the house endeavoured to laugh off, because he had lived a fortnight in it without perceiving any thing uncommon.

"This subject afforded one evening matter for a serious discourse among the officers. The Austrian veteran maintained, contrary to our expectation, that one ought not to treat with ridicule some events of supernatural a pearance, and no argument could make him relinquish his opinion. My heart panted for joy, for now I could hope he would not refuse to credit my wondrous tale.

"I was already going to relate the Strange events which I had witnessed at the Haunted Castle, when I suddenly was checked by the apprehension of drawing upon me the laugh of the company, or that some one or other would offer to encounter with me the nightly sportsmen, without being equal to that hazardous undertaking.

"The Austrian spoke with uncommon warmth, his eyes sparkled, and the wrinkles on his brow were contracting closer and closer, and when the company persisted in contradicting his opinion, he offered to enforce his arguments by undeniable facts, which he himself had experienced, requesting to be heard in profound silence, which could not but be granted to a man like him. We expected to hear something very uncommon, and for sometime gazed at him in dumb expectation, till he at length began as follows: —

"If I maintain that apparitions of supernatural beings ought not wholly to be rejected, then I must tell you, gen- tlemen, that I do not only mean that it is merely possible that departed souls, or supernatural beings of another class, can appear when and wherever they please; but I also promise to convince you by my own experience, that there are people who can affect apparitions of that kind, at certain times and under certain conditions.

"We stared at each other in silent wonder: the pre- amble of the Austrian gave us reason to expect some horrid tale, and the seriousness of his looks and the solemn accent of his words commanded general awe. After a short pause, our solemn narrator related the following tale: —

CHAPTER III

THE AUSTRIAN OFFICER'S TALE OF GODFRIED BURGHER'S GHOST

"IN a regiment of the garrison in which I served as Lieutenant, about twenty years ago, was a man who gave the most undeniable proofs of the truth of my assertion; he was a serjeant, about forty years old, and of a morose and gloomy appearance; he was respected by his superiors, prompt and exact in the service, and never would brook an affront. The unthinking called him a sorcerer, and people of a more serious cast of mind talked of his connexion with superior beings, taking great care not to offend that terrible man, whose name was Volkert. In the whole he was a very good sort of a man, never offended any body, if not provoked, was averse to company, and fond of solitude.

"He was reported to have performed many strange and wonderful exploits; an ensign, who had severely chastised him for a slight neglect in his duty, was said to have been deprived ever since of the proper use of his right arm; and a captain, who had scolded him without reason, to be afflicted with a deficiency in his speaking organs. In short, strange things were every where related of Volkert, and in so serious a manner, that no impartial man would laugh at those reports.

"I had not, as yet, got an opportunity of getting more nearly acquainted with that wonderful man, and I must confess I was not very desirous of being introduced to him, for I always treated with scorn such supernatural events, yet I never liked to make those matters a subject for ridicule.

"Some of my comrades were frequently inclined to have a fun, as they used to call it, and to request the sorcerer, Volkert, to raise up the ghost of one of their companions who had died suddenly in order to ask his departed spirit whether he had found pretty girls and good wine in the other world; but I always dissuaded them from it, endeavouring to direct them to some other amusement. Meanwhile the rumour of Volkert's ex- ploits increased from day to day, and some people would swear solemnly, that they had seen and conversed with their departed relations, through his assistance.

"Among those who related such strange things of Volkert, was a woman, whose husband had died sud- denly some months ago, and entreated her, before he expired, not to give her daughter in marriage to a certain tradesman who had courted her. The girl doated on the young man, and he likewise was exceedingly fond of her; the distress this young couple felt at that sad and cruel prohibition, cannot be expressed by words; their grief was unspeakable when they were thus unexpectedly removed for ever from the happiness of being united by the bonds of holy wedlock, just when they flattered them- selves to have reached the aim of their fondest wishes.

"Volkert was quartered in the same street where the unhappy girl's mother lived. She requested him to find out, by means of his supernatural skill, what reason might have induced her departed husband to forbid his daughter, on his death-bed, to marry the man of her choice, though he had not only never the least objection against the union, but also had always looked upon it with the greatest satisfaction. Volkert promised to take the matter into consideration and answered, some days after, that the deceased himself must be applied to.

"The poor girl was very much frightened at this declaration, however, the hope of being at last united to the darling of her love-sick heart, revived her spirits, and she consented at length to suffer the rest of her parent to be disturbed. The mother refused for a considerable time to consent to it, however, at last she agreed to Volkert's proposal, and the day, or rather the night, for the execution of the conjuration was fixed. — ' The mother,' added the Austrian, ' has related to me the whole transaction, and I will let her speak herself.'

"'It was on a Saturday,' said the good old woman, 'when we were assembled in a back room, the same wherein my late husband had breathed his last, myself, my daughter, her lover, and two of my neighbours being present. At eleven o'clock we began to sing, as Volkert had ordered us, penitential hymns and psalms till the clock struck twelve, when we left off singing, and Volkert entered the room, clad in a white garment, barefoot, and with a pale and disordered countenance; under his arm he carried a black carpet, a naked sword, and a crucifix, and in each hand a lighted taper. As soon as he entered the room, he beckoned us to rise, and made a sign not to utter a word; then he placed a table in the middle of the room, covered it with the black carpet, and put the crucifix and the tapers upon it, holding the sword in his hand: This done, he took out of his pocket a bottle with consecrated water, and sprinkled us and the floor with it. After we had pulled off our shoes and stockings, he burned perfumes in a chaffing-dish, and began the conjuration, mumbling many mysterious words, and brandishing his sword as if fighting with an invisible enemy; at once the combat seemed to cease, he grew quiet, and turning to- wards us who had been standing around him, exclaimed, 'I have succeeded, he is coming!'

"A thick smoke overdarkened suddenly the

room, the lights were extinguished, and a shiny figure, resembling in a most striking manner my deceased husband appeared.

"Ask him,' said the Necromancer, ask him before he vanishes.'

"I shuddered, seized with horror, and was unable to utter a single word: my daughter was in the same situa- tion; the phantom gave us a ghastly look, shaking his head, as if denying something. The Necromancer exhorted us once more to ask the spectre, and one of my neighbours took courage to question him. 'Who art thou?' asked he with a faltering voice. 'Godfried Burgher,' answered the phantom, in a hollow woeful accent.

"'May thy daughter marry Anthony Smith?'

"'No! no!' replied the apparition, gave a deep hollow groan and shook his head in a ghastly manner.

"'Why not?' resumed my neighbour.

"The phantom shuddered, lifting up his hands in a menacing manner, staggered back, and, when disappearing, added in a most rueful accent,

"He is her brother!'

"Night surrounded us, the Necromancer

pushed the window open, and the tapers began again to burn. Now I could breathe again, and looking anxiously around, beheld my poor child stretched on the floor in a fainting fit. The unhappy girl recovered soon, but alas! her reason was gone. We were seized by the chilly hand of horror when we beheld her roving like a frantic person, wringing her hands, in a grisly manner, tearing her dishevelled hair, and beating her breast in an agony of despair. A burning fever had disordered her mind, and, alas! after three days she was no more! Wild despair drove her lover into the wide world, and heaven knows whether he is still alive or has fallen a victim of his wretched fate. I am a poor disconsolate mother, and haunted by the agonizing pangs of a tormenting conscience, can find neither rest nor comfort here below; the spirit of my poor child, murdered, by my consent to that wicked infernal transaction, hovers constantly before my bewildered fancy; my peace is gone for ever; I dare not to pray to the supreme ruler of the world, for comfort and mercy, though he who dwelleth in heaven knows that I reluctantly consented to that wicked transaction, for no other reason but to promote the happiness of my murdered child, murdered by her own mother, who ought to have been her guardian angel! Oh! God of mercy, what! what will become of me, when I shall be called to the tribunal of the All-seeing! when I shall behold her standing before the Supreme Judge, and hear her accuse me in the face of heaven as her murderer? How shall I, how can I answer the stern questions of him who has entrusted her to my care, to watch with a mother's tenderness, over her life and happiness? I tremble, seized with chilly horror when my frantic mind anticipates that awful moment, when he who sitteth on the throne of majesty shall, with the voice of thunder, say unto me, Wretch who hast cruelly murdered thy child, depart from me into everlasting fire, prepared for the devil and his angels -Alas! I feel already within my breast, the worm that shall never die, and the fire that shall not be quenched."

Having thus given vent to her grief, she tore her hair in wild agony, beating her breast, and the tears of sorrow trickled down her cheeks-she appeared a grisly, ghastly figure.

"Her narrative, though incredible in the highest degree, made an unspeakable impression on me. I beheld the poor disconsolate mother standing before me in an agony of unutterable grief; saw the briny tears of her who had with her own eyes witnessed the apparition, and heard her bemoan her unhappy child. "Having mused awhile on these dreadful events, I felt an ardent desire to unfold the mystery hanging over that wonderful transaction; or, if I should not succeed, to convince myself by my own experience of Volkert's supernatural skill.

"I interrogated the woman about several circumstances, which had appeared to me rather suspicious; and asking her, at last, whether she had any reason to think that the lover of her daughter had really been a son of her deceased husband, she was prevented, by her tears and sobs, from answering that question, I therefore dis- missed her, with the firm resolution to make the strictest inquiries at her neighbours, which I did the same day, but all my endeavours to unfold that mysterious transaction proved abortive; they could tell me no more than what I had known already, repeating the unhappy widow's tale without any material alterations; I was left in the dark and found myself necessitated to check my ardent curiosity.

"I now waited with impatience for an opportunity of witnessing Volkert's skill, being determined to be present if he should perform another transaction of that kind.

"I went to him, requesting him to give me notice if he should happen to make a new experiment, and to admit me as a spectator. He hesitated not to give me his word, but seemed very little inclined to perform his promise, being terrified by the last transaction and its fatal consequences; the whole town talked of it, and the widow was sued at law on account of the death of her daughter. Volkert was prohibited by his General from making any farther experiment of that kind. He had not mentioned to me that interdiction of his commanding officer, yet I perceived that my request gave him some uneasiness, which I took for mistrust when I after- wards came to know that circumstance.

"A few months after my application to him, a new accident happened, which gave him an opportunity to exhibit an astonishing proof of his supernatural skill, and tempted him forcibly to disregard the earnest prohibition of his General.

"A friend of mine happened to fall out with a foreign officer, who had been visiting his parents, the foreigner challenged my friend, who most readily consented to decide the quarrel by the sword. Business of the greatest consequence obliged the foreigner to depart in the night preceding the morning on which the duel was to be fought — he wrote a note to my friend, promising upon his honour to appear at the appointed place on the ninth day, and my brother officer consented to the delay.

"I and a few more officers of our regiment paid a visit to my friend who had been challenged, two days before the duel was to be fought; we were in high spirits, played, ate and drank amid the cheerful laughter of merriment, not recollecting, that after three days our host, perhaps, might not be more. He himself appeared to have entirely forgotten the quarrel, 'till he at last, at the close of our merriment, recollected the duel he was going to fight, telling me who was to be his second, to remind him the following day of his killing business, lest his valiant adversary, Captain T-, might wait in vain for him.

"Upon my soul,' added he, heated with wine, 'I wish he was here now, d-n me if I would not send him to Paradise, to rest in Abraham's bosom.'

"'Why, brother,' exclaimed one of the visitors, could you not have him summoned hither by Volkert?

"That would indeed be excellent fun!' resumed my friend, but you know Volkert dare not do it, we must of course let him alone; yet, if the rascal does not come the day after to-morrow, Volkert must be applied to, and, even if I should be obliged to ask the General's permission he shall conjure him hither, that I may pierce his cowardly soul.'

"A unanimous bravo rewarded this unripe joke of our jovial host; we separated, and I went home, lost in profound meditation. Having some reason to suspect that Baron T would let us wait in vain, his departure having been so abrupt, I thought this would prove a fair opportunity of putting Volkert's super-natural power to the test. At last I resolved to wait quietly the issue of that affair; and if T should give us the slip, to try whether I should be able to persuade Volkert to give us a sample of his skill.

"Though I had unjustly doubted Baron T's courage, as it will appear in the sequel of my narrative, yet what we had suspected happened afterwards.

"The day fixed for the duel came, but no Baron T- appeared. We waited for him six hours, and still he did not come. Now I hastened to Volkert without telling a syllable of my design to my friends. The mysterious man smiled as I entered the room, and appeared to have a little more confidence in my honesty than when I paid him my first visit. I broke the business to him without circumlocution, and he seemed not unwilling to chastise the foreign officer for his want of courage, yet he endeavoured to make me sensible of the disagreeable conse- quences which likely would arise, if the transaction should transpire. I summoned up all my little rhetoric, and refuted his objections, by assuring him, that my friends would give him their word of honour never to betray him, and thus screen him from every disagreeable consequence; and that, if an unforeseen accident should unhappily make the transaction known, our joint interference should save him from punishment.

"These arguments, accompanied by golden encouragements, conquered at last all his remaining fear; he promised to serve me at any time; however, he entreated me not to invite too great a number of friends, that the danger of detection might not be increased without need. Having promised to act according to his desire, I left him with the greatest satisfaction, and went directly to my dis- appointed friend, who was railing with much asperity against the cowardice of his adversary.

"'What, brother,' exclaimed I, what will all this anger boot thee? It certainly will not give courage to Baron T— —, and thou canst not be blamed on account of his ungentleman-like behaviour, having not challenged him. There are a great many who would be glad to sneak off so cheaply and yet so gloriously; you rather ought to pity the white-livered fellow than to be angry with him, yet, if you like, we may hit him a blow when he least suspects it.'

"Not knowing whether my friend would approve my plan or not, I pronounced the last words in a jocose tone to secure a fair retreat, in case he should not relish my proposal.

"How else,' resumed I, 'could one get at him, than by forcing him to wait on us? Didst thou not lately swear to have him conjured hither by Volkert, if he should give us the slip ?'

"My friend seemed at first to be offended, looking upon my proposal as an unseasonable joke; but when I went on talking of Volkert, and his occult arts, he asked me at last, Seriously, friend, dost thou believe in the secret arts of that fellow?'

"'I believe nothing,' replied I, that I have not seen; let us make a trial how far the common talk of his supernatural arts deserves to be credited.'

"He stared at me with astonishment, asking me, after a short pause, 'Dost thou expect to prevail on that necromancer to agree with our wishes?'

"'What wouldst thou say,' replied I, 'if he had already consented to give us his assistance ?'

"My friend stared again at me, and exclaimed at last with visible satisfaction, 'Well then, let us see what honest Volkert can do.'

"Everything requisite for the accomplishment of our design was now talked over and settled. Two of our brother officers, whose discretion we could rely upon, were chosen to be of the party, and my friend agreed to win them over to our purpose.

"I returned to Volkert, and was not a little surprised when I found him less willing than ever to assist us in our undertaking. He pretended to have pondered my proposal, but thought it too dangerous to exert his supernatural knowledge in the present case, because the conjuring of a living person could have the most dreadful con- sequences, which very likely might happen on the present because the Baron seemed not at all to be over-stocked with courage. Though I could not contradict him, yet I endeavoured once more to dispel his apprehensions, by the repeated assurance to screen him, with the assistance of my friends, against every disagreeable consequence. At length he appeared to be easy in respect to that point; yet he did not think it convenient to execute our design in the apartment of my friend, but when I proposed my room, he consented, after many persuasions, to look at it. Having gained his consent, I left him with rapturous joy.

'Volkert came the next day to my lodgings, faithful to his promise, but having looked over my apartments, he raised new objections, telling me that none of my rooms were fit for the undertaking. I could not conceal my displeasure, which he, however, did not seem to notice.

"At last he made me another proposal before he left me, offering to speak to an honest tradesman, who had an empty room, which would exactly fit his purpose, and, as he hoped, be at our service, if we would but make a reasonable acknowledgment to its owner. I consented to that proposal, Volkert went away, and returned after half an hour with the joyful tidings that he had prevailed on the man to let us have the room, fixing, at the same time, the ensuing night, for the exe- cution of our design. He requested me to repair to the place of rendezvous after nine o'clock, describing the street so minutely that I could not miss it. Having reminded me once more of my promise, he left my room, and I went out to tell my friend and our two associates to resort in good time, to the place of appointment. At eight o'clock they came to my apartment, burning with impatience to witness the mysterious transaction, and we hastened a quarter before nine o'clock, to the house where our curiosity was to be satisfied.

"I knew the owner of the room which Volkert had chosen, as a worthy, honest man. When we entered his house he accosted us with much good nature, request- ing leave to be admitted to the experiment, which we the more readily consented to when he cautioned us to be on our guard against the cunning of Volkert, whom he very much suspected to be an artful impostor.

"'I, for my part,' added he, 'have taken all possible care to prevent the Necromancer from imposing upon us, and I would lay anything that we shall catch him in some foul play or other.'

"When we told him that imposition would

be impossible, because the gentleman who was to be summoned was still alive, he burst out into a loud laughter, requesting us to wait in his parlour till Volkert should call us upstairs.

"He will not be disturbed in his toilsome labour,' added he, smiling, and has made the whole evening such a tremendous noise, that one should think he had been hunting up and down the whole infernal crew of his satanic Majesty.'

"Time had passed quickly on in the company of that queer good-natured man, who fetched two bottles of excellent old wine, bidding us to be of good cheer. The clock struck ten before we were aware of it, and as soon as the last stroke was heard, Volkert entered the parlour, holding a lighted taper in his hand, his looks were wild and ghastly, his face pale, and every muscle of his countenance distorted, as if some horrid accident had filled him with terror. Every smile of merriment took its flight as he entered the room, our jovial mood was checked at once, and our faces grew deadly wan, like his, bearing all the marks of secret awe. He beckoned us to follow him, and we obeyed his solemn command like machines, forgetting where we were.

"He led the way, with tottering knees, in awful solemn 'silence, and we followed him with beating hearts, expect- ing to behold unheard and wondrous things. We stepped into a spacious room, in the back part of which we saw a little door. Volkert opened it, leading us through an empty narrow ante-chamber to a folding door; there he stopped, looking back with a ghastly boding aspect, and put the key in the lock-now he turned it slowly and carefully, the folding doors flew suddenly open, a thick smoke broke from it, as we entered, and darkened at first all the objects around.

"Ere long I observed in the back part of the spacious apartment a human figure clad in a white garment. The smoke evaporated by degrees through the open door, and the figure grew brighter and brighter, and, advancing a few steps towards it, I fancied to discern some known lineaments. The smoke was now entirely evaporated, and the vision hovered clear and discernible before our gazing looks; I shuddered back when I beheld the exact image of Baron T- before me. His tall slender figure, clad in a white night-gown, struck our senses with awe, as he stood motionless before us-his looks denoted a man in the agony of death, his long black hair covered partly his pallid woe-worn cheeks, floating in a grisly manner down his shoulders.

"The vision stared at me and my companions with a ghastly rueful aspect, it made my blood congeal, thrilling my soul with deadly horror; my hair rose up like bristles, and I staggered back towards my friends, who were standing by the door like lifeless statues, their faces wan, their looks bewildered-they resembled midnight spectres, just risen from the yawning grave. I collected all the small relics of courage, advancing again some paces towards the dreadful phantom, and saw the vision hovering nearer, making some feeble signs with his left hand. I made an attempt to speak, but what I said I do not know. The phantom uttered not a word, but was still making anxious signs with his left arm, Now I understood what he meant the right arm hung in a sling as if fractured.

"As soon as I comprehended this pantomime, the phantom staggered back, a dark mist arose from under his feet and surrounded the vision by degrees until we at last could see him no more. I panted for breath, my senses forsook me, a horrid humming noise filled my ears, my eyes grew dim, I staggered to the wall and was nearly fainting. At once I felt my senses returning, and, opening my eyes, beheld myself in a spacious, empty room, my companions around me, panting for breath like myself -Volkert was no where to be seen.

"It lasted a good while before we could entirely re- cover the proper use of our benumbed senses. My comrades were chilled with horror, and every one seemed to ask his neighbour, by his inquisitive looks, whether what our senses had witnessed had been a deluding dream or reality.

Part II, Chapter III

"The landlord was standing behind me, trembling like my companions, with crossed arms and downcast looks, buried in profound meditation, and exhibiting a woful picture of pallid fright; at length he begged us to follow him down stairs, and we went into the parlour with dejected spirits, he offered us a dish of tea, but we refused staying any longer, gave him two louis d'ors, and left his house.

"The next morning I awoke, wearied and dispirited, having had only a few moments of restless sleep. I expected Volkert would come to fetch his stipulated reward, but I was disappointed, and esteemed him higher for his seeming disinterestedness. At noon my friend who had been challenged paid me a visit.

"'Brother,' exclaimed he, as he entered the room, ´ tell me, what did the vision of last night mean by the anxious motion of his arm?'

"That his right arm was fractured,' replied I hastily.

"There, read that letter,' resumed he, throwing an open letter on the table; I took it up and read as follows:

"'Sir,-An unhappy accident prevents me from ful- filling my promise this day, having been thrown from my horse and fractured my right arm. However, as soon as I shall have sufficient strength to make a journey of twenty leagues, I shall insist upon your giving me satisfaction. I am fully persuaded that you would suspect me of foul play, though I should not have sent you the enclosed certificate; yet, not to give you the least room to suspect my honour, and to screen yourself by mean subterfuges, I send you the enclosed certificate of our Surgeon-Major. Within six weeks at farthest I hope to recover the use of my right arm, by the skill of that honest man, until then I remain, without either spite or enmity,

"'Baron T—.

'Signed with my left hand.'

"I gazed in dumb amazement at my friend, who was walking up and down the room with hasty steps and in a pensive attitude.

"Well,' exclaimed he at length, what dost thou think of that letter? It was, as I suppose, only owing to the carelessness of the postman, that I received it so late. The certificate cannot be suspected, and I would have believed the Baron though he should not have sent it.'

"I remained silent, reading over again and again the letter of the unfortunate T. The preceding night and the whole morning I had been wavering between doubt and belief, but now I was convinced of the Necromancer's skill, as I am still, and dreaded to see his face. At length I suffered myself to be persuaded by my friend to pay him a visit; he was not at home, and we went several times to his lodgings without seeing him, until we at last, on the third day, met him on the parade. I approached him, and my three fellow adventurers did the same, Volkert wanted to give us the slip, when he saw us coming towards him, however we came up with him, and with great difficulty persuaded him to come to my lodgings in the afternoon-having promised to meet us, he went instantly away with hasty steps.

"At three o'clock he made his appearance; we showed him the Baron's letter-having read it with apparent unconcern, he said, that he as well as ourselves had known the contents of it three days ago. We persuaded him with great difficulty to accept four louis d'ors for his trouble, and he promised to see us now and then, and to convince us of his warmest gratitude by every service in his power, if we would but promise him, on our word of honour, never to desire him any more to raise up ghosts.

"I have suffered very much,' added he, 'and I am determined to expose myself no more to like dangers. I am afraid some additional disaster awaits me. Baron T— is no poltroon, which I am glad of, but I fear, I fear lest—'

"Here he stopped, taking up his hat; we asked for the reason of his apprehensions, entreating him to speak without reserve; but all was in vain, and he left the room with these words, 'I wish all may end well.'

"We could not comprehend the meaning of these words, and did indeed not much mind them, my friend being quite unconcerned about the duel, which we thought Volkert had been hinting at.

"Eight days were now elapsed without any disagree- able accident. None of us had spoken a word, as well of our adventure as of the duel, but on the ninth day we were reminded of it in a most terrible manner. My friend entered my apartment at a very early hour, with a pallid, disordered countenance, flinging a folded letter on the table. I took it up, seized with terrible apprehensions, and saw that it was a second letter from Baron T— —. 'If you will give me leave, gentlemen, I will read it to you.' We all consented to it, and he read as follows:-

"Sir,-Having recovered my strength a little, I hasten to request you to acquaint me with the particulars of a dreadful accident, which you, without doubt, will be able to unfold.

"In the night succeeding the day which was fixed for our meeting, an accident happened to me which I cannot unriddle, and most willingly would suppose to have been nothing but the delusion of a disordered imagination; if not, many of my friends had witnessed the unspeakable sufferings I have endured. I was seized. after eight o'clock in the evening, with an agony more terrible and excruciating than that of a dying person, expiring amid the most pungent horrors and torments of a violent death. Drops of cold sweat bedewed my face, a chilly trembling shook my limbs violently, and the leaden hue of death rendered my countenance wan. I hoped to find relief if I was to walk up and down the room; how- ever, I was seized by the burning fangs of still greater, still more agonizing pains, and the despondency preying on my bewildered fancy increased every minute. I shivered and trembled in such a manner that the chattering of my teeth could be heard at a great distance; all my muscles were contracted by horrid convulsions; the pangs of excruciating agony increased for two hours of infernal torture, until at last, my friends, despairing of my life, carried me to bed; there I lay for half an hour as if my spirit had been separated from my body, which really has been the case. I can give no better description of the last degree of my agonizing pains, than by comparing my feelings with the torments of one whose whole frame suddenly is pierced with a red hot iron.

"'After that terrible shock I was in a state of lethargy, but I dreamed, a horrid, frightful dream. Methought I was violently dragged away from my weeping friends, and, on a sudden beheld myself in the company of some known persons, who seemed to be highly delighted with my torments, and inflicted still greater pangs on my woe- worn frame.

"Suddenly I recovered my recollection, to the utter astonishment of my afflicted friends, but I awoke in such a pitiful state of weakness, that every one present, and even the physician who attended me, despaired of my recovery. They all are of opinion that my enemies must have effected those infernal torments by supernatural means, and I myself cannot think otherwise. You certainly must have some knowledge of that shameless, horrid transaction, and it is you to whom I ought to apply for an explanation. I expect your answer by the returning mail. I repeat it once more, you must know the particu- lars of that infernal transaction, &c. &c.'

"The impression this letter made on us,' resumed the Austrian,' cannot be described. I read in the countenance of my friend the bitterest reproaches, for having seduced him to employ the infernal arts of Volkert to so shameless a purport.'

"The serious turn which this dark transaction began to take made us apprehend that it would end with a most melancholy catastrophe, yet all our apprehensions were trifles light as air in comparison to the dreadful anxiety which poor Volkert was overwhelmed with, when these tidings were reported to him. We now plainly comprehended the tendency of the mysterious words he had uttered, when we had seen him last-I never saw a man in a more distressing situation than he was as he perused the Baron's letter. His agony rendered him almost distracted when he came to the conclusion of that melancholy epistle. He wrung his hands in wild despair, was beating his breast, and tearing his hair, exclaiming in an accent of unspeakable agony, 'I am undone !'

"Then he fell on his knees, imploring us for God's sake to spare him, and to save him from ignominy and ruin. 'I have foreseen it,' groaned he, 'I have foreseen it; O, had I but that time not suffered myself to be deluded to lend a helping hand to that wicked, infernal trans-action!'

"We did all that lay in our power to make him easy, and promised him to take all disagreeable consequences upon ourselves; however, he would not listen to the comfort we administered to him.

"I am too much known,' exclaimed he, and left us in wild despair. "I now consulted with my friend what was to be done, and we agreed at last that it would be best not to answer the Baron's letter, but quietly to await his arrival.

"Volkert, who was now more submissive and humble than ever, came frequently to see us, and approved our resolution; but he was always in the greatest anxiety when the idea of the Baron's arrival crossed his mind. Meanwhile the time when we were to expect the Baron drew nearer and nearer.

"Six weeks were now nearly elapsed since we had received his last letter. One morning, as I was reading and smoking my pipe with much tranquillity, my servant entered my room, telling me a foreign officer desired to see me. Not suspecting that I should be the first person to whom the Baron would give notice of his being arrived, I was struck with surprise when I beheld Baron T- before me, and I cannot but confess that I was seized with horror when I saw him. The marks of a recent dangerous illness were still visible on his pale countenance; his gloomy, melancholy aspect strongly denoted the sufferings of a deeply afflicted mind, and his whole carriage horribly reminded me of the detestable, dark transaction of that unhappy, fatal night. He entered my room bowing silently, and began, after a portentous pause, to address me thus :—

"'Sir, you are the second of Mr. C, who has injured me in a most glaring and disgraceful manner; first, by having insulted me in public, and then by having employed infernal arts to torment me. I dare say you are no stranger to the horrid means your friend has made use of in order to let me feel his wrath. I will not publicly accuse your friend of that black, shameless transaction, the dreadful effects of which you can still read in my countenance; however, he shall answer me with his heart's blood for that ignominious transaction, and for the sufferings he has made me undergo. I have written to him, but he has not thought it proper to answer my letter, which is a certain proof of his having been concerned in that horrid deed, the reality of which I am now fully convinced of: I know everything, even the wretch who has assisted in the performance of that diabolical business. Do not ask me how I came to know it.'

"He spoke this with such an emphasis, that I was unable to utter a single word in defence of my friend, and he appearing not to expect anything of that kind, added, after a short pause,—

"'My arm is not yet fit to manage the sword, for which reason I request he may bring with him two brace of pistols. You may tell this, your friend: I hope he will not oblige me to force him to accept my terms. At seven o'clock next morning I shall be at the spot we have appointed long ago; till then farewell, and tell your friend that I have not waited on him, because he prefers to con- verse with unbodied beings, and that I have written to him no more, because he has not thought proper to answer my last letter.'

"So saying, the Baron rose and left me in

such per- plexity that I was not able to utter a word in reply. My friend was not less frightened than myself when I told him his antagonist pretended to know the whole of our secret transaction. The remainder of the day was spent in preparations for the duel, and in settling all the affairs of my friend, in case he should be killed.

"Volkert came in the evening as usual, being afraid of being known to have any connection with us. He trembled violently when we told him that the Baron was arrived, but understanding that he would not make public the dreadful wrongs which he had suffered, the poor fellow recovered from his fright, and offered to assist the Lieu- tenant's servant, who was scouring his master's pistols. This task was soon finished, the two brace of pistols cleaned and charged with bullets.

"We sat down conversing and drinking punch till midnight, when Volkert left us with the promise to see my friend once more next morning. He seemed little inclined to give us his opinion on the means by which the Baron could have got intelligence of the conjuration, and the man who had performed it; yet he promised to tell us next morning all he knew about it. I remained with my friend the whole night, and began to sleep a little towards morning. At six o'clock Volkert interrupted our slumber, telling us that he came to take leave of us.

Part II, Chapter III

"We gazed at him with astonishment and surprise.

"'Yes, gentlemen,' exclaimed he, 'I am going to leave this town, and I am very fortunate that I can do it in an honourable manner. I promised you last night you how Baron T has traced out his tormentor; know, then, that he has written to his family the same that he wrote to you in his second letter; his relations soon suspected me, being known here as a Necromancer these many years; they gave notice to the governor of the supposed transaction, and he bearing me a great regard, would not meddle with this affair; he has, however, requested my General to remove me to some other place as soon as possible, which my commanding officer was very willing to grant. He sent for me the day before yesterday, and when I appeared before him accosted me thus:

"'Volkert, I have warned thee several times to prac- tise no more thine infernal tricks, I expected thou wouldst show some regard for thy General, but seeing that all my endeavours to recall thee to thy duty are fruitless, I must send thee away, yet do not fear that I shall be unkind to thee. I know thou art a clever fellow, and I will give thee a commission as recruiting officer, which employment, I suppose, will not be disagreeable to thee, because it will afford thee an opportunity to make a proper use of thy talents.'

"'My heart was ready to leap into my mouth for joy,' added Volkert, 'when I heard these welcome tidings, for this is the very situation I had been hankering after. Yesterday I received my instructions, my commission, and plenty of money, and I shall set off as soon as I shall have seen the decision of Mr. C's affair, and begin my new employment with pleasure and vigour.'

"We were surprised to see the gloomy, melancholic Volkert on a sudden so cheerful and merry, but he did not give us time to disclose our astonishment, taking a hasty leave. Having wished success to my friend, he shook us heartily by the hand, and told us, that if Mr. C should kill the Baron he expected him to join him on the road, adding,

"'Perhaps I may then have a better opportunity to convince you of the love and high esteem I bear you.' Having promised to see me once more after the duel, if possible, he left us; however, I saw him no more. The hour fixed for the fight drew nearer and nearer. We now took a hasty breakfast and went to the appointed place, where we found the Baron awaiting our arrival in com- pany with a foreign officer, his second. He was impatient to begin the combat directly, but I begged him to have patience, and to remove a little farther from the town, into the field, lest the report of their pistols might be heard by the sentinels on the ramparts. Though the young spark thought it needless to be over cautious, as he scorn-fully called it, he consented at last to my proposal, riding a good distance farther. We thanked him for his readiness to oblige us, and alighted. '

"The combatants were placed opposite each other, within the short distance of four paces. My friend fired first, but missed his antagonist; the Baron doing the same was not more successful; my friend fired a second time, but he missed his aim once more; Baron T- -'s second ball grazed his antagonist's cheek; Lieutenant C- was vexed, and seeing him take up the third pistol, with a trembling hand, I asked the foreigner whether he was satisfied; he shook silently his head, and my friend missed him again: the Baron returned the shot, and his ball entered the shoulder of C—: I entreated the foreigner to desist from farther animosities, however he would not listen to me and turning with a malicious grin towards his second, he took the fourth pistol from his hand; my friend discharged his into the air, but the Baron, less generous, took his aim, and his ball whizzed through his antagonist's hat; then shaking my friend smiling by the hand, he mounted his horse, and rode in full speed to the town, accompanied by his second.

"The Lieutenant grew fainter and fainter from the loss of blood, and all my endeavours to stop it were fruitless. At length my servant, whom I had sent to town, arrived with a coach and a surgeon, who declared that the wound was of no consequence, and, having dressed it, we con- ducted my friend to his apartments.

"On our arrival we were told that the Baron with his second had been arrested as they had entered the town gate, but nobody could tell us who had been the informer. The auditor of the regiment made his appearance soon after, and examined me strictly, yet he assured me that we had nothing to fear. It is known,' added he,' that your friend has not been the aggressor.'

"When I begged him to tell me the name of that in- former, he paused awhile and then replied,

"'Well! I will tell you to whom you owe that kind service, he is no more here; it was Volkert, the noted Serjeant of Colonel R- 's regiment.'

"'Volkert!' exclaimed I, the words dying on my lips. "The auditor affirmed it and left me. I followed him to the door, inquiring whether Volkert had said anything else.

"I don't think he has,' replied he, 'he departed this morning on the recruiting business, and before he left the town has told the governor, that a foreign officer, a notorious wrangler, had challenged Lieutenant C, and that they were going to fight a duel this morning. The governor ordered a file of soldiers to arrest you, but they were too late.

Part II, Chapter III

When Baron T returned to town, he was arrested along with his second. That is all I know of the matter.'

"I returned to my wounded friend in a pensive mood, not knowing what to think of Volkert's strange pro- ceedings. I was inclined to look upon this step as a proof of his concern for my friend's safety, yet I could not conceive why he had not given earlier notice to the governor, having known the hour when the duel was to be fought.

"The wound of my friend was not dangerous, and he was able to go abroad after the tenth day, when he went to the governor to make his submission. Having expected to be condemned at least to four weeks' confinement, he was surprised when that gentleman, who was known to be very rigorous, dismissed him with a slight reprimand. Our General took not least notice of the whole transaction, and Baron Treturned to his garrison after having been arrested four weeks. All our brother officers spoke highly of his noble behaviour, telling us that he had rejected all the proposals of his relations to interfere in his behalf.

"'However," added the Austrian, "I will not abuse your patience any longer, and here conclude my won- derful tale, thinking to have fully proved my paradoxical opinions, by the account I have given you of Volkert's experiment, and I thank you cordially for your kind attention to my long mysterious narrative; you will excuse my prolixity, having been desirous to give you a faithful account of that strange man. Although I am not able to clear up his character in a more satisfactory manner, yet I am convinced that you now will believe that spirits can appear to the eye of mortals."

"Here he ended, seeming to care little what sensations his odd tale might have produced in the mind of his hearers. The serious tone in which he had been speaking, and the high respect we bore him, prevented us from making our observations on his tale; I, for my part, could not help thinking it very extraordinary and fabulous, yet I could not harbour the least mistrust in the narrator's veracity, in despite of the struggles of reason, being fully convinced of his honesty. My design of relating to him our adventures at the Haunted Castle began now to ripen, and I was determined to catch the first opportunity that should offer to impart to him my secret.

"The other officers sat in dumb silence, seeming to ponder how to abide by their first opinion without op- posing their reverend antagonist: 'It is a pity,' one of them exclaimed at last, after a long solemn silence, it is a pity that Volkert is not present, for I am sure he would convince us also, by ocular proofs, of a matter which bears such evident marks of impossibility, in the eye of the impartial friend of truth. I do not in the least suspect your veracity, being fully persuaded that you are convinced by your own experience of a reality of the strange incident you have related; yet you will not take it unkind if I assure you, that my reason will prevent me from becoming a convert to your opinions, until I shall have been an ocular witness of an experiment of that kind.'

"The Austrian replied not a word to that speech, but rose and took up his hat in dumb silence.

"'But, pray sir,' resumed another, have you had no further account of Volkert? did he never return from his recruiting business?'

"'He is dead,' replied the Austrian.

"'Dead!' we repeated with one voice.

"'He is,' repeated the veteran, coolly, he met with a sad misfortune in the second year of his employment; ten of his best recruits gave him the slip, and, being called to an account for his negligence, he fell a victim of wild despair, blowing his own brains out.'

"A sad exit for a Necromancer,' resumed he who had put the question to the Austrian.

"'But a common one with gentlemen of that line,' added another, rather forward.

"The Austrian gave him a stern, scornful look.

"'I wish Volkert was still alive,' said he who lodged at the haunted inn, 'I wish he was still alive, he soon would restore tranquillity to the house of my landlord, and put a stop to the disagreeable talk that is rumoured about, and so hurtful to the poor man.'

"The Austrian made a silent bow to the company, and left the room. I followed him with hasty steps, and, coming up with him, accosted him respectfully. 'You will excuse the liberty I am going to take to request of you a private hearing, wishing to impart to you something.'

"'That I will hear to-morrow,' interrupted he drily, and went away.

"The night being far advanced I went to my lodging. I awoke with the first dawn of day, arose, and, having put on my clothes, waited with impatience till it should Strike eight o'clock, at which hour I intended to pay a visit to the Austrian. It was about five o'clock when I got up, and the seeming slow progress of time was very painful to me. At length the wished-for hour arrived, and I went with hasty steps to the veteran's lodging. He received me as he was wont to do, with great kindness, giving me a pipe, and after I had lighted it he asked me what my pleasure was?

Part II, Chapter III

"After some circumlocution I broke the matter to him, giving him a full account of our adventures at the Haunted Castle. He listened with great attention to my tale, and hinting, at the conclusion of it, that I wished he would assist me in unfolding that mysterious matter, he looked seriously at me without uttering a word. Having waited some time for his answer with anxious impatience, he arose, and walked up and down the room in profound meditation.

"'Friend,' said he at last, after a long and painful silence,' what reason have you to engage in that dangerous undertaking?'

"'I have no other motive,' replied I, 'than to chas- tise the impostors, and to deliver my servant from their clutches.'

"'He shook his head: 'Are you certain,' resumed he at length, after a short pause, 'that your servant has not been associated with those nightly sportsmen ?'

"I stared at him and replied, after having meditated awhile, 'No, it is impossible, the fellow was too honest; and what motive-You are right,' interrupted he, it cannot have been a preconcerted plan.'

"He walked again up and down the room in a pensive mood, and then exclaimed suddenly in a determined tone, 'Well, I will be one of the party, and, if you like, we will set off instantly.'

"I eagerly accepted his proposal, and having put in readiness everything necessary, we agreed to depart in the evening. He proposed to take one of his serjeants with him, and I resolved to do the same. I returned to my lodging against noon, highly pleased with my success, in order to prepare myself for a speedy departure.

"We left F- at eight o'clock in the evening; nobody was privy to our design, and our serjeants fancied we were going on business, wondering very much how recruiting officers in the service of two different princes could act thus in concord. But on the road we undeceived them, and were much rejoiced that our hoary veterans did not dislike our enterprise.

"Three days after our departure from F— we arrived within a small distance from the place of our destination, without having met with any sinister accident.

"We were now on the skirts of the Black Forest, but could see no village; the spot where the houses leading to the castle had began was deeply impressed on my memory. I showed to my fellow traveller the rivulet, on the borders of which the old man had been sitting when we first had met him; we looked about for the houses but we could find none. I did not know

Part II, Chapter III

what to think of the matter.

"Pursuing our route, we ascended a rising ground. Gracious heaven! how was I shocked when I at once beheld a heap of ruins on the spot where the village had stood! We could still trace the marks of conflagration. In the back-ground we saw only a few miserable huts left, and a little further distant the castle presented itself to our view. We gazed at each other in dumb astonishment, and the Austrian alighted; I and our two hoary veterans did the same, and we climbed, after much difficulty, over the heap of ruins. As we approached the few remaining houses, the inhabitants came running towards us covered with rags, and exhibiting pale, woe-worn countenances. I never beheld such a horrid picture of wretchedness and misery; they wrung their hands, crying for alms, and wept bitterly.

"Having distributed money amongst them, I inquired when that misfortune had happened. Alas!' groaned they, who should have thought, when your honour left us, that you ever would see us in such a miserable State? We are all ruined; all our little property has been consumed by the flames. Good heaven! how shall we keep our little helpless babes from starving?'

"Repeating my question, when that terrible accident had happened, the poor unfortunate people told me their village had been set on fire the day after we had left them.

"Dreadful apprehensions filled my soul, and the Austrian's looks seemed to confirm them.

"When I inquired after my former host, I was told that he had lost his life in the flames. 'The fire,' said the poor people, 'broke out suddenly, in different places, in the dead of night; they had not been able to save their property, and a great number of the inhabitants, with their cattle, had perished in the flames.' This horrid tale made my blood run chill, being convinced that I had been the primary cause of that dreadful event.

"As we entered one of the miserable huts, we were met by the lamentations of people half-naked; they all recollected me, receiving me with hideous groans. All my money was not sufficient to comfort the unhappy sufferers, but I divided it willingly amongst them, feeling an inward pleasure in being able to ease at least their sufferings a little. The Austrian, smiling at me, followed my example as far as the expenses of our journey would admit.

"At last I ventured to inquire after the Haunted Castle; the poor sufferers shuddered at the question, telling me, without reserve, that they did not doubt that the last visit we had paid to that abode of horror had drawn upon them the dreadful ire of the revengeful spirits, which I in vain wished to be able to contradict. Unwilling to behold any longer the marks of sorrow and distress so deeply imprinted on the faces around me, and stung to the heart by the tormenting thought to have partly contributed, by my idle curiosity, to provoke the lurking tempest of woe that had thus cruelly crushed the earthly happiness of the wretched villagers, I hastily inquired for the next village, they showed us the way, and we bade them fare- well with a bleeding heart, riding away in full speed. resentment.

"But, alas! I could not escape the hideous spectre of self-reproach, pursuing me with icy fangs. The scene of misery which my eyes had witnessed hovered constantly before my gloomy fancy, the groans of woe which I had heard still vibrated in my ears, the haggard looks of these unhappy people, undone by my heedlessness, stared me in the face ever and anon, and I struggled in vain to shake off the grisly spectre pursuing me with unrelenting How comfortless and miserable is the man,' said I to myself, whom conscience accuses of having plunged into the gaping gulph of misery a fellow-creature!'

"The Austrian saw the painful workings of my soul, kindly striving to dispel the gloomy clouds hovering over my brow. 'How can you accuse yourself,' spoke the reverend veteran, of having been, though involun- tarily, accessory to the fatal blow that has thus cruelly destroyed the happiness of these people, whose fate you are bemoaning? It was the high decree of a superior power, that rules the fate of man. The ways of the All- wise are ever good and just, though surrounded some- times with impenetrable darkness. Men are but tools in the hand of Providence, and never ought to murmur against the Father of the universe. It is not you who have destroyed the happiness of these poor sufferers; your heart is good, and you could not foresee the dreadful consequences of your juvenile rashness; cheer up, young man, and trust to the Supreme Ruler of all things, that he knows best what is good and fit; he produces light from the womb of darkness, and leads sometimes his children to greater bliss over the thorny path of misery and woe.'

"I listened with eager attention to the soothing speech of comfort flowing from the reverend lips of my sage companion, and a heavy load was taken from my heart; when he had finished, the clouds of gloominess dispersed by degrees, and a ray of cheerfulness darted through my mind. After half an hour's ride we beheld a large village before us; we agreed to wait there the setting in of night, and then to visit the Haunted Castle secretly.

"Our host could not, or perhaps would not, answer our inquiries concerning the desolated castle, and we endeavoured in vain to know whether the mighty sports- men were still housing there or not; my serjeant went abroad to get some information, and was so fortunate as to draw from the schoolmaster of the village as much as we wanted to know; returning after an hour with the corroboration of our suspicion, that the spirits residing at the castle had set fire to the desolated village, and that they since that time had forsaken their former abode.

"Although the latter part of his intelligence gave us but little hope that we should succeed in our design to unfold the mystery of the ruinous castle, yet we determined to make at least a trial, the Austrian being very desirous to explore the noted building, and we went all four to the Haunted Castle as soon as it was dark.

"We arrived at the gloomy fabric after a short walk, lighted some torches we had brought with us from F————, entered the courtyard, and ascended the spiral staircase; the Austrian searched every corner, and I found all the rooms in their former condition, the seats and the table we had constructed were still as we had left them, un-moved, untouched.

"When the Austrian had carefully searched everything, we descended the stairs leading to the cellar, but found the iron door strongly fastened as before. We entered the garden, searching and prying round, till we at length espied the aperture of the cavern through which we had effected our escape from the grisly jaws of a lingering death. The hollow sound of our footsteps re-echoed horribly through the dreary subterraneous abode as we entered, and the light of our torches reflected grisly from the damp mossy walls of the deep and narrow passage.

"Stepping into the ruinous stable, we espied, with pleasure, the hole in the boards through which the Baron had fallen down, and detected in one of the corners a ladder, and above the place where it was standing a trap-door. Having ascended the ladder, I opened the half- decayed door, with one violent push, and entered with my fellow-adventurers the well-known spacious apartment, leaping over the gaping opening where the boards had given way. Looking around we beheld several small iron doors, one of which flew open at the first push of the Austrian, and presented to our eyes the avenue of a damp arched vault, from which a stone staircase led to that part of the fabric which faced the cellar door.

"Without stopping there, we pursued our way to the large folding door leading to the great hall under ground, but found it strongly bolted on the inside, and all our hopes of farther discovery were blasted at once. We made the utmost efforts to disengage the massy door from its rusty hinges, but all our labour was lost, its Strength proved superior to our united endeavours of forcing it.

"While we were standing before that door, consulting whether we should go back or not, we heard suddenly a distant noise, as if a lock was opening, and soon after a folding door seemed to fly open, with a hideous creaking, which instantly was followed by a terrible noise of numer- ous steps as if people in boots were descending. When the noise drew nearer, we could distinguish the clattering of many spurs, and the harsh voices of men; the whole subterraneous cavern was at length filled with a most tremendous noise, and we gazed at each other rather pleased than frightened, being four vigorous men, used to danger, provided with four sabres and as many brace of double-barrelled pistols. The Austrian, standing nearest to the door, retained his equanimity unimpaired and, ere long, a hollow voice, like the distant rolling of thunder, exclaimed, 'Come hither with the booty.' A confused bustle ensued, the tinkling of money was heard, some quarrelled and some cursed and scolded, but were soon reconciled. At length the bustle ceased, a door was opened close by us, and money locked up in a chest. Meanwhile the following discourse took place in the unknown assembly.

"FIRST VOICE. To-morrow we will waylay the gentle- men of Norrinberg, and ease them of their golden burthen. I trust you will behave like men, my jolly boys! It would be a pity if they should give us the slip once more.

"SECOND VOICE. By holy Peter! they shall not escape.

"MANY VOICES. They shall not, they shall not.

"THIRD VOICE. I wonder where our grey-beard may stay so long. I have not seen his holy face since our last fun.

"FOURTH VOICE. Take my word, brother, he sits by the fireside and chaunts penitential hymns. The fellow is of no further use to our community, we must send him to the devil.

"FIRST VOICE. Let him alone, my boys, he has ten- dered us many good services, has saved many of our brave companions from the hangman's ruthless fangs; don't grudge him a little rest, he will soon return and bring us joyful tidings.

"SECOND VOICE. He has procured us many a golden booty; has, by his cunning, extricated us from many neck-breaking difficulties; it would be ungrateful to be angry with him. What would become of our noble band if he did not guide our arm by his sage counsels?

"THIRD VOICE. Bravely spoken, my lad, he is a good sort of a fellow; it is a thousand pities that he begins to grow old and infirm.

"FIRST VOICE. Let him grow old and infirm, if he but escapes the gallows.

"Here somebody was locking the door of an adjoining room, a hollow bustle and humming ensued, and the robbers (for such they must have been) were going to withdraw.

"'Shall we break in upon the scoundrels?' whispered the Austrian to me.

"'By what means?' replied I, shrugging up my shoulders.

"'Through the garden, or the adjoining wing of the castle,' resumed he.

"'But the danger,' said I,-' Is fancy,' interrupted the Austrian; not so great as you yet it will be better to force the gentlemen to open the door; if they should refuse to do it, then it will be time enough to surprise them in the court-yard, for I do not think it prudent to venture on the staircase, because they would then have too much advantage over us.'

"Now all was silent in the cellar, till after a short pause a new conversation began.

"FIRST VOICE. I say, brother, what shall we do with the officer's servant we have entrapped? The dog is good for nothing, and we are in danger that he will betray us one time or other.

"SECOND VOICE. Let us knock his brains out.

"THIRD VOICE. Let us give him his liberty.

"FOURTH VOICE. Or sell him to a recruiting officer.

"FIRST VOICE. We will take thy advice, brother Rasch, and set him at liberty. If his master has saved his life, the servant may share the same fortune with him; but first the blockhead shall swear a terrible oath never to betray us, else I will break his rascally neck.

"MANY VOICES. Well spoken, Captain, let us break the scoundrel's neck if he refuses to swear.

"Now we heard them ascend the staircase with a terrible noise, and instantly the Austrian knocked with his hands and feet against the door; a momentary silence ensued. ·

"'Open the door, ye miscreants!' roared my friend with a thundering voice. Open the door, ye rascals,' exclaimed I and my fellow adventurers, but before the hollow sound of our voices had ceased re-echoing through the vaulted passage where we were standing, the whole crew was running up stairs with a tremendous noise, and we hurried with all possible speed through the long winding passage, with pistols cocked, but before we could reach the end of the subterraneous avenue, we heard the trampling of horses, which soon was dying away at a distance. A gust of wind had extinguished our torches, but the light of the moon was shining so clear that we soon beheld an opening in the garden wall leading to the field, where we could see at a small distance, a numerous troop of horsemen galloping away at a furious rate. On our return we observed that the horsemen had taken their flight through the garden, which appeared to have been their common in and out-let since the burning down of the village.

"I left the residence of these robbers very much dis- satisfied; the Austrian, on the contrary, was highly pleased, representing to me that we should not know much more of the matter than we had heard, even if we had surprised them; that I did wrong if I complained of having been disappointed, being now informed of my servant's fate, and the mystery of the castle; and that every wish of taking personal vengeance on these mis-creants was not becoming men like ourselves, because the hangman would have been defrauded of his perquisites if we had killed some of them.

"'All we could do,' added he, 'would be to give notice of what we have seen and heard to the magistrates of the next town; but I fear the gang is too numerous than that they could be taken prisoners; besides, they will take care not to suffer themselves to be entrapped; and if the magistrates were to take cognizance of our denunciation, and should fail in their attempt to destroy the whole crew, they perhaps would be made a second example of the revengeful daring spirit of these lawless wretches, and pay dearly for having enacted the laws against them. Remember the agony of grief you felt when you beheld the horrid consequences of opposition against these outlaws, in viewing the ruins of the village which but lately has fallen a victim to their cruel resentment, and then tell me whether it is advisable to inform against them? We had better leave their punishment to that supreme Judge who certainly will overtake them with his vengeance when their measure shall be full.'

"I returned to our inn at the next village, comforted by the seasonable reasoning of my worthy friend, and I never shall forget the wise instructions he gave me on the way; I never shall forget his tender exhortations to take care not to follow the first impulse of the moment, but always to listen attentively to the voice of reason before I should engage in any undertaking, and to bridle the youthful ardour of heedlessness by prudence and cool reflection.

"We entered our inn at two o'clock in the

morning, and we were met by the landlord, who had been very uneasy at our staying away so long, because many murders had been committed lately within the environs of the village. We told him we had taken a walk, but having missed our way, had strayed about until the dawn of day had assisted us in finding our way back. He appeared to believe our words and we went to rest.

"We awoke at eight o'clock, and departed at nine for F-, where our absence had not been much taken notice of, those secret journeys being very common among recruiting officers; yet some of my friends puzzled them- selves very much by various conjectures about the reasons of my connection with the Austrian; but neither we nor our trusty serjeants communicated our adventure to anyone of our acquaintance.

"During our absence a strange accident had happened to one of our comrades, which had made every one wish for the return of the Austrian, and no sooner were we arrived before all the officers repaired to my room to inform us of it.

"The officer who lodged at the haunted inn, coming home against midnight three days ago, sat down to finish a letter to his Colonel. As soon as it had struck twelve o'clock, he heard a tremendous rap at the door, which he did not mind at first, but continued writing. A second rap, more violent than the first, disturbed him soon after, but he still took little notice of it. A third, not unlike aclap of thunder, ensued after a short pause, the door of his apartment flew open, and a white figure was going to enter the room."

"Fearless,' these are his own words, ' did I start up, unsheath my sword and run towards the phantom; it retreated, but I pursued, and pierced it with my sword, it gave a hollow scream, but what further happened I cannot tell; I awoke as if from a deluding dream, and was lying stretched on the floor at the bottom of the stairs, surrounded by a great number of people with lighted candles; terrible pains had seized me, and my sword was still in my hand.'

"When the narrator had finished his wonderful tale, I perceived visible marks of its authenticity on his face, and inquired whether he had been hurt by the fall. He told me he had suffered no material injury except a few bruises.

"The Austrian began now to question him.

"'Have you perceived anything uncommon before that strange accident happened?'

"OFFICER.-Nothing at all except an insignificant noise, after twelve o'clock.

"AUSTRIAN.-Have you, perhaps, before you met with that misfortune, been thinking on my tale of Vol- kert's exploits?

OFFICER. (Vexed) I was writing to my Colonel; how could I therefore think on that fellow? Or do you think it impossible that any one besides you can experience things the possibility of which you have proved by facts?

"The Austrian, apparently lost in profound medita- tion, gave him no answer, but was walking up and down in solemn silence.

"Our companions acquainted us now with the purport of their visit, signifying a desire to encounter the kingdom of spirits and hobgoblins in pleno corpore, under the command of my serious friend. Thinking the veteran would relish their proposal as little as myself, I thought it would be agreeable to him, if I could prevail on the spirited sons of Mars not to urge the matter further, addressing them in a jocose manner : —

"'Gentlemen, it seems you do not consider that these airy disturbers of nocturnal rest are not fond of large companies; or do you suppose the apparition, which I suspect to be a female one, a second Semiramis ? '

"However, it was in vain to attempt persuading them to drop the adventure, their imagination having been heated too much by the Austrian's tale, as that they would give up their design. Turning their backs against me, highly displeased with my harangue, they solicited my friend with the greatest impetuosity to comply with their request. He inquired whether Lieutenant N- was still an inhabitant of the haunted inn, and being told that the valiant son of Mars had removed to another lodging the next morning after the nocturnal encounter, he refused flatly to yield to their entreaties, telling them he was sure the apparition would give them the slip.

"Well, well,' exclaimed the undaunted warriors, 'we will run the risk and watch the ghost, though we should sit up ten nights for it; we are determined to unfold that mystery.

"So saying they left the room in great hurry. "What do you think of the matter?' said I, when the visitors had left us.

"'Nothing,' replied he, with much sang froid, shrug- ging up his shoulders.

"'But the ghost,' said I —

"'Is an offspring of their childish fancy,' replied the Austrian.

"'The fall of Lieutenant N- ?' asked I.

"'Is very natural,' replied the Austrian; 'I could cite you more than one hundred incidents corroborating the truth, that people have a very confused idea when their senses are tied up by fear and anxiety. As soon as cool reflection gives way to the horrors of a disordered fancy, we are but too apt to create phantoms and spectres around us, we do not see what really exists, but what we fear to behold.'

"I could oppose nothing to this reasoning of his, founded so strongly on experience, and suspected the courage of our valiant Lieutenant very much, having no doubt but his fear had made him miss the staircase; I therefore took no farther notice of our bravado and his companions, not caring what would be the finale of their trifling adventure. My friend was likewise quite unconcerned about the matter, and, without mentioning it any farther, we went about our business.

"When night invited us to rest from the toils of the day, we dedicated the remaining hours to the mutual enjoyment of hallowed friendship's cheerful bliss.

"Eight days of peaceful happiness were now elapsed, when Lieutenant N- entered my apartment one morning, with a countenance exhibiting the strongest marks of horror.

"I come to you,' said he, 'because I apprehend a second refusal from your friend, if you do not support my request.'

"Asking him whether he intended to apply once more to my friend to encounter the ghost, he replied, it was his inten- tion to try his fortune once more with my obstinate friend.

"'Then you must excuse me,' exclaimed I, peevishly.

"Having stared at me awhile in profound silence, he began walking up and down the room, and at last seated himself by my side, resuming, in a cool and tranquil tone, "Hear what I am going to say before you refuse to inter- cede with your friend, and I will acknowledge myself to be unworthy of your confidence if you persist any longer in your resolution, not to speak in my behalf to your worthy friend."

"The solemn manner in which he pronounced the last words engaged my attention, and made me apprehend to hear a tale of horror. Having moved my chair closer to his he went on.

"You know what I and my friends intended to do; we have executed our design. All our efforts to make the ghost appear proved abortive at first; in vain did we watch, make a noise, search every corner of the house, and try to provoke the spirit for three nights; we could neither hear nor see anything uncommon.'

"I was going to interrupt him, and to argue

the imprudence of their proceedings, but he squeezed my hand gently, and begged me not to interrupt his narrative.

"The fourth night appeared," thus he continued after an awful pause, it still makes my blood freeze when I recollect the horrible scene of terror my eye beheld in that night of dreadful note. We all repaired to the abode of that airy disturber of the stillness of night, taking our residence in a lonely hall, in the apartment. We sat down to the inviting punch bowl after eleven o'clock, as we had done the preceding nights, filling our pipes and cursing the cowardice of the spectre, seemingly afraid of meeting an assembly of hardy soldiers; but it took ample vengeance on our forwardness, in so horrid a manner, that one must have been an eye-witness of its ire, if one will form a just idea of our situation.

"Our impatience increased as the punch began to heat our blood, we took the candles from the table, unsheathed our swords, and began to search every corner of the house and the cellar without success. My friends looked gloomy, the clouds of dissatisfaction were hovering over their brows, and a storm was gathering, which perhaps would have ended in a serious quarrel, if it had not been for the Austrian's tale, which, as yet, had sheltered me against their boiling anger, and from the suspicion of being an impostor or a coward. They began ridiculing the landlord and myself on account of our self-created fright, as they called it, declaring all we had heard and seen to be a mere phantom, the offspring of a deluded fancy ; however, they were soon convinced of the truth of our narration, in a most shocking manner.

"We were ascending the staircase, and the foremost had not yet reached the last step, when a sudden hollow noise arose. It was not unlike the howling of the tempest rushing through the chinks of an old ruinous building. The noise carried something frightful with it, which cannot be expressed by words. My hair rose up like bristles, an irresistible horror made my blood run chill, and my ridiculing friends became as serious as if a magic wand had touched them, gazing at each other in dumb astonishment. The dismal noise continued a few seconds, and then every thing was as silent as the grave.

"We pursued our way to the hall, and retook our seats, wondering what could have caused that dreadful howling, and one of the company opened the window to see whether a tempest had gathered in the air, but the sky was clear, and not the least wind blowing. Sensations of unspeakable awe thrilled our souls, the fumes of punch. evaporated, and solemn stillness swayed all around; nothing was heard save the violent palpitations of the heart, the chattering of our poor landlord's teeth, and the knocking together of his trembling knees.

"A few moments more of profound silence, and then the dismal howling arose again with redoubled force; a sudden violent gust of wind threw the windows open, and the door from its hinges, extinguishing all the candles; a tremendous clap of thunder shook the house, a terrible flash of lightning hissed through the room, and prostrated us to the ground; a hideous lamenting noise assailed our ears, and lifting up my head I beheld the phantom that once had frightened me, advancing with a threatening grin; grisly was its shape, and its eyes rolling like two flaming comets.

"I was the first who recovered the use of his senses, and, calling in vain for the landlord, my companions Started up, and we found the poor fellow prostrate on the floor, half frantic with terror. At length he also recovered a little from his fright, and after many persuasions ventured down stairs, accompanied by me, to strike a light. Every- body in the house was snoring, except our crest-fallen fellow adventurers, who exhibited a rueful ghastly group, being all as pale as ashes. Looking at our watches we saw it was past two o'clock, sat an hour longer without perceiving any thing farther, and returned against morning to our respective lodgings.

"I would not have troubled you with an account of this strange incident if an accident was not connected with it, which has happened last night.

"My recruiting business having called me abroad yesterday, I returned in the afternoon; in the dusk of evening I entered a thicket in a gloomy pensive mood, all around was lonely and buried in profound silence; no sound was heard except the dismal dirge of the screech-owl, and the shrill chirping of the amorous cricket*. At *The chirping of the cricket is a noise which the male one makes with his wings in order to attract the attention of the female.-Vide Goetze, "Ueber Natur Menschenleben und Vorsehung." length I heard a whispering within a small distance, and cocking one of my pistols, I rode on with the greatest circumspection. At once I saw a manly figure coming out of the thicket, but could not distinguish his dress; advancing a little farther, I beheld somebody in a peasant's garb, walking on briskly and talking to himself. As I came up with him I observed a black wallet on his back, and a thick branch of a tree in his hand, serving him instead of a walking cane. He seemed to take no notice of me, pursuing his way with hasty steps, and still muttering between his teeth. I saluted him but he gave me no answer.

"Whither art thou going, good friend?' exclaimed I.

"'To men!' replied he, to my utter

astonishment.

"'Very likely to F,' resumed I.

"'Yes,' said he, there are men.'

"Supposing him to be a lunatic, I passed him, pursuing my way in a brisk trot; when I came out of the thicket I saw that I was nearer the town than I thought, and made my horse quicken his pace; but how was I astonished when I beheld again the same figure walking before me.

"'Old gentleman,' exclaimed I, ' it seems thou knowest the road better than I do.'

"I think so myself,' added he drily; know many things better than you do.'

"' Strange being,' resumed I, 'who art thou?'

"' A friend of wisdom!' was his answer. Thy wisdom,' replied I, 'must be as odd as thyself! But pray what dost thou call wisdom?'

"'What you do not understand,' was his reply.

"Hearing the words friend of wisdom, I was suddenly struck with a suspicion which my readers will easily guess, and that suspicion was strengthened when the narrator informed me of his definition of wisdom. I strongly suspected that he was the same person I had met in the Black Forest, under the garb of a pilgrim, and I hardly could refrain from exclaiming,' Art thou here, impostor?'

"Every one may guess the conclusion of the Lieutenant's wonderful tale. I scarcely had patience to await it. The narrator being highly charmed with the hoary juggler, could not find words to express the sensations his reverend aspect had raised within his breast. He had fancied to be in a company with a robust countryman, but when he entered his house in the suburbs, to which he kindly had invited him, he beheld the countenance of an old man with silver hair, and a mien exciting awful respect. He offered him a glass of excellent wine, and began by degrees to become more cheerful and communicative.

"The old man's conversation on the road having betrayed a high degree of occult knowledge, had very nearly tempted the Lieutenant to communicate to him his adventure at the haunted inn; that temptation returning with redoubled force he could no longer resist, and told him everything that had happened. The result of the ensuing conversation was, that he entreated the old man to come and conjure up the apparition, to which he, after many seeming struggles, at last consented, under the condition that no more than six persons should be present, and the landlord's leave could be obtained. The

Part II, Chapter III

Lieutenant left him in high spirits, after having promised to fulfil strictly these two conditions.

"I could not bridle any longer my ardent desire to hasten to the Austrian and to get rid of my visitor, who now became exceeding troublesome to me, being tired of his overstrained encomiums on the old deceiver, I therefore, anticipating the renewal of his request to speak to my friend, promised that I not only would engage to persuade him to assist at the conjuration, which was to be performed the ensuing night, but I also assured him that I myself would be present.

"The Lieutenant's raptures exceeded all bounds, he almost stifled me by his embraces, and called me more than a hundred times his kind benefactor, and his dear obliging friend. I was, however, entirely indifferent to his raptures and endearments, pondering how I might best confound the vile dissembler, and put a final stop to his enormous cheats. I begged the poor hood-winked Lieutenant to give me leave to go directly to my friend, and to win him over to the party, which he instantly did, after having fixed an hour in the afternoon when he would wait on me to hear how far I should have succeeded with the Austrian.

"'Meanwhile,' added he, 'I will go to the owner of the haunted inn, in order to talk the business over with him, and to engage three able assistants more from among our friends.'

"Not finding the veteran at home I was vexed very much, but when dinner-time came I had the pleasure of meeting him. The recapitulation of Lieutenant N— —'s account of his late adventure at the inn, and his conversation with the hoary juggler, produced the desired effect. Though a man like him, who was of a cool temper, and never suffered his passion to get the better of his reason, could not be seized with a fit of amazement, yet I never saw him so violently agitated.

"Having with apparent emotion awaited the conclusion of my tale, he exclaimed at last, after a short pause, during which his desire for vengeance and punishment seemed to struggle with his reflection and prudence-

"'Friend, what do you intend to do?'

"To seize the Necromancer.'

"Before or after the conjuration?' asked the Austrian.

"'After it,' replied I.

"'Now the dinner bell rang, and he left me with the promise to repair at night to the place of action.

"Having accustomed myself by degrees to

examine minutely what likeliest might be the result of my noble friend's almost unfathomable considerations, before I determined on anything he was concerned in, I succeeded sometimes in my anxious endeavours to act in unison with his principles, and to coincide with his ideas, but in the present case I was quite at a loss how to proceed conform- ably to his wish, having not the least clue by which I could expect to extricate myself out of the labyrinths into which he had led me, leaving everything to myself.

"However, after much reflection, I was at last so fortunate to hit upon a plan which he fully approved, proposing to conceal myself until the whole transaction should be finished, and then to rush like lightning upon the hoary deceiver, to upbraid him with his glaring cheats, to force him to a confession of the dark, fraudulent means he had employed to play that infernal trick upon us, when he left us in the lurch in the cellar of the Haunted Castle, and then to make him a prisoner without farther ceremony.

"We both agreed to deliver him up to the civil power, after having convicted him of his roguery, and to order four stout corporals to rush into the room at the first signal, in order to arrest the shameless, cunning deceiver. Flattering ourselves with hopes of good success, we parted, after a mutual promise to repair to the place of action at eleven o'clock.

"Lieutenant N came to my lodging at three o'clock in the afternoon, to inform me that everything was ready for the performance of our nocturnal adventure. The landlord had made no difficulty to give his consent to the conjuration, and was desirous to be admitted one of the spectators, being elated with the hope that his house soon would be cleared of that troublesome being which had until now banished all his customers, and very much impaired his circumstances. He knew the reverend Necromancer, as the lieutenant was pleased to call him, and was in raptures that the honest old man was returned to F, and had consented to restore the tranquillity of his house, exclaiming,

"'Now I am easy; Father Francis is the very man. It is a thousand pities that he visits these parts so seldom, and that he, if present, buries himself in solitude.'

"'He could not tell me precisely,' added the lieutenant, 'how the old man employs his time, because nobody was on an intimate footing with him, nor could any one tell where he came from, or whither he was travelling so often, but that it was universally known that he possessed houses in most of the adjacent towns, where he was living in the same retired and harmless manner as here.'

Part II, Chapter III

"The lieutenant, highly pleased when I told him that the Austrian had consented to be present at our nocturnal meeting, went now to the other associates, in order to settle everything, and invited myself and my friend to supper, which I readily consented to.

"Having shifted my clothes, that the old deceiver might not know me so easily, I went to the Austrian, whom I, without difficulty, persuaded to sup with me and Lieu- tenant N- We repeated our orders to our trusty corporals and left the house."

"Strange sensations occupied my mind, spreading a gloom over my countenance. The expectation of seeing something extraordinary and wonderful thrilled my soul with awe, and an unaccountable chill trembled through my limbs; perhaps it was the effect of a foreboding of my approaching separation from my ever-beloved friend, who appeared as cool and unconcerned as ever. When he saw me so silent and gloomy, he said, 'So solemn, my friend, it seems you wish very little for your old acquaintance.'

"'It is no pleasant task to unmask an impostor,' said I.

"'But a useful one,' answered he, taking me under the arm.

"'I endeavoured to appear cheerful, in

which painful task I succeeded at length; however, there was still lurking in my soul an awful, strange sensation, quite foreign to my character, though the latter had been tinged with a sombre hue since I had frequented the company of my new friend.

"When we came to Lieutenant N- -'s apartment, we met two of his most intimate friends, who had been present at the late alarming apparition of the ghost, and were determined to engage the spectre once more.

"They all were rejoiced at the Austrian's coming, and soon began to recount the terrible visitation of the ghost, and the anxiety they had suffered, which they did in a most prolix and tedious manner. The Austrian begged them to talk of something else and not to deprive themselves of the necessary firmness of mind by the recollection of what was past; he at the same time endeavoured to give the conversation a more cheerful turn, and I cannot but con- fess that he never had been so amusing and pleasing since I had known him.

"The cloth being laid we sat down to supper, but none of us did honour to the meal except the Austrian ; the wine promised to dispel the clouds of gloominess from our circle; however, our host plied us in vain with bumpers, the heart-elevating juice of the grape could not raise our crest-fallen spirits, and the Austrian was the only one who relished it, and experienced its powers divine.' "The farther the night advanced the lower our spirits sunk, in despite of my friend's endeavours to spread the glow of merriment around, and to encourage us to join him heartily in his libations. Though he sounded the praise of the wine's excellence, by words and deeds, yet he kept within the bounds of soberness, and when it struck eleven o'clock, bade us drink a final bumper to good success, and then took up his hat and sword.

"I did the same, and our companions followed our example with fear and trembling. We went down stairs in solemn taciturnity, and groped our way through mid- night darkness to the Haunted Inn.

"The master of the house welcomed us most cordially, thanking us beforehand for the expected tranquillity of his house and the return of his prosperity; he led us to the hall where the above-mentioned dreadful apparition had appeared, enlarging with indefatigable garrulity on many horrible incidents which had taken place, within the space of a twelvemonth, in that disastrous apartment.

"The Austrian uttered not a word, but searched closely every corner of the spacious lonely room, and then took a candle and went out. Having been absent a good while, he returned at length, pulled his great coat off, and entered into a long conversation with the master of the house, asking him many questions, which betrayed his diffidence in the poor fellow's honesty. I was not much pleased with his unequivocal marks of suspicion, knowing the innkeeper as an upright, honest man, void of disguise and art, and that he himself had suffered the utmost damage by those nocturnal apparitions. His inn had been unfre- quented by travellers these many months, on account of that sleep-disturbing phantom which haunted the weary wanderer in the dead of night, and he swore by every thing holy and sacred, that he had never seen Father Francis (so he called the hoary deceiver) though he had heard of many deeds perpetrated by that wonderful man.

"'It is now,' added he, 'a good while since I have heard of that sagacious old man; they say he is gone to a distant place, offended at the ingratitude of the people of our country. Formerly he has told the people's fortunes, but without fee. My father, the late possessor of this house, has told me many marvellous instances of his astonishing skill in detecting thefts, and recovering stolen goods; as how he has been possessed of a wonderful sagacity to read in people's looks, at first sight, whatever they had done all their life long; discovered and solved the spell of witchcraft, and horribly punished the old hags that dared to bewitch the countrymen's cattle. In short, said my father, God rest his honest soul, Father Francis has indeed been a father and a friend to every one in distress, and a baneful foe to the Black Spirit and his infernal hosts.'

"The Austrian appearing still to harbour thoughts of suspicion against the simple innkeeper, watched closely all his motions, was always at his heels when he left the room, and ever busy to ply him with various questions. I and my companions kept close together, myself burning with desire for the beginning of the drama, and my fellow adventurers awaiting it with fear and trembling.

"It struck twelve when the innkeeper was still in close conversation with the circumspect Austrian. The door opened, and Father Francis entered the room; the sight of the hoary deceiver made my blood boil in my veins, and I clapped my hand involuntarily to my sword; the Austrian, who was standing at a small distance from me, hiding a part of his face under his hat, and holding a brace of pistols in his hands, seemed to ask me, by a side glance, whether Father Francis and my old acquaintance in the Black Forest were one and the same person. I affirmed it by a quick motion of my eyelids, and the Austrian turned his back to the Necromancer; I removed behind Lieu- tenant N, and peeping over his shoulders, watched the proceedings of the juggler, who advanced with solemn steps into the middle of the apartment, where he stopped, resting his inquisitive looks on the countenances of the company.

"Profound silence swayed all around, and we were fixed to the ground like so many statues, thrilled with anxious expectation, and scarce ventured to breathe.

"The old man was clad in a long robe of black silk, his snow-white head uncovered, a white silken sash, marked with strange characters, was tied round his waist, and the well-known black wallet hung on his back; having taken it down he untied it, and exhibited the mysterious instruments of conjuration: at his mute command the host carried a table to the centre of the room, put two lighted torches upon it and bolted the door.

"Now he gave us a signal to form a circle round him ; the Austrian placed himself to his left side, turning his face towards the door, Lieutenant N, by the conjurer's own desire, to his right; the innkeeper stood close by the Austrian, one of Lieutenant N- -'s friends took his station by the landlord, and I placed myself close to the latter. The Necromancer appeared to care little for the right wing, and I could clearly observe that his left neighbour raised his suspicion.

"However, he began his conjuration with apparent firmness, after he had strewed a reddish sand on the floor, and delineated a treble circle with his ebony wand. The particulars of the act of conjuring were nearly the same as in the cellar of the Haunted Castle, except his reading aloud the greatest part of the form of the conjuration, and his face being not so horribly distorted by convulsions as in the subterraneous rooms of that terrible haunt of robbers.

"Now the ceremony was finished, he cast his book on the table, and pronounced thrice the well-known mysteri- ous word. Suddenly a howling blast of wind rushed against our faces, a thick column of smoke ascended from the floor, overcasting the whole apartment, and extinguish- ing the torches. Darkness and horror surrounded us.

"Ere long a faint gleam was breaking from the floor, sparingly illuminating the objects around, and rising higher and higher on the opposite wall till it reached the ceiling. At once the floor seemed to shake beneath our feet, and we beheld with chilly horror a human figure hovering on the wall; its garments and face, bearing the grisly marks of corruption, appeared to have suffered by the flames. It shook its head and fiery sparks flew around. A sudden smell of brimstone almost suffocated us.

"After we had gazed at the phantom some time, with secret horror, the Necromancer exclaimed with a thundering voice, 'Who art thou?'

"PHANTOM (Staggering back). — A soul from pur- gatory.'

"'OLD MAN. — What is thy desire ? ' "'

"'PHANTOM. — To be redeemed from the flames.'

"'OLD MAN.-By what means?'

"'PHANTOM.-By the sale of this house.'

"'OLD MAN.-For what reason?'

"'PHANTOM.-Because I have got it by fraudulent means.'

"'OLD MAN.-How can the sale of this house expiate thy crime?'

"PHANTOM.-It can, because my children will be saved.'

"The Necromancer was silent and the phantom dis- appeared.

"A violent gust of wind rushed again in our faces, the smoke evaporated, and the torches began to burn. Lieu- tenant N- with his friends and the landlord, were struck with amazement, and unable to stir; the Austrian lifted his hat, which had hidden part of his face, staring wildly at the hoary cheat, and I expected with impatience the signal for seizing the rascal, who, with great tranquillity and unconcern, was busied with putting his again into his wallet.

"Now the Austrian came forth, and I clapped my hand to my sword; awful silence reigned around, and our companions were still fixed to their places, whilst the Austrian's sparkling looks rested on the Necromancer, who now had packed up the instruments of fraud, and thrown the wallet over his shoulders. Just when he was going to leave the room his eye caught the glowing face of my friend, and he seemed thunderstruck. Their looks evinced a mutual emotion of an uncommon nature: my friend's stern looks grew more and more terrible, and the old man was appar- ently grasped by horror's icy fangs : our expectation rose to the highest pitch, and we were standing around them in a grisly attitude, most of us thrilled with secret awe, and I not without chill.

"'Yes,' began now the Austrian with a trembling voice, 'yes, it is thou, Volkert! it is thou!'

"The old deceiver shivered violently, his face was distorted by terrible convulsions, he gave a hollow groan, and fell lifeless on the floor.

"We all seemed touched by a magic wand, and the Austrian was standing a good while in our middle, in a state of stupefaction; at length he recovered his recollection, drew with his wonted firmness nearer to the lifeless Necromancer, raised him up, shook him with all his might and exclaimed :—

"'Volkert, Volkert, return to life once more.'

But all was in vain, the old man gave no sign of life. Volkert, Volkert,' exclaimed my friend once more, but he did not hear him.

"The innkeeper ran down stairs, fetching a glass of water and some drops, but our endeavours to restore the hoary villain to the use of his senses proved abortive, and he remained senseless in our arms.

"Well then,' resumed the Austrian, his eyes flashing with anger, if amicable means will not do, then I must have recourse to violence.' So saying, he discharged a pistol, the door flew open, and four corporals rushed in with their swords unsheathed.

"Tie the rascal's arms and legs,' roared the Austrian, ' away with the villain, he is our prisoner.'

"Your prisoner!' replied the grey deceiver, who had recovered at last, 'your prisoner!' roared he with a ghastly grin, disengaging himself from our grasp.

"The corporals rushed upon him.

"I am a citizen of F- who dares to touch me?' of a free imperial town,

"The corporals retired hastily, and the Austrian's brow was covered with terrible wrinkles, his eyes flashed anger, his mouth foamed, and his whole frame trembled in an agony of furious rage. I never beheld a more terrible aspect.

"'Infernal spirit! hell-born villain!' roared he, gnashing his teeth, 'I am deceived! — deceived by thee, Volkert!-Volkert!'

"At once the thunder of his voice lowered to an entreating accent.

"'Volkert, Volkert, for God's sake have mercy on me ; save me from an ocean of doubts; spare me, O spare me ; save me from the disgrace of appearing to myself and my friends a fool and a superstitious fanatic! Tell me, O tell me, am I indeed deceived? O, I will forgive thee, I will pronounce thee my benefactor, my saviour, only speak- tell me I am not deceived!'

"The tears ran down his cheeks as he pronounced these words, spoken in a most violent passion.

"It is a terrible, awful sight to see a man weep. I turned my eye away from the affecting scene, not being able to behold it any longer. The rest of my companions were seized anew with dumb stupefaction when they saw the violent emotions of my venerable friend, and a pause of unutterable horror ensued after the Austrian's speech. The old man either would or could not speak, and the Austrian began once more to address the hoary deceiver in an accent of utter insensibility, and with a sternness of look not to be described.

"'Volkert, thou wilt not know me. I will spare thee the disgrace of confessing thine own guilt, but if thou wert in my power-

"His eyes darted flashes of lightning, and his voice was like the roaring of thunder.

"'If thou wert in my power, I would make thee confess thy cheats, and if I should be forced to beat thy old rascally limbs to atoms, and to draw thy black blood from thy diabolical heart by single drops, I would make thee con- fess; but,' added he in a more gentle accent,' thou art not within the reach of my power, and it is well that it is so. Volkert, here is my hand, I forgive thee. Thou not only deservest my forgiveness, but also my sincere gratitude, because thou hast given me a wholesome lesson, hast taught me, that everybody, though ever so wise, may be deceived; and I think I have not paid too dear for it.'

"Volkert wanted to speak, but he could not, being overcome by a sudden emotion, and hid his face with his hands. "Well, Volkert,' resumed the Austrian, I see thou art not quite so bad as I thought. I will not compel thee to a confession, though I am wishing most ardently to have my doubts cleared up, and trust that thou wouldst tell me more than I want to know. I will not distress thee any longer by my presence; I am going to leave this house and this town for ever.

"'Gentlemen,' added he, addressing us, 'I have de- ceived you, by supporting the reality of things which have been nothing but illusion; from this moment I have for- feited your good opinion, and the honour of being admitted any longer to a circle where I have been respected. You may call my resolution pride, caprice, or whatever you please, I cannot remain here any longer, and I am determined to depart this instant; farewell, live happy.'

"Having addressed us in so unexpected a manner, he hurried out of the room, taking no particular leave of me. Sympathizing with his feelings, I thought it proper not to pay him a parting visit, because I knew it would recall disagreeable recollections, and give him pain.

"A parting look which he gave me, when he was leaving the room, told me more than words could have done. Mine eyes were bathed with tears. I have seen him no more, and shall never forget that unhappy night which has robbed me of such a valuable friend, and deprived me of the darling of my soul. His

"When the Austrian and the corporals had left us, the Necromancer was likewise going to leave the room. appearance was sullen and gloomy, his looks cast down. My friends were also stirring and stopped him, forming a circle round him. "The landlord was still in a maze of silent wonder, not knowing what to think of what had happened. I was dejected and melancholy, and had banished from my soul every idea of vengeance; my companions, however, seemed not inclined to let him get off so cheaply, and insisted on his explaining how he had contrived to cheat us; but the innkeeper interferred, imploring them not to ruin him entirely, by quarrelling in his house.

"Lieutenant N- threatened at last to give him up to the civil power, if he would not confess, which I at first likewise had determined to do, how he had deceived us; however, his stubbornness could not be shaken, and he remained as silent as the grave.

"Seeing that every further means to break his obstinacy would prove fruitless, I interfered, advising my fellow adventurers to let him depart in peace.

Part II, Chapter III

"'Upon the whole,' added I, 'it matters not how we have been deceived; our friend the Austrian has set us an example how one ought to behave on such an occasion. Let us, like him, forgive the wretch, he is below our resentment.'

"These words produced the desired effect on the minds of my fellow adventurers, who were stung with shame and remorse, but none of them more than Lieutenant N. He blushed at his idle fears and his credulity, leaving the room abruptly, accompanied by his friends and the landlord.

"Being now left alone with the Necromancer, I flattered myself to succeed better than my companions, and to get informed of what I so eagerly wanted to know; but I was mistaken, his stubborn reserve baffled all my solicitations.

"'Farewell, Lieutenant,' said he, as he was going to leave the room, 'I did not know you at first, and I am rejoiced that you have escaped your doom. I do not deserve your noble, generous treatment: Farewell, and remember sometimes Volkert the Necromancer. If you could see my heart, you rather would pity than despise me; I may perhaps one time find an opportunity of being serviceable to you, and of proving my gratitude by deeds.'

"I went down stairs with him, and having

seen him to the door he squeezed my hand and hurried away. I left the fatal house in a strange situation of mind, and it struck one o'clock when I came home. I went to bed, but not to rest, my fancy being haunted by gloomy ideas, which kept sleep and repose at a distance. Early in the morning my fellow adventurers came to see me, requesting me to unfold the mysteries of the preceding night.

"We know,' began Lieutenant N, their spokes- man, we know that you are, or at least have been, very intimate with the Austrian, and you will, of course, be able to inform us, how your friend came to be acquainted with the cheats of the Necromancer. We have reason to think that he would have acted with more circumspection, if he had known that the Necromancer was no other person than Volkert his former intimate favourite. We hope you will be so kind to clear up the matter. The Austrian's firmness of mind, his solid character, and his unshaken belief in the possibility of apparitions, give us strong reasons to think that he cannot have acted thus without mature deliberation.'

"Being but ill-disposed to enter into a circumstantial narrative, and not at all inclined to inform the intruding gentlemen of our adventures at the Haunted Castle, I called one of my corporals, who had been on the watch in the fatal inn the preceding night. 'This man,' said I, ´ will tell you more of the matter than I know, having watched every motion of the Necromancer, and discovered all his secret machination.'

"The old veteran was very willing to satisfy their curiosity, and began a prolix narration of every proceeding in the lower apartment of the inn. The innkeeper was, he related, deceived like ourselves, but his servants had acted in concert with Volkert, and enabled by their assistance to impose upon us.

"Not being disposed to listen to his tale, I did not mind what he related, but my visitors, more attentive than myself, appeared at least to be fully satisfied and left me, after a profusion of thanks for having freed them of the doubts and errors.

"The separation from my venerable friend had spread a melancholy gloom over my mind, which nothing could dispel.

"The third day after his departure, I could no longer Stay in a place where every object reminded me of so many hours of bliss, and of the man, whose friendship had made me so truly happy; I bade my servant pack my trunks, ordered my corporals to keep themselves ready, and left F after a few days.

"My journey afforded me but little amusement, being not able to wean my gloomy mind from the painful recollection of the time past, the image of my friend rush- ing ever and anon on my soul, and I could not resist the ardent desire of being re-united to him.

"I sat in the stage musing on what was past, revolving in my mind the strange events of the Haunted Castle, and the inn, and examining minutely all the particulars, but I grew not a bit wiser: that Volkert was an impostor could not be doubted, but how he had managed his artful cheats and what his views had been in deceiving us, I could not unravel in a satisfactory manner; I examined singly all his transactions I knew, pondered with the greatest accuracy what the Austrian had related of his earlier exploits, but I was not able to dispel the impenetrable darkness which I was bewildered in.

"The final result of my meditations was, that anybody, though ever so circumspect and wise, would, like my worthy friend, have been deceived by his intricate machinations, and tempted to adopt the opinion that enlightened officer had once defended so stoutly.

"I was almost angry with myself for having let slip the opportunity of forcing that dangerous man to a con- fession of his dark and diabolical transgressions. It is true, I myself knew him as a hardened impostor, but could he not drag into the gulf of perdition many of my fellow creatures, who, like myself, would fall an easy victim to his deceitful hypocrisy?

"This thought overwhelmed me with a load of un- easiness, and I reproached myself severely for having imitated the over-generous example of the Austrian, and suffered the accomplished villain to decamp without punishment. I had, indeed, reason to apprehend that the magistrate of F would not have regarded much the information of a recruiting officer against a citizen, and that the innkeeper would have been induced, by fear or bribe, to contradict our denunciation; nevertheless, I should have had the satisfaction of having performed my duty, and cautioned the inhabitants of F that dangerous villain.

"Tormented with this and similar thoughts did I finish my first day's journey, struggling in vain to recover my wonted cheerfulness, my mind being then too much occupied by gloominess, and an entire stranger to joyful feelings.

"Not being able to get a wink of sleep all night long, I was haunted without rest, by the gloomy offsprings of my fancy, distressed by the appearing slowness of time, and entirely cut off from every comfort by the snoring dis- position of my fellow travellers, which made me resolve to leave the stage next morning, and to continue my journey on horseback. I left, therefore, my cheerless and sullen companions, with the first dawn of day, bought a horse in the first village where we stopped, and trotted briskly onward.

"I was not in the least acquainted with the roads in those parts, a circumstance which ought to have come sooner in my mind; I was obliged to ride back several times, and when it began to grow dark, found myself bewildered in a dreary forest, without knowledge which way to turn. My jaded horse being hardly able to stir; I alighted, leading the poor beast by the bridle, in order to advance with more expedition.

"It was now so dark that I could hardly distinguish the objects before my eyes, when a sudden rustling in the thicket made me start; I listened, but all was silent again and I pursued my way without apprehension, thinking it might have been a deer; but I was not gone far when I heard the rustling again much louder than at first, and close by me: I now beheld, on a sudden, a man with a sack on his back, and a staff in his hand, coming out of the thicket, within the short distance of two or three paces. This unexpected sight gladdened my heart, flattering me with the sweet hope of getting a friendly conductor out of that dreary wilderness, who would direct my weary steps to a place of rest.

"'Whither art thou going, good friend?' exclaimed I.

"'To the mill,' answered he, groaning under his burden.

"'Is the mill far from hence?' said I.

"'No farther than half a league,' he replied.

"'May I find shelter there for myself and horse?'

"'No,' replied he. "Why not?' asked I.

Because,' replied he, 'the miller does not admit Strangers.'

"'I am sorry for it; but is there no house hereabouts where one could get a night's lodging?'

"'O yes,' answered he, 'not far from hence, if you turn to the right lives a wood-cutter who lodges travellers.'

"'But do you think I shall be safe there?' asked I.

"'What do you mean by that?' said he.

"'Don't you know, good friend,' replied I, ' that this part of the country is the constant haunt for robbers?'

"'Would to God I could stay this night with good Master Max, I would not be uneasy on that score; but I must go on, and alas my burden is heavy.'

"'If my poor beast was not so jaded, and so much tired, I would be glad to lend it you,' said I,

"'Thank you, Master,' returned he; "I am used to hard- ships, and have laid in a good stock of patience.'

"Discoursing thus we went slowly on together, till we came to a foot-path, where the wanderer stopped to direct me to the wood-cutter's cottage: 'You cannot miss your way,' said he; if you pursue this path you will soon see light.'

"I hesitated a little while, whether I should follow the advice of the honest man, or not, but the increasing dark- ness, and a rising tempest, which shook the oaks around, fixed soon my wavering resolution, and I pursued the path, bidding the honest wanderer good night.

"I soon found myself on an unbeaten footway, ob- structed by brambles and underwood; my poor horse threatened every moment to sink down, and I could not resist the apprehension of having been sent on a fool's errand by the unknown man, and misled into an unfrequented lonesome part of the forest. This made me look about with more circumspection, till I had ascended a rising ground with great difficulty, my horse fell frequently on his knees, and it would have been impossible to proceed a mile farther; you may therefore easily think how rejoiced I was when the glimmering of a light, apparently at a small distance, bade me hope a speedy end of my distress.

"Quickening my steps, I soon perceived a small cottage, the owner of which made his appearance as soon as I had knocked at his humble door, hailed me with a hearty welcome, and bade me, with much good-nature, enter his hospitable abode.

"Not expecting much convenience, I was struck with wonder when he showed me into a neat little room, not in the least corresponding with the poor appearance of his hut; I had expected to be introduced to the residence of poverty, and found a habitation that bore evident marks of prosperity, and seemed rather to be the abode of a gentleman than that of a poor wood-cutter.

"Mr. Max-this he told me was his name-Mr. Max took no notice of my astonishment, but prepared, with much alacrity, to provide me and my weary horse with food and drink.

"While he was busy to prove his hospitality, I had full leisure to satisfy my curiosity, and to take a view of the objects around me, assisted by the faint glimmering of a lamp.

"The first object that struck my fancy was an enormous sword, hanging by his bed-side, which, as I thought at first, was rather an improper furniture for a wood-cutter's dwelling; but I soon made myself easy when I recollected, that he, living in an unfrequented part of the forest, might want sometimes an instrument of that kind to defend himself against unwelcome visitors, but my apprehension returned when I beheld a brace of pistols hanging on the wall, which I found were charged with ball.

"I went farther in my search, and saw a great number of guns, pistols, and swords in a recess close by the fireside; I was chilled with terror, and just as I had taken the lamp in my hand to have a closer view at this alarming furniture, Mr. Max entered the room, with a large plate of greens, a piece of ham, and a bottle of wine.

"'Well,' exclaimed he merrily, as he entered the room, 'there, I have brought you something to silence your grumbling stomach with; sit down, good sir, and take up with my frugal fare.'

"'Alas! my appetite was gone, but he fetched knives and forks and a large loaf of bread, and began to eat with great avidity, taking at first no notice of my backwardness to follow his example; perceiving at length that I did not eat, he exclaimed, 'Well, sir, why don't you eat? I think one must be hungry, if one has travelled far and missed one's way.'

"His joviality revived a little my spirits, but his country- like simplicity, and his seeming honesty, appeared to me very little corresponding with the great number of fire-arms and swords which I had seen, yet I joined him at last in eating and drinking.

"When supper was over I could no longer suppress my curiosity, and asked him why he kept so many guns and swords in his house.

"'What,' replied he rather angry,' what is this to you? I get sometimes visitors for whom I must keep them.'

"'But why,' resumed I, 'so great a number as I have seen in the recess by the fireside

"'These are fine doings,' said he angrily, 'who bade you to search my room? Is this becoming a guest ?'

"I arose, and asked him how much I had to pay for my supper? He fell a laughing, and exclaimed, with marks of astonishment-

"'You don't intend to depart in this dark and tempestuous night! Don't you hear how the tempest roars, and how the rain beats against the windows? I hope you don't think you will be shot or stabbed because there are so many fire-arms and swords in that recess? No no, good friend, you need not be afraid, all these things are not mine, they belong to sportsmen who have laid them up here, that they may have them when they are a hunting in this part of the forest; perhaps you may see them yourself to-morrow morning; and sword by my bed-side I bought some years ago from an Austrian deserter.'

"Though I was not inclined to stay for the sportsmen, I did not know whither I should go with my jaded horse in that dark tempestuous night, and dreaded to run the risk of escaping from an imaginary danger, only to fly in the face of a real one, which, at last, determined me to stay. I begged Mr. Max to show me the place where I was to sleep, intending to charge my pistols with balls before I should go to bed in case of accident.

"My host opened a side door leading to a small chamber, where a bed was.

"'Here,' said he, 'you may sleep till it is broad day, and rest your weary limbs at your ease; I keep this chamber on purpose for travellers; take this lamp, I will fetch it when you shall be asleep.'

"So saying, he left me, shutting the door after him.

"Taking a nearer view of my bed chamber,

Part II, Chapter III

I observed that it had no windows, and, in order to be prepared for the worst, I charged my pistols, which I had put in my pockets before I had entered the cottage. This done, I considered whether I should go to bed, and thus deceive my host, which, on mature deliberation, I thought would be best.

"With that intention I took my lamp to see whether the bed was fastened, lest I might sink down with it into the cellar. Though this apprehension was groundless, I made another discovery which filled my soul with horror. Perceiving traces of blood on the pillow, I was seized with a sudden terror, my hands trembled violently, the lamp fell on the floor, and I was in the dark.

"As soon as I had recovered a little from my fright, I searched for my pistols, groping about a good while before I could find them in the dark. My fear abated a little when I found them at last, after a long and fruitless search, and I sat myself down on a little stool by the bedside, listening whether anybody was coming. All was quiet at first, but after a quarter of an hour I heard somebody entering the adjacent room, and approaching the door of my chamber, which was gently opened, and the voice of my host called, 'Are you asleep?" I uttered not a word, and after a short pause the same voice resounded once more, Have you extinguished the lamp?' I still gave no answer, and the host retired.

"All was hushed again in profound silence, but it lasted not long, my ears being suddenly assailed by the sound of many voices, the tinkling of spurs, and humming noise, as if a number of people were discoursing; I could understand nothing, the discourse being held in so low an accent, that I was unable to distinguish the sound of their words. At once I saw, through the crevices in the door, somebody striking a light, which gave me some comfort. The discourse was still carried on in` that secret mysterious manner. At last, it seemed as if the company were sitting down, and I could now better distinguish the different sounds. The voices of those that spoke were rough, and the words seemed to belong to a foreign language.

"I sat near an hour on my stool, like a poor culprit who awaits his doom, but was determined to defend myself to the last drop of blood. I intended several times to rush into the room, and to force my escape through the company with cocked pistols, but something within my breast admonished me to stay where I was, and patiently to wait till they should think it proper to pay me a visit.

"My situation was exceedingly painful, and at the least noise which seemed to approach my chamber I started up, putting myself in a posture of defence. My fears not having been realized as yet, my apprehensions began to vanish a little, and I thought Mr. Max might be an honest man, and his company the sportsmen he had been speaking of, although their language seemed to contradict that opinion. Hope soothed my terrors for some time, till at length I recollected the traces of blood I had seen on the pillow, which recalled all my apprehensions with redoubled anxiety.

"Sleep, whom till now I had carefully kept at a distance, began, by degrees, to steal upon me, and shut at last, with his leaden wand, my heavy eyes. But I was scarce fallen asleep, when one of my pistols dropped on the floor, and went off. I started up, seized by the chilly fangs of terror, and in the same moment the other pistol slipped out of my hand. I had scarcely picked it up when the door suddenly flew open, and three fellows, of a gigantic size, entered my room with naked swords. Sleep, the report of my pistol, and the sudden appearance of those terrible men, had stunned me so much, that I, without knowing what I was doing, discharged my pistol, at which one of the villains dropped on the floor with a roaring yelp. A numerous crew, armed with guns, cutlasses, and daggers, rushed like lightning into my chamber, and before I could unsheath my sword, I felt myself in their clutches, bereft of all power of self-defence.

"A tremendous voice roared like thunder from the adjoining room, Hither with the rascal.'

"Before I could recover my recollection, I felt myself dragged out of my chamber, and beheld in an instant a man of the most terrible forbidding aspect, who, with a rough thundering voice, menacing looks, and sparkling eyes, asked me'If I could not have patiently waited my doom.'

"Tie the daring wretch,' added he in a rage, and throw him into the cellar, until sentence shall be pronounced against him.' His commands were obeyed, and Mr. Max himself assisted; I was seized with a despairing Stupor, and uttered not a word. I was shut up in a damp cellar; how long I remained in my dungeon I cannot tell, having been in a situation which suspended all my powers of reflection.

"After a long interval of the most desponding agony, I was at length dragged forth, and brought before the tribunal of the terrible looking man. The villain whom I had wounded was stretched on the bed, his head tied up, and his associates standing round him, bemoaning his hapless fate, and amongst them a venerable old man, whom I at first had not observed.

"Now the grim judge began to speak, and the whole assembly to dart furious and bloodthirsty looks at me. The old man likewise turned his face towards me, and it cannot be expressed by words what my sensations were when I discerned the features of Volkert. A poor culprit cannot feel greater joy when, under the hangman's merciless fangs, his guardian-angel appears to save him from his impending doom. I did indeed not know whether he could save me or not, however, the sweet soothing voice of hope silenced all my apprehensions; I had saved him once from ignominy, and, perhaps, from death itself; he had promised me to prove his gratitude, how could I therefore doubt that he would save me from destruction. 'Volkert!' exclaimed I, in a supplicating accent, Vol- kert!' The terrible man staggered back, staring by turns at me and him.

"'Volkert!' exclaimed I, again lifting up my fettered hands; he knew me, and without the least delay took a knife out of his pocket, and cut asunder the cords my hands had been tied with. The whole frightful assembly was fixed to the ground, seized with wonder and astonish- ment.

"Thou hast saved me,' began my guardian-angel now, in a solemn awful accent, thou hast given me liberty, take back thy gift, and life into the bargain.'

"'Friends,' said he, addressing the gaping crew, 'friends, he is the preserver of my honour and my liberty, what may he expect?'

"'Pardon, pardon,' was the unanimous cry,

'pardon, pardon, he shall live.'

"'Bravo, my boys,' said now their formidable Captain, who was sitting in judgment upon me, ' bravo, my honest lads, you are noble fellows: farewell Andrew,' added he, addressing his dying companion, ' farewell, Andrew, thou art avenged, art doubly avenged by the generosity of thy companions!'"

" At the same instant the whole crew hurried out of the room, leaving me alone with Volkert. Farewell, Lieutenant,' said he, shaking me by the hand, 'you hav wisely acted, in leaving F, like the Austrian; I shall never return to that town. If any similar sinister accident should happen to you, need but to pronounce my name and you will be safe.'

"I was going to embrace, and to assure him of my warmest gratitude, but he tore himself from my arms, and hastened to join his associates. Soon after I heard a confused noise before the door of the cottage, and, ere long, the whole band rode away in full speed. Now I was surrounded by midnight stillness, interrupted only by the groans of the dying robber. Max did not dare to enter the room while I was there.

"I was no longer able to remain in the house, the roaring of the tempest was hushed in silence, and the dawn of morn peeping through the windows; I found my horse sleeping in a corner behind the cottage, got on his back, and rode away in a slow pace.

"The morning sun rose in all his dazzling splendour, and still I was bewildered between trees and bushes, Straying about two tedious hours without being able to find an outlet, until at length I was so fortunate to meet a countryman, who, for a small reward, directed me to the road leading to N.

"Warned by my dangerous adventure, I now inquired at every village for the route I was to take, and thus reached at last the place of my destination without having met with any farther misfortune. Before I arrived at N- incident happened, which being connected with my adventure at the Haunted Castle, I cannot omit mentioning.

"Coming to a village about three miles distant from N- -, a great noise struck my ears, proceeding, as I soon could distinguish, from a great number of recruits, carousing and singing at the inn. I alighted and entered the residence of merriment and intoxication, in order to inform myself who the commanding officer was, in hopes to meet with an old acquaintance, but I was disappointed. Two serjeants, entirely unknown to me, conducted the transport, and, inquiring after their officer's name, I found that he was an utter stranger to me.

"Having surveyed the recruits, I was going to leave the room, when my eyes by accident fell on a man standing in a musing attitude by the fire-side, his looks fixed on the floor. Thinking to recollect his features I advanced nearer to him; he started up from his reverie, and, seeing me standing before him, staggered back with evident marks of astonishment; however, his terror soon gave way to rapturous joy; he ran towards me, caught me by the hand, and exclaimed, flushed with pleasure,—

"'Dear, dear Lieutenant, is it you? God be praised that you are still alive! God be praised that I have once more the happiness of seeing my kind old master!'

"His voice, his accent, and his transport, gave me no room to doubt that he was my late servant, whom I had lost in the castle.

"The honest fellow could find no words to express his joy, at my not having been famished with my companions in the cellar, as it had been the intention of the robbers. He expressed his joy in so noisy a manner, that we were soon surrounded by the recruits. I begged the serjeants to indulge with me with a private conversation with my honest servant, which they granted me with great politeness. I called for the host, requesting him to let us have a room to ourselves, that we might converse without being interrupted by the curiosity of his noisy guests.

"As soon as we were in private, I requested John to give me a brief account of what had happened to him after we had left him snoring in the great hall of the Castle; he was very willing to satisfy my curiosity, and related as follows:-

"I was aroused from my sleep by a violent shaking, and, recovering from my drowsiness, saw myself seized by two ill-looking fellows, who were employed to drag me forcibly away. Fear and terror bereft me at first of all power of utterance and resistance. I attempted several times to cry, but I could not pronounce a single word, and, as much as I could observe through the midnight darkness, saw myself carried down the spiral staircase, over the court-yard. When we were arrived at the gate, I was tied upon a horse, and surrounded by a numerous crew, who took me between them and rode away in full speed. My feet being tied together under the horse's belly, it was out of my power to stir, which rendered my situation exceedingly painful.

"The dawn of morn appeared, but not a single ray of hope cheered my desponding soul, being in the power of those merciless ruffians, who were still sweeping the field with all possible expedition, not caring for the excruciating pains I suffered, and forcing my horse to leap over hedges and ditches.

The swiftness of the race and my uncomfortable situation deprived me, at length, of all power of recollection, and threw me into a kind of stupefaction which prevented me from observing how long our journey had lasted. I was seized with a fainting fit, and when my recollection returned, observed that I was shut up in a subterraneous dungeon, an old hag was rubbing me with onions, and, when I recovered from the state of stupefaction, occasioned by the cruelty of my leaders, she fetched a bottle of brandy, admonishing me, in a rough uncouth dialect, to drink plenty of it, which I declined, requesting her to rub my lacerated limbs with it.

"Having performed my request with great alacrity she left me, and I had full leisure to contemplate the horrors of my dreary abode, the walls of which were blackened by the hand of time, and overgrown with moss; muddy straw spread on the damp ground served me for a couch, and the faint glimmering of a lamp heightened the horrors of my dungeon; the thick corrupted air made it difficult to fetch breath, to which were added most excruciating pains, not in the least alleviated by the use of brandy, but rather increased on account of the sores my poor frame was covered with; only the agony of my tortured mind surpassed the sufferings of my body; futurity stared me grisly in the face, and the consciousness being in the power of a set of villains, who would either sacrifice my life, to their thirst of blood, or force me, by threats and exquisite torments, to commit deeds of the most atrocious nature, filled my mind with dreadful apprehensions.

"I remained two days in a state of unspeakable despondency; although my bodily pains had abated, and I could move my limbs with more ease, yet the fear of futurity had weakened me so much that I could not stir from my miserable couch; my misery was augmented by the troublesome officiousness of the old hag, who every instant came to torment me. One time she wanted to apply to my sores poultices of roasted flour, and at another she would make me swallow a spoonful of disgusting nauseous drops; now she would force down my throat a soup of a most uninviting appearance, and a few minutes after she brought straw, which was half rotten, to place it under my head; in short, she tormented me so much by plying me with her unwelcome officiousness and kindness, that the gloominess of my mind hourly increased, and my little remaining strength was entirely spent by my efforts to resist her torturing care for my health and ease.

"On the fourth day of my confinement I was taken out of my dungeon, and my apprehensions were realised. The infernal villains intending to make me one of their associates in wickedness, ordered me to mount a horse, and forced me to follow them in full speed through fields and forests, notwithstanding the weak state of my body. My conductors, at first only three in number, and clad in linen frocks, blackened with coal dust, rode a-head, looking back now and then; their black faces and sooty hands evidently foreboded their dark design.

"After half an hour's ride my infernal guides stopped at a lonely public house, alighted, and bade me take care of the horses until they should return.

"I obeyed their stern command with gloomy silence, tied the horses to a tree, and sat myself down upon a bench before the house. The haunts of my disordered fancy made the time pass quickly on; I revolved in my afflicted mind my former occupation, the happy hours I had spent in the service of a kind, indulgent master, and the horrors of my present situation, the briny drops of sorrow and affliction moistened my pallid cheeks. 'What will become of thee?' said I to myself; a robber, and perhaps a murderer, too.' A chilly trembling glided through my veins, I started up, and was resolved to mount one of the horses, and make my escape, but the want of Strength reminded me soon of the utter impossibility of the execution of my rash design. I sunk down upon the bench, imploring heaven rather to put an end to my miserable life than to suffer me to become an associate of these hell-born fiends. After I had ejaculated this fervent prayer I felt my despondency abate a little, awaiting with impatience the re-appearance of my fell conductors.

"A short time after they came, accompanied by three more ruffians of a most frightful aspect, who, with the greatest expedition, fetched their horses from an adjacent stable, mounted them without delay, and rode away like lightning; my conductors did the same, ordered me to follow their example, and galloped over fields as fast as their coursers could run; coming up with our ill-looking companions we pursued our journey with all possible swiftness.

"Having, by accident, mounted the wrong horse, which was the fleetest of all, I kept always a-head, and could distinctly hear every word they spoke, though I could not understand a syllable of their conversation. After it had grown dark, we alighted again at a solitary public house, the horses being once more committed to my care, and I awaited with patience the end of an adven- ture that boded no good.

"I had been standing in the chilly air of night above an hour, musing on my deplorable fate, when the innkeeper brought me a piece of bread and butter and a mug of beer, but I could neither eat nor drink, shaking with cold. "The night was dark and the sky overcast, a thick dampish fog had wetted my clothes, and not one friendly star was to be seen in the firmament, which was as gloomy as my mind. After I had been exposed for half an hour longer to the inclemency of the chilly air, my conductors re-appeared, their number being increased to twelve, and their sooty dress exchanged for green hunting coats; every one of them was armed with a gun, a brace of pistols, and a cutlass.

"The feelings which were rushing on my mind at that sight admit of no description; the blood froze in my veins, my soul was harrowed up in dreadful suspense, and I mounted my horse more dead than alive, galloping over the heath with my conductors in senseless stupefaction, like a poor culprit who is dragged along to be delivered to the merciless fangs of the grim fiendly-looking executioner, till I at length was roused from my stupor by the sounds of horns assailing my ears from afar, and the loud clamorous shouts of our troop.

"The sound of horns drew nearer, and my conductors answered by blowing theirs. Now I perceived a powerful troop of horsemen, sweeping the heath like a hurricane. In an instant I was surrounded by a numerous crew on horseback, and rough dismal voices vibrated in my ear in a confused manner. One of them struck fire, a number of torches were lighted, and I beheld with amazement and dismay, a large troop of terrible beings around me.

"Whithersoever I turned my eyes, I was frightened almost out of my wits by stern, threatening looks. They soon perceived the workings of my desponding mind, laughed at my fear, and uttered terrible execrations. One of them, who bore a more tremendous aspect than the rest, came forth, the noisy crew was awed in solemn silence, and the terrible man began to address them thus:

"You know, my brave companions, that this rascal here,' pointing at me, is the servant of the wretch who has dared to watch in our Castle, with armed numbers. The daring scoundrel and his two associates are punished; famine and thirst have seized their victims with merciless fangs, tormenting them with excruciating pains, with agony and black despair; on our next visit nocturnal to the castle we shall see them lifeless on the ground. You know how the daring fools have been vexed, teased, and tormented by Father Francis. It was glorious fun, we have been amused with their foolish credulity, and are now amply avenged on these bold disturbers of our nocturnal assembly.

"The villagers are not yet punished,' continued he, 'for having assisted them, but they shall not escape their doom. Our future safety demands the destruction of the village, and its environs, but, tell me, what shall we do with that fellow there? He is well fed, and seems not to be without strength, my advice is to make him our companion.'

"'We will, we will,' roared the whole troop.

"Then their terrible leader resumed, he must give us tonight a specimen of his dexterity.'

"'He shall, he shall,' was the universal cry. I trembled like a wretched culprit who hears his sentence pronounced, when the speaker addressed me thus :- Fellow! thou hast heard what an honour we have conferred on thee, we expect that thou wilt be faithful to us, oaths are as little valued among robbers as they are in hell, and a hand-stroke will satisfy us, give me thy right hand as a token of unshaken fidelity.'

"Trembling did I obey his stern command, and he bade me to take courage, to abandon all fear, and to follow him. The torches were extinguished, the robbers began to converse in an unintelligible accent, the horns were sounded, the whole troop set spurs to their horses, rushing over the fields like a midnight tempest; I felt myself seized by the arm, and my horse pulled by the bridle after them. After a short ride the voice of the terrible leader ordered us to halt.

"'Here,' said he to me, ' is a gun and a

whistle! The former thou art to use in case of necessity, and the latter as soon as a waggon or a coach passes the road.'

"This said, he rode away, but methought I heard another horseman not far from me.

"Now I began to consult with myself what I should do, whether I should betray the innocent traveller, or suffer him to escape. My mind shrank back from the horrid idea of becoming accessory to the destruction of a fellow-creature, but how could I avoid it if I would not myself fall a victim to the cruelty of my infernal compan- ions? Life is the sweetest gift of heaven, and not easy to be parted with.

"While I was in deliberation with myself what course to take, I heard the rattling of a coach within a little distance from me, and a violent trembling seized my limbs : the coach came nearer and my trembling increased. Without knowing what I was about, I was going to apply the whistle to my lips, my hand trembled, a sudden stupor seized me, the whistle dropped to the ground, and the coach passed by in full speed; at the same time I heard somebody whistle behind me, soon after the report of three guns, accompanied with cries and lamentations, struck my ear; a female voice was praying for mercy, loud acclamations filled the air, and soon after all was hushed in profound silence.

"I was sitting on my horse in dumb stupefaction, when on a sudden I perceived somebody laying hold of the bridle of my steed, and pulling her forcibly after him. After a few minutes I saw at a distance a glimmering light shining through the bushes; as we came near to the spot I beheld in my conductor the terrible leader of the band, and we at length arrived at a place surrounded with bushes, where the robbers were seated round a fire, dividing the spoil; they all gave a loud shriek, as if they already knew how badly I had acquitted myself of my first task.

"'Let us pronounce sentence against the rascal !' exclaimed my conductor, with a thundering voice.

"'Let us knock his brains out,' roared one of the robbers.

"'Send him to the dungeon,' exclaimed a second.

"'The latter we will do,' resumed the Captain, 'punishment may, perhaps, recall him to reason.'

"Having said this, he ordered two of the gang to me to the place of confinement; they mounted their horses, took me between them, and hurried away with me at a furious rate. We arrived with the first dawn of day at the bottom of a hill, where I forcibly was dragged through the bushes and thorns fettered with heavy chains, and carried through a narrow passage into a dark dungeon ; groping about I found myself surrounded with straw, the muddy smell of which left me no doubt that it was half rotten.

"Having lingered many hours in that terrible abode of misery, without either hearing or seeing anybody, I at last was hailed by the distant, hollow sound of approaching footsteps, dying away sometimes, and then vibrating again faintly on my ear; at once they grew more and more audible, and the glimmering of a light began to illuminate the subterraneous cave.

"Turning round with much difficulty, I perceived that it emerged from a deep grotto behind me. The glimmering grew lighter, and the sound of footsteps drew nearer ; at length I beheld a figure more frightful than the robbers themselves; the old hideous hag, adorned with all the graces of hell, ascended with alacrity from the gloomy abyss, panting for breath; and now I had a full view of the horrors of my den: the faint rays of my lamp were reflected in a grisly manner from the lofty walls, hewn into the solid rock, and mixed with the midnight darkness, which was hovering beneath the high-vaulted ceiling. My dungeon was of a small circumference, but appeared to be far removed from the surface of the earth; the dreadful abode of horror was infected by a damp, pestilential air, through which the light was glimmering as if through a bluish fog.

"The antiquated scare-crow began to pity and to bemoan my miserable doom, exhorting me to obey more strictly the commands of my masters, and, having put a pitcher with water, and a piece of bread before me, unfettered my hands, admonishing me to submit patiently to my fate, and never to attempt an escape, which not only would prove abortive, but at the same time prolong and increase my punishment. I uttered not a syllable, and she left me to muse in solitude on my forlorn and unhappy situation.

"Three gloomy days of misery and dismay were now elapsed since I had been thrown into that terrible abode of silence and melancholy, before I saw anybody except the old witch, by whose visits alone I could guess the progress of time. No year of my whole life has ever appeared to me so long as those three days of woe; I strove in vain to loosen the fetters which chained my feet, the lock that confined them together baffled all my endeavours, and, after many fruitless efforts, I was obliged to bid a mournful adieu to every ray of hope of making my escape from the fangs of my cruel tyrants: black despair hovered over me with sooty wings, the greedy tooth of grief was gnawing on my vitals, and the recollection of former times of ease and tranquillity served only to heighten my misery.

Part II, Chapter III

"The fourth day brought me the visit of the Captain, who entered my dungeon with a lighted torch.

"'Well, rascal!' exclaimed he, how dost thou like this beautiful apartment? art thou tired of thy sepulchre, or dost thou prefer to be entombed alive for ever, to the honor of being one of our brave party? art thou sensible of the foolishness of thy stubborn disobedience, and may I expect that thou wilt be more obsequious in future?'

"I groaned a lamentable yes, the result of my resolution, which I had been driven to by despair and my forlorn situation.

"'Well,' resumed my tyrant, unfastening my chains, 'I hope thou art sensible that it is more eligible to be a gentleman of the high road than to be buried alive amid spiders and toads; I will try once more whether I can make thee a worthy member of our society, rise and follow me!'

"I attempted to get on my legs, but I sunk down again upon my damp couch; my legs, which were become quite useless by the pressure of the chains, were now pierced with most excruciating pains, and unable to support my miserable carcase. The robber seeing me struggle in vain to obey his command, seized me with a powerful arm, and dragged me forcibly over the rocky ground. I was trailed along the winding passage of the subterraneous fabric, like a victim to the altar, where it is to receive the finishing stroke. I was every now and then forced to crawl on my knees through narrow holes, and to climb with much difficulty over gaping chasms in the rock, till at length an iron door obstructed our passage; my conductor opened it, and I beheld a spacious lofty hall, illuminated with a great number of torches, where some of the robbers were seated at table, eating, drinking, and conversing merrily with each other, and some cleaning guns and pistols, and charging them.

"They all spoke kindly to me, inviting me to partake of their blithsome meal, and congratulating me on the wise resolution I had taken to become a sharer of their fortune. I relished the roasted meat, the turkeys, and hams exceeding well, and swallowed plentiful draughts of most delicious wine. Though I was not remiss to ply briskly the knife and fork and the cheerful goblet, and strove to do honour to the table, yet the robbers chided me every now and then, finding fault with my tardiness.

"The exhilarating juice of the grape spread mirth and cheerfulness around; the spacious cavern re-echoed their Jocund songs, the tales of their exploits gave variety to the entertainment, and it seemed as if the sting of conscience had entirely lost, with them, its pungent point. The cloth was at length removed, the beldam who had been waiting at table began now likewise to eat, and the robbers made themselves ready to leave their subterraneous haunt.

"To-day,' said the captain to me, before they departed, 'thou shalt stay at home, but to-morrow thou art to be of our party, and thy deportment must decide whether we can enlist thee in our noble company, or shall knock thy brains out.'

Then the whole crew sallied forth through the iron door, without giving me time to answer, and left me alone with the old woman, who was very assiduous to amuse me, relating with much garrulity, many stories of the dear gentlemen, as she called the robbers, and extolling their generosity to the skies.

Perceiving that I did not relish her tiresome tales, she fetched books, cards, and dice, leaving it to my choice what sort of amusement I should fix upon. I preferred reading to a tête-à-tête with the old witch, and endeavoured to dispel the gloom of my mind, by perusing an old book of chivalry.

"At night my rusty companion wanted me to sit down to supper with her, which I refused, requesting her to show me to my bedroom. Vexed by my refusal, she mumbled something between her few remaining teeth, and opened the door of a small side-room where I found a couch, made of clean straw, and covered with a blanket ; throwing myself upon it, I slept for the first time sweet and soundly after eight painful nights of horror.

"The next morning the old woman thundered at my door, telling me it was broad day, and past nine o'clock, and that our gentlemen would soon return to dinner. I got up much refreshed, and assisted her in the kitchen, which pleased her so well that she promised to recommend me to the good graces of the Captain."

"Thus far had my servant proceeded in his narration, without having been interrupted by me, though he had been very circumlocutious, and spoken above an hour. It gave me great pleasure to hear a circumstantial description of the robbers and their cave, and honest John's simplicy afforded me great amusement, which proved a very seasonable relief in my then gloomy state of mind; I therefore was very much vexed when one of the serjeants entered to tell him that they were waiting for him to pro- ceed on their march, and bade him make haste, just as he was going to give me a full account of the robbers' deportment towards him after their return, of the splendid dinner which the old woman had prepared, assisted by him, and of their discourses at table.

"I entreated the rough son of Mars to resign this recruit to me, and to accept from me double the binding money he had given him, but he did not relish my proposal, and John himself was little inclined to enter again into my service; at last I prevailed, by fair words and a small present, on the serjeant to wait a quarter of an hour longer, and he left the room after we had promised to be as expeditious as possible.

"When he was gone I asked John why he would rather be a soldier than enter again into my service.

"What else would you advise me to do?' replied he, with weeping eyes, ' my life is exposed to the danger in these parts, and would you like to have a servant who has been a robber?'

"You have not been a robber,' interrupted I the poor fellow, but recollected soon that he had not finished his narration, and perhaps might have been compelled at last, by menaces, to become a member of the gang, I therefore requested him to continue his tale, and to be as brief as possible, which he in vain strove to do, going every now and then astray. The substance of his confused continuation was as follows: 66 The robbers returned, treated John again with kindness, ate, drank, and left him once more, without mentioning a word about his going with them, which did not in the least displease him; he amused himself with reading, and when night invited him to sleep, he went to his couch with a much lighter heart than when he had left it in the morning. That manner of life he led eight days, during which time the robbers always returned to dinner, in greater or lesser number; the whole gang consisted of twenty-four stout men besides the Captain.

"On the ninth, tenth, eleventh, and the three succeeding days, the robbers did not return, but on the fifteenth they all appeared in high spirits, though with empty hands; John concluded, from this circumstance, and what he could gather from their mysterious discourses, that they must have had several other haunts, where they hoarded up their spoils; the old castle on the skirts of the Black Forest seemed, however, to be their usual residence.

"After dinner was over, and the goblet had freely circulated, the captain recollected that John was to give them a second sample of his capacity, ordered him to mount a horse, and conducted him, accompanied by two of his associates, to the high road leading through the forest, where he commanded him to lay in ambush, and to rob the first traveller he should see coming along the road.

"Poor John was thunderstruck at the stern command of the Captain, fell at his feet, and entreated him to have mercy on him; but the ruffians laughed at him, and their leader repeated his order, swearing he would kill him on the spot, if he did not instantly comply with his desire. The hapless fellow seeing there was no alternative, but to be killed, or to prey on his fellow creatures, concealed himself in a thicket, and the robbers posted themselves opposite to him, behind some bushes, taking the three horses along with them.

"The first travellers that passed by were two monks, and John thanked God in his heart that they were two. A little while after a ruddy countryman appeared, he was on horseback, as it seemed returning from the market, carrying two empty sacks behind him, and counting money. That will be an easy task, thought John, but when he was going to leave his hiding-place, his knees trembled he was unable to stir, and the clown pursued his way without being disturbed.

"The robbers began to hem, and poor John seized with terror, was going to run after the swain, but, thinking him too far advanced, resolved to wait for the next traveller, and to attack him vigorously.

"He had waited a good while for another opportunity to acquit himself of his task, till at length a travelling journeyman appeared. John rushed out of his hiding place before his prey was near enough and as soon as the frightened traveller saw a man running towards him with a pistol, he took to his heels and luckily got out of his reach.

"The Captain and his companions seized with a fit of roaring laughter, exhorted their awkward pupil, in a low accent, to have a little more patience in future.

"Before John could reach his lurking place, a Jew made his appearance; the sight of the poor Israelite fired the novice in robbery with an unusual courage; he rushed upon the terrified Hebrew like lightning, and, having seized him by the collar, demanded his money with a thundering voice. The petrified Israelite feeling himself thus roughly handled, shrieked and lamented most rue- fully, and stoutly refused at first to deliver up his mammon, but when he saw his life at stake, and John put his pistol to his breast, yielded at last, with a woeful visage, to the uncouth demands of his aggressor, 'I will give—I will give-all the money I have about me.' So saying, he untied a leathern bag with money, fastened round his waist, and offered it to the greedy robber, who, transported with joy at his success, was thrown off his guard, and the cunning Jew taking hold of an opportunity to recover his treasure, seized, with much adroitness, the pistol, wrested it from poor John's trembling hand, and ordered the affrighted fellow, who was almost petrified, to return him his money instantly, if he would not have his brains blown out; John hesitated not a moment to submit to the Jew's demand, restored him his bag, and took to his heels, but the two robbers sallying forth from their hiding-place, retook him soon, while the cunning Israelite got clear off with his money and John's pistol.

"The unfortunate fellow was instantly carried back to the robbers' den, and shut up again in the subterraneous dungeon which he had but lately left. Having been con- fined there some weeks the robbers took him one day out of his hole, and gave him his liberty, and a small sum of money, after he had sworn a dreadful oath never to reveal the least thing of what he had heard and seen in the cavern during his stay with them, and to leave the country as soon as possible.

"This is the substance of my late servant's narrative ; he had entirely forgotten his oath until he mentioned it, yet he silenced soon his murmuring conscience, persuading himself not to have committed perjury, because he had been intimidated by dreadful menaces to make it, and an oath of that nature could never be binding; he at the same time alleged, that the Captain himself had declared that among robbers swearing was of no importance, and thus soothed his conscience.

"I did not think it necessary to undeceive, but gave him a handsome sum of money as a token of my gratitude for his faithful services, and bade him an affectionate farewell. He thanked me with weep- ing eyes and left the room. When he was gone I mounted my horse, and arrived after a few hours at N — .

"Now I come to the last and most important incident I ever met with during the whole time of my recruiting business, which will clear up all the above-related events, and dispel the clouds which are still hanging over some parts of my wonderful tale.

"Two years were now elapsed since my last adventure, and I had heard nothing farther either of the Necromancer or his associates. The frequent unwelcome visits at the Castle and their alarming consequences, very likely had made both parties more circumspect, which appeared to me to have been the principal motive of those ruffians to release my servant, lest I might be induced to make a Strict search after him; whatever may have been their motive for doing so, I had no farther trace either of the robbers or Volkert, and even at F- the Necromancer's principal place of action, whither I went shortly after, even there, everything relating to our former adventures was entirely forgotten-the haunted inn had been sold. to a new master, the apparition was frightened away, and the house was a respectable auberge.

"I also began, by degrees, to forget the adventures which I partly had heard related, and partly experienced myself, being only now and then reminded of those incidents, when, in the lonely hour of solitude the recollection of the Austrian stole on my mind.

Part II, Chapter III

"My long overclouded serenity had resumed its wonted brightness, and the remembrance of my ever-regretted friend was no longer accompanied by gloominess and melancholy sensations; I could again partake of the pleasures which smile at us wherever we are, and could relish again the innocent sports of merriment.

"In that state of mind I arrived towards the end of summer at A, when the expectation of every inhabit- ant was engaged by the approaching scene of a bloody execution, which was to take place within a few days.

"A church having been robbed about six months ago, several suspected persons had been imprisoned and put to the rack, but could not be brought to confession, upon which the magistrates had been obliged to set them at liberty for want of such witnesses as the law requires, and to give up the inquisition until further proofs should be found. Many months elapsed before the enraged priests, aided by the eagle-eyed assistance of the magistrates, could trace out the sacrilegious robbers of their hallowed treasures, and feast their vengeance on the throes of the victims of their foaming ire, expiring on the flaming pile, until at length an accident delivered into their holy fangs the perpetrators of that daring deed, whom they in vain had endeavoured to discover by advertisements, tortures of the rack, and the promise of reward.

"There lived in a suburb of A-, an old unsuspected man, named Peter, loved by the children of the place, whom he oftentimes amused with little tales, and bribed with sweetmeats, but dreaded by the aged, who firmly believed him to be on an intimate footing with his satanic majesty, because he now and then displayed, when in good humour, proofs of his juggling skill, which they beheld with gaping terror. This hoary man, who lived in a mean cottage, in apparent indigence, and could not be suspected of possessing ill-gotten goods, went oftentimes abroad, but whither he journeyed, or what called him so frequently from his abode, nobody could tell with certainty; some said he went a begging, others, more superstitious, pre- tended to have seen him, through the chinks of the half decayed window shutters, stretched lifeless on the floor; and some insisted upon having seen him riding through the air on a broomstick, to pay, as it was supposed, his court to his infernal master, to whom his soul and body was said to be mortgaged.

"Very fortunately this man was not at A- when the church robbery was committed, to the greatest satisfaction of some who thought him to be an harmless man, and to the greater mortification of others, who pretended to have suffered many a malicious trick by his sorcery: for if he had not been absent at that time, his ill wishers would certainly have forged a pretext to deliver him up to the civil power, as a suspicious, because he never went to church, although he was supposed to be a Roman Catholic.

"Some days after the above-mentioned prisoners had been set at liberty, he returned to A- on a holiday after sun set. The children playing in the streets no sooner espied him, than they ran towards him, hailing their hoary benefactor with loud shouts, searching his pockets for sweetmeats, and teasing the poor old man so unmercifully, that he at last grew angry, and threatened to chastise the troublesome crowd with his staff; however, their demands grew still more clamorous, and some of them began to prick him with pins, which at length obliged him to put his threats in execution.

"When the mothers of those ill-mannered boys saw the old man plying the backs of their darlings with his staff, they attacked him like furies, to revenge their children's wrongs and the profanation of the holiday, and by their vociferations alarmed the whole neighbourhood. The husbands of the enraged dames came soon to their assistance; the children began terribly to roar when they saw their old friend in danger of being torn to pieces by their parents, and poor Peter was glad when he got off the clutches of the merciless multitude, after having sustained many a hard blow, and hastened with all possible speed to shelter himself from farther insult in his humble cottage.

"But who can describe the terror he was seized with, when he perceived that he had lost his wallet in the scuffle ! Raving like a madman did he rush out of his hut, to recover his property, which was carried away in triumph by the victorious party. He exhausted all the rhetoric he was master of, entreated them, whined, and swore, but alas! his adversaries had hearts of flint, and stoutly refused to give up their booty, and when he at last, half frantic with despair, endeavoured to regain it by force, a violent shower of stones drove him back to his humble abode, leaving his dear wallet in the ruthless hands of the furious and inexorable mob.

"The principal motive that had induced the assailants to retain the wallet, was an impulse of curiosity, to see what the old sorcerer, so they called him, had got by his journey; and the attack of the children was, very likely, a preconcerted matter, in order to provoke his anger,thus to give them an opportunity of satisfying their curiosity.

"The wallet having been opened the first object meeting their prying looks was an old pair of breeches, a tattered shirt, and some pairs of stockings, then followed a large book and some unknown instruments, and at last they found at the bottom a heavy leathern bag, the knot by which it was fastened, baffling all their endeavours to untie it, was at length cut asunder, and the amazement of the gaping multitude rose to the highest pitch, when their eyes beheld a great number of gold pieces.

"At first the whole crew was struck dumb with astonishment, but their silence was soon interrupted by a voice, exclaiming, 'We have entrapped the sacrilegious robber of our church!' which was the signal for the enraged multitude to break out in curses and terrible execrations against the old man; the air resounded with the universal cry, ' Church robber! church robber ! ' and some of them, hastening to the justice of peace, roared with a bellowing voice, We have found him out! we have detected the sacrilegious robber of our church!"

"The justice was astonished at the unexpected tidings, but his amazement increased still more, when he saw the large heaps of gold coin which had been found in the wallet of the old beggar, and instantly sent the beadle to seize poor Peter; meanwhile the rest of the furious mob had stormed the defenceless hut of the old man, dragged him forth, and conducted him towards the judge's house amid numberless blows and curses. He was now delivered up to the grim catchpole, who instantly carried him to the town prison.

"His trial began the following day, and he

was ordered to give an account of himself, and how he had got such a large sum of money. Refusing to answer that question, and pretending to have earned the money by honest means, he was put to the rack; yet he stoutly maintained his first declaration, and the justice, being unable to convict him of the charge he stood accused of, was obliged to set him at liberty, retaining, however, his money, until he should have proved that he had got by lawful means.

"Peter promised to prove his deposition within a short time, and returned to his hut, which, during his confinement, had been closely searched by his busy neigh- bours, who, however, had found nothing in it but some tattered coats, and broken pieces of furniture.

"The justice, being a prudent man, dissembled to have dropped all further inquiry, but secretly appointed some trusty people to watch all his motions. Their vigilance was fruitless a great while, until at length one of Peter's neighbours observed him, one morning, leaving his house, with a wallet on his back and a staff in his hand, setting off in full speed.

"The people of the justice, whom he informed of what he had seen, followed Father Peter in different directions, in disguise, and saw him at noontide enter a lonely public house. Having waited in vain for his re-appearance, they began to conceive suspicion, and concealed themselves behind some bushes within a small distance from the house, until it grew dark.

"As soon as night had spread her dun mantle over the face of the earth, they heard a distant trampling of horses, bending their course towards the spot where they were hidden, and, ere long, a numerous troop of horsemen alighted at the public house and entered it, upon which the spies crept forth from their lurking place, and stole softly to the windows of the house; there they had not listened six minutes, when they heard a jingling of money, and, peeping through the chinks of one of the shutters, beheld a table covered with dollars, and surrounded by a number of armed men, among whom was Father Peter, feasting his looks on the money which was spread before him.

"Having now got every information necessary, they mounted each of them one of the horses which the robbers had fastened to some trees, and hurried back to the town with all possible expedition. The public house being distant from A- only two leagues, they arrived there after an hour's ride, and having informed the justice of everything they had heard and seen, were instantly sent back with a great part of the town-guard, well armed, and mounted on the fleetest coursers that could be got.

"The whole troop arrived a little before midnight at the public house, where the robbers were seated round a table, eating and drinking in great security, and almost bereft of the use of their senses by frequent libations. They all started up as if roused by a sudden clap of thunder, when the town guard rushed into the room, seizing their arms, and threatening to blow their brains out if they should attempt the least resistance.

"Their hands having been tied, Father Peter, the land- lord, who had concealed himself under the bed, and all his servants were seized, and, having been properly secured, carried off in triumph.

"The robbers, amounting to ten, were clad in hunting coats, and their purses well stored with gold and silver coin; the whole train marching slowly on, with lighted torches, arrived at A before it was light, and the prisoners were safely lodged in the strongest dungeon.

"Their trial commenced early in the morning, and the youngest of the robbers, who was questioned first, refusing to confess, was put to the rack; his stubbornness being soon subdued, by the torments of the rack, he made evidence, that their gang was very numerous, and scattered all over the country, where they had a great many hiding places underground; their chief residence, he said, was the old

Castle, on the skirts of the Black Forest, where a great part of their spoils was concealed. He farther confessed, that Father Peter was in close connexion with all the different gangs he had no fixed abode, but resided sometimes in this, and at other times in that town, and enjoyed the burghership in several cities, where he pos- sessed houses and estates. He firmly denied to have had any share in the church robbery, but pointed out three of his fellow prisoners who had been concerned in it: whether Peter had been accessory in it or not he could not tell.

"The day following the three robbers charged with the sacrilege were brought to the bar, but none of them would plead guilty. Being put to the rack, the first of them, an aged man, bore the three degrees without uttering a word, and died a few hours after he had been reconducted to the prison. The second confessed at the third degree, that he had been accessory in the church robbery ; but declared that the third was innocent, and that he him- self had been persuaded by Father Peter to commit the sacrilege.

"Now the hoary dissembler was ordered to the bar. Having heard the charges of the justice with a firm counten- ance, he replied, with great equanimity.

"'Yes, I am guilty, and wish to God I had no other crimes on my conscience than that which

I stand accused of. The sluggish, gluttonous monks, who, in honour of an image of stone, have ruined and expelled from their own country a whole innocent family to beg their bread in the streets; these vile villains are far greater felons than myself, and I rejoice at having been an instrument in the hand of providence to avenge the wrongs of the hapless objects of their rapacity, and to restore to those innocent sufferers their property. If this action deserves punish- ment, you may tear my old limbs asunder, break these withering bones, and reduce to dust and ashes my poor worn-out frame; I will not complain nor utter a groan.

'The grim avenger draws near-I feel the hand of the Supreme Judge; he, and not you, poor mortals, forces me to confess my transgressions. I can brave the ire of men, and deride all bodily sufferings; but I must bend my aged knees to him who dwelleth in heaven, and the pangs of conscience are not to be trifled with.'

"The Judge and the Sheriffs gazed at each other in dumb silence at these words, and none of them were in- clined to question him any farther. Seeing this, he informed them voluntarily of every particular of the sacrilege, and of the family which had been plunged into want and misery by the rapacious monks whose church and convent had been robbed, by means of a forged will. He at the same time confessed where and in what manner the jewels, and the gold and silver furniture had been turned into money, and by what means the sums those articles had fetched had been conveyed to the family, without acquainting the innocent sufferers with the names of their secret benefactors.

"The astonishment of the whole court increased with every word the old man uttered, and as soon as he had finished his confession, he requested the jailor to reconduct him to the prison. It lasted a good while before the dread arbiters of life and death could recover from their astonishment, and debate on Peter's doom, which they unanimously agreed to mitigate as much as possible.

"According to the rigour of the law he should have been burnt alive, but he and the robber who had been convicted of sacrilege, were sentenced to be beheaded first, and then burnt. The rest of the gang were ordered to close confinement for further examination.

"When Father Peter with his fellow-sufferer was called to the bar, in order to hear his sentence pronounced, he behaved with the same firmness of mind as on his trial, and comforted him who had betrayed him.

"Having heard his sentence pronounced with the greatest equanimity, he thanked his judges for their clemency, and left the court, supporting with his arm his companion, who exhibited a ghastly picture of dismay and despondency. Father Peter did not lose his courage during his confinement, and took all possible pains to soothe the grief of his fellow sufferer, and to inspire him with sentiments superior to black despair.

"He was to be executed two days after my arrival at A— — — — —, -, and I hesitated long whether I should go and see this extraordinary man or not, although I was much solicited by my friends to do it; having a secret boding that this reverend old man, who faced the grim spectre of death so cool and undaunted, could be no other person than Father Francis, alias Volkert, and thinking it dis- ingenuous to distress, by my presence, a man who had saved my life two years ago.

"Curiosity and sensibility struggled a great while within my breast, until the last day before the execution, when an ardent desire of having cleared up the mysteries of former events got the better of my generous sentiments, and prompted me to see him early in the morning.

"Having mustered up all my fortitude, I went to the prison at six o'clock. Perhaps, thought I, the old man may now be more willing to dispel my doubts than formerly, being on the awful brink of eternity, and disclose the mystery of his former impenetrable transactions, and my presence may not distress the unhappy man so much as thou thinkest! Yet I could not get entirely rid of my apprehensions of increasing the sufferings of my benefactor, or being, perhaps, disappointed in my expec- tation.

"In this state of mind I arrived at the prison, which was opened by the gaoler after a violent knocking. I requested him to favour me with a short interview with the prisoner, but was denied access, because it was against the common rule to introduce company to the convicts the day before execution. I offered him a dollar, entreating him to make an exception with me, being a stranger, and having reasons of moment to wish for an interview with the old man. The sight of the money seemed to have more weight with him than my words; he mused awhile, and then said, 'Since you are a stranger, I will make an exception from the common rule, but I must insist upon your telling nobody of this indulgence.'

"So saying, he conducted me without farther ado to a narrow staircase, leading to a long and narrow passage; at length we came to a small black door, marked with three red crosses, through which I followed him into a dark gloomy room; the entrance was guarded by two men half asleep, and in the background close to the wall I beheld two human figures, of a ghastly woe-worn aspect, and drawing near with a beating heart, saw that one of them was

Volkert: his countenance was pale and emaciated, but still stamped with his usual dignity of mien; his head reclining against the wall, and his hands resting on his knees.

"He seemed not to perceive that a stranger was in the room until the gaoler said to him, 'Well, Father Peter, there is a gentleman who will be glad to speak to you and your comrade.'

"Hearing this, he slowly lifted up his head, staring at me.

"Volkert!' exclaimed I, 'Volkert!'

"His looks grew wild, his head sunk back, and he heaved a deep groan; whilst I was standing before him like a statue, thrilled with horror and pity.

"As soon as the gaoler had left us, Volkert began with a trembling voice, 'Lieutenant, are you come to embitter last hours, or to speak comfort to my afflicted mind?

"'The latter, good Volkert,' replied I.

"'Then,' said he, 'you are welcome, sit down, if you please, perhaps I may be able to be useful to you somehow or other, before I fall a victim to my crimes. I can cau- tion you at least against cheats like myself.

Part II, Chapter III

"'No idle curiosity has prompted me.' said I, 'to see you, nor am I come to distress you by illiberal reproaches, for having once endangered my life, that would be ungenerous. You have saved me once from imminent destruction, and that atones fully for all former injuries; yet you will not be offended if I earnestly request you to clear up some late events, which have happened to myself and the Austrian, who-

"Has been imposed upon by me,' replied Volkert, ' like yourself, whom I had given the lie at F, in your and your friend's presence. I will give you all the information you desire, and at the same time a short sketch of my life, as well as it is in my power in my present deplorable situation. I wish most ardently I had done what I always intended to do, and set down in writing those events, and the memoirs of my life; they undoubtedly would be very instructive, and greatly lessen the number of impostors, and those that are imposed upon.'

"Here he stopped, and, having mused awhile, began his narrative, which, indeed, was very defective, but satis- factory enough for me.

"'I am," thus Volkert began, "a native of England, my father died when I was not quite ten years old, and left me an helpless orphan, without either fortune or near relations. A rich

Dutchman being moved by my helpless situation, took me in his house, and, leaving England the year following, carried me over with him to the Hague.

"'This worthy man gave me a very liberal education, and when I was thirteen years old took me in his counting- house; but alas! he died before he could establish my fortune as he intended to do.

"'His son, who carried on his father's business, had never been partial to me, and found a pretext to quarrel with me, and to send me away. A rich nobleman, just going to set out for Germany, wanted a servant, who occasionally would act as secretary, and I was glad to accept his offer to take me in his service. He directed his way to K- where his father was one of the ministers of state.

"My young master appeared to be little inclined to qualify himself for state business, being possessed of a very small stock of ambition, and entirely addicted to the Study of the occult sciences, which had engaged his attention so much, that he was unfit for anything else. I soon was infected with an ardent desire to become his pupil, and, after a few months' instruction, was as great a fool as himself.

"It would be too tedious if I was to relate all our fruitless endeavours to effect the apparition of a spirit, and I was soon convinced that it lay not in the power of man to lord over these bodiless beings. My master, however, continued his mysterious operations day and night with an indefatigable ardour.

It is very natural, that it at length came into my head to profit by his superstitious enthusiasm, and that I eagerly seized every opportunity to impose upon a man, who promised to fall an easy sacrifice to art and cunning, having great reason to expect that such an attempt would ensure me his affection, and promote my fortune rapidly.

"One night as he was conjuring up his guardian angel with much impatience, I entered his room, telling him that all his efforts would be in vain, because he was not acquainted with the proper means of forcing the inhabit- ants of the other world to make their appearance.

"Gazing at me with wonder and surprise, he inquired whether I had improved so much in the occult sciences that I could effect what he so eagerly desired. I neither denied nor confirmed his question, but told him that I would give him the next day a specimen of my skill in Necromancy.

"It was an easy task to impose on my credulous enthusiastic Count, having secured the assistance of a fellow- servant. We resided at a country-seat his mother had left him, which was the fittest place in the world for the execution of our design. Having succeeded better than I at first expected, I made him my dupe above a twelve- month, and grew at last so bold and impudent that the Count could not but perceive my juggling tricks, and instantly sent me away.

The good credulous man has certainly been convinced afterwards, that the lesson I gave him by my cheats deserved the warmest gratitude.

"I had saved a pretty sum of money during my stay with the Count, and being used to an idle life, had not the least thought of looking about for another master. I went back to H- where I abandoned myself to gambling, drinking, and all sorts of dissipation, until all my money was spent, and no other means of getting an honest livelihood left, than to try my fortune in the army.

"A recruiting officer paid me a hundred dollars for my liberty, and I cheerfully enlisted under the banner of Mars.

"I had received the promise to be made a serjeant, but saw myself at first very much disappointed, being forced to serve as a common soldier. Being, however, a good penman, well skilled in casting accounts, and leading a sober and regular life, I soon rose so high in the good opinion of my superiors, that I was appointed serjeant after nine months' service. I certainly should have been promoted higher if I had continued to be zealous in the service, sober and attentive to my superiors, but my patience was exhausted, and I relapsed again into my former dissipations.

"A dissolute life requires money, and the desire of getting it plunges him who has once been led astray from the path of virtue soon into his former errors. I had once more recourse to my juggling tricks, pretending to possess a supernatural skill in detecting thefts, in tossing up the cup, and in telling people's fortunes; I conjured up spirits, dispelled the power of witchcraft, and raised up the dead. In short, I did everything in my power to drain the purses of the weak and credulous.

"This trade was profitable, and very advantageous in many respects; but it lost me the esteem of my superiors, Stained my character, poisoned my heart, and reduced me at last to that despicable sort of people whose heedlessness bids defiance to every obstacle, and who have nothing more at heart than how they may enrich themselves to the detriment of their fellow creatures. In short, I became a rogue of the blackest die.

"It was natural that my cheats now and again mis- carried before I arrived at that degree of skill, which, in later years, has crowned with success most of my roguish tricks. My superiors, who had warned me many a time against committing such villainous actions, became at last tired of admonishing and correcting me by words, and a spirit which I had conjured up played his part so bad, that they found themselves obliged to make an example of me, and to banish me the country."

A healthy well-made man of my age had no need to be uneasy about getting into the service of any foreign power. I had taken a liking to the life of a soldier, and found soon an opportunity of enlisting under the banners of Austria.

"A few days after I had began my peregrination, I met with a recruiting officer of that country, who pro- posed me to enter the Austrian service, but, being grown wiser by experience, I at first feigned to dislike the military profession, and succeeded so well that the officer at last threw a hundred ducats upon the table, assuring me, upon his salvation, that he never had paid such a price to a recruit.

"Now I thought it high time to strain the strings a little lower, agreed to his terms, and told him that I had been serjeant in the Hanoverian service. Having given him a specimen of my skill in penmanship, I requested him to recommend me to his commanding officer; he promised it and was as good as his word. The general received me exceeding well, and I occupied my former post, as serjeant, before a year was elapsed.

"Having been sent away with disgrace from H— —, I had taken a firm resolution to abstain in future from all fraudulent, juggling tricks, and kept my resolution firmly a long while, behaving eight years as it meets a good soldier.

"I abstained entirely from art and fraud, minded my duty, and thus ingratiated myself with my superiors to such a degree that I kept firmly my ground, in spite of many complaints which afterwards were made against me. An unhappy accident induced me to have recourse again to my former juggling tricks, and thus to acquire once more the title of a Necromancer.

"I will tell you all the particulars of that adventure, in order to enliven a little my tedious narrative, and to con- vince you that nothing but necessity could tempt me to engage once more in rogueries which already had destroyed my fortune once, and deprived me of my good character and a honourable employment.

"I was quartered in a house that was said to be haunted. It was rumoured about, that time out of mind it had been haunted by a spirit who disturbed the tranquillity of the inhabitants, though he never had injured anybody; he had now, for about six months, alarmed very much the people that lived in the house, and the report of that extraordinary perturbance had caused such a general fear that most of the rooms were unoccupied.

"Tempted by the cheapness of the lodgings, and desirous to get at the bottom of the alarming apparitions which had given so much uneasiness to the inhabitants of that house, I went to the owner, and agreed with him to pay five dollars a year for the best room; I instantly took possession of my apartment, and, to my greatest surprise, perceived a long while not the least trace of any supernatural inhabitant.

"My landlord always disappointed my inquiries by vague ambiguous answers; and his daughter, who, as it was rumoured, had suffered most from the dreadful apparition, replied with nothing but a deep sigh, when I interrogated her about the nocturnal phantom.

"That girl had attracted my attention in a high degree, as soon as I had seen her, being adorned with charms which conquered every heart, almost irresistibly, because she seemed to be entirely unconscious of their winning powers. Her face was rather pale, her constitution weak and sickly, and although she could not be called a beauty, yet I thought her very amiable, and more be- witching than any woman my eyes had ever beheld. I never had tasted the heavenly bliss of innocent virtuous love before my thirty-ninth year, but I must confess this girl had infused into my heart, at first sight, sensations I had always been an utter stranger to.

"Helen, this was her name, her father, and myself, occupied the first floor of the haunted house, and the second floor was inhabited by a young secretary; all the other rooms, a back parlour on the ground floor where the servants lived excepted, were unoccupied.

"The secretary seemed to have no concern for what was passing around him, his whole attention being engaged by his writings, and I happened only now and then to see him in the company of my landlord and his fair daughter, whom he treated as utter strangers.

"However, I watched my opportunity better than him, and was never so happy as when I could spend a few hours in conversation with the charming maid. I always pretended to have something to say to the father, taking care never to come to his apartment but when he was abroad. "However, all my anxious endeavours to make a tender impression on my charmer's heart proved abortive; Helen neither seemed to take the least notice of the attention I paid her, nor to be pleased with my eager zeal to engage her favour. The discourses I addressed to her consisted mostly in monologues, interrupted by frequent pauses; and her replies in a pantomime, composed of a silent shaking or nodding of the head, accompanied every now and then by a gentle sigh, which of course made me, by degrees, tired of conversing with her, though my heart at first shrunk back at the thought of giving up such a lovely object.

"I had now been many weeks in the house without either hearing or seeing the least thing of the phantom, the tranquillity of the mansion not having been interrupted for a single moment. The domestics of my land- lord were highly surprised, ascribing the peace which they enjoyed to me; even my landlord thought that I had chased away the dread phantom, and oftentimes thanked me warmly for having restored the tranquillity of his house.

"Dear friend,' said he one evening to me, shaking me by the hand with evident marks of satisfaction, 'to you I owe the peace and tranquillity I now enjoy; if the nightly phantom shall continue to stay away, my house will not longer remain unoccupied, and you shall live in it without paying rent as long as it shall be in my possession.'

"These words he spoke in the presence of his daughter, who fetched a deep melancholy sigh.

A few days after that trifling accident, as it appeared to me, I came home late in the night, and was going to lay myself down to rest without calling for a candle, every body being gone to bed, when I heard gentle foot- steps before my door; I started up, and the steps advanced nearer and nearer. Now they seemed to retreat, and silence reigned around a while.

"I listened with eager expectation, and at once heard again the sound of fearful steps and somebody moving the latch of my door, which now was opened slowly and shut again. I was just going to see what these strange proceedings meant, when a white figure entered my apartment.

"Who art thou?" exclaimed I, with a furious voice, seizing the phantom with a powerful hand.

"Jesu Maria!' groaned the apparition, for God's sake be quiet.'

"Methought I knew the voice, and, asking again who it was that dared to disturb my rest, the ghost whispered, in a faltering accent, 'Be quiet, dear Sir, I am Helen!'

"Half frantic with rapture, I pressed the trembling girl to my panting bosom, printed a glowing kiss on her sweet lips, and asked her what fortunate accident had procured me the happiness of seeing her so late in the night.

"Oh !' sighed the lovely girl, 'you shall save me from destruction.'

"With all my heart,' answered I, ' if it is in my power.'

"'It is in your power,' resumed my sweet visitor, ' my father confides in you; O, save me! save me ! '

"I entreated her to tell me the source of her affliction, and how I could be serviceable to her, upon which she sat herself down and began as follows:-

"The apparition which has lately disturbed the tran- quillity of our house is my lover, Henry-the secretary in the second floor. Last autumn he asked me in marriage from my father, who refused to comply with his suit, and the unhappy man has been hurried by despair into a resolu- tion which has destroyed the peace of my mind, and has made him likewise miserable.

"'Our house has been reported to be haunted by a ghost these many years, because it was formerly a cloister. My Henry took hold of that superstitious rumour, turning it to his advantage, and, alas! accomplished his design without difficulty. My heart was thrilled with terror at first, and several nights elapsed in unspeakable horror, before I knew that my Henry was the spectre that visited me every night, and made my blood run chill with awful dread. At length he undeceived me, but, alas ! it was then too late; my virgin honour was gone for ever. I feel the dreadful consequences of my guilty connexion with the unhappy man, and disgrace and ruin will seize me with merciless fangs, if you do not save me. O, Mr. Volkert! do not refuse your assistance to a poor helpless girl.'

"Moved by this woeful speech I promised to procure the consent of her father to her marriage with the secretary, might it cost whatever it would. Her gratitude. knew no bounds, she almost suffocated me by her endearments, and left me with these words :- My happiness, my life, and my honour, are in your power; without your assistance destruction will seize me, and eternal misery will be my dreadful lot.'

"After a cool deliberation, I grew sensible that I had engaged in a very difficult undertaking. By what natural means could the father of the seduced girl be persuaded to sanction her love? How was it possible to shake the firm resolution of a rigorous head-strong man, if a medium congenial to his manner of thinking was not to be employed which might surprise and prompt him to come to our terms for the sake of his own interest. This medium was no other than what he himself had suggested to me-his belief in the supernaturalness of the apparition, and the power he supposed me to have over it.

"I could not get a wink of sleep during the

remainder of the night, racking my brain and tormenting my imagination in vain. Whenever I fancied to have hit on a feasible expedient, it soon vanished like a deluding dream, as soon as I applied the undeceiving torch of reason, and I saw but too clearly that nothing would extricate me from the maze I was bewildered in but the magic wand.

"I was engaged for three days in a most distressing conflict with my rebelling conscience, and several times on the brink of shifting quarters, and taking a house far enough removed from my then abode, but my resolution was always shaken as soon as it was formed, when the doleful situation of the poor distressed girl recurred to my mind, imploring my assistance with a pallid, ghastly look.

"It is true the lover of the afflicted, disconsolate girl did not deserve my assistance; however, poor Helen would certainly have been lost without my assistance. These considerations conquered at last every hesitation which reason and honesty had suggested to my troubled mind, and on the fourth morning I went to work.

"I entered at nine o'clock the apartment of my landlord, and could not but observe that Helen's cheeks were tinged with a crimson hue of inward satisfaction; her aspect and her looks supported my resolution.

Part II, Chapter III

"'Sir,' said I, the tranquillity of your house is dear to me, and I have had the good fortune, last night, to hit upon means, the application of which will certainly secure it for ever.'

"The simple, superstitious man embraced me with visible marks of gratitude, exclaiming in an ecstasy of joy, 'O, tell me, tell me, what must I do?'

"Then he ordered his daughter to fetch a bottle of Hungarian wine, pressing me to drink; but I declined it, resuming-

"Sir, the ghost that disturbs the peace of your house-'

"Have you seen him?' he interrupted me, with a ghastly look.

"I will see him,' replied I; he is a malicious being, and has given me much trouble; yet I trust I shall be able to get the better of him by the assistance of the occult knowledge which I possess." ·

"How, how!' stammered the simpleton; then you are indeed the man I always took you for: then you are really one of those great mortals who understand the wonderful art of necromancy. How happy I am to meet at last, so unexpectedly, with the man I have always most ardently wished to find out. Tell me, dear friend, what must we do?'

"Nothing in the world,' answered I, 'but conjure up in due form that turbulent spirit.'

"And will you undertake to perform that difficult, dangerous task?'

"'Why not?'

"And when, dear sir, do you intend to do me that inestimable favour?'

"The ensuing night, if you will consent to it, for without your leave I can do nothing.'

"O, that you have! that you have! You may do whatever you please; I will consent to anything, if I can get rid of that infernal disturber of my nocturnal rest!'

"I left the credulous man with sensations which sprung from pity rather than exultation at my easy-gotten victory. I instantly made every preparation for executing my roguish plan, being assisted by the secretary, and having won over to my purpose the servants of the house, every- thing succeeded to admiration.

"A little before twelve o'clock all the inhabitants of the house resorted to my room, and an intimate friend of mine acted the ghost admirably well: benumbing per- fumes deprived the spectators of the proper use of their senses, and the landlord had previously been made unfit for investigation by a powder mixed with his wine.

"The ghost appeared, or rather stepped forth, from behind a partition of paper, which I had contrived to make.

"When I asked why he had dared to disturb the tranquillity and peace of the house, he answered, in a tremulous, hollow accent, 'Out of resentment to the female sex.'

"On my further inquires, he related in short answers, that, a century ago, the cruelty of a lady he had been in love with had driven him to despair, and hurried him into the rash resolution to shut himself up within a cloister's hallowed walls; but having profaned his holy order by entering into it with a worldly heart, polluted by the loose desires of sensual love, he had been condemned to purgatory until a certain condition should be fulfilled.

"All these queries and answers, previously set down in writing and got by heart, produced the desired effect on the blinded mind of the credulous father, who at length stammered out the question, by what means could he be relieved from his torments? The ghost replied, that he was doomed to suffer the agonies of purgatory, and to haunt his former abode in the midnight hour until an unhappy couple, separated by a parent's cruel tyranny, should be united in holy wedlock.

"Having related his fictitious tale, he disappeared behind the partition of paper, under the cover of a thick smoke, leaving my landlord in a state of mind which seconded our design to the utmost of our wishes.

"When the credulous man had recovered a little from his astonishment, I asked him if he could explain the mean- ing of the ghost's answer, and whether it was in his power to perform the condition he had hinted at; upon which he silently nodded to me, and promised to pay me a visit early in the morning, which he did at six o'clock, con- fessing his cruelty towards his daughter, which he believed had provoked the resentment of the monk, and pleaded the poverty of the young man, and the cool indifference he had treated his daughter with ever since his offers had been rejected.

"Now,' added he, 'I see everything in its proper light; the ghost has entirely opened my eyes, blinded by avarice. God be praised that the young man has not yet left my house, as he intended to do, for it would give then much room for scandal, if he should marry my daughter, which I am very well convinced cannot be avoided, if the tranquillity of my house shall be restored.'

"In short, the secretary was married to the girl, and the ghost appeared no more.

"This beneficial fraud-for so I may justly

call it, the honour, and perhaps the life of the father and daughter, having been saved by it, and the young man, who was sober and industrious, proving a tender and affectionate husband-this beneficial fraud was the first step, which afterwards led me to ruin and disgrace.

"Possessed of a large stock of knowledge of the human heart, of experience, and art, I was no longer satisfied with confining myself to trifling juggling tricks, but I soon began to act after a more extensive plan. In spite of all the precautions I had taken to keep the above-mentioned transaction from the knowledge of the public, it soon transpired, with the usual additions, and everybody thought me to be a sort of supernatural being, and so many opportunities of preying on the credulity of man- kind were thrown in my way, that I could not stand the temptations which frequently occurred to profit by the superstitions of my fellow creatures.

"I hope you will spare me the distressing task to relate all the transgressions I committed afterwards; suffice it to say, that a complete account of my frauds would swell many volumes. The few remaining hours of life allotted me prevent me from relating all the subsequent tricks which I committed, I therefore shall confine myself to the two criminal transactions by which your friend, the brave Austrian has been imposed upon; they will afford you ample means of forming a proper idea of those I am obliged to bury in silence.

"I had, for the space of six years, carried on my juggling tricks with so much secrecy, that few of my criminal deeds were known. Although I had been betrayed several times by my associates, and reprimanded by my superiors, yet I always suffered myself to be blinded by the too powerful charms of gold and false ambition, and was ever ready to lend my assistance to deeds of the blackest hue.

"One day the widow of an honest citizen sent for me and, having bribed me by some pieces of gold, requested me to assist her in the execution of a most criminal design.

"Her husband, lately deceased, so she told me, had promised her daughter in marriage to a man whom she could not suffer to become her son-in-law, because he had behaved very disrespectfully towards her while her husband had been living, and scorned to apply for her consent; moreover, she told me, he was a lazy drunkard and a gambler; in one word, a good-for-nothing fellow.

"I know, Mr. Volkert,' added she, 'that you are in high favour with the Devil, and entreat you to raise up one of the angels of darkness, commanding him to appear to my daughter, and to threaten her to carry her to hell if she will not desist from her intended marriage.'

Part II, Chapter III

"Shocked at that infernal proposal I was going to throw the money at her feet; would to God I had done it! but three ducats more soothed my indignation, and allured me to promise that I would take the matter into consideration, and inform her of the result of it the following day.

"I kept my promise, enjoining the woman to tell her daughter, as a secret, that her deceased father had, on his deathbed, compelled her to make a solemn promise never to consent to that marriage. She readily executed my order, and the poor girl was overwhelmed with grief.

"Then I bade the inhuman mother assume a melancholy aspect, to treat her daughter with more kindness than ever, to mingle her tears with those of her child, to inveigh now and then against the caprice of the deceased, to inflame the girl, by degrees, with a desire of knowing the reason her father might have had to forbid, on his death-bed, her union with a man he had always seemed to be fond of; and, after these preparations, to mention, as if by accident, my name, and my skill in necromancy, yet to take care, not to betray her design of having conjured up her deceased husband.

"The cruel, unnatural mother executed my orders with all possible dexterity and art, wept with her afflicted, disconsolate child, and, by these means, beguiled the unsuspecting heart of her unhappy daughter. The poor victim of a mother's infernal cruelty listened eagerly to the deceit- ful speeches of her artful parent, and her curiosity was soon raised to so high a pitch, that she one evening came to my lodgings trembling and shivering to acquaint me with her woe, and to implore my assistance, which I instantly promised to grant her. "The rest you very likely know from the relation of your friend. One of my comrades, who was always ready to execute my commands, acted the ghost, and every thing succeeded, alas! too well. 66

"But suffer me to drop the dreadful, horrid tale; this black, infernal deed lies heavy on my conscience, for it has rendered me guilty of the murder of two innocent persons.

"Your friend requested me, soon after, to give him a specimen of my talents, which I readily promised to do as soon as an opportunity should offer; but, God knows, I did not mean to perform my promise.

"However, the quarrel between the two officers afforded me very soon such an alluring opportunity to display my skill, that I could not stand the temptation to perform the most cunning and subtle trick. The whole transaction bears such strong marks of the marvellous, that you will expect a long explanation, but the contrivance was so simple that a few words will suffice to unfold to you that strange affair.

"One morning a foreign officer sent for and requested me, to compose an ointment which would make him invulnerable. I stared at him with wonder and astonish- ment; however, when he covered the whole table with gold, I was tempted to profit by his folly, and asked him who his antagonist was. Being told it was Lieutenant C, I would not run the risk of exposing myself to his resentment, and left the valiant son of Mars without listening to his proposal.

"The succeeding day your friend visited me; 'Volkert,' said he, as he entered the room, I have a job for you: I can give you an excellent opportunity to favour me with a proof of your skill, and to get a handsome sum of money into the bargain.' "I pricked up my ears, made a few faint objections, and at length suffered myself to be persuaded.

"As soon as your friend had left me I went to Baron T-, who was still in bed, without having the least inclination of fighting a duel.

"Baron,' exclaimed I, as I entered his room,' give me the money, I am ready to execute your orders; you shall not only be invulnerable, but also leave the field of battle and this town as a man of honour, provided nobody knows that you are returned from your journey.

"That is charming!' exclaimed the undaunted Baron, ' nobody besides you and my landlord know that I am returned, and him we can easily silence if secrecy is necessary.'

"Then he jumped nimbly out of his bed, and gave me the money. I laid my plan before him, and he joy- fully submitted to every thing proposed. His landlord and the owner of the house where the conjuration was performed, were bribed. The Baron, who acted the ghost, was concealed in a small closet, to which he, when the whole transaction was finished, retired, under the cover of a thick benumbing smoke, which concealed his retreat, and left the town that very night. The postman had likewise been bribed to deliver the letter, composed by me and copied by the Baron. The certificate of the surgeon-major was forged, and everything succeeded to our satisfaction.

"As to the duel, everything was effected by natural means. I cleaned and charged the pistols of Lieutenant C———————, and took care to spoil the locks of one brace, and to charge the other with wrong bullets. I informed the governor of the duel, that Baron T's courage might be known, and he returned, for the same reason, to town, as soon as the duel was fought, delivering himself into the hands of the soldiers who had been ordered to arrest the combatants.

"That he might be thought generous, he

supplicated for the enlargement of his antagonist, and procured him the governor's pardon.

"The heinousness of this deed of mine will be lessened in your eyes, if I tell you, that the bullets in the Baron's pistols were likewise too small, so that Lieutenant C———— could not be wounded dangerously, and the baron took care not to hurt him materially."

"Volkert had as yet spoken with great hilarity, and it almost appeared as if he had entirely forgotten his impending doom; but suddenly he grew more serious and solemn. Gloomy clouds of sorrow were gathering on his brow, the paleness of his countenance increased, his lips were contorted, he gave a deep groan of anguish, and after an awful pause of inward agony, he went on in a faltering accent-

"Oh that I here could conclude the dreadful tale of my transgressions! Oh, that I had not to relate deeds more glaring and abominable! Deeds which thrill my soul with anguish, and pierce my guilty heart with a thousand daggers, pointed by unutterable pangs of a polluted conscience. However, I promised you a sketch of my whole life, and will be as good as my word. Al- though I shall not be able to give you a full narrative of deeds which fill my soul with horror, yet I will go on as Iwell as I can.

"The intercession of Baron T in my behalf had so much weight with the governor, that he suffered me to escape without punishment, and sent me on the recruiting business, in order to get rid of me without provoking my anger. O that he had rather loaded me with his resentment than with his bounty, and punished me as I deserved; perhaps it would have opened my eyes and brought me back to the path of honesty.

'My ruin was now completed. I began my recruiting business with great alacrity and cheerfulness, and found but too many opportunities of exerting my plotting skill, which I did with so much success, that my comrades were astonished, and my superiors so highly pleased with my zeal, that they put the greatest confidence in me, and entrusted me with sums which enabled me to abandon myself to all manner of dissipation; the few remaining sparks of honesty and virtue were extinguished by degrees, and I was hurrying with rapid steps into the abyss of destruction.

"My dissipations tempted me to defraud my superiors, and soon intricated me in a maze of embarrassment, where I found myself entirely bewildered. I got acquainted and intimately connected with the most dangerous sort of people, with robbers and their infernal associates. Allured by my cunning and artful tricks, they did every- thing in their power to gain my confidence, and to win me over to their party, which, alas! laid the foundation to my ruin. I became a spy, a traitor, and, at last, their accomplice in the perpetration of the most shocking crimes.

"My recruiting business was neglected, and my superiors were going to call me back. Being not able to give an account of large sums that had been intrusted to me, I could not appear before my commanding officer, and no other means were left me to escape the impending storm, but to disappear entirely, which I effected in such a manner that every one firmly believed I was no more.

"I conducted ten robbers, disguised as recruits, through a large town, where many of my profession resided, and, as soon as we had reached the adjacent wood, they took to their heels. I ran to the next village, raving like a madman, related my misfortune, wept, cried, and then returned to the wood, dissembling to be in the greatest despair.

"The robbers, who were waiting for me, made me pull off my uniform, dressed a dead man in it, who, perhaps, had been murdered for that purpose, put a pistol in his hand, and disfigured him by blowing his brains out.

"Now I was no longer Volkert the serjeant; I was Volkert the robber and murderer. I painted my face, feigned to be twenty years older than I really was, and thus escaped being known by my former acquaintances. I soon became famous under the name of Father Francis, bought houses in several towns, and everybody took me for what I appeared to be, an old, harmless man. Yet I was known at length by one of my former messmates, when in the H-n service, who was recruiting in the empire, and forced me to assist him in his business.

The cunning rogue had not forgotten my skill in executing deceitful plots, and his expectation that I should be of great service to him by my artifices did not deceive him. I never spread my nets in vain when I wanted to catch a well-made young fellow, and we had enlisted within a short time a great number of recruits. How easily I could remove every obstacle I will prove by a single instance, which will give you a true notion of my intricate artifices.

"A well-made, young, and amiable Livonian, lodged with me, at the same inn, at T—, and my associate took such a liking to him, that he offered to acquit me of all farther services, if I could ensnare this young man.

"I promised to do my utmost, and went instantly to work, ordering some of the gang I was connected with, and who then resided at T- on account of the great fair, to purloin his ring, snuff-box, purse, and watch, returning him the latter in a public place, telling him that

Part II, Chapter III

I had detected the thief admirably well.

"This done, I left him suddenly, without giving him time to make farther inquiries, my sole view being to excite his curiosity, and to gain his confidence, in which I succeeded admirably well.

"The Livonian became very anxious to get acquainted with me, watched my return to the inn several nights, and attempted to converse with me; in short, he was very impatient to draw from me an information of the means by which I had detected the thief, but I always shunned him, and baffled his endeavours a great while, until, at last, I found it necessary to pay him a visit, in order to console him about the loss of a bill of exchange which my myrmidons had got in their power, along with his pocket-book.

"This bill having contained all the little wealth he had got about him, he was under the necessity of either remaining some time longer at T, or of selling his linen and everything of value, and thus return to his own country, in a most distressing condition. I gave him two notes, each of a hundred dollars, the binding money from the recruiting officer.

"My unexpected visit and my seeming generosity put him into the greatest astonishment, and I left him again abruptly, without entering into conversation with him.

He was now enlisted without suspecting it, but I did not, as yet, know how I could put him into the power of my employer; however, my inventive genius soon suggested to me the proper means of effecting my purpose. By some letters from his mother, which I had found in his pocket-book, I had learned that she had died a little time before, very ill satisfied with his conduct, on account of his dissipations when at the university.

"The characters engraved on the inside of the ring which I had taken from him, being the same with those the letters of his mother were signed with, put it out of doubt that the miniature picture of an old lady it was adorned with, must be the likeness of his mother.

"One of my associates, whose features had by accident some resemblance with those of the picture, concealed himself at the inn, painted his face with chalk, wrapped himself in a sheet, and went at night into the room of the young Livonian, who seemed to wait for my return, to inquire, as I suppose, some particulars about the two notes I had given him the preceding day, and was not a little frightened when he saw the ghost of his deceased mother entering his room. The phantom walked through his apartment, looked at the watch which was on the table to signify that it wanted rest, sighed, gave him a menacing look, and left him thrilled with horror and amazement.

Part II, Chapter III

"The day following I ordered my myrmidons to watch every step of the Livonian and was informed that he was gone into a tea garden, after he had changed the two notes.

"I hastened after him without delay, and found him sitting in a lonely bower; he did not see me, though I was standing close by him, being bewildered in gloomy meditations, and talking to himself. Suddenly he ex- claimed, 'No, it was a dream!' 'It was no dream,' replied I instantly. He looked up, seized with terror and surprise. I promised to unfold, at ten o'clock at night, all the mysterious accidents which had happened to him at T——————, and, having appointed to meet me at the city gate, which was within a small distance from our inn, disap- peared suddenly.

"My spies continued to watch his motions during the remainder of the day, and one of them carried every thing that he had lost to the landlord of the inn where we lodged, that he might be the more eager to meet me and to satisfy his curiosity, which had the desired effect.

"He kept the appointment very punctually, but I made him wait above an hour. Just when he was on the point of going home I came walking towards him with hasty steps, and conducted him to a lonely public house within a small distance from the town, which was the usual haunt of the recruiting officers and their associates.

"Having conducted him into a pleasure-house in the garden, built over a cellar, to which a trap door led from the room where we then were, I asked him what he desired to know, and seeing him hesitate to fix on a question, I inquired if he should not like to know his benefactor, who had interested himself so much for him? he consented to it, and, having drawn a circle round the trap-door, which could be let down from below, I placed him in the centre of it. Some of my associates, who were concealed in the cellar, imitated the roaring of thunder, during my conjurations, opened the trap door, and caused him to sink down into the cellar: he, who already had acted the ghost of his mother, appeared again in his former disguise; some blew powder of calophony through the windows of the pleasure-house, and everything succeeded as well as I could wish.

"The poor young man was stunned with wonder and surprise and seeing the ghost of his mother as he was sinking down into the cellar, lost all power of recollection. He was instantly carried in a coach, one serjeant of the recruiting officer seated himself by his side, and another mounted the box, driving on with all possible speed, but being a very indifferent coachman, the vehicle was suddenly overturned and one of the unhappy young man's legs was broken.

"When the serjeants saw it they disengaged the horses from the coach and rode away. This was indeed a great disaster, but still it turned out very fortunate for the young man, for a neighbouring nobleman, who saw him in his deplorable situation as he passed the road, took him to his castle, sent for proper assistance, and took so much care of the young man, that he, after a few months, was able to return to his native country, where he safely arrived without having met with any farther sinister accident.

"The recruiting officer, vexed at the miscarrying of our design, now dropped all connexion with me, and I abandoned myself entirely to a life of rapine and plunder.

"You will now expect me to unfold your adventure at the ruinous Gastle, on the skirts of the Black Forest, but I hope you will spare me the disagreeable task of enlarging on the particulars, since you have a clue, by the assistance of which you will easily extricate yourself from the maze of mystery and wonder in which you have been bewildered.

"As to the strange apparitions in the subterraneous vaults, they have likewise been effected by the assistance of the robbers. Some of them were concealed in the vaults joining to the principal cellar, and the burying vault, blowing the artificial flashes of lightning through the chinks in the wall, and others being concealed in the hidden recesses of the subterraneous fabric, produced the thunder by means of large kettle drums. The lid of the coffin was opened by a cord, which the darkness concealed from your sight; the female figure was the son of a neighbouring publican, closely connected with our gang, who already had acted the ghost several times, when curious travellers had visited the castle: the light shooting from the coffin was effected by a dark lanthorn, which previously had been placed to it: the bluish glimmering you saw in the other wault, came from a lanthorn composed of blue glass, and placed on the staircase of the cellar.

"The second ghost was one of the robbers; his fractured, disfigured head was made of a hollowed pump- kin. Our sudden retreat we effected through the iron doors, and the ruinous side building opposite the cellar door.

"'The stench you smelt was effected by some brimstone we had left burning on the staircase; the extinguishing of the light in the lamp, hanging over the cenotaph, and of that which you had taken with you was caused by a certain spirit I had poured in it as we descended the Staircase; perhaps you will recollect that I took it from you before I began my juggling tricks, as I was leading the way into the cellar. The spirit in the lamp over the cenotaph had previously been poured into it by one of my associates; and the smoke caused by the artificial lightning smothered the light until it evaporated in the arched vault. After the second apparition had disappeared I overturned the lamp; and the rest you will be able to unravel without my assistance.

'Now I come to the incident which gave you and your friend an opportunity of seeing me in my real character, and of detecting my juggling, cheating tricks. Every thing has been carried on and executed under my direction; here is the key to it.

"'Ever since the H- -n recruiting officer had known me at T I visited that town very seldom, though I possessed a house there, and was esteemed by my neighbours and fellow citizens.

"An acquaintance of mine who kept a public house within a small distance from T, took a large inn at that town, and expected to do very well, but an adjacent inn which was in great renown, disappointed all his hopes, and reduced him soon to very distressing circumstances. He disclosed his distresses to me as I once happened to come to T- and I advised him to ruin the neighbouring inn by the introduction of a ghost.

"The owner of the house had died a little time ago, and his son, a young inexperienced and simple lad, carried on the business. We bribed some of his servants to make a noise in the night, and to spread the rumour about, that the house was haunted, and that the late possessor of it appeared at midnight, frightening the guests in a terrible manner.

"This artifice succeeded to the utmost of our wishes, and when I left T——, a few months after, the inn of my friend, which always had been empty, was crowded with travellers, while that of his neighbour was the lonely haunt of the disguised spectres.

"Having great reason to apprehend that out machina- tion would be detected sooner or later, I promised my friend, who dreaded the same, to return within a twelve- month, and to procure him an opportunity of purchasing the haunted inn on reasonable terms. I was as good as my word, returned to T————, and what farther happened T- you know.

"'At first I was rather uneasy that the foreign officer had taken lodgings at the haunted inn, and prohibited every nocturnal disturbance, apprehending the whole artifice would be detected; but just as I was going to leave T, without having attempted anything, the cowardice of that officer gave me an opportunity of executing my design.

"His comrades, chicken-hearted like himself, pro- posed to watch with him in the haunted house, and their imagination played them a trick which most unexpectedly favoured the execution of my plan.

"They had watched three successive nights without either hearing or seeing anything uncommon; the fourth night a tempest was raging, without their perceiving it, being prevented from doing it by the great quantity of punch thay had swallowed, and the roaring noise which was the natural consequence of their inebriation.

"When they entered the room, after having been frightened by the howling of the storm, on their return from the search they had been making, the tempest ceased for a few seconds, and it was natural that one of them, who very wisely looked out of the window, could perceive nothing. Being chilled with dread and apprehension, he forgot to bolt the window, his companions had, from like reasons, neglected to shut the door, and the first gust of wind finding no resistance threw the window and the door suddenly open, the lights were extinguished, and their disordered fancy effected now, what I, perhaps, would have attempted in vain, with all my juggling skill. Flashes of lightning illuminated the room, the tremendous roaring of thunder shook the house, one of the company overturned the table in his fright, and they really fancied to see a phantom, which only existed in their disordered imagination, harrowed up by fearful apprehensions and superstitious terror. What farther happened I need not tell you.

"My spies informed me of the departure of the officer who had resided at the haunted inn, and of the route he had taken; they likewise apprised me of his return. I hastened to meet him on the road, and the conjuration of the ghost was agreed on.

"Being no stranger to the cowardly disposition of his friends, I apprehended not the least danger from their being present at the experiment, and willingly consented that he should bring with him some of them. However, I was very much mistaken, because two of them were gentlemen for whom I was not prepared, and who had been already once deceived by Volkert; yet I did not entirely miss my aim, and the haunted inn was sold soon after to my friend on very low terms; the simpleton who had been the owner of it, and who believed still in the reality of the apparition in spite of what he had seen and heard when I conjured up the spirit, and in spite of reason and good sense, having no peace nor rest until he had dis- encumbered himself of the possession of ill-gotten wealth. The apparition itself was effected by means of a camera obscura in an apartment beneath that where I performed the cheat, some boards in the floor having, the night be- fore, been sawed through, after we had made a hole in the ceiling of the lower chamber. The boards which covered the opening close to the wall were replaced in such a manner that they could be removed from below, by means of which the smoke could ascend from the lower apartment, and represent the picture in the machine- smoke and darkness put the finishing stroke to the deception.

"I left, like your friend, T— the next morning, with the firm resolution to return no more, apprehending to be delivered up to the vengeance of the civil power, in spite of your generosity, and having lost my good character for ever. On my journey I happened to come to the house where you was confined, and felt the highest satisfaction when I had it in my power to make you some atonement for the many wrongs you had suffered by me. My intention was to live here in A- in solitude and retirement, and to dedicate the rest of my miserable life to repentance, and thus to make my peace with God. But my former lawless companions soon found out my retreat and forced me to renew my crimes, and to assist them in their infernal deeds.

"The crime for which I am confined here you very likely know. All I can say in order to palliate this last transgression is, that it is one of the noblest deeds I ever performed, and it would not give me the least uneasiness if the execution of it had not brought destruction on other people beside myself.'

"Here Volkert stopped fatigued and exhausted by the long narrative. I conversed a good while longer with him on his conjurations, and could not help mentioning, that I was very much surprised that his deceptions could have been kept so concealed, though he had always been obliged to rely on the assistance of other people, to which he replied-

"Your observation is very just, but your surprise will vanish, if you consider that my assistants in cheating people bore their share in the frauds I committed, and, of course, would not have escaped punishment if they had not kept secret all transactions of that nature. "It is more surprising,' added he,' that one is always certain to find people who will lend their assistance in cheating their fellow citizens, and it is almost incredible how willing every one is to assist any impostor in deceiving others; yet I do not think that the source of that intriguing disposition, so common among all classes of men, springs from the depravity of human nature; I rather would attribute it to the pleasure every one feels when he can prove the superior powers of his genius, which is the head spring which animates us as well to good as to bad actions, and, if guided by a benevolent heart and good principles, raises us above the common herd, and leads us to honour and glory.'

"As I rose and was going to leave the

prison, Volkert squeezed my hand, and said, with a faltering voice-

"To-morrow, at this hour, I shall be no more, — to- morrow, at this hour, I shall have seen the Supreme Judge of human kind. I shudder when I think that I must appear before His awful throne. Yet, there is one con-solation supporting me,-one consolation, that, as yet, has warded off the deadly arrows of despair, and, I trust, will comfort me in my trying hour, and when He who dwelleth in heaven shall speak to me. This consolation, friend-give me leave to call you by that sacred name- this consolation is not the vain, groundless expectation that I shall atone for my sins by suffering the punishment that awaits me. No; if I had a hundred lives to lose, I could not atone for my manifold crimes. This consolation consists in the persuasion that I shall be made a warning example of the dread consequences attending the criminal abuse of the intellectual powers the great Ruler of the universe has given us, and that the world will be warned against impostors like myself.'

"When he had finished, I bade him a last farewell, in a faltering accent, and left the unhappy man, who said to me, as I opened the door-

"'Come to-morrow to the place of execution, your presence will give me comfort 1'

"I left the prison lost in gloomy thought, and with a bleeding heart. The dismal idea of the awful scene which was to be exhibited the next day haunted me wherever I went, and I struggled in vain to chase it from my mind. The solemn stillness of the night rather increased than diminished my uneasiness, and sleep en- tirely fled from my weary eyes. The dawn of the rosy morn cheered the whole creation, but my soul was pierced with horror when the first ray of the rising sun hailed me on my couch.

"At length the solemn sound of bells announced the approaching hour of execution. I wrapped myself in my cloak, and repaired with trembling steps to the place where Volkert was to atone for his crimes. The streets were crowded with a noisy multitude. Haunted by secret awe did I arrive at the place of execution, and horror made my blood run chill as I beheld the dreadful pile which soon was to reduce to ashes the preserver of my life.

"A gaping multitude was standing around, awaiting with cruel insensibility, and with more than beastly satisfaction, the dreadful catastrophe which was to terminate the life of their fellow creatures.

"Without recollection was I standing amid the crowd, when suddenly a confused noise was heard, and every eye directed to one spot. Lifting my downcast looks, I be-held the funeral procession drawing near with slow solemnity. Volkert was walking in the front with firm and manly steps, followed by his ghastly-looking fellow sufferer. The procession stopped at the enclosure en- circling the scaffold, and Volkert's eyes were anxiously looking around; at length he saw me, nodded to me with a grateful smile, and entered the enclosure.

"His trembling fellow sufferer was first sacrificed by the avenging hand of justice. I cast my eyes to the ground until I perceived by the murmuring noise around that his sufferings were over. Now I directed again my melan- choly looks towards the dread place of execution, and beheld Volkert undressing himself, and approaching with firmness the stool stained with the smoking blood of his friend. Now he was seated, the sword of the executioner lifted up-now it glittered in the morning sun ready to Strike the fatal blow. I shut my eyes involuntarily — a sudden hollow humming told me that Volkert had con- quered. Awful sensations thrilled my palpitating heart, and I forced my way through the gaping multitude without looking once more towards the horrid place where Volkert had expired.

"At the city gate I looked back and beheld with horror a thick column of smoke ascending aloft and darkening the pure, serene air; I could not stand the horrible sight, and hastened to my apartments, determining to leave a place immediately in which my peace of mind had been so much disturbed.

"But being informed that the Captain of the gang would be examined the following day, curiosity got so far the better of my impatience to leave as soon as possible a town where every object recalled to my mind the hapless State of my preserver, that I resolved to stay one day longer, and very glad I am that I took that resolution. The account this man gave of himself being so singular and remarkable, that I was amply repaid for the melancholy and grief which haunted me with unabating fury, whilst I tarried within the walls of the town where my benefactor had been executed.

"The trial began at six o'clock in the morning, and I took care to be in the town house before the terrible leader of the robbers had made his appearance at the bar. Every one present seemed struck with terror when he entered the hall.

"He was of a gigantic make, near seven feet high, his robust limbs corresponding with his extraordinary size; his black and bushy hair covered part of his sun-burnt face, which was disfigured by two gaping scars across his left cheek. His eye, for he had but one left, flashed like lightning when he beheld the dread arbiters of life and death eager to pronounce his doom. The judge exhorted him to speak the truth, and not to aggravate his guilt by stubbornness. However, nobody expected that a wretch of his appearance would pay the least regard to gentle admonitions, and perhaps remain silent even under the tortures of the rack. His savage look and lofty mien seemed to betoken a haughty spirit, not easy to be subdued. I at least had entertained not the most distant hope of having my curiosity gratified in so satisfactory a manner as he really did. Imagine therefore my astonishment when, contrary to all expectation, he began :-

"My Lord and Gentlemen,-I am in your power, and well aware that nothing can avert my impending doom; I scorn the tortures of the rack and bid defiance to every human effort, to force me to a confession of my crimes. You might tear my limbs asunder, and kill me by inches, and yet would never extort a single word from my lips if I had no other reasons to deal candidly with you However, I will spare you that trouble, and honestly con- fess my crimes, their origin, and their progress; being strongly persuaded that the history of my life will afford a useful lesson to judges, and teach the guardians of the people to be careful how they inflict punishments if they will not make a complete rogue of many a hapless wretch, who would have been recalled to his duty, and preserved to human society, by gentle treatment. I never should have become a robber, had not the too great severity of laws made me an enemy to the human race, and hurried me to the brink of black despair. I know my doom is fixed; however, if your heart is no stranger to pity you will at least not refuse a tear of humanity to a poor unhappy man, who has been dragged by dire fatality into the path of vice, and forced to commit deeds his soul abhors.'

"Here he stopped. Awful silence swayed around, and my curiosity was harrowed up to the highest degree, when he began nearly in the following strain : —

"I am the son of an innkeeper at A- whose name was Wolfe, and who died when I had reached my twenty- fourth year. I succeeded him in his business, which being indifferent, many of my hours were unemployed. Being the only son, I had been spoiled by my parents, who were delighted with my wanton pranks and indulged me in everything. Grown-up girls complained of my impudence when I was but twelve years old; and the boys of the village paid homage to my inventive genius. Nature had not dealt niggardly with me in respect of bodily endowments; however, an unfortunate kick from a horse disfigured my face in such a manner, that the girls of the village shunned me, and my play-fellows took frequent opportunities to make me an object of their merriment. The more my female acquaintances avoided me, the more the desire of pleasing took root in my heart. As I grew up, I was given to sensuality and persuaded myself to be in love. The object of my flame treated me with scorn, and I had reason to apprehend that my rivals were more successful than I; however, the girl was poor, and I had reason to hope that her heart, which was inaccessible to my vows and prayers, would yield to presents, which I knew not how to procure, the small income my business afforded me being entirely swallowed up by the vain efforts I made to render my person less disgusting. Being too much addicted to idleness to exert myself in amending my circumstances, and too ambitious to change my expensive mode of life, I had only one means left to improve my fortune, which thousands before me had tried with more success.

"The village in which I lived gave me an oppor- tunity of committing depredations on the game, and the money I raised in that way wandered regularly into the hands of my mistress. Robert, a gamekeeper to the Lord of the Manor, was one of the admirers of Jenny, which was the name of my paramour; he soon observed the advantage which my presents procured me over him, and being spurred by envy and jealousy he watched me closely. By degrees he began to resort to the Sun,' which was the sign of my inn, more frequently than ever, and his prying eye soon detected the source of my liberal gifts.

"A very rigorous law against game-stealing had been renewed not long before, and Robert was indefatigable to find an opportunity of getting rid of his rival. He succeeded but too soon; I was caught in the very act of shooting a deer, and condemned to be sent to the house of correction. It cost me all my little remaining fortune to buy off that punishment. Robert had gained his aim, and Jenny's heart was lost to me. 66 6

Glowing resentment rankled in my breast, and I was determined to be revenged as soon as a proper oppor- tunity should offer. Poverty and want, hunger and des- pair, tempted me once more to have recourse to game stealing, and Robert's watchfulness surprised me a second time. Being reduced to the lowest degree of poverty, it was not in my power to gild the hands of justice a second time, and I was committed for a whole year to the house of correction in the residence. Every lash of the gaoler's whip gave new strength to my resentment, the separation from my mistress increased my passion, and I hastened on the wings of love and revenge to my native place as soon as I had been set at liberty. I flew to Jenny, but was denied admittance and treated with scorn. The pinching want having subdued my pride and laziness, I offered my services to the rich, in the village, but nobody would employ a fellow who had been imprisoned in the house of correction.

"Pressed by hunger and dire necessity, and foiled in all my attempts at getting an honest livelihood, I renewed my depredations on the game, and was entrapped a third time through Robert's watchfulness. The repeated infringements on the game laws had aggravated my guilt. The judges looked into the records of the law, but not into the heart of the transgressor, paid no regard to the plea of want and dire necessity, and sentenced me to have the mark of a gibbet burnt on my back, and to work three years in the fortifications.

"At the close of that term I recovered my liberty a second time, and here begins a new period of my life.

"I was entirely changed, having entered the fortress as a common transgressor, and left it as a consummate villain. I was not entirely divested of all sentiments of honour when I was confined; however, the few remaining sparks of ambition were soon extinguished by ignominy, Deing confined in one room with twenty-three malefactors, two of whom were murderers, and all the rest famous thieves and vagabonds. I was laughed at when men-tioning the name of God, and urged every day to utter blasphemies against our Holy Redeemer! My fellow prisoners sung obscene songs to me, which I could not hear without disgust and horror, and committed actions which I could not behold without blushing. Every day new rogueries were related, or wicked designs fabricated.

"At first I avoided the company of that abominable set of wretches as much as possible, hiding myself in the remotest corners of the prison; however, I wanted a companion in my solitude, and the cruelty of my gaoler had refused me even the poor consolation of taking my dog with me. My labour was hard and my health declining: I wanted assistance, and, to be sincere with you, I was in need of comfort, which, scanty as it was, I could not obtain without sacrificing the last remains of my conscience.

"Thus I used myself by degrees to hear without dis- gust the most horrid language, and to behold without aversion, and at length with secret pleasure, the most shocking actions; before the termination of my confinement I was superior in wickedness to my instructors in villainy, and began to thirst with increasing impatience for liberty and revenge. I hated the whole human race because every one of my fellow creatures was either happier or less wicked than myself; I fancied to be a martyr to the natural rights of man, and a victim of glaring injustice. I rubbed my chains against the wall in a fit of frenzy, grinding my teeth when the sun was rising behind the rock on which the fortress stood, and experienced with unutterable agony, what a hell an extensive view creates in the bosom of a prisoner.

"The free air whistling through the iron

gates of my window, and the swallow perching on the massy bars, seemed to mock me with their liberty, and rendered my imprisonment more hateful and horrid to me. Seized with the burning fangs of despair, I vowed unrelenting and burning revenge to the whole human race, and have been as good as my word.

"The first idea which rushed upon my mind as soon as I saw myself at liberty, was that of my native village. I had indeed not the least glimmering of hope to meet there with the smallest assistance in my distress; however, I entertained sanguine hopes to glut my revenge, which gave wings to my steps. My heart beat violently when my impatient eye beheld the steeple of the village; how- ever, it was not that sweet satisfaction which I had felt on my first pilgrimage, which was now heaving in my bosom. The recollection of all the misfortunes and cruel persecu- tions I once had suffered there awakened me suddenly from a kind of stupefaction; all my wounds began to bleed anew. I quickened my steps, anticipating the pleasure it would afford me to strike my enemies with terror by my sudden appearance, and to feast my eyes on the of the devoted victims of my vengeance.

"The bells were ringing to summon the inhabitants to the church when I went to the market-place. I was soon known by the inhabitants, who were going to church, and every one who met me started back at the sight of me. -Having always been very fond of children, I could not resist the involuntary impulse of giving a penny to a boy who was skipping by; he stared at me for a moment and then threw the money in my face. If my blood had not been heated so much, I should have recollected that my long and bushy beard had frightened the poor boy however, my polluted heart had infected my reason, and tears, which I never had shed in my life, were trickling down my cheeks.

"The boy does know who I am, nor whence I came, said I, half aloud to myself, and yet he avoids me like a wild ferocious beast. Is my black heart marked on my brow, or have I ceased resembling a human being, because I am sensible that I hate all human kind? The contempt of that boy grieved me more than my long imprisonment, because I had treated him kindly, and could not accuse him of personal hatred.

"I seated myself on a large stone opposite the church. What intention I had I do not know; however, I remember very well that I rose up in a fit of burning rage when I saw that all my former acquaintances passed by with visible contempt, and scarcely deigned to look at me.

"I left my station in an agony of vexation, to find out a lodging, and as I was turning round the corner of a street I met my Jenny. My dear Wolfe,' she exclaimed, and offered to embrace me, 'God be praised that you are returned at last; I have shed many a bitter tear during your absence!' Hunger and misery were marked in her face, and I beheld with horror that she was infected with an ignominious illness. Her tattered raiment and her whole appearance told me plainly what a miserable wretch she was. I soon guessed the origin of her abject situation, concluding by the sight of some dragoons that soldiers had been quartered in the village. 'Soldier's strumpet ! ' I exclaimed, and turned my back to her with an exulting laughter. It gave me some satisfaction to see her infidelity rewarded in so shocking a manner. I never had loved her sincerely.

"My mother was dead, and my house had been sold for the benefit of the creditors. I had no friend, no money, except a few groats; everybody fled me like a mad dog; however, I was dead to shame and disgrace. After my first imprisonment I had shunned all human society, because I could not stand the contempt I met with everywhere. Now I intruded upon them, and it afforded me a malicious satisfaction to drive them away by my appearance; it gave me a pleasure, because I had nothing farther to lose, and nobody to care for; I had no farther occasion for the least good quality, because nobody believed I had one left; the whole world was open to me, and perhaps I should have been able to recover the character of an honest man in a distant province. However, I had no courage to assume even the mask of honesty ; despair and disgrace had forced these sentiments upon me, and I persuaded myself that every sense of honour was useless to me, since I had no claim to the smallest share of it. If my vanity and pride had maintained their dominion over me, I certainly should have put an end to my existence. I did not know myself what my intentions were ; I wanted to do mischief-so much I knew; I wished to deserve my fate. The laws,' said I to myself, ' are the guardians of human happiness, and therefore I will do whatever is in my power to subvert them. Necessity and thought- lessness had once compelled me to sin, but now I did it voluntarily, because it gave me pleasure.'

"I had again recourse to game-stealing, for hunting had always been my chief passion, and life called for support; but this was not the sole motive which prompted me to reassume my former favourite occupation; the desire of bidding defiance to the laws, and to infringe the prerogatives of the prince, was an additional impulse. I had no apprehension of being taken up once more, for now I had a ball in readiness to stop the mouth of my informer, and was sure I could not miss my aim.

"I killed all the deer which came in my way, selling only a few pieces on the frontiers, the remainder I left behind to rot. I lived very sparing, in order to be able to afford the expenses for powder and shot. My depredations, and the havoc I made in the forest, caused a great alarm, but nobody suspected me, my miserable appearance screened me from suspicion, and my name was forgotten.

"This mode of life I continued for several months without being detected. One morning I was rambling through the forest, pursuing the traces of a deer; having hunted without success two tedious hours, I began to give up every hope of coming at my prey, when I saw it at once within the reach of my gun. I took my aim, and was going to fire, but started suddenly back, when I saw a hat upon the ground not far from me. I looked around with great circumspection and beheld Robert, the game- keeper, standing behind the trunk of an oak, and aiming at the same deer which I intended to kill. My blood froze in my veins as I beheld the author of all my misfortunes; and this very man, whom I hated most among the whole human race, was within reach of my fusee. Infernal joy thrilled my whole frame, I would not have exchanged my gun for the universe; the burning revenge which till then had been rankling in my bosom rose up to my finger's end, which was going to put an end to my adver- sary's life; however, an invisible hand seemed to retain my arm to prevent the horrid deed. I trembled violently as I directed my gun against my foe-a chilly sweat bedewed my face-my teeth began to chatter, as if a fever frost had seized my frame; methought I felt the icy fang of death upon my heart, and every nerve was quivering.

"I hesitated a minute-one more elapsed-and now a third. Revenge and conscience were struggling violently for victory, the former gained, and Robert lay weltering in his blood!

"My gun dropped on the ground when Robert fell. 'Murderer,' stammered I, with quivering lips. The forest was as silent as a church-yard, and I heard distinctly the word murderer. Creeping nearer to the spot where my enemy was swimming in his blood, I saw him just expire. I stood a dreadful minute of grisly horror before my murdered foe, as if petrified; a yelling laughter restored me to the use of my senses. 'Wilt thou any more tell tales, good friend?' said I, stepping boldly nearer, and turning him upon his back. His eyes were wide open. I grew serious, and every power of utterance fled; strange and horrid sensations chilled my heart.

"Till then I had been a transgressor of the laws on the score of the disgrace I had suffered, but now I had perpetrated a deed for which I had not yet atoned. An hour before that horrid action, no man living would have been able to persuade me that there was a more abject being upon the earth than myself, but now I began to fancy that I had been enviable an hour ago.

"Not the most distant idea of God's judgments came in my mind; however, I had a confused notion of halter and gibbet, and of the execution of a murderer which I had witnessed when a boy. The idea of having forfeited my life froze my very soul with dreadful fear. I wished ardently that it might be in my power to restore to life my slain enemy, and racked my brain to recall to my recollection all the injuries he had made me suffer, but, strange to tell, my memory seemed to be entirely extinguished, I could not recall a shadow of all the ideas which, but a quarter of an hour ago, had filled my soul with glowing revenge, I could not conceive how I could commit such a horrid deed,

"I was still standing by the corpse in a kind of stupe- faction, when I was roused from my desponding reverie by the cracking of whips and the creaking of waggons on the high road, which was about a mile distant from the spot where I then was.

"I went mechanically deeper into the forest, and re- collecting on the way that Robert had been used to wear a watch, I wished to get it in my possession. I wanted money to reach the frontier, and yet I had no courage to return to the place where the corpse lay; the idea of the devil and the omnipresence of God rushing suddenly on my mind, I struggled a few moments, and having summoned all my boldness determined to go back and fetch the watch in defiance of God and the devil.

"I found what I had expected, and in a green purse a little more than a dollar, silver coin. As I was going to put both in my pocket, I started suddenly back and considered whether I should take it or not. It was no fit of shame, nor was it fear to aggravate my crime through robbery; it was rather scorn which prompted me to fling the watch upon the ground, and to take only one half the money. I wanted to be thought an enemy of the gamekeeper but not his robber.

"Now I fled deeper into the forest. I knew that it extended itself four German miles* towards the north, where the frontiers of the country began. I fled on the wings of fear till noon; the swiftness of my flight had dispelled the agony of my conscience; however, it returned with redoubled violence as my strength began to be exhausted: a thousand grisly phantoms tortured my fancy and filled my soul with dreadful bodings. I had no other choice but either to put an end to my wretched existence, or to drag on a life embittered by a continual * A German mile is five and a half English, fear of dying under the hand of the executioner. I had not the courage to rid myself of a painful existence, and shuddered at the idea of leading a life of never-ceasing torments.

Part II, Chapter III

"Hemmed in between the certain tortures of life and the uncertain horrors of eternity, equally averse to life and to death, I finished the sixth hour of my flight, an hour abounding with agonies which no living man can form an idea of.

"Gloomy and slow I had pursued a narrow footpath which led through the darkest thicket, when suddenly a rough commanding voice ordered me to stop. The voice was not far off. Agony and the horrors of despair, which had assumed their dreadful sway over me, had made me entirely regardless to the objects around me ; my eyes were cast to the ground, and I had covered part of my face with my hat, as if that could have hidden me from the eye of the lifeless creation. Starting and lifting up my eyes I saw a savage looking man coming towards me; he was armed with an enormous club, his figure was of a monstrous size, my first surprise at least had made me think so, and the colour of his face was of the mulatto hue, which gave to the white of a squinting eye additional terrors. Instead of a girdle he had his green buttonless great coat tied with a thick cord, to which an enormous knife and a brace of pistols were fastened. I had quickened my steps when his terrible voice assailed my ears, but he soon came up with me and stopped me with a powerful arm. The sound of a human voice had filled my soul with terror, however, the sight of a ruffian raised my spirits. In my miserable situation I had full reason to tremble at the sight of an honest man, but none at all at that of a robber.

"Who art thou?' thundered the frightful apparition in my ear.

Thy equal,' was my reply, if thou really art what they appearance bespeaks.'

"This is not the right way. What business hast thou here?'

"And what right hast thou to question me?' I replied n a determined accent.

"The terrible man measured me with his looks from top to toe. He seemed to compare my haughty answer with my defenceless situation- Thou art impudent like a beggar,' he resumed at length.

"Very possible, I have been one but yesterday.'

"He laughed, exclaiming with a horrid grin, 'My honest friend, I hope thou dost not presume to be thought something better.'

"That is nothing to thee;' so saying, I wanted to pursue my way.

"Fairly and softly, my dear boy, why in such a hurry ; what weighty business is it which makes thee run so fast?"

"I mused a moment, and cannot conceive what prompt- ed me to reply in a slow accent, 'Life is short and hell everlasting.'

"He stared at me with a ghastly look, 'I'll be d — d,' he resumed at length, if thou hast not stumbled against a gallows on thy way.'

'I may come to that one time; farewell, comrade.'

"Stay a moment longer,' he exclaimed, taking a tin bottle from his hunting pouch and offering it to me after he had swallowed a large draught. The hurry of my fright and the dreadful agonies of mind I had undergone had reduced my strength very low, and my parched lips had not been moistened with one refreshing draught that whole unfortunate day. Famine had already stared me horribly in the face, in that extensive forest, where three miles around no refreshment could be procured; you may therefore easily think how joyfully I accepted his offer. I swallowed greedily the contents of the bottle, and new strength animated my whole frame, my heart was expanded with new courage, and hope and love for life returned in my desponding heart; I began to fancy that I was not wholly miserable, so much relief afforded me that welcome draught; and I must confess that my situation began to appear less dreadful to me, since, I after a thousand miscarried hopes, had found at last a being that bore some resemblance with me. In the desponding situation in which I was, I would not have hesitated to pledge the health of an infernal spirit, in order to have a confidant.

"Meanwhile my new companion had stretched himself upon the grass, and I followed his example.

'Thy brandy has given me new life,' said I, 'we must be better acquainted with each other.'

"He struck fire and lighted his pipe.

"Is it long since thou hast carried on this trade?'

"He stared at me- What means that question?

"I took the knife from his girdle, resuming, ' Has this instrument done much execution?'

"Who art thou?' he roared in a terrible accent, flinging his pipe on the grass and starting up.

"A murderer like thyself-but only a beginner.'

"He gazed at me and took up his pipe.

"Thou art no inhabitant of these districts,' he resumed at length.

"I am; hast thou heard of Wolfe the inn-keeper, at A----?'

"He started up as if frantic, exclaiming in a rapturous accent, Wolfe the inn-keeper, who has been punished so severely for game-stealing?'

"That very man I am.'

"Welcome, comrade, a thousand times welcome!' many, he exclaimed, shaking me joyfully by the hand, 'how glad am I that I have found thee at last, I have been many months in search of thee; I know thee very well, know all that thou hast suffered, and have been longing for thy assistance this great while.'

"For my assistance? To what purpose?'

"Everybody speaks of thee. Thou hast many enemies, hast suffered glaring injuries, hast been entirely ruined, and persecuted with unheard-of severity.'-He grew warm. They have immured thee in the house of correction, have treated thee like a galley slave at the fortress, have stripped thee of thy fortune, and reduced thee to beggary, because thou hast killed a few paltry deer, which the Prince suffers to prey on our corn, and to rob us of the fruit of our diligence. Is it come to that, brother, that a human being is valued less than a hare or a boar? Are we not better than the wild beasts of the field? And a fellow like thyself could brook not such injury.'

"What could I do?'

"That we shall see. But, pray tell me, whence dost thou come, and on what errand?

"I related my whole history to him, and, without awaiting the end of it, he jumped up with joyful im- patience, pulling me after him with all his might.'

"Come along, brother,' he said, ' now art thou ripe, art the very man I wanted for my purpose. I shall reap great honour by introducing thee to our commonwealth. Make haste and follow me.'

"Whither art thou going to conduct me?'

"Don't ask questions, but come and see;' so saying, he dragged me forcibly after him.

" As we proceeded, the forest grew more and more intricate, impenetrable and gloomy. None of us spoke a word until I was suddenly roused from my apathy by the whistle of my leader. I looked around and beheld myself at the declivity of a steep rock, projecting over a deep cavern. A second whistle answered from the womb of the rock, and a ladder rose slowly from the abyss; a thundering voice hallooed from the deep, and the winding cavern echoed to the sound. My leader descended, first bidding me to wait till he should return. 'I first must secure the mastiff which guards the entrance to our abode,' he said, ' thou art a stranger, and the ferocious beast would tear thee to pieces.' So saying, he disappeared.

"Now I was standing alone before the precipice, and was well aware of it. The imprudence of my leader did not escape my notice. It would have cost me no more but a resolute effort to pull up the ladder, and I would have been restored to liberty, and effected my escape without the least danger of being overtaken by the inhabitants of the cavern; I cannot but confess that I had some temptation to do it. Looking down into the abyss I was struck with an obscure idea of the bottomless gulf of hell, from whence there is no redemption to be expected. I began to shudder at the new course of life which I was going to commence. A sudden flight only could have saved me. I was half determined to effect my escape, and already stretching out my hand to pull up the ladder, when suddenly I fancied to hear a thundering voice as if from the womb of hell, 'What has a murderer to risk?' and my arm lost its hold and every power of motion. My doom was fixed, the time of repentance past, and the murder I had committed was towering behind me like a mountain shutting up for ever my return to the path of virtue.

"My leader reappeared the same moment,

bidding me descend into the cavern. I had now no other choice left but to submit to necessity, and climbed down. Having advanced a few steps under the excavated rock, our passage grew larger, and I beheld some huts at a distance, and as I approached nearer, a round spot covered with grass appeared to my view. About twenty people were sitting round a blazing fire. Here,' my leader exclaimed, 'here I bring you a new member of our society, whose name is not unknown to you; rise and welcome the celebrated Wolfe of A-

"Wolfe!' they all exclaimed with one voice, starting up and forming a circle around me, men, women, and children. Their joy was unfeigned and cordial; con- fidence and even respect was marked in their looks; one squeezed my hand, the other clapped me on the shoulder in a confidential manner; all seemed sincerely rejoiced at seeing me, and the scene was not unlike the meeting again of an old beloved acquaintance.

"My arrival had interrupted their dinner, they retook their seats and pressed me to partake of their inviting meal, which consisted of venison of all kind and stewed fruits. The goblet filled with delicious wine wandered from hand to hand, and spread merriment and joviality around; plenty and concord seemed to reign in that little society, and every one strove to manifest his joy at my presence.

"I was seated between two females, which was the place of honour at table, and having expected to meet with the refuse of their sex, how great was my astonishment when I found amid this gang of robbers the most beautiful female figures my eyes ever beheld. Margaret the eldest and handsomest of the two, was called Miss, and could not be much above eighteen; her language was very licentious, and her looks still more so. Maria, the youngest, was married, but had run away from a husband who had treated her ill; her form was superior to that of my other neighbour, however, she was pale and of delicate constitution, and on the whole less striking at first sight than the lively Margaret. They seemed to rival who first should kindle my desires; the beautiful Margaret strove to dispel my timidity by wanton jokes : however, I soon conceived an invincible dislike to that woman, and the modest Maria fettered my heart for ever.

"'You see, brother,' said the man who had been my con- ductor to that place,' you see how we live here, and every day passes like the present. Is it not true, comrades?'

"'Yes, every day passes like the present,' the whole gang exclaimed.'

"If therefore you think you can accustom yourself to our manner of life, then stay with us and be our captain. Do you consent to it, comrades ? '

"An unanimous Yes,' rent the air."

"My imagination was fired with wine and loose desires, my reason fettered, and my blood heated. Human society had banished me-and there I found brotherly affection, good living and honour. Whatever might have been my choice, I could not escape the hand of punishing justice; however, in a situation like that which was offered me, I could at least sell my life dear. Voluptuousness was my ruling passion, and I had till then always been treated with scorn and contempt by the other sex, but here I could expect to satisfy my desires, and to be received with pleasure. My resolution cost me but very little, and I exclaimed, after a moment's consideration, I will stay with you, comrades, if you will cede to me my beautiful neighbour.

"All of them agreed to consent to my request, and I then became unexpectedly the avowed possessor of a whore, and the chief of a gang of robbers!

"To be revenged on the prince in whose dominions I had suffered so much disgrace was the chief desire of my heart, and to effect that purpose was the first use I made of my new acquired authority. Our gang con- sisted in eight stout fellows besides myself, the rest was composed of women and children. My new associates had contented themselves, till I was joined to their society, with clandestine depredations in the pantries and cellars of the rich peasants, and game-stealing, and never had recourse to violent means. My views went farther. I proposed to declare open war against the game, which had brought on my disgrace and ruin, and to rob the houses of the judges who had punished me so severely.

"To effect our purpose we wanted horses, the frontiers where the dominions of my former sovereign terminated being three miles distant. By means of house-breaking and some highway robberies we soon got possession of a sufficient sum of money, with which we dispatched one of our associates to a distant town to buy four horses, fire-arms, powder and ball. The houses of the hated judges were pillaged in a tempestuous night, and whenever the face of the earth was covered with midnight darkness, we sallied forth from our den to destroy the game in those parts where my misfortunes had commenced, and I took care to let my persecutors know that it was Wolfe who committed these depredations.

"Meeting with success in our nocturnal rambles, our temerity increased, and we waylaid the traveller on the high road; however, I took great care not to perpetrate a second murder. The terror of my name soon spread itself all over the country, and the neighbouring magistrates tried every means to get me in their power; a great reward was promised to him who should take me, dead or alive, and if one of my associates, a full pardon; however, I was so fortunate as to elude the watchfulness of my pursuers for a considerable time, and to frustrate every attempt on my liberty.

"I had carried on this infernal trade a whole year, when I began to be tired of it. The gang whose leader I was having disappointed my sanguine hopes, I soon perceived, with terror, how much my fancy, heated by wine and loose desires, had been imposed upon when I consented to become the captain of my associates. Hunger and want frequently supplied the place of superfluity and ease, which I had expected, and I was necessitated many a time to risk my life in order to procure a scanty meal, which hardly sufficed to appease the violent cravings of my empty stomach. The visionary image of brotherly concord disappeared, and envy, suspicion, and jealousy stepped in its place, loosening the ties of our society; the solemn promise of a full pardon to him who should deliver me into the hands of justice was a powerful temptation to lawless robbers, and I was well aware of the dangers which surrounded me. I became a stranger to sleep, a victim to never-ceasing apprehensions; the phantom of suspicion pursued me everywhere, tormented me when awake, laid down with me upon my couch, and created frightful dreams, when my weary eyes were now and then closed by the hand of slumber. My conscience, which had been lulled asleep, recovered its power by degrees, and the sleeping viper of remorse was roused by the general tempest which was raging within my breast; the hatred I bore the human race turned its dagger against myself I was reconciled to human kind, and cursed nobody but myself. The dreadful consequences of vice stared me grisly in the face, and my natural good sense dispelled at length the delusions which had led me astray from the blessed path of virtue. I felt how deep I had fallen, and gloomy melancholy stepped in the place of gnashing despair. I wished, with weeping eyes, to have it in my power to recall the times past, and was convinced that I would make a better use of the hours I had dedicated to the vile service of guilt. I began to hope that I yet would reform, being sensible that I should be able to effect a reformation. On the highest summit of depravity I was more inclined to tread in the steps of virtue than before I had committed the first lawless deed. "

"A war had broken out in Germany at that time, and recruits were raising everywhere, which gave me some hopes to retreat in an honourable manner from my associates, and turn a useful member of human society. I wrote a letter to my prince, the copy of which you will find in my pocket-book.

"The letter was produced and read by the

clerk; the purport of it ran, as much as I can remember, as follows :—

"If your Highness does not think it beneath your dignity to condescend to a villain like myself—if a criminal of my atrocity is not entirely excluded from your mercy, O then do not reject the humble petition of a repenting sinner. I am a murderer and robber, have forfeited my life, and am pursued by the avenging hand of justice. I will deliver myself into the hand of the executive power; but I, at the same time, am going to lay a very strange prayer at the feet of your throne. I detest life, and do not fear to die; it would, however, be dreadful to me to die without having lived. I wish to live, in order to repair my crimes past, and to make my peace with human society, which I have offended. My execution will be a warning example to the world, but will not atone for my wicked deeds. I hate vice, and have a strong desire to try the path of honesty and virtue. I have shown great capacities to become a terror to the state, and I flatter myself that I yet have some abilities to render services to the country which I have injured.

"I am well aware that I supplicate for something quite uncommon. My life being forfeited, it does not become me to propose conditions to punishing justice; however, I am not yet chained in fetters, am yet at liberty and fear has the least share in my prayer. "It is mercy that I crave, and if I had some claim to

justice I would not attempt now to enforce it;
yet there is one circumstance which I have
reason to recall to the recollection of my
judges. The period of my crimes commences
with that rigorous sentence which has deprived me of my honour. If my judges had not
been too severe, if they had listened to the
voice of equity and humanity, I should
perhaps not have been reduced to the necessity
of craving the mercy of your highness — their
want of feeling has plunged me in the fatal gulf
of guilt. "

"Let mercy supply the place of justice and
spare my life; if it is in your power to intercede
with the law in my behalf, the remainder of my
life shall be entirely devoted to your service. If
you can grant my humble prayer, let me know
it by way of the public prints, and I will throw
myself at your feet, confiding in your princely
word; if not, then justice may proceed as it
shall be deemed proper, and I must act as
necessity shall require.'

"This petition,' thus resumed the
delinquent,' was not taken notice of, as well as
a second and third, and having not the least
glimmering of hope left to be pardoned, I took
the resolution to leave the country, and to die
in the service of the King of Prussia as a brave
soldier.'

"I gave my gang the slip, and began my
journey. My road led me through a small

country town, where I intended to stay the night. A few weeks previously a proclamation had been published through the whole country, commanding a strict examination of every traveller, because the Prince had taken a part in the war as a member of the German Empire. The gatekeeper of the town which I was going to enter was sitting upon a bench before his house as I rode by; my forbidding countenance and motly dress raised his suspicion, and as soon as I had entered the gate he shut it and demanded my passport, after he had first secured the bridle of my horse. I was prepared for accidents of that sort, having provided myself with a passport, which I had taken from a merchant whom I had robbed. However, this testimony would not satisfy the eagle-eyed gate-keeper, my physiognomy being in contradiction with it, and I was obliged to follow him to the bailiff's house. He ordered me to await his return at the door.

"The passport was examined, and meanwhile a rabble began to assemble around me, attracted by my strange figure; a whispering arose among the multitude, and some of the crowd were pointing alternately at me and my horse; the latter having been stolen by one of my former associates, my conscience gave the alarm. The gate-keeper returned with the passport, and told me that the bailiff, understanding that I came from the seat of the war, would be glad to have half an hour's conversation with me, and to get some information of the situation of our army. This message increased my apprehension of being known, and fearing the invitation of bailiff to be a snare to get me in his power without resistance, I clapt spurs to my horse without returning an answer.

"My sudden flight gave the signal to an universal hue and cry: A thief! a thief!' exclaimed the whole multi- tude, pursuing me with all possible speed. The iron hand of punishing vengeance seemed ready to grasp me my life was at stake, and I redoubled the swiftness of my flight, goading the sides of my horse without mercy.

My pursuers were soon far behind me, panting for breath, and liberty promised to gladden my heart again, when the fleetness of my flight was suddenly stopped by a dead wall. My pursuers gave a loud shout when they saw me entrapped, and I had given over every hope of effecting my escape, when a sudden thought struck me that the wall might be the city wall, and that perhaps I would regain my liberty through a window of one of the houses on the bottom of the street. The door of that on the left side was open; I jumped from my horse, and entered it with a pistol in each hand, bolting the door after me, and hastening up stairs without being seen by any one of the inhabitants. My pursuers were close at my heels, and thundered at the door when I was rushing into a room where nobody was but an old woman. Seeing a man with a brace of pistols, terror fettered her tongue, and she fell into a swoon. I opened the window, and imagine my joy when the open field hailed my anxious looks; I bolted the door, placed chairs and tables against it, threw the bed out of the window, and concealed myself in the chimney to await there the setting in of night.

This was the work of a few moments, and I was safely housed in my hiding place when the door was forced open with a thundering noise. My calculations had not deceived me, and my plan succeeded as well as I could expect it. My pursuers, seeing the window open and the feather-bed lying in the field, believed firmly I had effected my escape: some young men jumped boldly down, and others went to pursue me on horseback; the old woman who could tell no tales, was carried to another part of the house, and I was left alone to muse on my awkward situation.

"Soon after, the owner of the house came into the room with some of his neighbours, and confirmed by his discourses my hope that nobody suspected my hiding place. One of the company thought I might be concealed under the bed, but his idea of my still being in the house was, to my inexpressible satisfaction, treated with ridicule. At length my situation became extremely painful to me, and I wished fervently my unwelcome visitors might be gone.

Part II, Chapter III

"After two tedious hours I was at length released of my fear to be detected by some unforeseen accident, when the landlord and his friends left also the room where I was hidden. As soon as the coast was clear, and the tranquillity of the house restored, I climbed higher up into the chimney, with the intention to get upon the roof; however, on maturer consideration, I thought it safer to remain where I was, hearing many voices in the field, which made me afraid of being detected.

"The time crept slowly on, and I thought the wished-for hour of midnight would never set in; hunger and thirst increased the horrors of my situation, and that ever- watchful remembrancer of the mortal race, conscience, began to remind me of my wickedness, and the punishments of never-sleeping justice, which sooner or later would overtake me. My resolution of leaving the path of vice acquired new strength, and I vowed fervently never to sin again if I should escape once more.

"Amidst these salutary meditations and resolutions night began to set in, and I breathed freer. At length the feather-bed was brought back, but nobody came to sleep in it that night, and the room remained unoccupied.

"As soon as midnight silence announced to me that everbody was gone to rest, I slided softly down the chimney, tore one of the bed sheets and twisted it in a line to make use of it in getting into the field. No sooner had I touched the ground than I took to my heels to reach, before daybreak, the Black Forest, which I knew was only two miles distant, being well aware that the whole country would be in a hue and cry after me, as soon as my nocturnal escape should be known. Fear gave me strength and winged my feet; fatigued and entirely spent I reached the skirts of the Black Forest, and threw myself into the first thicket to rest my weary limbs.

"Fatigued by the long journey I had made and the anxiety and fear which continually had harassed my mind, I fell asleep. I had not slept two hours, as I could guess by the sun, when I was suddenly roused by the distant barking of dogs: I started up and listened, when the hallooing of two huntsmen vibrated in my ear. They seemed to direct their course towards the spot where I was concealed, and no other means of escape were left me but to climb up an adjoining oak tree, and to hide myself amid its thickest branches, where I fancied to find security.

"However, all my fears and apprehensions returned with redoubled force, when the dogs came to the tree which sheltered me, and began to bark in a terrible manner. The hunters were close at their heels, but seeing no game, they recalled my new persecutors and pursued their way. Fear of falling into the hands of my enemies obliged me to remain where I was until the dark mantle of night should cover once more my flight.

"Hunger and thirst had hardly left me sufficient strength to keep my situation any longer, when I, to my inexpressible joy, espied the nest of a raven in the top of a tree, and six eggs in it. This unexpected relief gave me new strength, new life, new hope, and I awaited with patience the setting in of night, when I got down, pursuing my way through the forest.

"The night was dark, and a rising tempest shook the tops of the lofty oaks; the distant lightning and the hollow voice of the thunder announced a dreadful night. The thunder soon began to shake the firmament, flashes of lightning illuminated, by intervals, the dark and dreary forest, and to increase the miseries of my situation, a storm of rain rushed down with such violence as if all the flood-gates of heaven had been opened at once. I sought shelter beneath an ancient oak, but, alas! a flash of lightning which shivered to atoms a lofty beech tree, not above fifty paces from the spot where I was standing, made me soon quit my dangerous asylum, and drove me to an open spot, where I was exposed to all the violence of the storm. I was soon wet to the skin, my teeth began to chatter, and all my little courage fled on the wings of despondency.

"I had stood the fury of the elements two horrid, dreadful hours; no sound was heard but the screech of the owl, the croaking of the raven, the roaring of thunder, and the howling of furious winds: midnight was past, and the hurricane still raged with unabated fury. My wounded conscience brought all my crimes to my recollection: I fancied the day of judgment was near, and was seized with a violent trembling. My tortured soul divined a thousand horrid thoughts, and I vowed fervently to pursue the steps of virtue.

"My whole frame shaking with cold I began to run without knowing whither I was directing my course, in order to warm my blood, which was almost chilled, when suddenly the ground gave way beneath my feet, and I fell into a deep pit. My fall was violent; however, I received no other hurt except a few bruises, my coat being entangled in the root of a tree about four yards from the bottom of my subterraneous dungeon. I strove to climb up the wall, which appeared to be horizontal, but all my endeavours were fruitless, and the dreadful spectre of famine stared me grisly in the face. I sat down upon the damp ground and began to muse on my forlorn situation, when a sudden flash of vivid lightning illuminated my prison, and disclosed to my eyes a narrow passage; groped along the winding passage with fearful steps, not knowing whether it would lead me upwards or down- wards.

"I had walked above half an hour and not

yet found an outlet, the little hope I had to extricate myself from my subterraneous dungeon began to die away by degrees, and seemed to be entirely frustrated, when a massy iron door suddenly obstructed my way. I exerted all my little remaining strength to force it open; however, the impenetrable darkness which surrounded me rendered all my labours abortive. The punishment of my crimes seemed to be arrived, and I sunk down upon the damp ground in a fit of despair, entirely spent, and incapable to attempt any farther efforts to open the fatal door; cold drops of sweat bedewed my wearied limbs, and I began, the first time in my life, fervently to pray.

"At length a thought struck me, that perhaps the flash of the powder would disclose to me an outlet, if I was to fire a pistol. I hastily took one out of my pocket and discharged it; my hope had not deceived me entirely, and I beheld another passage to the left, which I instantly pursued with alacrity. Ere long I came to a second iron door, which, however, soon yielded to my efforts to open it, and let me into a spacious vault.

"Having groped about half an hour longer I was thrilled with unutterable joy when I discovered, after many fruitless researches, a narrow staircase, which led me into a roomy hall, faintly illuminated by the rays of the moon, who was peeping through the lofty windows, composed of stained glass.""

"Here the robber gave a full description of the Haunted Gastle, on the skirts of the Black Forest, which you, my dear friend, know too well to require a repetition of the faithful picture he drew.

"Having explored every corner of the ancient fabric,' thus he continued, without meeting a living soul, I descended into a spacious court-yard, from whence a lofty gate-way led me into the open field. The dawn of morn began to break in the east from the purple clouds, and I heard the crowing of cocks within a small distance. He only who has been in a situation like mine can form an idea of the rapture which rushed on my soul when I perceived myself to be so near an inhabited spot.

"Quickening my tottering steps I saw two country wenches with baskets on their heads coming from the adjacent village, which seemed to be not above a quarter of a mile distant. I was just going to inquire of them the name of the village, when both of them raised a dreadful scream, running back as fast as possible. Being desirous to know, previous to my entrance into the village, where I was, lest I might unknowingly run into the hands of my pursuers; I summoned up all the few remains of strength, which hunger and fatigue had left me, in order to come up with them, but when the frightened girls perceived me close at their heels, they threw down their baskets, and fled with the swiftness of an arrow.

"Fearing to be known, and apprehending the wenches would alarm the village, I was obliged to desist from my pursuit, and to seek a hiding-place until I should be able to advance a mile farther. No place promising a safer asylum than the desolated castle, I resolved to return, but previously to examine the baskets the girls had dropt, whether they might not contain some victuals to appease the pinching hunger which tormented me.

"It seemed they had been on their way to the market, their baskets containing some lumps of butter, two earthen jars with milk, some small cheeses, and two large pieces of coarse bread. The milk, which was not all run out of the earthen vessels, quenched my thirst, and the bread and cheese I took with me to the castle to satisfy the pressing demands of my stomach.

"On my arrival in the great hall of the castle I struck fire with the help of a steel I had in my pocket, and the flint of one of my pistols, and soon was seated by the blazing flame drying my wet garments and appeasing my hunger. Casting my looks accidentally on my hands, I saw that they were as black as those of a coal-heaver, from the soot of the chimney where I had sheltered myself against the first onset of my pursuers, and having every reason to believe that my face must be of the same hue, I easily could account for the sudden flight of the two girls, who very likely took me for the devil. This idea silenced my fears of a visit from the alarmed villagers tolerably, and the soothing hand of sleep began to close my eyes.'

"Thus far the captain of the robbers had related his extraordinary tale, when the chief Justice commending the apparent sincerity of his voluntary confession, broke up the court, ordering the prisoner to be reconducted to his dungeon until the following day, when he would hear the continuation of his adventures.

"My business not allowing me to stay a day longer, I departed reluctantly at four o'clock in the afternoon. However, before I left N- I obtained the promise of a friend of mine whom I accidentally had met, that he would send me the continuation of the robber's further confession, and four weeks after I received the following letter, which contains everything you may wish to know.

* * * * *

CONTINUATION OF WOLFE'S CONFESSION, AND THE FINAL ISSUE OF HIS TRIAL.

"My worthy friend,

"It is with the sincerest satisfaction I am going to give you a faithful account of the remainder of Wolfe's confession, and the final issue of his trial, according to my promise.

You will remember that he closed the narration of his singular adventures which he gave on the first day of his trial, with his reluctant return to the castle, where he intended to stay till the darkness of night should shelter him against the pursuit of his persecutors. The great fatigue he had sustained on his flight soon closed his weary eyes, and he slept till after sun-set, when he left the castle to pursue his way to F, where he intended to enlist in the Prussian service.

"Directed by the silver rays of the rising moon he soon found his way to the high road. At the first well he fell in with he cleaned his sooty face and hands and then went briskly on. Being well stocked with provisions, he determined not to enter any inhabited place before he should be obliged by necessity to do it, lest some new misfortunes might cross his military scheme. With that view he left the high road whenever it led through a village, walked all night long and slept in the day time. Thus he travelled onwards two nights without having met with any accident, when he, at the close of the third day, was obliged to direct his course to a small hamlet, in order to provide himself with provisions. As soon as it was dark he went with fearful steps to a baker's shop to purchase some bread, but great was his terror when he wanted to pay for the small loaf of coarse bread he had bought, and could not find his purse, which must have dropt out of his pocket when he dried his garments in the hall of the castle.

"Being entirely destitute of money he offered one of his pistols, which he took out of his pocket, in lieu of payment. The baker viewed him from top to toe, and after some hesitation agreed to the bargain. Unfortunately the house of this man had been robbed some weeks before by a gang of thieves, and Wolfe's savage look, joined with his singular appearance, rendered him suspicious to the baker, who, ever since the robbery had been committed in his house, took every ill-looking Stranger for a thief.

"Prompted by that notion he ordered one of his people to follow Wolfe at some distance as soon as he had left the house, and went instantly to the bailiff to inform him of his suspicions, and the strange bargain he had just concluded.

"The magistrate who had been indefatigable in his researches after the daring robbers, without succeeding in his endeavours to find them out, soon fell in with his opinion, and ordered some stout fellows to follow the suspected robber, and to secure him by surprise.

"Wolfe, who had meanwhile struck again into the forest, seated himself behind some bushes by the banks of a rivulet, and began to appease the demands of his grumbling stomach, not observing that he was followed, when suddenly four sinewy arms seized him from behind.

"The unexpected surprise, the continual fatigues he had undergone, and the strength of his adversaries rendered it impossible to disengage himself from their powerful grasps, and he was dragged before the magistrate of the hamlet, who demanded his passport. Having been obliged to leave it behind when his alarmed conscience had drawn upon him his late disaster, he had no other choice left but to pretend being an Austrian deserter, who wanted to go into the Prussian service. The bailiff, mistrusting his veracity, ordered him to be searched, when a loaded pistol and a large knife were found upon him, which increased the suspicion of the zealous magistrate, who, without farther ado, sent him to the prison.

"New apprehensions of a dreadful nature assailed now the unhappy man. The fear that all his former crimes would be detected filled his desponding soul with black despair; however, his lamentable situation took soon a turn more favourable than he could have expected. A transport of Prussian recruits passing through the village in the afternoon, the bailiff ordered him to be delivered to the commanding officer, thinking this to be the most commodious way to rid the country of a fellow whose whole appearance bore evident marks of his thievieh profession, and to spare himself the trouble of a tedious examination. His size and the robust make of his limbs rendered him a very acceptable acquisition to the recruiting officer, and he was enrolled as a Prussian soldier, to his unutterable joy.

'Wolfe, the robber, was now at once appointed to fight the battles of Frederic the Great, and make a solemn vow to fulfil cheerfully the duties of his honourable calling.

"The transport arrived safe at Magdeburg, and the new soldier was with his companions instructed in the art of killing lawfully his fellow creatures. The Corporal who was appointed to instruct him in the manual exercise was famous for his severity, conforming strictly to the military principles of his royal master, who, as it is universally known, had it laid down as a rule to inspire his martial bands with heroism by the frequent application of wooden arguments. Wolfe, who was not in the least partial to that sort of reasoning, found it very difficult to brook the brutality of his drilling master, who seemed to have a particular predilection for him, plying his back so frequently and so severely that the new soldier was soon rendered too sensible of his instructor's partiality for him.

"Wolfe exerted himself to the utmost of his ability to please the rigorous Corporal and to shelter himself against the frequent heavy showers of blows and cuffs, but not being able to attain his end, resentment and hatred began at length to rankle in his heart, his whole stock of patience was exhausted, and he began to have frequent recourse to drinking in order to dispel the gloominess of mind which haunted him incessantly, and to drown the recollection of his forlorn situation.

"One day as he came half intoxicated to the parade, he acquitted himself so badly of his task that his military mentor plied his back most unmercifully. Wolfe's anger was roused, his blood was boiling, and he called his chastiser a savage beast, a bloodhound, and many other names of the same stamp. The fury of his tyrant being raised to the highest degree by that language, he inflicted his blows with so much violence that Wolfe, in a fit of despair, struck him to the ground with the butt end of his gun. He was instantly seized, carried to the prison, and sentenced by a court martial to run the gauntlet.

"The day of execution appeared, the soldiers were drawn up, and his back was bared, when lo! the mark of his ignominy was seen between his shoulders. It being evident, by the sign of a gallows which was seen between his shoulders, that he had been under the hands of the common hangman, he was declared unworthy to undergo military punishment, and sentenced to work in the fortification.

"Confined with the dregs of human kind, and ever in company with the basest of villains, his weak virtuous resolutions died away by degrees. He once more began to consider himself as the sport of injustice and barbarous cruelty; his belief in the Providence of the benevolent Ruler of the world soon gave way to atheistical principles, and his former desire for doing mischief returned with redoubled force, when he saw his sincere endeavours to become a useful member of human society were thwarted again in a most cruel manner. He began to think that he was doomed to be a villain, and being driven to despair by hard labour and frequent blows, he concerted plans of effecting his escape.

"One of his fellow-prisoners, a most consummate ruffian, joined with him in devising means of regaining their liberty; and after many fruitless efforts they at length effected their escape, assisted by an impenetrable fog which covered their flight. As soon as their escape was known in the fortress, the cannons were fired and the country roused. However, they happily eluded their pursuers, and reached, at the close of day, a wood, where they resolved to conceal themselves in the tops of the trees till the heat of the pursuit should have abated.

"In this uncomfortable situation they remained as long as their small stock of provisions lasted, consulting with each other by what means they could best procure an independent livelihood, and at last agreed to resort to the Haunted Castle in the Black Forest, and there to commence robbery. After many fatiguing rambles and alarming fears, they arrived at length at the wished-for asylum.

Wolfe's inventive genius begot the scheme to render that desolate fabric more secure against the intrusion of unwelcome visitors, by raising an idea in the fancy of the neighbouring villagers of its being haunted by evil spirits. In order to accomplish their design, they set up a dreadful howling and doleful lamentations whenever they perceived some of the villagers near the environs of the castle. The gloomy appearance of that half-decayed fabric, aided by the superstition of the credulous peasantry, rendered their artful schemes successful, and in a short time none of the villagers dared to approach their lurking- place, from which they sallied out every night, disguised in the skin of goats, which they had stolen and fleeced, and committed numberless robberies in the village. Having procured a sufficient stock of money, Wolfe's associate was dispatched to a neighbouring town to pro- cure fire-arms, powder, and ball, and then they began to prey on the unwary wanderer. To relate the numberless robberies they committed before they were joined by new associates would swell volumes. As their numbers augmented they became more daring, and extended their depredations many miles over the country, till after a series of thirty successful years their infernal society sustained a deadly blow by the nocturnal surprise which delivered them into the power of punishing justice. Wolfe has since confessed that they have a great number of hiding places besides the solitary castle, and that their gang consists of fifty-three ruffians, who are dispersed all over the country. The useful information he has given to his Judges has enabled them to secure a great number of innkeepers and publicans, who were leagued with that infernal set of ruffians, of whom six more have been taken up since you left me; however, their money, and the great booty they have hoarded up, has not been detected as yet, and is supposed to have been removed on the first alarm by the rest of the gang. Wolfe's life will be spared on account of his faithful confession, and the great assistance he has afforded his Judges in putting a final stop to the depredations which have been committed for a series of years in the environs of the Black Forest; he is to be committed for life to the house of correction, where he will have ample scope to reflect on his life past, and to prepare to meet that eternal Judge who sooner or later overtakes the wicked in his vile pursuits. Thus I have executed my task as well as it was in my power, and trust you will kindly overlook the defects of my narrative, and always believe me to be, with the greatest sincerity,

Your affectionate friend,

"P

—."

FINIS